MOSCOW 5000

MOSCOW 5000

by DAVID GRANT

HOLT, RINEHART and WINSTON   New York

Published by Holt, Rinehart and Winston,
383 Madison Avenue, New York, New York 10017.

Library of Congress Cataloging in Publication Data
Thomas, Craig.
    Moscow 5000.
    I. Title.
PZ4.T4543Mo   PR6070.H56   823'.9'14   78–14183
ISBN 0–03–046680–6

First Edition

DESIGNER: Joy Chu
Printed in the United States of America
10 9 8 7 6 5 4 3 2 1

for LYNN, pure Gold

PROLOGUE

Oleg Kazantsev could reel off their names, their ages, their backgrounds, though he had never seen any of them except in photographs. Grainy snapshots of people climbing into cars, walking on crowded streets, at protest rallies; lurid, misty infrared shots of people ducking into the doors of derelict houses, scuttling across darkened streets. He knew their parents' names, even grandparents. The Kiev office of the KGB knew all about them. Until the moment when he'd arrived outside that crumbling tenement in Donetsk, he had known everything about them. Only the first flat crack, and the slow, wobbly collapse of one of his men in the gutter, had informed him that the group had guns, and had chosen the glamorous futility of an end game—something he had not known before. Explosives, yes—which was why he had decided to finish them quickly, before anyone got hurt. They were tired of rallies, of leaflets, of sit-ins, of flags, these successors to the *Banderovtsy*, skimpily linked to the Ukrainian Separatists in Munich, the *Narodny-Trudovoy Soyuz*, and all the little émigré satellites that orbited round it. They wanted action, some radical dream of hitting back, carrying the torch, waging the good war.

He screwed up his eyes against the rain that beat into his face, hunched his huge shoulders against its insidious passage between collar and skin, as if to protect himself against some personal experience which might emerge from the mockery of a row of tidied bodies lying on the pavement, arms folded on their chests, waiting for the meat wagon. Damp gray smoke still emerged from one of the upstairs rooms of the tenement where the grenades had gone off. He had ordered their use—door in with the boot, the little green tins rolling across the floor—

One of his men had covered the shattered, limbless lower torso of the youth nearest the detonation with a gray blanket, which now lay sopping and flush with the pavement.

Kazantsev turned away, looking at the tidier bodies. A girl, no more than nineteen, training to be a teacher, and a man of maybe twenty-six, a research student. Clever, bright people. His sympathies were with them, lying alongside them as if they, too, had died. The Ukrainian Separatist Movement—whatever its manifestation—had killed three policemen, two of his officers, and wounded eight others in the six days of the siege, before his men had gone in in a wet, dark predawn, driving a wedge of men up the rickety stairs to the third floor, bodily heaving the barrier of old furniture out of the way—the first of the dead falling back against his colleagues then—yelling and firing, the amplified calls for them to surrender being ignored, then the grenades and the machine guns. And soon over.

There had been no hostages, just the desire not to make martyrs and a fellow-Ukrainian reluctance to use a tank or a rocket launcher against the building. Six days of endless, sapping talk, persuasion and threats, waiting for the group to fall apart after the first man had been shot at the beginning of the thing. Then the capture attempt, and the realization that the siege had achieved nothing and they were going all the way and would have to be wiped out.

In Kiev, and then in Poltava, they'd had no trouble. Meek surrender after wordy defiance. In Donetsk, the bloodbath.

At the top of the stairs—megaphone in one hand, gun in the other—he knew the call to surrender would be ignored as his men crouched, ready to move again. He saw one of his best officers with both hands full of grenades and his face pleading that they get it over—he was kneeling over a corpse Kazantsev hadn't had time to identify—and he knew he could no longer identify with, have the least sympathy for, the ersatz terrorists along the corridor, and he'd given the order. Finish it.

The noise of the meat wagon. He could hear it distantly, a high, keening wail. If only, if only—

He was a policeman, a bomb expert forced by location and circumstances into being an antiterrorist expert. Nobody liked Russians, everyone shared something of the *Banderovtsy* spirit, the little spark of separatism, and remembered the myths of the famines in the thirties, Stalin's purges, the crushing of the movements after the Fascists had been defeated, the iron control that never relaxed—

Everyone shared something of it, as he did; every Ukrainian.

But this lot—the tidied, dead children—were different. Bombs, guns, outrages, massacres. Bank robberies, arson, kidnapping—these children had learned the lessons of the West, all right. A year before they'd put down the gang in Kharkov—*Zoop*, they called themselves, Russian for "toothache," not even using their own

Ukrainian language. And they were anarchists, Trots, Maoists, and God-knew-what. And kidnappers, gangsters, bombers. After them, things had gone quiet before the rumblings of leaflets and protests presaged—

This lot lying in the street, all dead along with five of his own and another eight wounded.

Lieutenant Oleg Kazantsev of the KGB knew he had lost something. He could not decide whether it was of value, even whether it any longer possessed sentimental worth—but it was gone. They'd helped him when they'd opened fire, and he'd finished the job when he ordered the grenades to be used and the machine guns put on automatic. And he was also chilled, not with the cold rain as much as with the perspective of the future.

Escalation. The nice, unemotive word people used when the body count began to go up, and up. Escalation. For him, it meant—*what next?* As if the gutter where he stood were a ledge over some bottomless, sheer drop, and he was teetering.

Then the siren of the meat wagon drowned further thought.

Feodor Yelisavich Shubin was crying, but whether for himself or for the others he could not distinguish. He hated his role of Ishmael, the lone survivor, as he listened to the flat, unemotional news item which described the police action against "criminals" in Donetsk. And he was shaking with relief at his own survival, when the rest of the group was dead. He, youngest but one, last to join, errand boy and not really taken seriously, hadn't been in the building when the KGB arrived. He'd been shopping, because no one knew him, he was still totally anonymous. And, coming back with his arms full of tall paper bags, he'd heard the megaphone bellowing first, then seen the ruddy flicker of an idling police-car light.

He'd dropped the parcels, and run; hidden with a girl in her college flat in Kiev after the bus journey through the rest of the night and the morning from Donetsk. Cowered, cringed, hidden.

Trying to explain his cowardice—or excuse it—within the imagery of a torch that now had been handed to him, the sole survivor. Successful, even, while the siege went on; successful until the announcement that his friends, his heroes, had been wiped out, labeled criminals, and dismissed.

He switched off the radio. The girl was washing up in her tiny kitchen, and he thought that she, too, was crying. He was about to call her name, his hand still on the radio switch, but then, almost by its own volition, the hand became a fist which swept the radio off the table, onto the floor by her bed. The back of the radio flew off, and two batteries rolled under the bed. Shubin stared at the innards of the radio in fascination, as if tracing some flow of energy or a pattern of events in the circuit board and the transistors.

All the time promising himself—and the dead—that something would be done. Something big—

Rudolf Ivanovich Belousov was on his knees in his garage, patiently, carefully sweeping at the concrete floor, making patterns in the omnipresent concrete dust as if running a comb through sand. He brushed each little hoard of dust, metal filings, and curled shavings into the dustpan, emptying the pan long before it appeared likely to spill back what he had collected onto the floor. He brushed round the small spillage of engine oil from his small Volga, so that none of the metal flakes adhered to its black stickiness. He brushed under the workbench, then moved the two garden chairs stacked next to it, opened and brushed them, then returned to the floor to brush up whatever had become removed from the canvas of the chairs. Their gaudiness was almost appropriate to the spring weather in the garden. Lowering his eyes from the window, where the unkempt garden seemed to reproach him for ignoring it, he studied the concrete floor. Everything seemed—

No, no. Impatiently, hot and relieved, he brushed very gently behind the paraphernalia of a beer-making kit he had used once, unsuccessfully, and three curling flakes of dull metal were ushered out by the nylon brush. His breath sighed audibly in the little garage. Yes—

He flicked them into the dustpan. Then he stood up and emptied the dust into the bread bin filled with sand which he would later dump outside the town. The gray concrete dust, the winking little shards of metal, he mixed in with the sand. Then he turned his attention to the saws, cleaning the blades, inspecting each millimeter until he was certain there were no traces of the metal they had been cutting. Not sufficient even for forensic examination to reveal.

When he had replaced his tools in their appropriate drawers, he brushed the surface of the workbench thoroughly—one flake of metal caught in the fleshy ball of his thumb. He watched a single tear of blood ooze out, then very gently removed the metal, wiped it clean, then dropped it singly into the sand bin. After that, he ignored his finger.

Then, when he was satisfied he had removed all traces, he stood in the middle of the garage, hands on hips, as if admiring some newly completed work of art. Almost ready, almost ready—

With the weekend coming up, he could make good progress. The beginning of July, almost certainly.

PART ONE

GLADIATORS

CHAPTER 1

Interval running. A technique pioneered by Emil Zatopek in the late forties and early fifties, and followed now by most middle distance runners. Raising the heart rate to 180 beats a minute. Federenko could almost count them mounting. Two hundred meters, down the back straight of the track, stop, let the heart fill with blood during the next half-minute, another thirty seconds until the expansion stimulus dies away, then another half-minute—

Then run another two hundred meters, stop, let the heart fill again. Do that twenty times, after running three miles that morning, and before running five more miles. He felt the heart rate dying down, and looked across to where his coach, Vladimir Oos, stood with a stopwatch. Meticulous Vladimir. Always to the second, adhering strictly to the training schedule they had worked out together, to the sheets of squared paper on which they had laid down his self-imposed regime. Charts and notes that would help him win an Olympic medal.

Because he would have the Silver, he told himself. Whatever they intended for Tretsov and the Gold—and he had little clear idea of their scheme because he had no desire to understand it—he wanted the Silver.

At least.

Two hundred meters, heart rate going up, stop. He was round past Vladimir now, who had hardly acknowledged his passage, but strutted a little with the watch held conspicuously in front of him. His little chest thrust out. Vladimir had never been topflight, not that it mattered. Federenko didn't need a coach—most middle distance runners didn't, except where they were lazy, or stupid. You did it all yourself, in the end. They were timekeepers, chart drawers, voices shouting abuse or encouragement. Five thousand meters you ran in your own head.

Last one. Two hundred, stop, feel the heart expand, close up again. Just the run left. Of course, Vladimir wouldn't like his missing the next day's training, three miles in the morning, eight miles *fartlek* or track running in the afternoon. But his mother was ill in Tripillya, and that was that. Zenaida, his sister, had telephoned him. No, not dying, but ill, and old, and a little afraid of the strange, plucking old heart under her ribs that seemed to float upward. His own heart stilled. Vladimir was watching him, still regarding the timepiece, then himself, in a sequence of rapid bird movements of his head. Behind his stumpy little form, the Tsentralny Stadium was virtually empty, except for some girls in bright track suits or provocative shorts and tight running vests fooling about in the stands while their sports teachers took coffee in the next-door Palace of Sport. One or two of them had recognized him, and waved. He had not waved back, preserving what Vladimir thought the proper distance between a Soviet international athlete and his audience.

There were other people training, of course—for field events. But that morning the adjoining park had been his, except for early joggers who had insinuated their smiles into his routine, winked in complicity as their faces reddened and their breaths roared, and this afternoon the track of the Tsentralny Stadium was his. Arkady Timofeyich Federenko, second in the Soviet Olympic Trials to Tretsov, because he'd had a cold and was still getting over it, fastest man in the Soviet Union the previous year over 5000 meters. Now, in early May, 1980, in Kiev, he thought, almost tasting already, so bad was the need, that race in Moscow in July—the Olympic Final.

Vladimir was getting impatient, and was beginning to strut. Federenko walked over to him and made a business of studying the logged times on the sheet attached to Vladimir's all-weather, plastic-covered clipboard. It pleased Vladimir if he did that, then looked up, slightly puzzled, slightly abashed, waiting to be instructed.

"You should have done *each* of the two hundreds fast," Vladimir said, pointing with his pencil halfway down the list of times. "Not just the second ten—look at the pickup here—" His pencil tapped on the clipboard. "Mm?" It was the rhetorical tone of a schoolmaster.

"I agree," Federenko said. "But last month was when I should have been doing this stuff—"

Vladimir looked appalled. "The schedule—" he began.

"I wanted to rewrite this two-week cycle, from the beginning. But you said no." Federenko's voice was calm, there was little or no accusation. "This is right for beginning the season. I'm repeating what I did in April."

"You need to repeat it." Vladimir didn't usually assert

things with quite so much vehemence. Federenko was surprised. "I'm taking tomorrow off, Vladimir—" Vladimir was beginning his head shake. "Yes, I am. I have to see my mother—she's not bighearted like I am. Didn't do enough interval running in her young days." Still there was nothing in the voice that was unpleasant—just the lightest touch of irony. Vladimir seemed to anticipate a storm still to come, and seemed even smaller; he made more and more of an effort to study the figures under the clear polyethylene sheet. "When I come back, redraw the schedule—put in, oh, put in day four straightaway—three, five with the fast two miles, then five again." Vladimir was shaking his head.

"You *must* follow the schedule, Arkady Timofeyich—" he pleaded.

"Who says so?"

Vladimir's eyes were too quick to smile—recovering remarkably quickly from their moment of wide-open shock, suspicion.

"I do—"

"No, you don't." Federenko, four inches taller than Vladimir, grabbed the small man's arms just above each elbow.

"Put your track suit on," Vladimir pleaded.

"Not yet. What is it, Vladimir? *Who* says so?"

"I do—for Heaven's sake, I do. I'm your coach, your trainer, whatever you want to call it—" Was that betrayal in the little man's eyes—couldn't be, could it?

"Insurance?" was all Federenko said. Then he concentrated, visualizing the training schedule they had drawn up together. It was as if he had looked at it for the first time, and as if he heard for the first time Vladimir's insinuating amendments, his whole *slowing-down operation* on the schedule. He knew it had been there, all the time. He had not wanted to consider it before, did not want to now. But he had already voiced his suspicions, stopped merely going through the motions. He added, "Vladimir Borisovich, what are you supposed to be doing to me?"

"Arkady Timofeyich—" he began, but Federenko held up his hand.

He released Vladimir's other elbow, scooped up his track suit trousers, tugged them on. As he did so, he said, "At this rate, I'll be ready for July—eh? Ready to run the good race, fight the good fight. Up the Ukraine, and all that bullshit—" Still the voice was even, unmarked by any violence of reaction. But each syllable was distinct and cold. "I won't win many races, will I? Perhaps a couple just before Moscow, to keep everybody guessing? Any I do win will take all I've got, and a bit more—won't it, Vladimir? I wouldn't make it in the Final though, would I? Mm?"

He was standing, arms folded, looking intently at Vladimir, who saw the young, handsome face uncreased by bitterness or anger, even though he knew.

"Arkady Timofeyich—believe me—!"

"Yes, yes, Vladimir. After all, I'm participating. I don't know why I suddenly objected to the masquerade. What about all the fifteen hundred stuff I've been doing—uh? And you want me to run another competition at fifteen hundred this month? While Tretsov runs in a ten thousand? I let you persuade me, for the sake of finishing faster. But that's not it, is it?" Vladimir shook his head, and that small, naked admission chilled Federenko to the bone. "When is the scheme to be explained to me, Vladimir—when?"

"I don't know—believe me, I don't know!"

Federenko studied him intently for a moment, his features sharp, the light blue eyes seeming to read the inside of his head. Then he turned away, walking off toward the changing rooms. Vladimir, clutching the clipboard to his chest, trailed after him.

He didn't seem angry, he thought—did he? Perhaps he'll go along. Perhaps he'll behave.

"It's May already. You're two months behind schedule. You say you can do it, messing about in your garage. Your business is to make those devices—not poking your nose into my end of things!"

"Feodor Yelisavich—I *can* do it. However, you do not seem to appreciate the difficulties I have had and am having. You think I'm making something a lot more primitive than current models—maybe I am. But it's more sophisticated in its way. I'm adapting existing types to do the job you want—and there's the necessary disguise. Do you realize how much difficulty that caused just by itself? Not to mention the timing mechanism. Where do you think I can *test* these things, eh?"

"All right, right, right—"

"No, it isn't *all* right. In just over a year, I've come close to completing my part of the deal. And you? All you've done is collect around you a group of hotheaded kids. You can call them *Do pobachenya* if you want, you can dress them up to look like patriots and freedom fighters—but are they really any good when it comes down to it? Answer me that."

"They'll do, they'll do. God, Rudolf, keep your nose out of *my* business. I need a group like them because they're not known, they haven't done anything, yet. They're willing hands, and they're my cover. There just aren't the *quality* people about anymore, since Donetsk and Kharkov and Poltava and Kiev. The bastards have wiped them out, or locked them up. Remember?"

"Very well. I'm sorry. But when I promise to complete the devices, I mean what I say. You can collect them—in July."

"But that's too—"

"*Late?* Not at all. The beginning of July, I should have said. You will have plenty of time. By the way, that girl you're living with?"

"Zenaida—what about her?"

"Something about her. Is *she* reliable?"

"Reliable enough—for what I need her for. Don't you realize I *need* students, kids, call them what you like. *Clean* people!"

"Will they be so reliable after the event?"

"They won't want to tell, will they?"

"Perhaps not."

"Make it June."

"The beginning of July."

François Diderot, with the tartan track coming up at him, felt his legs going but managed to turn on his back as he sank toward it so that his decline appeared merely from effort and not exhaustion. But he did not sit up straightaway. From where he lay he could see the great curve of the Olympic Stadium pressing overhead so that he saw the Munich Stadium closing over him like a great eyelid.

He knew he had almost blown it, thrown the race away. To win it, he had had to summon reserves that now left him spent and weak. He had never felt this bad after a race. And just to be three meters in front of Holmrath and an unknown Czech, after five thousand meters. His third race of the European season.

He should have coasted the last couple of laps, after he passed Holmrath, who didn't have a finish. He had almost enough, Diderot decided, seeing the German bending over him, breathing heavily but smiling. He winked at Diderot, and walked away—*walked!*

Diderot sat up. Winner of the Munchenerbrau Invitation Meeting 5000 meters event—he could hear the public address system informing the crowd, as if they needed to be reminded, that the sagging, seated figure in a blue vest by the trackside was the winner. There was applause, some French cheering, and a great deal more noise for Holmrath finishing second. Diderot got to his feet, felt his legs almost buckle—raised his hands as if trying to support himself on the air, but in reality to acknowledge cheering that was not really for him but for the distance of a German javelin throw in the center of the field. He trotted carefully off the track toward the tunnel, the noise in the huge stadium suddenly dulled and made distant. He felt awful.

Jorgensen, the Norwegian who had been European record holder two years before, was sitting on a bench in the tunnel, as if unwilling to board the bus that would take them back to their hotel, and a shower. He stood watching the quiet, patient Scandinavian for a moment as he stared at the floor in front of his feet, replaying the race on some inward videotape—seeing the times he had been boxed in, the moment he had lost contact with himself, Holmrath, and the Czech. Diderot shook his head and, even though it was warm and sunny, he shivered as he stepped out into the parking lot, as if he had seen some disturbing personal vision.

He looked around for the bus, and heard a car horn, arrogant and Italian. The car was parked near the exit from the stadium, where an eye could be kept open for his appearance.

Loriot. In a very expensive Cardin suit and Givenchy sunglasses which made him sinister in a high fashion way. Not that Loriot was sinister, he was just a businessman. When he smiled, he appeared nothing more than intelligent and affable. He held out his hand, which Diderot reluctantly shook as he climbed into the Alfa, and said, "You were hard-pressed today, François."

"That's true." Diderot looked around the parking lot. Hardly anyone going home, as yet. The parking lot was full of cars, empty of people. Still—

"I know what you're going to say, François," Loriot remarked. "I'm here as a representative of France-Allemagne Sporting, which is partly sponsoring this meeting—since we are part of Dumas-Quenelle, which has a considerable holding in Munchenerbrau, as you well know. And I am congratulating the winner of the 5000 meters. I am a sports fan."

"You're a sports businessman, Loriot. What do you want?"

"I do not intend to bribe you, here and now in the official lot. So relax—"

Diderot sat back in the seat, closed his eyes, and stared at the reddened sunlight behind his lids. He wished that Loriot would go away, but he could not tell him to do so.

A million francs.

The sum, staggering even now, began to spin in his head as if from the effect of alcohol. Dumas-Quenelle—cosmetics, drink, clothes, sports equipment through France-Allemagne, custom cars, hotels, travel firms. The whole range of luxury, of comfort, of acquisitive envy. Dumas-Quenelle—a life-style, their advertising called the company. And he was part of it. His cleared debts, his new car, his expenses, all proclaimed his employment by Dumas-Quenelle. He shivered. When he had felt like that before, he had called it the ghost of Avery Brundage. And had tried to laugh.

Not that Dumas-Quenelle didn't want him in Moscow, didn't want him to win. They did. If he was to spearhead their campaigns to sell holidays, after-shave and talc, beer and wine, cars—the Dumas-Quenelle life-style—then he had to be a medalist.

A million francs. Just for being François Jean-Marie Diderot, Olympic medalist. One Gold would be enough—he didn't have to win three, like Killy. Even a Bronze. Killy, Killy—they had taken all his medals away—they might have prevented him entering if they'd acted earlier. They could do that to him.

"It's not as if I'm corrupt—" He realized that he had spoken aloud, that Loriot was smiling, and cursed himself for the weak stupidity he had displayed. It must be the aftereffect of the race. Indeed, he felt light-headed in a rather disturbing way. "What do you want?" he snapped as gruffly as he could.

"Just to know that things are well."

"You're a trainer, a coach?" Diderot asked, his mouth contemptuous.

"Just a fan. A disappointed fan. You've been wasting the money you've had. You're living the Dumas-Quenelle life-style in *anticipation* of your triumph in Moscow. You must slow down, François—early to bed, and alone to bed, perhaps. Or more early mornings and fewer late nights."

"Mother of God—you're an *expert!*"

"Not at all. Except in money—and money is what this is all about, isn't it. We have given you some money, and we intend giving you a great deal more—but not for nothing. You only came first in our little competition to find an athlete to promote our interests because this is Olympic year. There were other *strong* contenders." With a hackneyed sense of drama, Loriot removed his sunglasses, tapped one arm on Diderot's chest. "Last season, you were a winner. You won almost every race in Europe. But you were hungry, and greedy, and vain. Don't blame us for pandering to your weaknesses, François. Blaming France-Allemagne or even Dumas-Quenelle might give you the impression that you still possess freedom of decision, freedom of action. You don't."

Diderot looked into Loriot's eyes as if for a remission of sentence. They had his name on the contracts, locked away in a Paris office, so secure that it was stupid to be frightened of the Federation Française d'Athletisme, even more stupid to be frightened of the International Olympic Committee—but he was.

For a bleak moment, as if a cloud had hidden the warm sun and the parking lot had gone gray and dull, he realized how much he wanted to win a medal—any of the medals—in Moscow. And how afraid he was the IOC would find out, sometime in the next two months.

"What if they found out?"

"Make sure they don't," was Loriot's only reply.

Every day—and it did not matter what his training schedules said or officious coaches and trainers tried to impose upon him—Winston Ochengwe ran the ten miles from the government office in Kabale, where he was a clerk in the provincial office of the Ministry of Works, to his hut in the village of M'seka. In the early mornings, perhaps, he enjoyed the running better, on the way to work. Yet, coming home, the thought of his wife and son was always before him, like a tape, or a cheering crowd or someone with a stopwatch and good news.

Ochengwe was a Tutsi refugee from Rwanda, from a village only forty miles across the border from his present home in Uganda. He had come as a child, with his family, in 1964, when the Hutu massacred several thousand Tutsis, the traditional ruling caste of Rwanda. His uncle and his elder brother had been killed by a drunken mob as they left their place of work. He did not remember the incident, being no more than a child and told nothing by his stern father, the strong man he had emulated all his life—whose memory he had emulated because that strong, wise man had died three years after they transplanted themselves, as if he had been a great tree uprooted in a storm that had overwhelmed him. His mother had instantly become old—a crone who shared a room of their hut now with memories and a goat.

By the time his father died, Winston was at school, and passing examinations set by people in England who could not be corrupted or bribed or frightened. You passed on merit. Winston had passed, as he had then passed the civil service examination, which was easier than the one about *Julius Caesar* and the book of poems about green fields and fat cattle and sheep and great cities full of factories, and that African novel, about Kenya, in which he had had even less interest.

But the thing he did best, so that he knew it even on the day he started his job in a clean pressed white shirt—Sarah, his wife, said he would cut his throat on the open collar—and his best shorts and creaking boots that had belonged to his father, was running. For miles and miles and miles. Running—untiring, strong—a champion.

Ahead of him, as he pounded down the dirt road—his shoes round his neck since he could not leave them at his office to be stolen by the cleaners or one of the office boys—the Mufumbiro Range stretched into the evening sky. Blue peaks thrust up out of the uplands. He began to labor up a long slope of the road, sensing the greater effort, delighting in the ease with which his body provided the extra effort without seeming to waste energy or begin to tire.

Schoolboy champion of Uganda at sixteen, Ugandan record holder at seventeen, African champion and record holder for the last three years—titles that impressed him only in that they measured his absorption by his new country, measured his strength and his fitness. Between his shoes, the little gold cross that declared the Catholicism he had brought with him from Rwanda bounced on his dark skin. He smiled, lifted his head as if to shout something. If you could run, religion didn't matter, nor did the fact that you were an immigrant. He would never be kicked out like the Asians.

He shook his head. He felt a vague disloyalty in even remembering the lighter skins and narrow faces that he no longer saw in the shops in Kabale and Kampala. President Idi Amin had sent them to Britain—and they did exploit the Africans, there was no doubt of it.

The long slope down—the last slope. Sarah would have the meal ready for him. There was a slight haze from cooking fires ahead of him. He began to notice the buzz of insects.

He moved off the road as a car horn sounded behind him. A battered Ford passed him, covered with dust. In it were three laughing Africans, probably policemen heading for a tour of duty on the Rwandan border. He could have had a car himself, he thought, as he watched it disappear round the bend toward M'seka. They had promised him one. But the gasoline cost too much, and his village was proud of him now because they could still come up to him, talk to him, watch his body, and wonder how a champion differed from them—the boys, especially, did that. In a car, how could they look on him except as someone reminding them that he was different. Sarah would be shunned by the other women. For similar reasons he had never fully thought through, he had refused a job in Kampala, where the best training and facilities were. Even though they had tried to put pressure on him, he had refused—always deferentially, politely, but nevertheless refused.

Perhaps the mornings were better, the air still cool, the running shoes supple from the evening's attentions, the sky not yet leached of color. But the dust of the old car's passage had settled again, and he could smell the smoke from the fires. And Sarah and his son were waiting for him, and that made the evening run best of all.

Federenko was waiting for the local train to Tripillya, in one of the waiting rooms of the Central Station, drinking coffee and reading a Kiev evening paper, when Shubin found him. Shubin made the meeting appear accidental, as if he, too, were waiting for a train, but he noticed that Federenko was instantly alert, as if his senses had been heightened by danger, or some change in the middle of a race.

"Arkady Timofeyich—!" he exclaimed, extending his hand, which Federenko seemed to inspect for dirt or a concealed weapon before he lightly returned the grasp. To Federenko, the patronymic distanced them rather than claimed familiarity.

"Feodor Yelisavich," Federenko said quietly and without enthusiasm, and then they went through a hand mime of indicating the empty chair opposite Federenko before Shubin sat down. He unbuttoned his jacket—plastic masquerading as leather, Federenko noticed, over a pair of faded jeans. Black market, no doubt. He smiled. From some visiting athlete or holidaymaker.

"They must have cost you something," he said.

Shubin pouted dismissively. "Not too much."

"Still requiring badges of office, then?"

"Like yourself, Arkady Timofeyich—with your times and your medals—mm?"

Federenko smiled. He shied away from something he sensed in Shubin, something like a secret life; avoided, too, when he could, the knowledge that Shubin and his sister, Zenaida, had been lovers and that the relationship was not over yet; avoided most of all the sense of envy he always felt from the other man. Shubin was a failure, a brilliant engineer caught up in student and poststudent Ukrainian Separatist politics who had lost his lucrative job in the Donets basin in the hydroelectric industry because of pamphlets and letters and a small-circulation newspaper avowedly anti-Russian. Shubin was a bitter man; always sharp, clever, idealistic, he had thrown away promotion and relative prosperity—the very things Federenko now represented as a favored Soviet athlete.

He sat silently, studying Shubin's narrow bearded face, the smudges under the eyes, the eyes themselves quick and bright with observation and contempt. Shubin was an uncomfortable man—he had known that at university, known it since Zenaida had gotten mixed up with him.

"Well, Arkady Timofeyich, this is pleasant—" Shubin said eventually when the strained silence had been sufficiently prolonged to make his remark an obvious fiction.

"Indeed—pleasant." Then Federenko seemed to relent, and added, "You're still employed at the power station?"

"Oh, yes. I worked in the electricity industry before, so I do so now. I have a white coat, too, together with my broom and my mops." Each word came like a jabbing finger, seeming to pain Shubin, as if they had been extracted with dentist's tools.

"Mm."

"Mm? Your concern does you credit, Arkady Timofeyich."

Federenko looked at his watch. Still twenty minutes before his train.

"Let's talk about something else, shall we?"

"About you, perhaps? And the Olympics? Much more interesting, of course." Shubin was openly sneering. Federenko felt hurt, but not so much by the tone as the subject broached. He shook his head.

"No, not that either. Why not talk about Zenaida?"

Shubin's eyes flickered.

"Truly, why not? Your sister."

Federenko looked out at the station concourse. Commuters heading out of the center of Kiev were passing the window in droves. The crowds made him strangely impatient, in anticipation of his journey.

"Are you going to marry her, or live with her, or what—?" he blurted out.

Shubin smiled unpleasantly.

"Or what, I should think," he remarked.

Federenko felt humiliated, not in control of himself or the

conversation. But the subject was broached. He didn't like Shubin, not anymore, and he did care about his sister.

"Do you care about her, or don't you?" he insisted.

"Of course I care!" Shubin leaned toward him over the table. His sleeve knocked against the spoon in the sugar bowl, and the table was suddenly gritty with sugar. Shubin traced his finger in it, making snow tracks, as he added, "But not in the way you think might be nice, the *nondangerous* way. The arse-licking, pat-on-the-head, scratch-my-back way you've chosen, Arkady Timofeyich." He seemed to stare at the table, or at his tracing finger which had spread the sugar into random streaks. Then he looked up into Federenko's tight features. "You go on being the good boy, Arkady—you don't deserve your patronymic. You know that, don't you?"

"Because my father got himself sent to one of the camps as a *Banderovtsy*?" Federenko felt betrayal cut as deep as a long knife, twist in his stomach, at the casual, contemptuous tone he adopted to hide his real feelings. "That was thirty-two years ago. And he came back—after a *short* sentence."

"And after breeding you and Zenaida, he went away again, and didn't come back!"

Federenko looked at his watch. Just over ten minutes. He made as if to rise. Shubin shot out a long, thin hand and grabbed his sleeve.

"Sit down, arse-licker!" Federenko shrugged off the grip, but sat down. "Good. Do you know why I'm here, consorting with someone like you? Because Zenaida asked me to. She wanted me to talk to you, sensibly. Enlist your help, your heart. But we never talk, do we? We just scratch at each other's faces like cats in an alley. You and me—opposite poles, but we don't attract."

"Once we were close—" Federenko felt compelled to lighten the mood of Shubin's conversation, or distract it.

"A long time ago, when *I* didn't know any better! Before you discovered you had a bigger lung capacity, a stronger heart, than most of your fellow Ukrainians. And became a *pet* in Stalin's house."

"Stalin's dead."

"I don't believe it—in *his* case, there's reincarnation."

"How long are you going to harangue me like this?" Federenko was calm now. He could view all this not as a personal attack but as a species of polemic, the sweeping dialectical frenzy of student days.

"What's the use?" Shubin replied, sitting back in his chair, flinging his arm toward the window. "I've done what your sister asked. You're just gutless, or you love comfort too much. I don't know which it is, and I don't care, much. Just go and catch your train, Arkady Federenko, stateless person and international *nothing*. Tell your sister I tried, will you?"

Federenko stood up, and looked down at Shubin's face. The man looked tired, as if some inner effort had left him weak and exhausted. No, he corrected himself, Shubin always looked like that, worn away from within by some torrent of anger. Federenko shivered. He suddenly wanted his sister to have nothing more to do with Shubin. Shubin was, in some obscure way, dangerous.

"Good-bye, Feodor Yelisavich," he said, and walked out of the buffet, heading for his platform.

For most of the journey, the local train ran alongside the Dnieper. Federenko watched the barges and the tourist boats, glass houses afloat, heading downriver on their week-long cruises to Odessa. Federenko had been to Odessa—courtesy of the Light Athletic Federation of the USSR. He had been able to take his mother and Zenaida for two weeks. As a Master of Sport, International Class, it was one of the privileges.

He dismissed the thought, and focused his attention on the other good things—for good things had come out of it, and remained, he reminded himself. His mother had a house of her own—at least, she had it at a low rent, and for life, and shared it with only a farm laborer and his family—which was good, because the man cultivated the large kitchen garden and two other private plots which association with the family of Arkady Timofeyich Federenko had brought his way. His mother ate well, and the man's wife looked after her while he ran and Zenaida finished her studies at the teachers' college.

All on the plus side. He breathed deeply, and looked out of the other side of the compartment. Barley, still green, waving in a slight breeze. He turned back to the Dnieper. A motorboat, leaving behind it a herringbone wake. A Party official, beginning his long weekend at his dacha on the riverside, screened by trees from the *narodniks*, the peasants. Federenko screwed up his nose. He was beginning to think like Shubin—and he with a new flat in Moscow waiting for him when he moved up from Kiev next month.

Damn it, but Shubin really got under his skin—!

So did Vladimir—and perhaps that cut closer and deeper. He knew something, something not very nice at all. Federenko tried to feel his strength, his prowess, as a current in his muscles. Compared himself with the overweight clerk across the compartment, with the fat woman, the dumpy girl, the pudgy child. It seemed that the whole compartment was full of fat people; perhaps the whole train was—? Yet he was no freer than they were, though had they known his name they would have envied and respected him. But he was reduced to picking out excess kilos that others carried round with them as an antidote to the creeping sense of paralysis he first felt showering after his training. He had forgotten the evening run, and caught the early train to Tripillya.

They were going to *use* him, in some way. Not to win a medal, either. Apparently, that was out. His training program, ever since the winter, had emphasized speed, not stamina—as if he were training for the 1500. Too much short work, fast repetitions, ever since December, when he had given up most of the distance work. He had been entered for the 1500 in the indoor championships in March—a point at which suspicion deteriorated into fear—as if he were being prepared for a peak *before* the Final in July. Cross-country? Early winter was the last time he had run a cross-country race. Vladimir had conned him out of any more, all winter.

At first, he had gone along willingly; later, he had gone along unquestioningly, because he did not want to ask questions. Then why had he asked, that afternoon? He tried to picture the scene exactly—

Vladimir, strutting like a pigeon, watch held out, about to criticize— Yes, that was it. Something in him had been aroused by that sight, by the *presumption* in Vladimir, the control he thought he exercised—*had* exercised.

He could do nothing, he admitted, as the train disgorged more city workers at Vitachiv station, a country halt, where the stationmaster grew cabbage and cucumbers under glass instead of merely pretty, and inedible, flowers. Federenko watched with amusement as he worked in the garden plot, half-obscured by the station nameboard, while his son or daughter, presumably, collected the tickets at the exit. He did not look up from his weeding even as the train pulled out. Only once had he been distracted. He had paused, then cut and handed over a lettuce to the driver of the train, who had hurried across to receive it.

He could do nothing. The thought pressed in on him again as Vitachiv was left behind and he looked down on the river from a greater height. Just play along, be a good boy. *Arse-licker.* Shubin was right.

He squeezed his eyes shut—to encourage or prevent the prick of tears, he could not be certain.

His mother was sitting up in bed, drinking thick *rasolnik*—pickled vegetable soup—when he arrived. He kissed her leathery old cheek, sat with her while she told him about Fedukhin and his family downstairs, and the death toll among her acquaintances since his last visit, asked him about himself and his health—as if he were a clerk who never saw the sun. He diagnosed to himself that her illness was probably indigestion complicated by loneliness now that Zenaida came home less often, and two of Fedukhin's girls worked in Kanev, in the Taras Hill Hotel and Restaurant, and he hardly appeared during the athletics season.

So he held her hand, stilled his impatience, and listened and agreed.

It was dark by the time he sat down in the next room, a comfortable sitting-dining room, well-furnished and with a small TV in one corner—*the* corner, he supposed, since so many families still sat round fireplaces rather than televisions. Zenaida had cooked his supper, *pyelmeni* in thick gravy, and *blini* pancakes with butter to follow. As he ate the meat dumplings, he realized that he took the food for granted. He, as an athlete, was on a special diet—good, regular, nourishing food. He was special. When he had arrived, old Fedukhin downstairs had greeted him almost by touching his forelock, like some kind of serf to his master.

When he had finished, and washed the last of the meal down with a bottle of imported East German beer, he watched his sister through the open door of the small kitchen adjoining. She appeared absorbed in the simple task, so much so that he recognized her tension, and supposed he had better begin the conversation. He picked a piece of meat from a back tooth, then said, "I met Feodor Shubin today."

"Oh, yes?"

"Yes. Apparently at your suggestion."

Something slid back into the washing-up water, probably a plate, and she came to stand in the doorway. She was wearing pink rubber gloves and a plastic apron promoting the newspaper *Komsomolskaia Pravda*—he assumed it was a joke. She appeared nervous.

"What—what did he have to say?"

"The usual bull—only this time more forcibly—" He saw her

face pucker as he decried Shubin, as if he had physically hit her. "He's off his head, if you ask me—"

"I didn't!" she snapped.

"O.K., O.K., *Zenushka*—" She seemed instantly to resent the diminutive. "All right. He tried to sell me some hackneyed line of nationalist claptrap. Then he spat all over my Master of Sport award, my life-style, and me. That is exactly what happened."

Now he could see that she was torn between him and Shubin. Shubin should not have insulted her brother, the international athlete. For however critical of the Soviet setup she might be, Zenaida seemed to have the trick of excluding him from any of that comment.

"He always goes too far, he's lost—"

"Lost something or just lost?"

"Lost his sense of humor," she ended lamely. "He's very clever, but it makes him very serious. And he's very bitter for what they did to him." She came toward the table where he was stretched out on his tilted-back chair, sat down opposite him so that he viewed her dark hair and eyes, her fine bones, her high color, almost from the vantage of a lover. She *was* beautiful, and intelligent. And Shubin was inside her head, as no doubt he had been inside her bed, inside her—

He choked off the thoughts, and took her hand, turning the pink rubber glove palm up, palm down. He did not look at her as he said, "Zenushka, he's a dangerous man. I don't care about his insults—well, only a little—but I do care about you. There's something wild about him—" He looked up at her now, his light blue eyes disconcerting her with their stare. "Do you have to go on seeing him, Zenushka?"

She dragged her hand from his light grip. Her color had risen, and her dark eyes were focused with resentment.

"Arkady—you mustn't tell me who to see and what to do! No longer, Arkady. I'm not your *little* sister anymore. I'm not in a greenhouse, growing up with all the other lettuces or pretty flowers—" He remembered the stationmaster at Vitachiv, bending over his private-enterprise garden plot, and smiled. She mistook the expression. "Don't patronize me, my big brother, from the lofty pinnacle of a red vest and the good life!" He heard Shubin speaking with her voice, and grabbed her hand at the wrist. She winced with pain.

"Don't talk to me as if you were Shubin. He's a madman. He can kill himself with drink or politics or get run over by a bus because he's too self-absorbed to notice it. I don't care what happens to him—but I do care what happens to you. Understand?"

She pulled her hand away, rubbed her wrist, grimacing.

"You've settled for your life, for things as they are. Some of us, we haven't—"

"What? You're talking just like him now!"

"He's right about you, Arkady. You're blinded by the *things* your running has brought you—blind to everything else. If you were like Father—"

He stood up, his face chalk-white with rage.

"I hardly knew my father, and you knew him even less. Don't use him as a stick to beat me, or as a myth to believe in. He may have been a nationalist, a *Banderovtsy*, but if you listen to our mother sometimes, you'll realize that he was also a drunk and wasn't above beating the daylights out of her while fighting for an independent Ukraine!"

"Keep your voice down. She'll hear you!"

Federenko came close to the table, and leaned his head toward her. She seemed suddenly small in the chair.

"My father may have died in the camps—our grandparents may have died in the famine of '32, along with five or six million others—but *I'm alive*—and so are you. And I'm afraid that Shubin won't be for very long."

It had been half-anger, used to elicit reaction. As he finished the final sentence, he saw her face crimson, sensed the whiff of danger, the obscene glamour of secrecy and plotting—and *action*— about her. She was too like Shubin, much too like, for her own good. In a quiet voice, he said, "What the hell are you up to, Zenaida— what, in God's name?" As he said it, it was as if the emphasis had become a prayer. His eyes flickered to the icon on the wall, above the vase of flowers.

Ben Greenberg was about to leave the office when a junior editor came up from the newsroom, a teleprinter sheet with a torn edge in one hand. Greenberg looked at his watch, because junior editors had a habit of detaining him for sporting reminiscences, and he had a plane to catch for Los Angeles. Unfortunately, he considered, he had too much time to get to Kennedy.

"Ben," the editor said. "Thought you'd like to take this with you." The man was grinning from ear to ear. "Show it to Gutierrez, your boy wonder. Make him choke on his ego, shouldn't be surprised!" He broke into a deep belly laugh. Greenberg ignored the insults to the athlete he had championed in his column ever since his freshman year, and took the sheet of flimsy. Then he looked up.

"Last night?"

"Sydney, under floodlights. His last race of the season, too."

"Jesus Christ," Greenberg breathed. "Jesus Christ, Lord of all the Athletes—what the hell are you *doing* to the United States of America?" He raised his eyes to the ceiling, then looked down, screwed up the paper, and threw it across his office. It landed in a wastebin with a click. "I won't say thanks, Sam."

"Thought you'd like to know—uh?"

"Uh."

The teleprinter sheet had contained the completely unexpected news that Kenneth Irvine, Australian champion at 5000 meters, had broken the world record in the last competitive race of the Australian season.

CHAPTER 2

Greenberg watched from the press box for the moment that Gutierrez would choose to leave the field for dead. He had bet MacDonald, athletics columnist for the *Examiner*, which lap, even which bend. MacDonald, who was more objective about Gutierrez, had taken his hand with a sigh and a shake of his gray head. He had foreborne to comment.

But Greenberg knew not only that the kid would win, but that he would win well. Perhaps the others did see Gutierrez objectively—or objectionably, because the kid really was that—and he saw him through rose-colored glasses. He nodded to himself, watching the track below the glass box in which he sat and in which the clichéd cigar smoke of the press contingent curled like a blue fog—but it was like watching your own son, even yourself, down there.

Most of the press in the box were, with one or two exceptions, major columnists from the dailies. After all, it was the National Collegiate A.A.U. Championships, a good guide to the Olympic Trials which would be held in Eugene, Oregon, in mid-June. This was the time, the place, for an American athlete to impress, wave a flag that he could carry through the Trials. And Greenberg knew that Gutierrez would wave a bigger, brighter flag than most.

There were senior East Coasters there, like Shane and Huckfield. And himself. Benjamin Joseph Greenberg, syndicated columnist, best-known for his years of faithful reporting in the *New York Enquirer*—best-known outside Olympic circles, that is. In the record books, just a footnote to say that B. J. Greenberg of the U.S.A. dropped out of the Olympic 5000 meters Final in Rome—with a damaged tendon. Somebody had spiked him when he was boxed in on the fourth lap, well tucked in, brain going like an advanced IBM computer.

Forget it, he told himself. Blow your nose and get rid of the smell of wintergreen and self-pity. Watch the kid—let him do it for you. Because however good they said Prefontaine was, or Mills, this boy was the best middle distance runner he had ever seen. That there had ever been.

The door opened behind him, letting in the noise of the crowd for a moment. Someone whistled—a wire-service stringer, probably, because everyone of any standing or years in the press community would have recognized Karen Gunston immediately. The door closed behind her, shutting out the atmosphere of the meeting. Funny, he thought. Live broadcasts like the ones she does pack the place with all-round mikes to pick up the atmosphere— while we sit in a cone of silence, detached. Don't we *like* the atmosphere—?

"*Mizz* Gunston!" Greenberg exclaimed, standing up, bowing to her. Karen Gunston, top live-action anchorperson-cum-producer for CKR-TV, wrinkled her nose, which made her freckles slightly more evident beneath the makeup, and attempted not to be amused, or put down, by Greenberg. In fact, she attempted to consider his behavior always in the light of the ending of their affair, which she had wanted, but which he had resented. To her, he was still trying to wound her.

"Mister Greenberg," she said levelly, running her eyes over him before prodding him in the area of his recently developing paunch. "You must take some of your own advice to the citizens of our country—go jogging."

"It's you," he said maliciously, and loud enough for the younger members of the press community to hear. "You used to be my ideal exercise—"

Her green eyes flickered. Then, deliberately, she brushed her hand through her short auburn hair, and said, "Benjamin—you mustn't be a greedy boy."

"What do you want, Karen?" Greenberg was unperturbed— yes, he observed to himself, I feel almost affable toward her, certainly I'm not uptight when she's close anymore. He turned back to the race. "Lap?" he said.

"Four to go," MacDonald answered him, chuckling. "Start worrying, Ben. That black kid is still with him, and your boy don't look too happy."

Greenberg studied Gutierrez for a moment, adjusting his field glasses so that he could see the young man's face. Then he smiled. Gutierrez's pace had dropped, since he had led the field for the first five laps, and he looked tired, as if he should never have led. Bluff. He decided not to say anything to MacDonald.

"Do you want me to answer your question?" He had forgotten, momentarily, about Karen Gunston. He turned back to face her, briefly, before his attention returned to the track. The leading group of runners were on the back straight now, Gutierrez just behind the Berkeley runner, Anderson, black and stringy, his vest flopping loosely on his back, with a blond from Kentucky tucked in behind Gutierrez, waiting to pounce. Then two others, dropped a lap ago, and fading, and the strung-out bunch just entering the straight, perhaps sixty meters behind.

"Sure," he said. "What d'you want?"

"An interview with your Golden Boy, for openers." He did not look at her.

"Not *my* boy, Karen—he doesn't run for the University of Greenberg—my colors are pink and lime."

"I want him on my part of the show—after he runs."

"Oh." He looked over his shoulder at her. She seemed little interested in the result of the race—Anderson seemed to be dropping Gutierrez on the bend. The Kentuckian was out of it, seizing up slowly and five meters back. Gutierrez looked worn-out. "What angle are you using?"

"I just want to dig into his ego a little."

"Jump on his bandwagon?"

"How's that?"

"CKR-TV—have they decided who goes to Moscow?" He looked at her swiftly, then back—Gutierrez hadn't dropped another inch. Karen Gunston's face was sharp with confession. "Wait a minute—wait a minute. CKR wants to send *you*, but you have to prove your bona fides by doing some sports—uh?"

"You're way off—"

"I don't think so—" Two and a half laps to go. Anderson looked good, head up, arms swinging rhythmically, long legs increasing the stride. Gutierrez looked awful, dropping back. "No—they won't let TV news people in there, just the genuine sports characters. That's what you have to be to get your visa. Karen Gunston, fearless social commentator, is just a cheerleader at heart!" He chuckled. "What a laugh."

"Will you get me the interview?"

She was close to his ear, her voice deliberately soft, insinuating. Greenberg burst out laughing. Looking at her, he raised his hands in mock self-defense.

"O.K., O.K.—for that gag, I'll try to get him to talk to you. My influence on him? About two percent."

"Thank you, Benjamin."

"Sure. Let me get you in another fine mess sometime, uh? Just to say thank you nicely."

When he turned back to the track, smiling, Gutierrez had already opened up a gap of five meters on Anderson. Greenberg looked at MacDonald, who commented, "Last gasp."

"A lap and a half—some gasp." He turned back to watch. Gutierrez was magic—magnetic, mesmerizing. The tabloids had used all those words. And they were true. Each stride now seemed to leave the tall black looking ordinary and slow and in another race. The blond from Kentucky had been finished for a long time.

"You told him about Irvine?" Karen Gunston asked, now watching the race.

"He knew. That's his answer—looking as if he isn't trying, but really saying two fingers to the guy. I can do it as easy as a training run."

Gutierrez passed underneath them, and the bell went for the final lap. He had overtaken two of the trailing runners who had become detached from the gritty, ordinary little bunch over half a lap behind. Gutierrez had moved into the kind of gear people expected of an 800 or 1500 man, up the last back straight. Greenberg glanced at MacDonald, who seemed to be thrusting the field glasses against his eye sockets as if he could not believe what he saw.

"Looks bushed, uh?" he said. MacDonald growled something inaudible, and prepared to part with ten dollars. Gutierrez came off the bend, and Greenberg could faintly hear the cheering—the kind of cheering that goes beyond partisanship; rather, applause for somebody doing something no one else could do, coming home with his superiority stamped on his event. Long, easy strides, then arms aloft still ten meters out. The tape fluttered away behind him. Greenberg applauded, laughed, then turned to Karen Gunston.

"Come on—let's see if he'll talk to you." He grinned at MacDonald as they went out of the door of the press box.

Irena Witlocka, in a gymnasium of the Palace of Sport in Warsaw, kicked her long legs like a dancer, warming up. Grachikov, her Russian coach, was watching her like a policeman—which she half-believed he was. After all, he had replaced Jerzy, her coach since schooldays, last year when she had tried to stay in America after the Poland–U.S. meeting in Dallas.

She kicked her left leg up at the wall bars, then the right leg, all the time watching Grachikov, who watched her. He made her warm up for twice as long—train twice as hard, even though she had entered fewer competitions than ever before. It was some kind of punishment, she supposed, the only way they could try to make her life more unpleasant—along with the smaller flat she now had to share, and in a workers' suburb of Warsaw. Her parents had had to move out of their apartment, and back into the dilapidated block from which they had come. It should have been marked for demolition, but it was still there, in a narrow street near the center of Krakow—picturesque rodents, peeling stucco, everything the tourists admired.

She tried not to think about her parents. She wanted—what she wanted had nothing to do with them, and would hurt them even more. But she still wanted it, like something sinful or self-indulgent. Wear lipstick and go to Hell, the nuns said to her as a little girl. Masturbate and go to Hell. Disbelieve and go to Hell—there was only the one punishment, it seemed. Love an American and go to—America. This time, she would.

They would have thrown her over, she knew that. They had wanted to. It had been a scandal that they hadn't been able to keep out of the papers, even though they hushed it up and she had been forced to apologize to the American authorities and tell the world she wanted to go back to Poland. But she was still the best high jumper outside the DDR and the U.S., and this was Olympic year.

"All right—you're warm." Grachikov never smiled, always brayed his orders like a donkey. "Start running—forty meters, and stay *relaxed*. You are not relaxed, Irena." He bared his teeth at the last remark, but it was nothing like a genuine smile. "After that, thirty minutes' weight training, then forty jumps over one meter seventy-five." This was her two-hour training session, repeated six days a week throughout the year. Compared with her regime of preparation, a runner had it easy.

She had to run as fast as she could, training for the approach run, building up speed but having to stay relaxed—stop, turn, run again—until Grachikov was satisfied. The gym echoed to the pounding of her training shoes.

"Relax, relax!" he bellowed over the sound of her shoes coming back off the walls. Why did the noise make the place sound damp, hollow and unused, she wondered. She tried to loosen her body, or at least imitate relaxation. That was the trouble, she told herself. When she had decided her course of action, lying awake the previous night, staring at the ceiling and hearing the snoring of Nadia, the typist, she had chosen for herself a life of deception. Having made her decision, she had made a little prison for herself—inside which she would be perpetually afraid of the prying eye at the hole in the door.

"Relax, relax! You bitch!"

Which was what came of loving Martin Gutierrez, she reminded herself, but choked off the thought because it might open a perspective of futility just when she needed to believe in him, more than ever before.

The papers were handwritten, difficult to decipher, but that was not *Burgoyne*'s business. The felt pen's blue ink, the deletions, the rearranged paragraphs, the more hurried scrawl of qualifying thoughts, the careful script of the main thrust of the argument for a ten-percent increase in the research and development appropriation—the Deputy Defense Minister in command of the Strategic Rocket Forces was forceful, persuasive, imperative in tone. But *Burgoyne*, pushing the next sheet of handwritten notes into the light of the desk lamp, gauging the camera's focus, pressing the shutter release, had no interest other than to get the job completed, get out of the office, and return the notes to the locked safe in the office of the secretary of the Deputy Minister.

The material was one of the first indications of the content and intention of that year's defense budget, and the CIA were insistent, impatient. With SALT II signed, the first defense budget of the Soviet Union to follow the treaty was of paramount importance to the Pentagon and NATO. Thus, instead of waiting for the minutes of the first meetings of the Military Council and the Politburo, or the agenda for those meetings, *Burgoyne* had obeyed instructions to photograph draft material before it was typed and worked into papers and made available to the members of the Military Council and the Politburo a week before the first meeting. The thoughts of the Defense Ministry were gold to Langley.

Burgoyne shuffled the photographed sheet out of the way, slid another into the center of the lamp spill, the page starkly white, the hieroglyphs anonymous until initials and cryptonyms insinuated themselves—SS-20s, the costing of development of SS-21s and -22s during the next year—*Burgoyne* pressed the shutter release twice, ignored the appended pages of detailed costings since they were summarized on page 21 of the notes, pushed another of the Deputy Minister's sheets into place, clicked twice, and pushed the page aside.

New storable fuels—a new ABM system about which the

Deputy Minister was skeptical but which he wished funded as efficiently as possible—*Burgoyne* wondered about that, since it might be a deliberate throwaway when the estimates came to be pruned by the moneymen in the Politburo, then pressed the release. A click that was as loud as a door being locked.

Pause. Next page, the advanced cruise-missile program requiring billions of additional rubles. *Burgoyne* snapped that page eagerly, almost lovingly. Page 18, 19, 20—

No footsteps, few noises on that floor of the Ministry. And *Burgoyne* had every right to be there, the name on the office door proclaimed that. And, for safety, the main light switch was on the desk, next to the lamp, and a heaped bundle of files were ready to be toppled across the incriminating papers on the desk should anything disturb the anxious silence.

Battlefield support missiles, AS and AA missiles, ICBMs, MIRVs, supporting evidence from field trials—*Burgoyne* could not entirely suppress a sense of excitement, of self-congratulation, at the comprehensiveness of the material, at the good judgment that had selected the Deputy Minister's initial notes as a target.

Page 29. The last. A loud exhalation in the darkened room, then the camera dropped into an open drawer, the papers collected into their original bundle, replaced in their envelope, light on, a moment to steady oneself. And the mind reaching ahead to the drop, the passage of the information to Langley, its dissection, the judgments made—then the demands upon *Burgoyne* for more information, always more and more information.

Burgoyne was worried. There was a new hunt for the double agent they knew had to exist inside the Defense Ministry. The secret verbal bargaining in the final stages of SALT II—something *Burgoyne* had worked for, after which they had falsely promised a speedy exit—had ironically helped to confirm the plant. The Second Chief Directorate had put Leonov in charge of the new investigation. And *Burgoyne* knew how good, how persistent, how dedicated, Leonov could be.

It was something to worry about. The time was coming to press the OUT button in earnest. No taking any more polite delays. Hence, perhaps, the risks with these notes, now clutched tightly—release, take the pressure off, the envelope's creasing—a preliminary bribe before *Burgoyne* pressed that button and yelled down the tube to Langley to be lifted out of Moscow. Surely, surely it's been *earned* by now, that new American identity—?

Burgoyne returned the envelope to the safe, collected the

camera, handed in the ID tag to the security staff, and left the Defense Ministry, wary already of being tailed.

All the time he was in the girl, Gutierrez was thinking of Karen Gunston. It was involuntary. He wanted to think about the girl, wanted the kind of trip that sex with her usually supplied. She was good—moaning softly, moving slightly back and forth on top of him while he stroked her waist, her hips, her buttocks. She was thin but he enjoyed the angles and planes of her body, enjoyed the small breasts now above him, just out of reach. He could feel himself coming—even if he'd wanted to prolong it, she was too good to let him.

All the time he stared at the ceiling, knowing she couldn't see his face, and cursed himself for being led on by the Gunston woman to the point where he half-admitted the hash smoking. She'd led him on, even tried to turn him on—just so he'd say it, admit to something more newsworthy and dramatic than winning a race. What had he stirred up? What the hell could he do to counter what he'd done?

Damn it, damn the fucking woman! The girl leaned forward, pressing her breasts down toward his mouth. He raised his head, reluctant and in the wrong mood for a moment. She moved, so that her breasts undulated just out of his reach. He suddenly wanted to stop it, slap her backside, roll away and get himself a smoke. He'd been taken, conned, just a mark for a news story about athletes on soft drugs. Millions of people must have heard him, for Christ's sake, bragging about hash.

He came, and it seemed that he had been holding his breath all the time, because it suddenly roared in the dark room. The girl giggled softly, satisfied with her success, he thought. And the whole thing turned sour on him; even having the girl astride him, which he usually enjoyed with her, was a reduction of himself. The look in Karen Gunston's eyes was another reduction—buck, stallion, stud. Show us what you can do, running boy. Sometimes he loathed sex, and women, and their attempt to get to him, get with him, get on him, get him in them.

And sometimes he loathed himself for the view they sometimes gave him of himself, when he could see his ego jutting like a rock up out of his life.

He pushed the girl, none too gently, and she rolled away from him. He felt the slight trickle of semen in his crotch, ignored it, though he was normally fastidious, and rummaged in his strewn clothes until he found the joints. He opened the flat tin, and removed two of them, expecting that the girl would indulge. For him, it would be an escape from the pressing sense of her presence. He fumbled for matches, and heard the girl's voice.

"I've got some stuff."

"What?" He had a ridiculous and diminishing picture of himself hunched on the edge of the rumpled bed, lighting the joint. And the ignored girl behind him, naked, staring emptily at the ceiling. It really wasn't what his life ought to be about, he told himself. But sometimes he had to stop running.

"Some stuff, Marty." The diminutive grated on him.

"For Christ's sake, stop being earth mother mysterious—what stuff?"

"Like vintage champagne—some tablets from the Welsh connection." She giggled. "I paid top price—rarity value."

He puzzled over her words. Then, "How many times before?"

"Once—only once, Marty." Most of all, he affirmed, he disliked such child imitation. All right, so he knew people who talked to each other like that most of the time—his own parents still did—but perhaps love excused it, made something out of it. Cohabitation of a strictly temporary kind wasn't enough. "A good trip," she added. "Want to try?"

He turned on the bed and looked at her: a pale little smudge of face, waiflike, and the boyish little frame stretched out on the bed. Her hand was close to him, and he could see the green tablets.

"I can't afford the fare."

"I'll treat you."

"No thanks." He wanted nothing to do with LSD. He could retain control, even when one joint followed another—he was stretched out and floating, sure, but in control, not wandering round the inside of his head afraid of what he might meet. He had seen bad trips, and didn't want them. More, he couldn't take the physical and mental time out the trips required. He added, "No vacation this year. Just business, business—"

He lay back on the bed, and lit the joint. As the match flared, he thought of getting rid of the girl, taking her home, then he drew in the sweet smoke. He felt it curling round his body like a gas, enlivening senses, relaxing muscles and nerves. He drew again, already beginning to forget the presence of the girl.

It must have been late in the night, perhaps no more than an hour before the quick African dawn, that the sound, whatever it was, awoke Ochengwe. He listened, but there was no repetition. But in a dream of running, he was certain that the noises were those of a creaking bicycle, then footsteps, pace and sound so different from his dream that he knew they were not imagined.

He eased his arm from around his wife, who stirred but did not wake, and rose from the cot. He padded across the wooden floor of the hut, past his sleeping son, through the tiny, cramped kitchen that they promised would be modernized soon, and out onto the back porch.

He was naked, and his posture was almost instinctively that of the primitive hunter—as if smelling and hearing were his only senses. He did not know why he was disturbed, even afraid, his body chilly and goosefleshed as if some old and buried fear had come out of the night. He stepped carefully down off the porch, sensing the direction as if still listening to his dream.

M'seka was a small place, a haphazard arrangement of huts of wood, some still of mud and straw, each with a dusty strip of garden; one main street and three side streets meeting at the village square like the points of a broken star. Without understanding what he was doing, he moved toward the newest dwellings, three or four huts hammered out of gasoline cans and corrugated tin and chicken wire. Here some recent immigrants from Rwanda and Tanzania had settled. The village was close to the point of accepting them, but not quite.

An old, rusting woman's bicycle with a slack chain and one flat tire. It looked innocent, innocuous. He thought for a moment of turning back, stepping carefully over the bottle tops and bits of bright cloth strung out to keep the birds from what grew in the gardens—then he was fully aware of the possible significance of a stranger arriving quietly in the late night in his village.

One tin and chicken wire hut belonged to a young man and his family—it also housed two ancient relatives, perhaps his parents, even grandparents. Ochengwe was spurred to move closer by an inward picture of the young man seeming to sneer, to adopt a superiority, as Ochengwe passed him on the run. Winston Ochengwe had not been more than surprised, but he had often thought of the young man's evident assumption of superiority.

He could hear low voices, talking urgently. He was no more than five yards from one tin wall of the hut. He could see the hammered emblem of an oil company, could almost reach out and touch it. He saw the light of an oil lamp from the gap under the ill-fitting board of a door. He had a sense that the conversation was almost done, that the voices had risen to a note of agreement and satisfaction. He moved quickly, stepping high to avoid any of the bird lines, and concealed himself behind the angle of the hut.

Two men came out, followed by the young man whose hut it was. He seemed pleased, but Ochengwe sensed a relief of nerves in his grin as much as genuine pleasure. The other two men he did not know. All three shook hands, then the smaller of the visitors climbed on the handlebars, while the other made ready to ride the old bicycle. Ochengwe watched them wobble away from the hut—then something fell from one of the two men, and they stopped, retrieved it, and set off again. The young man watched them until they were out of sight, relieved himself against the hut, and went back inside.

Ochengwe stayed a long time before moving. The gun that one of the visitors had dropped disturbed and frightened him. The men were obviously guerrillas from across the border in Tanzania. Why were they in M'seka—with guns?

His stomach felt heavy as he went back quietly to his own hut.

"*Burgoyne*, I am being tailed. Were you tailed to the last drop?"

Burgoyne had been shown how to remove the KGB bug from the telephone whenever expecting a call, and how to replace it later. The man at the other end of the line, ringing at his appointed time, knew it was safe to talk. *Burgoyne* had lifted the receiver after the tenth ring. Twelve rings, and the contact would have asked for a different, wrong number.

"No—no, I wasn't." Nervousness, a schoolboy's eagerness to avoid blame. "Are you certain?"

"Yes—I'm too old a hand. But you're safe—?"

"As far as I can tell. You've reported to Control—?"

"Not yet. He can come to me. I lost them on the metro—as usual. Remember last year, when it looked as if—"

An old man, a very good, but old, man. Reminiscing in the middle of things, taking time out to recollect old dangers. *Burgoyne* was angry, then guilty at that anger. Life depended on this old man's cleverness, his ability to use the metro system to wash himself clean of any tail.

"Yes, yes, I remember. But you're clean—?"

"Yes, I've washed." A chuckle. Then more serious. "I'm just

warning you, as you warned me. Something is building, *Burgoyne*. Busy, busy—you know the KGB. Be careful, otherwise only the Americans around us will live to tell the tale."

"Yes, yes—thank you, I'll be careful. *You* be careful—"

The dead tone of a disconnected line. *Burgoyne* put down the receiver as if reluctant to admit that the fragile contact between them had been severed.

The evening darkened, the lights of Barnsley and the glinting ribbon of the M1 were behind him, as he climbed up toward Hugset Wood and the golf course. His hair flattened, dripping the rain onto his face and neck, the track suit heavy and sloppy in the sleeves with the weight of the rain being blown on a mild evening wind. Peter Lydall paused at the edge of the wood and looked down. Cars, headlights like great washes of light, streamed north and south on the motorway, as if hurrying past his hometown. The motorway was like a barrier of modernity beyond which the gray and wet town lay humped and shabby. To his left, a mine, to his right, another— two encroachments on Hugset Wood by the town, as if catching it in a pincers. Dodworth, this side of the motorway, was like another eruption of the town. He looked at his watch, peeling back the wet sleeve of his track suit. The time was disappointing—not that he could assess performance over his personal cross-country course with any degree of accuracy, but a couple of years ago he would have been quicker to this vantage point.

And the leg was beginning to ache dully. An old man's arthritis brought on by the weather. As soon as he acknowledged the ache, he turned back to the wood and began running again. Under the trees, the ground was drier, but great drops dripped like some pastoral version of a water torture from the leaves above him. In there, unseen birds called to each other, as if remarking his passage. The ache in his leg subsided, held down below the conscious level by willpower. And by his attention to his whole body—heart, lungs, thighs, arms, back. As if he had taped himself with sensors which now went about their business of recording his condition.

He was two months—perhaps more—behind his schedule for the season. The bloody car accident and the broken leg last year had seen to that. So, he was really a year and two months behind his Olympic schedule. Last season he had sat with his leg in plaster while the newspapers sympathized, criticized, wondered, and finally wrote him off.

Has-been.

He gritted his teeth as he came out of Hugset Wood and swung southeast toward the folds of the golf course, now dying into shadow. To the west, briefly in front of him, the sun was sinking behind bars of heavy cloud—more rain on the way. It was lighter on this side of the wood, looking toward the sunset and the Peaks, without the motorway and the town to darken the perspective.

He had three weeks before the Crystal Palace meeting. There was an omission in the Great Britain team, in the 5000 meters event. The British first-string had been picked, but there was room for another man. It had to be himself—that's what the unusual omission meant. Either that, or it was to prove to the great British public, who had a sentimental recollection of his failure to reach the Final in Montreal, that he was finished.

He could see the clubhouse away to his right, huddled against the clouds, as he crossed the fairway of the tenth. The ache came back a little as he went down a gentle slope, then disappeared as he topped a further rise.

This time, this time—

Like a litany, part of a ceremony in which, at odd times, perhaps in front of a class or after a training run, he had a sense of losing all belief. So that, at thirty, he confronted the compromises, the lost opportunities, the sacrifices of career—and happy marriage, some voice muttered in him—that he had made in ten years of international running; and tasted a bitter, compacted food that he could hardly digest, the mess of pottage that was his track career.

He pushed on, the rain lightening, passing the slaty, grubby mine, wheel and coaltip heavily impressing him, toward the B road and the motorway again, the slashing bright lights seemingly greater in number and moving faster, running away from him.

He did not want to go home. Not that the place was empty. Just frosty with the presence of his wife and their long silences. And the tinge of contempt which she would show when he appeared bedraggled and weary.

God in Heaven, he didn't even like the Russians, and wouldn't pay twopence for a holiday in Moscow.

The car was waiting for him, pulled onto the verge of the B road. A three-year-old Lotus. The man standing by it was vaguely familiar, a bright blob in the last of the daylight in his red-and-white car coat and light slacks. As Lydall pounded up the road toward the car, the driver raised a hand in greeting.

Lydall stopped, studying the tall man for a moment. Then he said, "Dave—Dave Allardyce." He consciously wiped his wet hand on his wet track suit before taking the other's proffered hand. Allardyce, fair-haired, handsome in a youthful way, seemed pleased to see him, and Lydall responded without, for the moment, wondering why a man he had not seen for more than three years should suddenly appear on the route of his training run, evidently there so that they should meet.

"Peter. How are you?" Allardyce had the ability to command situations, a social ease and authority that Lydall had often envied—though those qualities had never been displayed in order to declare any difference between the two of them.

"So-so. Not so bad, really." Lydall was aware, momentarily, of his local accent, his ordinariness alongside this man—well-off, Oxbridge, journalist by inclination, amateur athlete who had been content with a three-year stint as British number two in the 100 hurdles, and then retired. An unenvying man.

"Good—look, if we stop and chat, have a drink, am I interrupting anything vital?" The question was languidly put, but well-intentioned and without irony and indifference. Lydall shook his head.

"No—just on me way home. I can jack this in for tonight. Bloody awful weather for it, anyway!"

"Good. Anywhere you recommend?"

Lydall nodded over his shoulder.

"Pack Horse in Dodworth is closest. No carpets on the floor, mind."

Allardyce smiled.

"Trendy then, is it?"

Lydall laughed.

"It might be to some—but not to you. Still, you can give me a ride in this old banger of yours, can't you?"

"Don't laugh—I am going to get rid of it. The ashtray's just about chockablock."

"Shame."

"Isn't it?"

Both men seemed pleased to have fallen into an old habit of talk, as if they had met only recently, and then regularly. Allardyce appraised Lydall carefully as he drove down to the village, and parked the Lotus in the cramped little patch of concrete at the back of the unprepossessing pub. The athlete seemed older—in experience rather than years; and as if there were some inner fire burning his flesh, slowly eating it away. He was almost gaunt, and he looked tired. Allardyce acknowledged the way Lydall must be driving himself to competition fitness. And doing it by himself, determined to do it alone. He felt an admiration that he left unvoiced, aware of how it might seem patronizing.

When they were settled round a stained table in one corner of the tiny, stone-floored Lounge Bar, Lydall with orange juice, Allardyce with a whiskey and soda, Lydall said abruptly, "Well, to what do I owe the pleasure? Cheers." He sipped at his drink. Allardyce inspected the smudges of inadequate washing on the tumbler, then swallowed half of his whiskey.

"Cheers—cold out there, waiting for you."

"Why wait then?"

"Ah." Allardyce's eyes sparkled. "I want to interview you, if you're willing."

"Me. I'm no terrorist or politician. What's the angle, the threat I pose to the IOC?"

"I'll explain. David Allardyce, fearless foreign correspondent, is being asked by his newspaper to cover the athletics front at the Moscow Olympics."

"What?"

"I'm eminently qualified. I failed to reach an Olympic Final— sorry, that wasn't a dig. I kept coming in fourth in all the internationals in which I ran—who better?"

"True. And I suppose, if you just happened to come across some inside-the-Soviet-system gems, the paper would print them *after* you got back?"

Allardyce nodded. "Quite correct. Everyone is at it, trying to discover sports correspondents at their foreign desks. One TV company that shall remain nameless has, it is reported, reached the depths of the Thames Valley Extra-B team in its search for people with the right background."

Lydall grinned. "So, I have to prove to the public that you can do in-depth profile stuff on deadbeat athletes?"

"Self-pity?"

"No."

"Strangely, I believe you. Are you willing?"

"Buy me another orange juice, ducky, and I'm yours." Lydall held up his glass. Allardyce swallowed the rest of the whiskey, and went to the bar. The landlord studied him and over his shoulder the dripping figure of Lydall, and was obviously puzzled. The only two other occupants of the Lounge, a silent man and his silent wife who stared communally into the unambitious fire in the black grate, paid no attention to their companions. Allardyce took the drinks back to the table.

"All right—tell me about the opposition in Moscow."

"Background—you're supposed to research this."

"I am. Consider yourself my technical adviser."

"Mm. O.K., you want to know who's going to win?"

"If *you* know."

"Irvine, the Aussie—he'll be over here from now on, running in every race he can get. Psychologically, he's riding a wave. I'll be running up against the bugger at Crystal Palace, no doubt. He'll be there—unless he spreads himself like Viren over two events. He might not have the grip for both. I don't know."

"What about Gutierrez?"

"California Dreamer? He's good, and he knows it." Lydall shrugged. "I didn't run last year, and the year before that he was all over the place tactically. But you should have seen him last year, competing in Europe—cashing in on the big meetings in Scandinavia. Besides, he's so bigheaded he has to be in with a good chance."

"Diderot?"

"Playboy—he's half-fit—like Lydall of Great Britain, if you're interested. The Russians are strong. Tretsov won their trials very well, but I reckon Federenko is better. It might depend which one Mr. Brezhnev favours there."

"What about the Africans?"

"Only one of them—Ochengwe. He's—incredible. He'll be there, whoever else is there, when they roll off the last bend. He may run for one of the most godforsaken countries in Africa, people may think he runs by instinct rather than brains, which isn't true anyway, but he'll be there."

"You admire him?"

"Yes. He's not a perpetual student, nor is he in the Red Army or a Master of Sport. He runs to work, and back home again. If anyone represents what it *should* be all about—it's him."

"Rather like yourself, then?" There was an edge of irony in the level tones now. Lydall wrinkled his face in irritation.

"Not like me. He's uncomplicated. He *enjoys* running. Not winning, not being feted, not breaking records—just *running*. I don't feel like that—never have done."

"And what about *you*?"

"Ah." Lydall put down his glass, and pumped his arms, imitating running as he sat. "I know what you want me to say. Well, I've said stuff it to Tom McNab and the Dubai professional circus. So, I'll be there—gallant old Great Britain—" He smiled, then his face slipped into gaunt, serious lines. "And I won't be far behind, either. Come and see me at Crystal Palace, Dave. I'll make it."

CHAPTER 3

The Lenin Stadium, Moscow, first site of a modern Olympiad to be in existence before the home of the Games had been decided. It had been built in 1955 and 1956, in the southern loop of the river Moskva where the marshy wastelands of Luzhniki—a name still given sometimes to the stadium, though not in Olympic year—were filled in and leveled, and planted with thousands of trees and laid with asphalt walks, all now widened and improved. The park complex extended over 175 hectares (432 acres), and included the main stadium with its 100,000 seating capacity, the covered Sports Palace, a competition swimming pool with room for 13,000 spectators, tennis courts, and the smaller stadium for 15,000 capacity, where Federenko now watched Tretsov in training.

The statue of Lenin erected in 1960 had seemed to follow him with its stone eyes as he passed it on his way through Luzhniki Park, to be officially renamed Olympic Park by the Soviet First Secretary the following week, when the cosmetic work would be complete. New security barriers and brighter lighting were being added to the stadium complex on its splendid site across the river's loop from the University and the Lenin Heights.

He had been summoned by Party and Soviet Olympic Committee representatives, just five days after his arrival in Moscow. His new apartment was on Rusakovskaya Street, out near Sokolniki Park, in a discreet block in pink stone that housed a number of government officials as well as athletes and sportsmen and -women who lived permanently in Moscow. He had traveled through from Sokolniki to the Sportivnaya station on the metro, his kit in a leather bag which he wore over his shoulder like an emblem of success.

Something of a hollow boast, he considered, looking down at Tretsov going through his training routine, twenty-sixty to sixty-two-second laps. Tretsov had done a couple of warm-up laps, then gone straight into the routine. Willing workhorse—or tool, if you wanted to be unkind.

Vladimir had not traveled to Moscow with him. Which did not bode well, he reminded himself, especially now that Tretsov's coach had told him what part of his act he wanted to see—four very fast laps with no warm-up other than that he would do before the beginning of a race. And then he was to go on, and they would time him for each succeeding lap, until he went above seventy—

Burned himself out.

He felt cold on the bright afternoon, sitting on a crush barrier, his feet dangling over an exit tunnel, staring at his training shoes, looking up occasionally to measure the effort Tretsov required to perform.

He was going well, burning off imaginary rivals like someone leaving a swarm of insects behind. Tretsov must feel good, he thought. Better than I feel.

The pacemaker. The blowtorch. Strip off as many coats of rival paint as you can, before the paraffin runs out. Then Tretsov takes over. They hadn't said it, yet. But he knew it was what they wanted. Had he won the Trials, they might have done it to Tretsov—but, as it was, Tretsov the slogger, the everlasting slow-burner, was who they had backed to win the 5000. He was only the torch leading the way, burning out before the end of the race.

And he wanted to win. So much that the thought of not winning made him nauseous and weak, and he hated the old men he knew were behind it just as he hated Tretsov.

When Tretsov's coach waved in summons, he jumped down onto the tiered gangway, picked up his bag, and went down toward him.

Tretsov continued to circle the track like a puppet, a depressingly regular mechanism.

Gutierrez studied the white envelope, turning it back and forth in his left hand, the coffee cup still, poised, in his right. It was as if he hoped its anonymity might rescind the details of the letter it had contained, which lay, acquiring butter and toast crumbs, on his breakfast plate. A summons by the U.S. Olympic Committee to appear before a disciplinary subcommittee in two days' time.

It was not the embossed letterhead, nor the signature, not even the contents of the letter in bold IBM script—simply its origin. Since the stupidity of his half-admissions on TV, he had expected action from the college authorities, even his track club—leading, perhaps, to action by the USOC. But they'd jumped those early hurdles, coming for him before he expected it. And the college had kept in the background, hiding in the brush and leaving him the only fool standing up when the shooting started.

He crunched the envelope into a tight ball in his fist, as if testing the strength of his body, or asserting something. If the USOC was about to wave him good-bye as they got on the 747 for Moscow, this would be the way they would do it. Three weeks before the Olympic Trials at Eugene, they wanted to see him—and at the moment he was nothing to do with them, none of their business.

And maybe that's what they wanted to tell him—you're none of our business. Good-bye. He felt weak with fear. The emotion was undiluted, acid. They were going to dump him because the Russian press had taken up the story for propaganda reasons, and some of the more high-toned of the West Coast papers were sticking it to him, notwithstanding their usual pussyfoot approach to his membership of an ethnic minority. Everyone—except Greenberg—seemed satisfied to shaft him, and twist the knife. Just because he had boasted of something everyone did, everyone knew about.

Christ, what if they excluded him from the team—?

He picked up the letter, wiped the butter and crumbs from it with the edge of the tablecloth, as if by showing respect to their instructions he might ingratiate himself with the U.S. Olympic Committee.

"Chief, we've found him!"

"Ilya—take a breath. Found who?"

"The old joker who slipped us on the metro, Captain. He was picked up collecting his pension, of all things—" The excitement tailed off as the young man remembered that it had been Leonov's idea to use Identifit in the post offices, welfare service departments, library reading rooms, on and around pension day. Leonov laughed into his receiver, placed his free hand flat on the desk blotter. He studied the strong fingers, letting his subordinate fumble an apology, stew in his mistake, for a little while.

"It must be my own advanced age that made me think of it," he said finally. "Someone followed him home?"

"Yes, sir—"

"Give me the address." An anonymous block in the heavily industrialized Lenin suburb beyond the Novospassky monastery. A lot of people lived there on their state pensions of fifty rubles a month. The rents were some of the lowest in the Moscow conurbation, and the apartments some of the oldest. "What's he doing?"

"Sorry, sir, they don't know. Surveillance is impossible—not an empty flat in any block overlooking his. We've checked all of them out."

"O.K."

"Do we lift him, Captain?"

"Let me think—?" Leonov could not help the little catch in his voice, the tingle of excitement in the hand pressing on the blotter. This was the closest they had got, after months of careful, unglamorous, unrewarded work. One or two drops, dead-letter boxes, and two embassy possibles who might be the double agent's control. No nearer the double. "Does he have anything?"

"By now?"

"Right. We'll set up as good a surveillance as we can, and run it for a couple of days. If nothing happens, he makes no move and no one contacts him—then he's going into the bag, and through the mincer."

"Great." Leonov was surprised at the young man's enthusiasm. Perhaps he was only embracing the long-withheld tangibility of the investigation. God help the old man, he added, to himself. When he went through the mincer, there'd be nothing left of him, so desperate were they for a lead.

Stop it, stop it dead, they'd said to him. *It's been going on too long, and because of SALT II the area is becoming too sensitive for high-grade leaks of this kind. Stop it dead.*

Once they got their hands on anyone, the Center was going to chew them up.

"O.K., young man. Tell them well done from me—and that I'll be out to inspect their efforts tonight."

"Sir."

Leonov put the receiver back grudgingly in its rest. Once the contact was broken, the intangibility that had permeated the investigation came back to him, and persisted.

Irvine's fellow Australian, who worked as a film editor for the BBC, had stitched the film together for him within a couple of days of Irvine broaching the idea. Then he had smuggled the film can out of Broadcasting House, and back to his flat in Earl's Court, where he had a projector and screen. Kenneth Irvine had arrived in England only a week or so before, from Europe, eager to race as often, and as hard, as possible during the English athletics season and greeted by the national press as a threat to anyone else's hopes of an

Olympic Gold at 5000. Already he had one six-mile race and two at 10,000 lined up, a couple of invitation three miles, and a shorter 1500 at club level to sharpen his speed. Irvine had raced in a number of the big meetings in Europe, collecting the anticipated generous expenses, and he intended returning there before the Olympics.

"What's the order of appearance?" he asked as his companion switched off the lights in his lounge, and then flicked on the projector.

"Lydall first—just some training film from a 'Grandstand' profile last month."

"Shit, he's out of it, Don. What about the African, and the Russians?"

"Yes—but the Russians are from last year. Soviet Olympic Committee won't release any film of the Trials—and the rest of Eastern Europe's gone remarkably dumb when it comes to enquiries about Soviet athletes. The African's from a couple of weeks ago."

"What about the Yank?"

Don looked at the back of Irvine's head as he sat on an upright chair facing the screen, and pulled a face. "Yeah, he's in. Winning that collegiate race a while ago. Clever bastard he is, too!"

"The Frog?"

"Got him falling down knackered at the end of that race in Munich."

"Good—run it, then."

Irvine heard behind him the little explosion of the pull top of a can of beer, then the throaty swallowing which was intended to convey Don's independence. Then the projector started to roll, and he became totally absorbed by the screen.

Lydall—so the scratchy sound track told him from the speaker sitting under the screen—was training on a local track in Yorkshire. Irvine watched him with almost obsessive analytical attention for a couple of laps, watched the tactics the man was employing, fitted the images with mental images from races, from other films. Lydall looked old, and tired, and a loser. Part of Irvine, existing outside self-confidence, weighed him objectively, and came to the same conclusion as the ego. Lydall was behind time, behind schedule.

Flickering numbers, running down to a flare of blank screen, then Federenko, the Russian number two. Two years before, in the World Student Games, Federenko had beaten him, because he had failed to realize his tactics then until it was too late. Which was why he studied the films Don brought home on the q.t. Federenko had run a fast early half of the race, slowed the pace, then kicked explosively and killingly in the final two hundred. Since then, the Ukrainian had got nowhere near his best times. Tretsov was older, canny and dogged—but unworrying to Irvine. Then Ochengwe, color film but bad African camerawork for the most part, easily winning a race in Kenya, against the two best Kenyans and a promising Tanzanian.

Don popped open another can of beer. Irvine watched the screen intently, learning what he could of opponents he had either never met or who had previously beaten him. And, in the case of Gutierrez and Diderot, and the German Holmrath, opponents he had beaten. More than once. Whenever Don's film allowed a whole lap to be studied, the stopwatch in Irvine's hand clicked on, clicked off over the whirring of the projector.

The film ended with the shot of Diderot lying painfully exhausted on the trackside in Munich at the Munchenerbrau Invitation. Irvine knew the time for the race—much too slow.

Don switched off the projector and turned up the lights. He swigged at the beer can, then said, "Well? What you wanted, mate?"

"Near enough. How's the ten thousand film stuff coming along?"

"Christ, Kenny! You can watch the stuff on telly next week. 'Sportsnight' is doing a profile of the leading contenders—including your good self."

"As long as you get me the stuff they don't use, Don—"

"Bleeding hell, Kenny! I'm not your slave. I'm not supposed to bring film home from the Beeb, you know!"

"Do it for Aussie, mate—do it for Aussie." Irvine was smiling. Don, tossing his head in mock disgust, handed him a can of beer. "Ta."

"You going to do both races—seriously?"

"I reckon to. Ten thousand's a lighter field. And I'm favourite for the five."

"Good luck to you, mate. Don't bust a gut doing it. That's something the folks back home won't forgive you for! They never forgave Clarkie for not winning a major championship, and they bloody well won't forgive you either!"

"The old sod's hanged himself!"

Leonov turned on the man who had spoken, his face suffused with rage and frustration, his hands curling into fists at his sides as if trying to grasp something that eluded him. The young man who had spoken—more in surprise than contempt—blanched, turned his glance aside.

"You didn't *see* it! None of you saw it! Shadows on the curtains, activity as he went from room to room—they always wander around before they do themselves in! Christ—I'm surrounded by kids!" He looked at Georgi, the senior detective in charge of the duty surveillance team. Georgi's lips were pressed tightly together, as if resisting the insinuation of shadows that moved across his face— someone had bumped into the old man's legs as they burst into the room, and set the body swinging. Georgi shook his head.

"He looked out of the curtains a couple of times, as if waiting for someone—"

"He saw you—!"

"*No*—sir. I don't think he did. Not tonight. Perhaps—well, perhaps before tonight, but not this team." Professional pride rather than buck-passing, Leonov perceived. Irritated, he turned to the scrawny, elongated body with the sideways head, some plaster dust still in the white hair and beard like bits of meringue and his tongue was sticking out as if to lick the nearest pieces into his mouth. Leonov caught hold of the legs and stilled the body. He noticed that Kostya, two years' experience, and Ilya, six months, were looking uncomfortable, mesmerized by the distorted face, especially the bulging eyes—at a loss.

"All right, all right—" Leonov was looking up to the ceiling, where the old man had knocked out the plaster to expose a joist from which to suspend the rope. Then he'd climbed on a chair, kicked it away, and strangled himself slowly. On a sudden impulse, Leonov went into the bathroom, and ran the taps. Then he studied the one glass shelf. No razor. He felt the water trickling from the hot tap. Tepid, no more. He glanced into the kitchen, saw the tiny electric stove, and nodded as if he had discovered an important piece of evidence.

He paused at the door of the lounge. The old man's back was to him. He almost—dangerously—admired the thoroughness, the single-mindedness, the decisiveness of the man's action. Suspended above his team, he seemed to suggest a mocking advantage. Then he was just an old man who'd hanged himself to avoid being interrogated.

Leonov already had a feeling about the investigation. He was pressing—just as he was being pressed—like a hand squeezed round a bar of soap. If he could make the soap pop up, and watch for the helping hand that reached for it before it fell—

It was, he believed, all he could do. However small the number of suspects, the agent was clever and there was nothing, no trademark or giveaway, that would further narrow the field. And, at that level in the Ministry or the Secretariat, there was no excuse for arrest without proof. If he squeezed, though—like this old man and the others who were contacts, cutouts, postmen, pickups—he might panic the double, and the Americans would try to lift him. Then, perhaps.

And only then. He wanted to do damage to the old man who had been so calm, so assured, so methodical. And so unafraid of dying. He might have been able to bargain for his life, if he'd told. Instead, he'd known they were closing in, and he'd protected the agent in place.

"Cut him down," he said quietly, for by now the room with its one dim lamp and faded strips of carpet and sagging furniture had become religious in its heavy silence. "Cut him down—then search the place thoroughly."

François Jean-Marie Diderot, French champion at 5000 meters, sat at his ease in the small television studio RTF used for its weekly sports program, watching the camera, waiting for the red light to operate. The program presenter was introducing him, voice-over on a piece of video of his last race, in Düsseldorf. Holmrath had beaten him in front of a partisan crowd, but he had come in second, ahead of the rest of the Europeans, Anderson the American number two, and Jorgensen the Norwegian—in better form, but struggling with the years as much as the opposition.

Red light.

". . . François Diderot is with me here in the studio. François, though you finished second to Holmrath in Düsseldorf, you seem to have run a much more tactical race, and have more to spare at the end."

Diderot cleared his throat, smiled into the camera.

"I think that's true. Although I was second, my time was faster than in Munich, when I beat him. This time, the tables were turned—you saw how he collapsed on the track after the race. It was my turn to smile down into his face." He grinned toward the host, who nodded sagely, returning the smile.

"Are you satisfied with your preparations for the Olympics, now we're in the middle of the season?"

"I think so," Diderot replied expansively. "My program is worked out in detail—the races in which I shall run, the opposition I will face. And the training—" He grinned ruefully into the camera.

"Ah, yes. In the past, you've been much criticized in the popular press for not training hard enough. That's no longer true?"

"Not at all. The playboy image is a thing of the past. I am going all out for a medal in Moscow."

"François—if I can ask you this—?" Diderot was slow to perceive the surprise that was coming.

"You've recently changed your job, isn't that so?"

"Yes—?" Don't be hesitant, evasive, he told himself. Just tell them calmly. He felt the lights above his head as if they pressed down on him. His body felt hot and damp inside the new suit. A bead of sweat popped out at his hairline, just above the light makeup the girl had dabbed on him. "Obviously, I had to make a decision—not in terms of my future, but in terms of winning a medal for my country—"

The interviewer smiled, and inclined his head as if Diderot had won a point.

"Quite so. Your new job, with France-Allemagne Sporting is not on the sales side?"

"I am merely a consultant. *I* have *not* used it as a means of advertising." Better. "I would not be allowed to become part of the sales force, or appear in any advertising material, of course."

"Of course not. Thank you, François Diderot—and the best wishes of 'Le Sport à Huit,' and no doubt of our audience, to you in Moscow—"

"Thank you—" but the interviewer was already turning to another camera and another item. Diderot looked at the studio manager, who mimed that he could move out of the chair. He did so gingerly, and crossed the floor of the studio behind the three cameras. The studio manager shook his hand, spilled superlatives like sweets over him, then showed him into the corridor.

"A moment," he said. "You'll stay for a drink?"

"Uh—sure."

"Good. I'll get one of the girls to show you up to the bar. We'll wrap up, and Jacques and the others will meet you there. Excellent, excellent—"

Diderot was left alone in the corridor for a moment. And he wondered how much they knew. He felt as if a huge bowling ball were rolling down the empty corridor toward him—at the moment, it was invisible, but he was just learning that it was there, and how fast it was moving.

Zenaida had made little sandwiches for them, and tea. It was, Shubin thought, as if he'd been invited to meet the parents of a girl he was soon to marry. There were times when he could not ignore his contempt for the girl, even though he never failed to be aware of her malleable enthusiasm, and her admiration for him. She was the most loyal member of the cell he had called *Do pobachenya*, the Ukrainian word for "Good-bye." One of his rare, and bitter, flashes of humor. Laughter, like most recreations of his angry spirit, became twisted and black in him, part of his constant sense of superiority to others.

There were six of them in *Do pobachenya*. Four of the others had already arrived, and seemed absurdly pleased and at home with the thin sandwiches and the cups of tea. He watched Zenaida, framed by the afternoon light through the net curtains she had erected at the window of her college room, serving the sandwiches and cut bread and pickle, then bringing small pancakes from the kitchenette, and wanted to laugh aloud, except that he had important things to say, and he wanted them compliant, enthusiastic. Thus, the little bourgeois custom of taking tea.

They were all young, from this teachers' college or other higher education institutes in Kiev. Kostya, Ilya, Ferenc, Lyudmila—and Yakov who had not yet arrived because of a late economics lecture. All of them *clean* people, without records with the KGB for anything other than student demonstrations of the peaceful kind. The sort of people he needed, and—he admitted the fact only occasionally to himself, when, as now, he was confronted by their eager, childlike faces and responses—the only kind he could get. He preferred to think that it was because of the purges of the previous year, the tough line by the KGB which had rolled up, or liquidated, cells in most of the major cities of the Ukraine. He buried the thought that others with more experience did not trust him completely, or regarded him as natural subordinate material. He never recollected the one or two unsuccessful attempts at recruitment more than a year ago, when they had smirked at his ambitions and his proposals and would not consent to be led by him, returning instead to the underground presses and the leaflets and broadsheets. The Separatists became quiescent volcanoes awaiting some future eruption.

To Shubin, they had all been cowards.

With these people—the children—he had satisfied himself. They were with him because of his magnetism, his ideals, and because of nothing of their own. And he was satisfied with the foreknowledge that they would do as he suggested, so that he reached out for one of the remaining sandwiches—though he refused an immediate offer of tea—and tried to ignore the satisfaction of Zenaida's smile as she saw the half-furtive act.

Eventually, Yakov arrived, suitably apologetic and anxious in case he had missed anything. Shubin luxuriated in the way in which Yakov immersed himself in the group, in their chatter about lectures, lecturers, their growing irreverence that seemed to pass from one to the other of them like an igniting spark, their political slogans bandied about like rational thoughts. They delighted in belonging to their own little secret society. It amazed Shubin still the way people wished to sink their identities in that of a group, give themselves over completely to something. So different from himself, never surrendering for a moment what he knew to be his self, not even in bed with the girl; rather, expanding the self into others like growing additional limbs or hearing himself, multiple-voiced, in an echo chamber.

Look at them now, he instructed himself, giggling over some exaggerated imitation of a teacher. Lyudmila, catching his eye, putting her hand to her mouth as if caught in some misdemeanor, but Kostya and Ferenc continued silently mimicking the imitative Yakov—while Ilya helped Zenaida with the washing up. Despite his irritation, he would wait until they fell progressively silent and turned to him as to their yogi sitting in the corner of the room.

They were his assistants, the instruments he required to perform his surgical operation. Belousov had the technology, he had the brain—these were the hands and other limbs, the respirator and the knife. They would allow him proximity to the body he was about to dissect. He did not concern himself with the nature of the medical imagery as fiction or mask, but accepted its truth. And perhaps he did not understand the inner necessity to surround himself with an admiring group of enthusiastic amateur terrorists.

Zenaida and Ilya returned from the kitchen, and the others fell silent as if on cue. The moment was precisely right, and he stood up dramatically and took a folded map from his inside pocket. He allowed it to drape down one plain wall while he fixed it with two dabs of masking tape from a roll in his pocket. Then he stood back for a moment as if to admire a painting, and watched the children nod with impersonated wisdom. Then he stepped back in front of the map. It would be a short speech, and he had thought a good deal about it. He was not a good exhortatory speaker—too much impatience, perhaps too much contempt for any audience he addressed.

"We have talked and talked in this cell, but to this moment we have not acted—though all our talk has been about action." He watched the smiles become sheepish as he regarded each face intently. "I have a cure for our idleness, and a means of letting the whole world know of our struggle." He paused for a moment—as if adjusting some imperative in himself to a perspective that belonged to other people. "A means of telling everyone about the Ukraine, and what we want—making *Do pobachenya* a household name, putting us on everyone's lips." Now they were eager, puzzled and excited like children awaiting the unwrapping of parcels. And like children, they would do it, because they were fundamentally child-amoral, lacking the adult sense of consequences and the adult hesitancy about complete commitment. "We *can* terrify the Kremlin gang into granting the Ukraine what it wants, go farther along the road to separate and autonomous identity—" He stepped aside from the map with a conjuror's flourish of his hand. "All we need to do—" He let the words drop like stones in their minds, let the easiness his tone implied win them over. "We need to plant two bombs—one here—" His finger dabbed at the center of the street map of Moscow. "And one here!" His finger stabbed again at the map, a little to the southwest of the previous point. "The television cameras of the world will be in Moscow for the Olympics, and that's when we do it. Two bombs are all we need!"

He stopped, and the silence in the room struck him—a long moment of charged, tense silence before the anticipated babble of questions, suggestions, qualifications. Then the children started clapping him, each one taking up the applause Zenaida had initiated. It was that easy—easier than he had thought, or hoped. The children wanted a bonfire party and loved him because he promised them one more spectacular than they could have ever imagined.

CHAPTER 4

David Allardyce watched the clock in the corner of the screen ticking away, utterly removed from the efforts of the men on the track below the commentary box. He leaned against the back wall, studying the runners through the glass and between the shoulders of the race commentator and his expert adviser, John Millichip, a three-miler of the late fifties. Irvine, as expected, was out in front, long fair hair streaming behind him, green and gold vest determinedly advertising his presence as a visitor in this invitation event. Lydall was thirty yards down, on the seventh lap. The commentator seemed galvanized into new life as a crane shot of the track at Crystal Palace revealed the gap between Irvine and the field. His remarks were pertinent, couched gently, suitably complimentary to the Australian—but Allardyce was suddenly irritated by the concentration on Lydall, marking off his performance against the clock, and creating the drama of his attempt to achieve better than the Olympic qualifying time for the first time in eighteen months.

Someone had leaked it to the press, and it had been simmering, then boiling, in the newspapers all week. The Olympic selectors had made it clear to Lydall that he had to achieve better then thirteen-thirty in the Crystal Palace race—eight seconds better than the Olympic qualifying time—if he was to be selected. Even then, it was understood that he would still have a great deal of ground to make up before Moscow.

The touts had been selling cheap stopwatches outside the stadium all that day. When he inquired, Allardyce had been told— "Selling like hot cakes, guv!"

The camera zoomed in on Lydall, running bunched up above the waist in his usual style, and as Millichip added his experience to the emerging drama, Allardyce slipped out of the commentary box, to make his way down to the OB unit in its green van. An Oxford contemporary, now an OB producer for the BBC, had invited him up to the box, then back to the van. It was an invitation that Allardyce knew might lead to some television work in Moscow, and he was flattered by the possibility. Also, it allowed him to talk and listen to people close to the contemporary athletics scene—and a stint as foreign correspondent in southern Africa had put him rather out of touch.

He climbed down the ladder, the wind flapping his jacket and slacks, blowing high white clouds and their shadows quickly over the stadium. Irvine passed beneath the commentary box, then Lydall, who appeared to have dropped another five yards. He was slipping back toward the strung-out bunch, as if responding to a siren call not to be foolish, not to try. Allardyce felt a quick stab of sadness for him, watched for a moment until Lydall began to round the far bend, then continued down the ladder. Perhaps he would watch the rest of the race from the terraces, he decided. The runners might not be so close out there, one couldn't see their faces, know what must be in their minds. Especially, he wouldn't be able to read the expressions on Lydall's face as the laps ebbed away, and the time lengthened. Irvine looked stronger with each lap that passed, confident, riding the ego like a great wave since his record-breaking run under lights in Sydney, and his subsequent wins in Europe.

Clouds scudded, obscuring the sun for a moment, and it was as if that sudden shadow was both appropriate, and ominous. Allardyce was suddenly aware of the man standing next to him at the back of that thinly populated part of the terrace.

"David—my dear fellow!"

Simon Maulle. The sun reemerged, and Irvine passed across Allardyce's view as he turned back to the track. Below them, only a few heads turned, then moved slowly from left to right as Lydall came round the bend into the straight in front of the main stand.

"Simon," Allardyce said levelly. "Fancy meeting you here—like this. I didn't realise you had such a passion for track and field."

"David—I have to admit my interest in this affair is much more—shall we say *localised*?"

"In that case, you can fuck off," Allardyce said levelly, with perfect diction and an innocent smile. "Unless you're chasing one of the younger competitors."

Maulle's handsome face creased as if it were folded, then unfolded again. He smoothed a long hand through his dark hair, adjusted the tiny knot in his narrow tie. Allardyce looked down. Yes, the inevitable suede shoes. Maulle's suit was lovat, and a Daks lightweight.

"Not today, old boy. Today I'm chasing you."

"I'm working."

"Don't sulk, David. It does nothing for your looks."

Allardyce leaned back against the concrete wall at the back of the terracing, letting the body do its own relaxing, concentrating on not allowing his features any mobility of expression.

"Simon—what is it?"

Irvine's back retreating down the straight—Lydall coming round the bend, face looking white and strained, his whole appearance as bedraggled as on that occasion outside Barnsley. Just over two laps to go. Allardyce found himself absorbed now, just as television viewers must be, encouraged by the commentator and Millichip, just like the large crowd at Crystal Palace. He could feel an electricity of tension unearthed by the concrete under his feet, as if transmitted through the seating, or in the air. Lydall passed the finish with two laps to go.

Allardyce looked at his watch. Lydall had to do two laps at sixty—no, better than that, to qualify. Everyone else knew it, too, by the murmur of the noise as Lydall went into the bend. As he passed across the face of the far terracing, voices began to urge him on. Irvine was running in a different, lonely race.

"He isn't going to make it," Maulle observed.

"Not committing yourself to something, Simon?" Allardyce observed lightly.

"To something—maybe. So might you." He smiled with an intended mysteriousness, and put one long hand inside his jacket. He took out an envelope, and passed it to Allardyce. "Have a look at my snaps, would you? Tell me if you recognise anyone."

Allardyce quashed the rising curiosity, opened the buff envelope with a steady, indifferent hand, and studied the two photographs—one a studio portrait he had seen before on a mantelpiece, and the other a street crowd with that same face in the foreground.

"Of course," he said. "Why show me those?" He wished he didn't sound so amateurishly belligerent, but he was helpless to avoid betraying his feelings—just as he wanted to shout, in the same moment, at Lydall, who was moving smoothly round the bend below them, now having cut loose from the straggling rest of the field, and having rendered Irvine as good as invisible to the crowd.

"Source *Burgoyne*, the CIA calls our friend there," Maulle remarked. "But, of course, you knew that."

"Yes." Allardyce looked at his watch. Last lap in fifty-nine. Bell for Irvine, then the long, long time in which the crowd seemed to hold its collective breath until the bell rang for Lydall. Then the crowd released its tension, and breath, in a roar of encouragement. Allardyce, who had always observed the transience of athletic or sporting fame, felt something in him respond to that. Wish fulfillment, collective identification with the individual, chauvinism, envy, hysteria, ignorance. Just a wall of sound rising up around the runner. Applause for Irvine as he came up the back straight, transmuted to shouts and bellows of encouragement as Lydall moved past the same spectators. Maulle was irrelevant, his bringing up of the past nothing more than irritation. He made as if to move away.

Raising his voice above the noise, Maulle said, "The CIA seems to think our friend may be in trouble—*big trouble*, as they put it to me."

Allardyce, barely attentive, said, "Trouble?" Lydall was at the bend, Irvine already past him and beginning the home straight, to modest cheering, as if he were an event that had to be done with before they could concentrate on Lydall.

"They feel—the CIA, that is—that our friend has become the subject of a new drive to root out the agent the KGB knows is there." Maulle paused for effect, but the silence was filled with the roar—now that Irvine had broken the tape—that ebbed and washed against the stadium as Lydall came off the bend into the straight. Now, it was little more than hysteria—the crowd was, each individual, running the last hundred meters out on the tartan.

"You're going to Moscow, aren't you—?"

Allardyce, as if stung, turned to Maulle.

"Yes—"

He looked at his watch. Lydall was going to make it, just—he was going to make it.

"And you helped recruit our friend—in a modest capacity."

"Yes!"

Lydall, thirty yards, twenty—the noise boiled up around him, as if he were running down a tunnel of sound. Head down, he sprinted the last ten strides, flung his chest forward, then stumbled just beyond the finish, rolling onto his back on the track. Allardyce smiled as someone ran to him, cradling a stopwatch, shouted something down at him, and the thin white arms came up, fists clenched. He had done it, and knew it. The crowd applauded and bellowed as if he were doing a lap of honor lying there on the track.

"You may—" Maulle, having waited impatiently for the conclusion of that particular piece of futility, showed his teeth as he spoke, and his eyes gleamed. "You may be required to assist us to get our friend out, if it comes to that. And I'm afraid we can't accept no for an answer."

Captain Gennadi Mihailovich Leonov at forty possessed the face and posture of a man of deliberation, without sudden movements or hasty decisions. Which, he supposed, was why he had taken so long finding another woman after Esfir had died, and why he had resisted all pressures to find, and marry, a housekeeper and stepmother for the boys. Why, certainly, he had resisted involvement with Anna until this last year. He sat in the warm sunlight of a Moscow noon, in the Gorky Park of Culture and Rest, idly watching his younger son, Maxim, playing football with schoolfriends it was his turn to chaperone. Boys who lived in the same block of apartments; sons of civil servants, actors, even one Soviet film star. And idly watching the girls in summer dresses, reflecting on the desires he might have felt creeping over him in the past, and the smug way he could now afford to regard them as little more than the most pleasant part of the scenery.

Captain Leonov, Second Chief Directorate of the KGB—that concerned with the internal security of the Soviet Union—had always been bored as a junior officer on duty with the Moscow Police at football matches, international athletics meetings, swimming matches. And, fifteen years later, he did not look forward to sharing the bunch of tickets, mostly for the athletics, that Anna had been able to obtain by pulling strings, paying over the odds. Colleagues of his he had seen in frenzies over duty rosters, black-market tickets, allocations to officers of rank; buying the tickets, not arresting the touts. Ridiculous. But the thought of Anna's enthusiasm made it, if not less ridiculous, certainly something that he could simply accept.

He reminded himself to smile, nod his head, as Maxim pushed the checkered ball past a diving boy in shorts and inside the precarious little heap of bottles and shoes that formed a goalpost. Maxim, he reflected, must have picked it up from school, or his friends—like the Muscovite accent that now overlay his Minsk twang.

He saw Anna Borisovna Akhmerovna entering the park, under the gigantic stone porch with its architrave bearing the emblems of the Party. She was dwarfed and shadowed suddenly so that the image disturbed him, then she was out in the sunlight, carrying her jacket, wearing a light skirt and navy blouse. A bob of fair hair, expensively cut. He watched men—and women who might have had hair under their armpits and who were lumpily dressed—turn to stare after her. She carried their eyes as she carried the jacket and the shoulder bag—carelessly, confidently, with the ease of a mannequin, the elegance of money and position. As befitted a member of the Secretariat—the civil service of the Communist Party of the Soviet Union—working in one of the most important Ministries.

Laughing, he reminded himself how he hated embassy party duties, had almost not gone to a function at the British Embassy, would have missed her, perhaps finally and for always. Stupidly, he felt a lump in his throat at the idea of it.

He stood up, eager as a schoolboy, and saw the moment of cool appraisal as she took in his eagerness, his pleasure, as if she needed that reassurance, then she moved into his embrace, and lifted her face to kiss his cheek. Then she was at arm's length again, appraising him, her head slightly on one side, her eyes keen and amused. He could see the light dust of freckles beneath her face powder, was aware of those freckles on her naked shoulders, her throat, and felt stupid and doglike and randy and delighted, and superior to the men who passed with their shabby women or bits of girls.

"Well? Taxi fares, a missed lunch, walking in these shoes—?" She sat down, crossed her long legs, took off one of the smart shoes, and rubbed her instep. Leonov watched her perform the ordinary action as if he had never seen anything of its kind before, or as if he had been warned to memorize every detail about this elegant, intelligent woman.

Maxim walked across to them, breaking off from the game, his football boots—Dynamo First-Class, strictly birthday-occasion products—clattering on the concrete path. Anna smiled, inclined her head, and Maxim pecked at her cheek. Then he moved back, his mouth working as if he were savoring the taste of the face powder. Leonov felt no older than his son at that moment, and pleased also that the boy had taken to her—fallen under her magic might have been a more accurate description.

"Back to the game," Leonov said, smiling at his son, who nodded, then winked outrageously, and ran off. Leonov laughed. Anna leaned back on the bench, shading her eyes, then seemed to remember her sunglasses, which she fished out of her bag and put on. "I'm sorry you had to miss lunch. Perhaps a hamburger, or a hot dog, and Coca-Cola—that's what we're having." He waved his hand in the direction of the red-faced, intent junior footballers.

"Sportsmen's lunches? No, thank you. Perhaps the one disadvantage of the Olympics in Moscow is the invasion of American eating habits!" Leonov sat back, folding his arms, as if by assuming the same posture he became closer to her. She added, "The ladies in the office were very impressed with the appearance of Captain Gennadi Leonov when he visited the other morning. I really oughtn't to tell you, you look so smug at the moment. However—"

Leonov smiled, inclining his head in a little bow. "Thank you, beautiful lady. You have addresses?"

"More in your line of work, I would have thought."

The amused remark ruffled his mood of well-being; as if it had been no more than an interlude, or deception.

"Which is the real me? The KGB officer sniffing around your Ministry for a double agent—or the doting father chaperoning the full complement of kids from our apartment block?" By the time he had finished, he was smiling again, realizing the foolishness of resentment, defying the tiny moment of fragility he had seen, like a ladybird balanced on the last edge of a frond of fern, about to topple.

"Both—and the man in my bed, that's you, too. And the young boy who jumps up from his seat when he sees me. I am flattered to be loved like that—" He looked at her. She could always disconcert him by her honesty, her bluntness—the way she dug down beneath moods to explain them to herself, and to him. Never content, it seemed, with the moment, or with mere response. She had to understand, to be *aware*—like keeping her eyes open, studying his face, when they made love, even when they reached the climax. She would squeeze them shut, as if diving into herself, for a moment then. But not otherwise.

"Tell your ladies that the handsome, intelligent, *unmarried* Captain Leonov will be visiting again later in the week. And he will be bringing some younger men with him, also."

Her face darkened; at the mention of marriage, he presumed.

"More questions?"

"More questions—but, continuing our deference to the Secretariat and the Ministry, we are conducting them at your offices rather that at ours."

"Dzerzhinsky Street isn't my favorite restaurant."

"I'm coming on Thursday—can we have lunch?"

"I should think so—if you're a very good boy."

"When—tonight?"

"Put your tongue back in, Gennadi Leonov. I'll come and cook supper for you and Maxim, after work."

Leonov, as if shutting off from her, sat back on the bench. He closed his eyes, and Anna watched the smile of deep satisfaction spreading over his face, as if the sunlight were bringing it out like a flower. And she felt choked with the witness of his happiness.

Oleg Georgevich Kazantsev, his wife Valentina looking on indulgently, was momentarily buried under the combined weights and arms and legs of his two children, Misha and Tanya, spluttering with laughter, his big hands ruffling them, yet holding them as they struggled on his lap. They had been in bed when he got back from Kiev on the express, a journey that had taken most of the day, and now they had interrupted the moment of calm he always felt as he sat in his chair and Valentina stood at his side, he just holding her hand as if that were the only physical contact he needed, a reminder of the way in which he was part of her, she part of him.

He could not resent the noisy intrusion of his children, who had not seen him for five days. When they climbed down from his lap, hair untidy, faces red, it was the traveling bag that became the focus of their attention. He sighed theatrically, raised his hands in the air. Presents from Kiev—which he had bought in Moscow, at Detsky Mir (Children's World, the largest toy shop in the world) on Marx Prospekt, just before it closed, on his way from the station. Since they would not be interested in hand-embroidered shirts or tablecloths—he had one of those for Valentina, and a beautiful blouse—then their presents had to come from Detsky Mir.

He unzipped the bag, dipped his hand in, fiddled about secretively, and his hand came out as a fox's head, red tongue lolling, mouth opening and closing as he operated the glove puppet. Tanya screamed in delight as the fox tried to bite her ears. Then she grabbed it, cuddled its suddenly deflated form, and Valentina showed her how the puppet worked, but more gently, ingratiating it with the little girl. Then the model of a satellite launch vehicle, together with a detachable Voskod capsule. The boy took it reverently, careful to keep the whole toy together, walking carefully to the table so that he could stand it upright, then making it blast off with his hand, using the other hand to detach the capsule. The launch vehicle fell back carefully in his right hand while the capsule continued in its orbit. Kazantsev was satisfied.

When the children had been put back to bed, Valentina served the Ukrainian dumpling stew she had been warming in the oven. After the first mouthful, he waved his fork and said, "Better Ukrainian cooking here than in Kiev."

"Thank you, kind sir." He looked at his small, dark wife, in whose image he was thankful his daughter was made, rather than his own beefy, high-colored, clumsy-looking appearance, and even with his mouth full she understood the meaning of his smile. "You look tired," she said.

"Must be the train—stops everywhere. I don't know why they call it an express—" He saw the look in her eyes, and remembered with her the first journey to Moscow a year before, when he was transferred from the Kiev office to Moscow Center and the KGB Antiterrorist Squad, for his work on identifying, and arresting, two Ukrainian cells based in Kiev and Poltava. And he remembered Valentina's not wanting to come; then the surprise of the privileged apartment on the Sadovaya-Spasskaia, with double glazing to keep out the noise of the great motorway ring and its traffic; and the promotion and salary rise, and prices in Moscow—

Everything.

"You've been busy?"

He nodded his head, his mouth too full to speak. Valentina pulled a deprecating face. "Yes," he said eventually. He watched her demonstrate polite eating, amused, then added, "I met Federenko, the runner."

"He's not mixed up in anything you might be interested in, is he? Not *this* year—"

He shook his head. "I don't think so. Just routine. It's his sister who's mixing with the wrong types—you know, student enthusiasm and all that. There were plenty of those a year ago, when—" She nodded, as if to blot out that time. "I know, I know," he said soothingly. "Some of them got themselves killed with their silly, romantic enthusiasm."

"You're not getting into something like that again, are you, Oleg?"

Again, he shook his head. This time, it was a calculated gesture, and he was careful about the expression in his eyes, and whether his ears would go red as he told a half-lie.

"No. I don't think so, no." One of the reasons she had at first resented his promotion to Moscow was her view of it as some kind of reward for rounding up, shooting—blood money. Kazantsev had regretted that shoot-out in Donetsk, the silly, self-glorification of the amateurish terrorists not much older than teenagers which had led to the crumbling apartment house and the siege and the death toll of officers, police, and terrorists; all of whom had lain dead in the gutter, waiting for the meat wagon, looking little more than children, untidy and beatific. But it had happened. "No," he reaffirmed, more strongly for her sake. "I only met Federenko because he was visiting his mother. He's living in Moscow now, training. The sister—hotheaded, but not dangerous. And you know the Kiev office. Send for their expert, Lieutenant Kazantsev—just to blow their noses for them!"

He laughed, and plowed into the remainder of his meal with an assumed, and distracting, gusto.

The reprimand still rankled—four days and a hundred miles from Los Angeles. The members of the U.S. Olympic Committee and the AAU had sat in judgment on him, mouthing platitudes about the adverse publicity, and objections to his being part of the U.S. team because of that publicity, because of public knowledge of his use of marijuana. The fattened former athletes, gray-haired men of principle, satisfied themselves by issuing a reprimand, widely circulated—the Russians had been delighted, so some U.S. newspapers had reported.

All through the meeting of the USOC disciplinary committee, he had sweated with the fear of losing his place on the team, his scholarship, or both. They hadn't gone that far, but it still rankled.

Now, he stood in an orange grove in southern California, the dappled shade a cool illusion, the scent of the fruit heavy, dust rising slowly from the road beyond the grove as cars passed. His father continuing his work of patient inspection of the crop—even to picking off insects from the immediate branches and fruit, and crushing them with dry snapping sounds between his fingers. Old, dark, dirty-nailed Mexican fingers.

José Gutierrez, his father. Thin, corded with veins and with a life of physical labor, back bent, brow furrowed under the floppy sombrero he wore like a declaration. A clichéd old peon. It was hard to love his father, hard even to be grateful for the work, the opportunities, to turn him into an American. Because his father insisted, always, on his own Mexican-ness, his origins as a wetback, a taco-head, a greaser. He made Gutierrez feel he had betrayed something, or somebody, or gone on a long journey with no clear idea of his destination.

"Your mother was upset what she read in the newspapers about her son," his father said without looking at him, moving aside the leaves of the tree with a long pole, disclosing the ripening fruit in which he seemed to have sole interest.

"I'm sorry about that—Pop. I wouldn't want to upset her."

"I'm saying you did—it's too late for you not to want it." The grating accent, the almost-whining twist given to words that Gutierrez pronounced with a Californian's voice. *Ees too late fohr you not to warnt eet* rolled around in his head. And his mother in black; ageless, timeless peon-woman, vaguely unsettled by the invention of the car and the television. Ignorant and loving. Christ, why did they give him such hang-ups, such clouds of contradictory feelings that seemed to close on him chokingly whenever he thought about them, was with them? His sister, Inez, had no such feelings, moving with natural grace and effortless ease between her Santa Barbara suburb and executive husband and her parents' home—still speaking in Spanish to them, not just his grudging occasional word in his first language.

"O.K., I'm sorry anyway."

"Good. You tell your mother. She worries about that—the drugs."

"Christ, Pop—it's hash, once in a while. I'm not shooting stuff!"

The old man turned on Gutierrez then, and beneath the brim of his hat his eyes lurked like two bright spots in the shadow.

"This language—you think I send you to school to talk like somebody on TV?" Gutierrez saw that the free hand at his side was shaking, that there was a quiver in the pole as it stood beside him. He saw the depth of his father's anger with him, given occasion for expression in the matter of his jargon.

"Why did you send me to school? You cut me adrift, then, Pop—"

"You cut yourself adrift, Martin. What you do now, uh? You spend your time running. What job you going to get when you're too old to run anymore?"

Gutierrez saw that they had jumped into a hole together, one that had been waiting for them for two, three years. He wanted to climb out, and suspected that so did his father. But the narrowness of his father's view, something he might have expected more readily from his mother, the *constrictions* it seemed to place upon him—to wear a suit to work, to get on, and up, in something with an obligatory American accent, and the key to some executive washroom and a company car. The old man's vision was thirty years out of date, and through the wrong end of a telescope. He wanted to explain.

"It's maybe the only talent I have," was all he said.

His father moved on, crossed a splash of sunlight, into the deep shadow beneath the next tree.

"Only talent?" He snorted, spat. "You, the top boy in his high school class—"

Gutierrez moved to him urgently.

"That kind of thing counts for nothing these days—don't you understand that?" He was breathing as after a long run, or a weight workout.

"Then why you want to win a medal in these Games? Tell me that. You want to be top there—for a piece of gold smaller than the size of your palm?"

Gutierrez's hands worked at his sides, open-closed, open-closed. Trying to press the untidy lump of the conversation, its suggestive ugliness, into something aesthetic and harmless.

"Pop—" he said, as if pleading.

The old man turned away, poked the pole up into the branches, uncovering the fruit, suggesting wisdom that Gutierrez could not comprehend; or a dumb old Mex who ought to be despised. He folded back leaves, and Gutierrez stared up at the oranges, and the flash of sunlight that his father let in.

"You'll watch me? On TV?"

The old man turned back, as if denying the gulf between them. He nodded. "Your mother—she will pray, and I will think, and we will both watch. But—no more drugs, uh? No more!"

Gutierrez nodded. He could mold it now, to some kind of satisfactory conclusion. "No, Pop. No more newspapers, no more drugs. The next time you see me in the newspapers, I'll be wearing a medal." He grinned, cajoling his father into acquiescence. The old man nodded.

"Good. Good. Now—go see your mother. I have work to do, and she will be anxious—"

As he walked away, Gutierrez looked back at the patient, shrunken shape with the long pole. It seemed to suggest meaning, significance to him, but he could not interpret the sight.

Irena Witlocka, on a Warsaw thoroughfare, trying to check, in her status as an amateur of the secret life, whether there was any professional presence. It was the day. She had postponed, vacillated, rejected, and desired, until she had worn out all the great urgency, and all the reluctance. Now, it was a kind of automatism, or something that was simply inevitable, beyond emotion.

She wanted to think herself unfollowed, and was afraid that desire had outrun caution and observation. There didn't *seem* to be anyone following her. All the same, she was deliberately on the other side of the street from her objective.

The American Embassy.

It could not wait until Moscow. At one time she had wanted to postpone it until she met Martin once again, could be certain that it wasn't vanity—no, not that word, because there was no doubt of her own feelings; rather, she could not quite be certain of her image of him. She had had to find her propulsion from her own feelings, and it had been sufficient, until she began to imagine clearly meeting him again. Through the welter of images of their relationship, bed, coffee shop, park, or beach, and those that bookended that untidy sequence of recollections, the dreamed-of future life, she had had to envisage the *actual* him, the manner of his greeting, the nature of his feelings.

Because he had never written, and they hadn't met for a year.

So—?

She crossed the street like a fugitive, heels clattering, a few heads turning as she gained the pavement to look at the tall, dark girl, almost five-ten, with the shock of curling black hair. And sharp and guilty gray eyes.

No one stopped to study her. She was the only still thing on the street. Black gates, a glass box inside, a short little drive into and beneath an archway. Once she was through the gates, there was no problem—except when she reemerged. And she was expected. The marine would have her name on his clipboard.

So—move.

The marine inspected his list, then picked up his telephone. He spoke into it briefly, while Irena moved her head from side to side, studying with peripheral vision the people who passed the gates. No one stopped.

"Sir," the marine finished, then smiled in a clipped, momentary way at her. His eyes were level with hers. "Just go through under the archway, Miss Witlocka—" He pronounced it badly. "Ask the porter for directions there." His white-gloved hand pointed the way. She nodded, as if having forgotten his directions in an instant, then hurried away from him.

Once under the archway, she felt her chest less tight, her breathing didn't roar in her ears as if she were unfit, or old. The porter was helpful, unsuspicious. Fourth floor, turn left, right, left again—room 416. She nodded almost after each word, and her breathing quickened again as she tried to attend to his words so utterly she could not possibly go wrong. She suddenly knew she had to make the meeting as brief as possible, that she had to be out on the street again as quickly as she could, and back into the pretense. Here, she had no pretense, no disguise. She was declared to anyone, naked for all to see. That there was no one to see her except Americans, that she was certain she had not been followed, held no power over her imagination. All the time she was absent from the street outside, from Warsaw concrete that qualified as "Polish soil," it was as if there were a gap in the air, an outline of her shape she might have stepped out of, which attracted attention like a signpost, yelled out that she was inside the U.S. Embassy making her arrangements to defect to the West.

She wanted the elevator to go faster—saw herself in a bikini on some dream Californian beach, and almost giggled at the incongruity and superficiality of her images of life with him—hurried down the corridor, to the left turn; blank doors, discreetly numbered but bearing no names; the right turn, and it was left again almost at once—not so quickly, surely? But there was room 412 and she came to herself in front of the door of room 416. She told herself not to be stupid, arranged her hair a little less untidily, smoothed her skirt, plucked at her blouse—then knocked with the timidity of an applicant for another way of life.

"Come," she heard a man's voice say, and she pushed open the door, stepping into a small room that overlooked the central courtyard of the embassy building—a room impermanently furnished from some central warehouse with a light, veneered desk, two functional easy chairs, a plain carpet, unremarkable curtains. The room was dim and undersea, the light filtering through the venetian blinds. A young man—she was surprised at his age, he couldn't be more than thirty—stood up and held out his hand in greeting. He seemed genuinely pleased to see her, put her at her ease.

"Miss Witlocka—it's nice meeting you." He waved her to one of the two easy chairs, arranged away from the desk, and sat in the other himself, hitching his trousers to preserve the crease as he crossed his legs. With his short fair hair, squarish good looks, lightweight suit, he could have been one of the young men she had been interviewed by last year, when the whole thing had gone ridiculously wrong. She had wondered for a moment whether in fact she had met him before.

"Now—you want to defect, right?" She was shocked by his directness. The idea that she had kept secret for a year suddenly lay like a harmless pet on the carpet at her feet, to be cooed over by the two of them.

"I—I—" she began, feeling her color rising.

"I've had your file sent over here—" He did not explain its point of origin. He was smiling blandly, brushing at his trouser leg as if smoothing the harmless idea he had broached. "So I understand your great desire to get to the United States." He emphasized the smile. Irena relaxed and allowed him to talk because he seemed to have settled everything, carrying her along, his words like visas. "Your telephone call the other day—asking to speak to someone in the CIA. They usually have orders on the switchboard to deflect those, or cut them off." He grinned. "But, your name, naturally— that's why we gave you an interview with the man in visas. But since I'm what's called the Third Secretary round here, you can assume that I know what you want, and I'm the guy you have to talk to—"

She was about to say something. But he offered a pack of cigarettes, which she refused, and put them away again. He went on almost immediately, "I got right onto it, Miss Witlocka. You would have—difficulty in making a normal application. We understand that—" He rubbed his nose, and when his hand came back down to the arm of his chair, he was no longer smiling. "You present us with a problem, Miss Witlocka. Moscow is definitely a no-go area for us during the Games. That order's come right down from the top—the very top." He nodded sagely, almost as if imitating an older man with more *gravitas*. "I'm instructed to say at this stage that we can't see how we can assist you, Miss Witlocka. Not at the moment, not during the Games, and not in Moscow. I'm sorry."

"Mr. Director, the President would be very unhappy if this proposed operation were to take place—" The Secretary of State raised his hands, palms outward, to forestall interruption. He had pounced upon the meat of his brief suddenly, and would not let the two less political animals on the other side of his ornate desk share the meal until he was ready. Behind his head, in the bright early summer sunshine, the flags stirred distantly along the facade of the

Kennedy Center for the Performing Arts. The Director of the CIA studied the view, unsurprised at the statement the Secretary had just made, and prepared to listen in silence while he gathered his own arguments. Beside him on a Louis XV chair similarly drawn up to the huge desk the Director of the CIA's Covert Action Staff was obedient to the silence they had agreed to in the car from Langley. His was a merely supporting role, though source *Burgoyne* was his agent.

"The President—rightly in my opinion—" the Secretary of State continued in a voice more detectably authoritarian. "The President is concerned that the Russians are just ready for some clandestine operation they can expose to our embarrassment at this time. Something this large would be—just what they might be looking for."

The Director could just see the far end of the Theodore Roosevelt Bridge where it crossed the Potomac, if he craned his head slightly. He ignored the Secretary of State while he did this, sensing the politician's embarrassment as he was kept waiting and the weight of his utterance dissipated in the quiet room. The quiet hum of the air conditioning was all he could hear. When he spoke, the Director intended surprising the Secretary.

"We've rehearsed the priorities for an hour, Harry, before you got to the bottom line. And I'll be damned if I'll let an agent of *Burgoyne*'s importance go down the drain!"

The use of his first name, the blunt phrasing, the indifference to the Presidential quotation, all conspired to make the Secretary of State uncomfortable, angry—and suspicious. The President had picked this Director himself, dumped him on the intelligence community two years earlier, and asked him to sweep clean. He'd done that, and grown into the job of revitalizing and rebuilding the CIA, while retaining the respect of his President. Now, the President was worried, but the Secretary found himself uncomfortably in the middle. The President wouldn't issue a direct order to the CIA—perhaps because he expected it, even wanted it, to be ignored. The Director seemed, at the very least, extremely confident of his standing with the President.

"*Burgoyne* came to us, Mr. Secretary, like manna from Heaven. The source hasn't gone stale, and I won't throw the source away."

"If we let *Burgoyne* go to the wall, sir—" the Director of the CAS put in on cue, "then every other possible double agent or any future Company *unofficial* will get the idea we don't look after our own. I can't afford for that to happen to my department, Mr. Secretary."

"I know that, and so does the President," the Secretary retorted sharply. "It is regrettable, but in this case—"

"Look, Harry—I'll give it to you straight." The Director leaned forward, long, slim fingers on his knees, the eyes behind the tortoiseshell glasses kindly, patronizing, aloofly adult. And designed to irritate the Secretary of State. The voice and the blunt, outspoken clichés did not fit the academic manner and appearance. "We should have got *Burgoyne* out last year—your team of negotiators at SALT II were bandying stuff fed to us by the source all over the place—*jeopardizing* the source." And he held up his hand in mockery of the Secretary's earlier gesture, as he concluded, "*Burgoyne* was a fact for the Russians as soon as we started using material from the source in our negotiations. But we asked the source to stay on, and tell us what the first post-SALT defense budget would look like. And we promised—*real* promises—that the source could come out like an express once it was done."

"What sort of danger—?" the Secretary proffered, knowing he was being led, that a maze of detail, of expertise to which he was not privy, was being erected round him whichever way he moved. He began to think more consciously than before that the President wanted *him* convinced by the Director because he was already himself convinced, wanted *him* to give approval—

"The on-scene officer has already closed down the network to protect the source. There was a man who committed suicide just before the KGB got to him. The KGB may know of others, but they're cut out now, and can't lead back to the source. That right, John?"

The Director of the CAS nodded.

"The source is safe from detection for the moment, but the Russians know the prize that we want—the defense budget details—and they know we have a high-level source of information. They'll use everything they've got to find the source and eliminate it."

"How—*long* before things become critical?" The Secretary was riding with the current for the moment, awaiting an opportunity to reverse the trend of the argument, which might present itself once they returned to the international repercussions, the diplomatic realities.

"July will see the first series of meetings, Mr. Secretary," the Director of the CAS replied. "We have to have details of those, at least. So far we have some preliminary indications that the Soviets are going for some massive research and development quite out of line with—"

"July? How does this cutoff source supply you with the information?"

"*Burgoyne* will bring it out."

"With everything shut down, how do you check it's not just panic?"

The Director watched the Secretary seizing upon his assistant with the ferocity of ignorance. And knew he had him, and through him, the President. Enmeshed in thrashing out details, the Secretary of State would not easily return to the diplomacy of the situation.

"We'll use a case officer who can evaluate the material— samples will have to be provided."

"When would you expect—to *lift?*" The Secretary used the jargon with exaggerated quaintness.

"Sometime at the end of July," the Director said flatly, unemphatically. The significance of the date did not, however, escape the politician.

"Definitely not, gentlemen—not during the Games."

"The best time. Sure, the KGB will be on full alert working forty-eight hours a day—but they'll be stretched so thin you'll be able to *see* through them!" It was not an opinion.

"This becomes more and more dubious a proposition the more I learn, gentlemen. What else is there?"

As soon as he heard the reply, he was certain the Director had briefed the President personally and independently, and the President *was* using him as a potential scapegoat. He would not advise the President that the operation be canceled—he knew he would not. Silently, he damned the unholy alliances of successive Presidents with their chief intelligence officers.

"The *salesman* would be a Brit—" The Secretary stopped brushing his hand through his gray hair in an affectation of calm. His bushy eyebrows lifted in genuine surprise, not untinged with alarm. He was suspiciously Anglophobic.

"A what—?"

"A Brit who has no current connection with any of their intelligence people. A journalist who would be in Moscow by *right*, his real job the only cover he would need."

"Explain your desire to jeopardize the whole operation by using this amateur, Mr. Director—if you please." The Director removed his thin smile. The Secretary was still making diplomacy where he could, fiddling while his Rome burned.

The Director of the CAS said, "We got *Burgoyne* in the first place because the Brits couldn't handle it. This man Allardyce used to be a courier for them at the time *Burgoyne* was recruited. He knows the source, the source would trust him."

A moment's pause, then the Secretary said, "The President would, of course, disavow the Company if anything—anything at all—were to go wrong. No waves, not even a ripple, must reach the surface. The State Department will not go anywhere near it—" His face indicated he was speaking of a source of infection. "If you blow it, then you will be buried alongside the source. On that basis, do you still consider it worthwhile continuing?"

The Director paused before he replied. He knew that the Secretary of State had agreed, and had already protected his rear. The State Department would beat the White House to the news-stands in denouncing the operation if the Russians exposed it. And, he knew, the President would let it happen. The President, his old friend, had made himself unassailable. The Secretary of State had sniffed enough of a rat to protect himself in advance. So the Company was out on its usual limb—

He wanted to smile. Something moved in him that made his posture in the seat, the previous movement of his blood, seem sluggish and half-alive. The academic life was light-years behind him now. His renaissance had come with his appointment to the Director's job at Langley. He really didn't mind being stuck out on the limb they thought they'd prepared for him. He'd always expected to end up there, anyway.

"Oh, yes, Harry. We can't afford to get a reputation for mere politics, for not caring—mm?" And he allowed the smile to rearrange his features to those of someone much younger, a child with thinning hair.

The Lenin Olympic Stadium in the Luzhniki Olympic Park, on a bright warm day, the crisp new flags standing out, unfurling slowly in the light breeze off the Lenin Heights. A group of men, flanked as if being herded by an impressive security cordon, inside which the few permitted press photographers subjected the group to a hail of flashbulbs; the group of men appeared to have little in common besides their uniform sobriety of suiting. Black faces, white, brown. A jumble of ambassadors, consuls, or their representatives, being shown the improvements to the Olympic complex for the benefit of the world's press, and for the practice of the Soviet television crews recording the event for the evening news programs.

Stress was laid upon the remodeling of the grandstands in the main stadium, the sums involved in bringing the competition swimming pool up to and beyond Olympic standard, on the renovations and additions to the Palace of Sport—now the Olympic Palace of Sport—for the indoor competitions.

Ambassadors, studious and learned in the ways of not appearing bored, or ignorant, though not necessarily skilled in the finer points of sport or architecture, listened and looked and approved as their governments intended. Moving in an untidy phalanx where their host and master of ceremonies, Mr. I. T. Novikov, chairman of the organizing committee of the 1980 Olympiad, directed them, they stood for required periods of time before buildings, inside buildings, beneath ranks of flagpoles, and on the steps of one of the main aisles of the stadium, above seventy-two tiers of seats, all newly painted, newly covered, looking down at the athletics track and the bright artificiality of the grass's color.

Then the rehearsed spontaneity of the descent to the stadium floor, the shuffling assembly into a tight group on the grass, the firing squad of flashbulbs, the scurrying men with handheld TV cameras—before the official party adjourned to the Yunost Hotel at the entrance to the Luzhniki Olympic Park, for the champagne reception. Reflecting on the morning, Mr. Novikov and his aides pronounced themselves satisfied with the elaborate publicity exercise they had conducted with the ambassadorial party. And they raised their glasses to July, and the Opening Day ceremony of the XXII Olympiad of modern times.

July, July—

Hang on until July. In the darkened apartment, it was almost as if *Burgoyne* could hear the words being whispered—in an American voice—in the silence. Just after opening the door, hand pausing on the light switch as if sensing there was someone there, or being afraid there was, the words were so clear in *Burgoyne*'s mind they seemed spoken that moment, not something encoded and left at a drop.

The defense budget. The first series of meetings, the details, the mood, which way things are likely to go—

Then come out, and welcome, welcome. *Burgoyne* could hear

words expanding the simple message, as if a persuasive, tempting figure sat in the dark lounge, speaking in an amplified whisper.

Burgoyne switched on the light. The flat, of course, was empty. Silly fears, almost womanish. *Burgoyne* giggled in the aftermath of nerves. A sense of being followed which was entirely illusory, a need to check and recheck desk and filing cabinets in case some clue remained, a need to change taxis or metro trains—

A sense of an old man hanging from a joist newly exposed, to protect a source the CIA seemed content to leave in danger. A lurid image *Burgoyne* had come by accidentally, from a conversation, though the death itself had been reported in *Pravda*—page 11, two paragraphs, mostly the neighbors' reactions to the arrival of Leonov's men. *Burgoyne* shuddered, poured a drink, swallowed the bile and the Scotch together. Never that way—

What if there was no hot water, no razor? And the stove was electric in this apartment. A short laugh, abrupt and mirthless; reminiscent of a series of exercises, each successive sound marking a return to fitness, to equanimity.

They wanted the minutes of the first series of meetings—and suggested a new drop pattern, new letter boxes, with contact made dangerously direct between the source and the embassy. Against time, and in such a short time—and not trusting *Burgoyne* more than they need—it might work. It would serve to expose them rather than their source, so *Burgoyne* could accept it.

To miss something of the Olympics—that would be a pity, *Burgoyne* thought, dropping eggs into a bowl, preparing to mix a heavy *blinchiki* pancake mixture. A tub of cream cheese stood by the mixing bowl as filling. *Burgoyne* had had a heavy lunch, and nerves had not increased hunger, only caused a mild indigestion.

But the nerves were there, inside but eruptive, betraying.

Care, care, *Burgoyne* thought as some of the *blinchiki* mixture splashed on the vinyl work surface.

Winston Ochengwe was running home in the hot, dusty evening, perhaps for the last time, or almost the last; his swift passage along the baked road effortless, shoes around his neck, laces knotted, crucifix bobbing on the dark, gleaming skin between the shoes. Arms moving just to balance, leg cadence correct, knee lift unexaggerated, mind floating but aware. He smiled, knowing exactly what point in his journey he had reached, seeing it in terms of the sequence of 5000 meters he had set himself to run that evening in the middle section of his journey, knowing that now he should begin the middle race sequence of gradually accelerating laps—he did five or six faster laps in the middle of a race, something he had developed himself. Which meant that he appeared to be left behind at first by those using strict time laps of sixty, sixty-one, or the like, but which would put him up with them, past them, before he had finished his mid-race sequence.

He found delight in his strength and stamina—an arrogance of self-discovery rather than a wish to prove himself. It was as if his body were some great tree, outside himself, whose bark he could touch, and his eye trace each intricate, thick branch. The body represented a kind of permanence of self, his prowess something lasting, not fleeting or merely the result of constant training. To run a 5000-meter race in the middle of his evening run home, and within that to run his mid-race sequence, was something to delight in.

First lap, he told himself, knowing it almost exactly, about sixty-three. His mind coasted, riding on the gleaming body in the track suit, the regular slapping of the training shoes on the packed dirt of the road the only noise, except for some evening birds trying to outcall the blood in his ears.

Second lap—sixty-two.

Third lap—sixty or sixty-one.

Fourth lap—sixty.

Fifth lap—fifty-eight.

Sixth lap—fifty-nine.

And he felt no more tired. He was poised, the mind set to close upon the race he was now in like a steel trap. Two or three laps to go now, depending upon when he had begun the sequence. Two, he told himself, as if he had shouted.

He would run the rest of it now, finish the race without settling into a lap of more routine running. *Strike.*

He lengthened his stride, his breath seeming to labor for a moment, the body protesting like an engine that had been put in too high a gear—then the revs picked up, everything settled, and he began to pull ahead.

He heard no cries, no applause, in his mind, only the wind, the roaring of his blood. He felt every part of his body moving, making the effort. He saw no competitors he would pass. There was just himself, expressing himself.

He was into the final three hundred meters of his imagined race when he saw the pyre of smoke ahead of him, hanging above the road like the sign of an explosion. As if his physical efforts had prepared his mind for a brilliance of comprehension he did not normally possess, he understood the signal from beyond the last rise.

A gun dropped in the bright moonlight, two men wobbling away on a bicycle. And an old Ford with three noisy policemen heading for the border. And the government civil servant who was really a secret policeman who had offhandedly asked him questions about M'seka at his place of work.

And Sarah trying, in her determined way, to make the wife of the strange young man visited by friends with guns in the middle of the night feel more at home in their village, when the other women thought of her as an outsider, with no commonalty.

He topped the rise.

At first, it appeared that the whole village was on fire—as if the gasoline-can houses had been filled with liquid still. The smoke was oily and thick and rolled above the roofs. He hardly paused, his eyes darting as quick as his thoughts and fears. His own house, his own house—? Smoke obscured it, parted like a curtain to reveal a thin black shape in shorts lying on the ground.

Fifty yards. Fifty yards from the first oil-can house, from the old British AT105 personnel carrier parked across the main street—another waving curtain of smoke, and through it some wailing and the sight of another personnel carrier at the other end of the village. He saw the Ferret scout car, and an officer standing up in it, hidden to the waist. The machine gun was pointing at the sky, like an arm waiting to drop.

He cannoned into a soldier, who looked suddenly wild-eyed and afraid as he stared into Ochengwe's face. The Swiss SIG automatic rifle waved feebly in the air, a harmless stick. Ochengwe pushed him out of the way, the growl in his throat something he did not recognize as belonging to him.

Then he was in the smoke, trying to sweep it aside with his flailing arms. He heard the wailing, and headed for it as if drawn by a compass. He heard orders shouted, including an order not to fire into the smoke. His eyes watered, his chest heaved and labored in the dense atmosphere inside the pall of smoke—he felt sick, and unfit, and spent.

Then he was through it to clearer air, and saw one or two wooden huts spurting smoke and sparks like old locomotives, but the rest of M'seka intact. Including his own house.

He stumbled, eyes watering, over something in the street. He rolled, was up immediately, and saw the strange young man whose visitors carried guns, bleeding almost unnoticed into a red pullover and the dust. He was lying on his face, thin legs stretched out in baggy trousers the color of the street. Ochengwe wanted to kick the body as it lay there, because that inert thing was to blame for this—

He ran on toward his own house, heart heaving with effort and with the desire for the illusion that his own house was untouched, safe.

A soldier came out of the hut carrying a machine gun. He looked surprised to see a track-suited figure, but before he could move, register anything but suspicion, Ochengwe was on his porch, flinging one arm at head height, knocking the skinny soldier aside, flipping him over the rail of the porch so that the tin overhang of the roof rattled like gunfire.

It was dark inside—he wiped his eyes clear of the tears of smoke and sweat and anticipation. He ignored the shouting outside and the footsteps, when he saw the oilcloth had been dragged sideways off the table. He lifted it, and found it in the dead hand of the girl, the body that was married to that other body in the red pullover. She must have run for help, for safety—

"Sarah!" The voice came from very far away, and was ridiculously like that of a woman, as he noticed the way little drops of sunlight were spilled on the floor, like drops of blood, because there were neat round holes, in lines and curves, in the wall of the hut. Little flashlight-beams of sunlight shining through the holes. He became obsessed with them, as if their significance escaped him, or he wished to escape their meaning.

Sarah was in the kitchen beyond his mother's body—the strange young man's young woman must only have reached the table, and been shot. She had not had time by her cries, her fearful breathing, to get Sarah from the kitchen. Sarah had fallen by the enamel sink, and what she was preparing for supper lay in her lap as she half-sat on the floor, as if she had vomited. He could see the pink sole of his son's foot, just inside the door, and his thin little leg. The rest of his son had been shoved through the door and to one side by the force of the bullets.

A great revulsion shuddered through him. He could not move from the spot, as if God had struck him with paralysis, and he could not touch them. They had been transformed into hideousness. He backed away.

A voice shouted at him, a gun waggled threateningly as he turned to acknowledge it. Bulky shadows in the doorway, one rubbing its head, and a small, thin-faced officer just in front of him, waving a pistol, hiding any sense of events under the issuing of orders. Ochengwe found his hands automatically on the man's throat, in a natural expression of shock or grief, and the officer dropped the gun in surprise. And Ochengwe squeezed, until he was hit over the back of the head—three times—by the butt of a rifle.

When he regained consciousness, the pain flaring in red sheets behind his eyelids, his head pounding, he found he had been dragged out into the street. Almost as soon as he opened his eyes, the officer began talking to him, standing above him, walking round and round him as if casting some spell. He was explaining—he knew who Ochengwe was, knew what he had done to Ochengwe's family, had to justify himself. But he could only shout, only bluster, in order to escape the reality of what had been done. Shouting made the words belong to someone else—perhaps to the President.

Under orders. You understand, man. This village, used by insurgents—he used the word as if it was fraught with weight and significance—keeping guns in two of the huts, signaling across the border—enemies of the President, man—he understand, uh? Woman running—one of his men young, you understand, uh, man? Machine guns, wooden walls. You know. Village being used by insurgents, can't be permitted, can't be, no way. You understand. In war, accidents they happen. You understand. This a staging post for these people, the enemy.

It went on and on. Ochengwe listened inside himself, to his blood dying down, to his heart steadying. His proud body settling down, growing smaller again after his running. And he was aware, for the first time in his life, of the great hollow spaces in there when his body was still.

The officer, realizing that he should put his justifications in a report, not spend them profitlessly on this hunched man on the ground, walked off. As the evening deepened, and the smoke died away, and the wailing, too, became more ritualized, lost in the activities of mourning, and the bodies were tidied away, Ochengwe went on sitting in the street, arms clutching his drawn-up knees, head on his thighs, listening to the great empty silence in his body.

CHAPTER 5

It was a hot morning, the sky bleached already and little eddies of dust rose from the concrete as Irvine stepped out onto the tarmac for the semiofficial posing, knots and groups imitating the congealed, squashed lumps in wedding photographs, before the press boys and the Nikons and handhelds infiltrated them, picking out the few the people expected to see in the papers or on the evening news. Sydney Airport, and the departure of the smiling, bronzed Australian team. Irvine had a quick, hardly noticed perception of how healthy they all looked, how white all their teeth were—like a commercial promoting the Australian way of life or breakfast cereals that kept you regular—before a banner fluttering between two sticks stretched out so that he could read it—

Good luck, Kenny. Punctuation of clicks from the multitude of cameras, the press photographers standing, hands over their heads clutching the imported cameras like a group of arrested, frantic terrorists, jostling for the shelter of other bodies. Then another banner—

Bring the bugger back, Kenny.

Then another—

We love you, Kenny Irvine.

He was a celebrity. The crowd looking down from the observation roof of the departure lounge declared it to be so. The way in which he was cut from the blazered herd, together with a few of the swimmers and the better-looking girls, the blonde ones, demonstrated that he was one of the select few in that group of three hundred or more heading for Moscow. And he felt no weight of responsibility, no foreboding of failure. A sudden row of cameramen closed in a crescent, jockeying him into a smile with chatter, and he raised his arms above his head as if he had just won a race, and the clicking increased in tempo and he heard the crowd on the roof make itself heard, picked out his name, turned to them, then, fists clenched, arms working above his head—they loved it. He wanted it.

He could have traveled direct to Moscow from the U.K. without coming back for this official team flight from Sydney. But when he had left Australia a couple of months before, he had bought a return ticket for this occasion. World record holder at 5000 meters, undefeated in Europe at 5000 and 10,000—he had beaten all the competition except Ochengwe and Gutierrez, and them he had beaten before. He had a right to it, this adulation, this moment. It did not make up for the effort, the expense, the years behind him. But it was his by right.

"ABC, Ken—" A TV camera settled as if a bird on the shoulder of the cameraman, and a sports stringer—the number one was already in Moscow—thrust a mike under his chin. "Anything for the whole of Aussie before you get on the plane?" Irvine, looking at a face hardly older than his own, but the hair already thinning above it, being tugged by the breeze, saw envy mixed with the facade of professionalism. They acknowledged each other for an instant, winner and trier.

"What do you want me to say?" Irvine grinned, relaxed. "You want me to say I'm going to win both medals?" Other mikes, other resting camera parrots, surrounding him. "I'll say this—I'm the one they'll be trying to beat—I'm the one they *have* to beat."

Then, quite consciously, he moved to one side, allowing the cameras to trail him, the interviewers to press behind with their questions. He looked up at the roof again, at the girls and the kids gobbling and waving as they leaned out over the rail—heard the questions at his back—and wondered why, just for a moment, it all seemed unreal, and far away, as if his hearing had failed him.

Winston Ochengwe was at Entebbe. There were still pockmarks in the facade of the main terminal building from the assault of the Israeli commandos, though the one Ugandan Airlines 707 out on the tarmac, steamy and insubstantial in the boiling noon, the only aircraft there, held no hostages. Winston Ochengwe felt imprisoned, nevertheless, as he waited with the other Ugandan competitors for the arrival of Field Marshal Idi Amin Dada, the President. Outside the badly air-conditioned lounge a little knot of soldiers from the Revolutionary Suicide Mechanized Regiment, now in effect the Presidential bodyguard, waited anxiously for the arrival of the Presidential Mercedes.

The regiment had acted, until two years before, almost as a freelance unit dedicated to the harassment of Christians, confiscators of Christian property, thugs—operating out of their base at Masaka. Too far from M'seka to have been the men who murdered Sarah and his son. Winston Ochengwe had nothing to fear as a

Catholic, as an immigrant, as a government official—as a family man. Not only because the President himself had apologized for the *misunderstanding*—had offered to show him the head of the officer who had tried to explain what had happened in the dusty street of his village. Not because of anything except the fact that he no longer wanted to live. He was a prisoner inside his own body, which now seemed heavy and overmuscled and spectacularly futile at its peak of fitness; a vehicle for which his spirit had grown too old—an old man leaving a sports car in the garage because he had lost his taste for it.

Ochengwe knew that the other athletes were leaving him alone, like some species of dangerous animal rather than out of respect for his feelings.

A fly droned around his head, where a bead of sweat rolled slowly down his cheek. He seemed to pay no attention to it, as if he were a yogi retreated from sense impressions. The fly, perhaps emboldened, or confused by inanimation, settled on the gray material of his uniform flannels. His big hand slapped down on his thigh, hard enough to hurt him, and when he lifted his pink palm, there was a tiny mess in the center, like a blob of woodland on the map of his hand, straddling his lifeline.

Federenko was puzzled by the visit of Kazantsev, the KGB officer, until the man identified himself as a member of the antiterrorist squad. Then he instantly became afraid for Zenaida, afraid so complexly that he was aware he might be overacting his feigned surprise, and that, too, was a cause of fear.

He slowly became aware that the big policeman—for him, the KGB had always been no more than a branch of the police force—was diffident, awkward, respectful. And the pleasure of childhood gleamed in his ingenuous eyes, meeting a hero, a celebrity. It relaxed Federenko.

He watched the policeman weighing, studying the furniture of the apartment, measuring the size of the room—not as a policeman, more as someone who lived in a similar place making comparisons. Since he was a lieutenant, Federenko was unsurprised at the tinge of envy, the gesture of resigned expectation with which he seemed to stroke the material of the sofa after he had sat down.

"They do you well, then," Kazantsev observed. Federenko nodded carelessly.

"Temporary—better than the place I had in Kiev." He was at

once sorry he had broached the subject of Kiev, as if the Ukraine ought to be some distant country out of both their minds.

"When are you moving into the village?"

"Next week sometime, I think."

"Tell me—"

"Y—es—?"

"What do *you* think your prospects are?"

Federenko breathed audibly, as if he had just stepped back from the edge of something.

"I don't know. I really don't."

"You're short of races, wouldn't you say?"

"Maybe—" Federenko was bemused.

"Your sister, Zenaida—you've got her tickets, of course?"

"Mm—?"

"She isn't a fan?"

"No—"

"She's coming to Moscow, though?"

"Is she—?" Federenko felt himself embroiled in something, as if he had agreed to some stupid, risky act while drunk, and was now sobering up and realizing what he was involved in.

"I hoped she might be—" Kazantsev spread huge hands on his knees, looking up into Federenko's face with the ingenuous eyes. "Look, let me be straight with you. I'm—doing a favor for the Kiev office—mm?" Federenko nodded. "They—well, they're not really interested in her, but some of her companions—a funny lot, don't you think. Student hotheads, of course—but—"

Federenko felt impelled to speak.

"I warned her—"

"About what? About who?"

"Shubin—"

Kazantsev nodded, his glance averted but intent, like a dentist examining a successful extraction. Federenko was appalled at the ease with which it had happened, felt an acute pain as if he had been struck.

"Ah, yes—our friend Shubin. Kiev is interested in him." The ingenuous eyes again. "Your sister—she's having an affair with him, right?"

"I—I'm not sure."

"A technicality, sure. But she's in love with him, then?"

"I—look, has my sister done anything, Lieutenant—?" The room seemed hotter, or he was, as if he had been working out.

"No, no—" Kazantsev spread his hands. "Look—straight, I

said. I meant it. Have a word with your sister. Break it off, if you can—"

It was only at that moment that Federenko realized how carefully the big policeman had been walking through the mined conversation. He had been warned not to upset him; the realization caused him to grow back into himself, cooled him, too. Zenaida was safe, far safer than he had thought anyway, because of what he was, and the proximity of the Games.

"I'll try," he said with assumed nonchalance, wary of offending, of having his realization proved false. "Yes—I'll be seeing her."

"We—have some tickets for the Games—"

"I've got those—"

"No, these—these are better ones, and any day you like. Persuade your sister and your mother to come to Moscow. It won't cost you anything."

"Something's going to happen to Shubin—is that it?" Federenko snapped, closing his mind on a sense of complicity he disliked.

"I'm not sure—maybe, maybe not. If your sister's not with him, then—" Kazantsev stood up, startling Federenko. He seemed suddenly huge, threatening, in the room. "Look, I'll get those tickets for you, and we'll get accommodations—they could have this place while you're in the village—" Envy again, perhaps for the tickets which the policeman would have liked for himself, or his wife and kids. "Just you get them to Moscow for the Games—mm?"

Peter Lydall stood, looking into the wardrobe in the spare bedroom, not hearing the noises of kids skateboarding down the gentle slope of Wordsworth Drive on the new, scrubbed estate on the southern edge of Barnsley—not a tree above six feet, and most of the cars left on the blacktopped drives and not in the narrow garages where inherited, big old furniture resided because it threatened the proportions of the bright little rooms of the identical houses. This wardrobe—her mother's—should have been in the garage, but he, fastidious in the rear garden and with the strip of lawn at the front, always put the Mini away.

A blue blazer and gray flannels, squashed between miniskirts and old summer dresses, and two out-of-style Regency-type evening dresses, for the end-of-term dinner-dances he always seemed to have to organize for the staff at school. Old pointed shoes, his and hers, tumbled in the bottom of the wardrobe. His hand, as if possessed of nostalgia, ruffled the skirts, the dresses, the box-jacket suits—she never threw anything away, or gave it to the Women's Voluntary Service—but was drawn to the blazer. Fin-gered the relief of the thread, some of the wiry thread coming loose now. Hadn't he caught the badge with his traveling bag, getting off the plane in Montreal? MONTREAL. GREAT BRITAIN TEAM. 1976 OLYMPICS. He could read the badge like braille.

He slammed the door of the wardrobe shut. The tiny key fell from the lock to the floor. He ignored it. Outside, a year after the craze had died, the sons and daughters of reps and clerks and car salesmen and *teachers* stubbornly insisted that skateboarding was the only thing to do and be doing. *Teacher.* Joan said it like that, more and more often, measuring each new car on the estate, each new outfit at the supermarket, each promotion mentioned there or over the fence or when walking the dog—

She had, of course, taken the dog with her.

Lydall walked out of the spare bedroom, back into the room with the double bed and the open suitcase—his, this time, but he could almost perceive it resting in the impression on the bedspread left by her case. Their bedroom overlooked the back garden, and the back gardens of every house in the cul-de-sac. He lit a cigarette, sneering at the defiance it represented, or the cowardice of memory confronted by her disapproval, and stood at the window, looking down at the overturned tricycles, buckets, teddy bears, rubber ducks—a chopper bike, one skateboard. His garden was tidy, green, bright with flowers, empty of the detritus of children.

There had been one occasion—he was forced to be accurate, even fair—*only* one occasion when she had said it, that obscenely hurtful twist to the cliché, call yourself a man—*Call yourself an athlete?* He had drawn the line at treatment, courses of hormone pills, the regimen of making himself more potent. That would have interfered with his training; last year it would have hindered his hope. And for that, she had never forgiven him, could never, perhaps. Qualifying for the Games had been a slap in the face for Joan, an assertion of impotence, some sort of vasectomy.

He let the images idle and dwindle, tired of them, gripped with a sense of the mess he had made of things, and aware of a dim perception—so neat it might have been false, but could have been a gleam of truth—that his inability to father, to do what every other male in Wordsworth Drive past the age of puberty could do, had done, was what made him the competitor he was, gave him the will to succeed, and blinded him to age and unfitness and the way he had dropped behind people with fewer qualifications, less experience but more trendy courses in making a career.

Joan would come back—would she? Might come back, when he returned from Moscow. There was no one else, anyway. She had returned to mother, not run off with her lover. *Would she come back?* He tried to make himself ask the question as if it mattered, really mattered.

The cigarette stub burned his fingers, and he put it out in a green Wedgwood jewelry tray, on the crinoline of a shepherdess. Then he looked at the gaping suitcase—new leather look from Woollies—and his mind went to packing for London, and to the clothing and equipment issue, to the send-off, and 350 competitors in two wide-bodied jets taking off for Moscow. His wife faded in his mind, much as her presence in the house, marked by a last cigarette in the kitchen and the scent of her perfume in their bedroom when he had first come in from school, had begun to retreat.

Cheremetievo Airport, flying the flags of all the competing nations, as if the main passenger lounge was the United Nations building. From the Pan Am 747, as it rolled to a halt, parked with no more difficulty than a car in front of the glass expanse of the lounge, Gutierrez watched the flags stand out in a stiff breeze, and shadows of clouds chase each other across the bright, dusty concrete. And the faces of Russians, official and unofficial but *organized*, gathered at the main doors and pressed against the glass so that they were like little clouds themselves between the reflected stretches of blue sky.

Officials of the U.S. Olympic Committee first, adjusting blazers and hats self-consciously in the doorway, coughing in anticipation of speeches; then the team captain, Avery the long jumper and the first black to be Olympic team captain; then the remainder. Gutierrez had no interest in the protocol or precedence of going down the passenger ladder of a wide-bodied jet, and remained in his seat while the girl swimmer in whom he had taken a preseduction half-interest throughout the flight collected her bags and scarf.

He thought, briefly, now that the girl's warm arm was no longer against his, of Irena Witlocka, and the CIA spook who had spoken to him in New York about his relationship with her—Gutierrez snickered at the memory of the man's overdramatized approach, his jargonized conversation, his bungling inquisition. All to find out if he was in love with Irena, had ever been so, would be so again. And when he asked why—the girl wanted to defect, and he, apparently, was the reason.

The spook had been surprised, even offended, by Gutierrez's laughter. A laughter of surprise, and disbelief; beneath that, hardly acknowledged, a sense of self-disappointment that he normally refused to admit. The laughter had swept that away, together with the images of Irena, especially those of her face, the echo of her words. He left himself with the skinny naked body which seemed to help him consider the matter as closed, the episode over. He made himself refuse to take it seriously, this business of Irena's defection. She was just a long-legged girl from the Student Games who had no hold on him. How could she—in 1980—how could she be so *hick* as to believe in Romeo and Juliet?

He satisfied himself with amused contempt—and he chased the thoughts away by getting up, pulling his travel bag down from the rack, feeling the rump of the swimmer against his hip as she bent to shove things in her bag. He smiled again, felt himself stir a little, looked down at his trousers like a kid amazed at a first erection, and knew that there was nothing wrong, nothing going to go wrong. Even a couple of the old bastards on the committee that had disciplined him had greeted him with handshakes at Kennedy—forgive and forget and go and get us a medal, kid. A gold one.

All the way to the door, he pressed against the buttocks of the swimmer—Peggy?—rubbing slightly like a skinny pubertal kid in a line for ice cream at the beach who suddenly finds his trunks contain a stiff lump of something he didn't expect, but likes a lot. Gutierrez smiled at the image that was almost a memory.

The sun glanced off glass and steel, and the passenger gangway was hot to the touch. *Christ, were they all going to be introduced, one by one?* But he was shepherded with the other athletes through the main lounge, suddenly and gratifyingly cool after the tarmac, while passengers and the huge gathered crowd of Russians allowed into the terminal to spectate, and kept back from the concourse by white, braided ropes, gaped. He thought of the hash in his luggage, right down in an old pair of training shoes and not really enough for the two weeks but all he dared risk bringing, and he wondered whether assurances about the sanctity of athletes' luggage had been anything more than a con. He should have asked Greenberg, maybe—but Greenberg would have been searched, as a news-paperman.

He saw the team officials and manager surrounded by a surge of Soviet newspapermen, TV cameras bobbing, moving in, quicker than NBC and CBS. A carnival of public relations, which was why the crowd of Russians was there, allowed to gape at these people arriving from the country that had been the enemy as long as most of them could remember—and be seen by half the world as gaping and innocent.

He picked out Karen Gunston in the melee of TV people, and his thoughts recollected Irena uncomfortably, a nagging reminder of her thin, dark, intense face flickering in his head. Karen Gunston suggested other possibilities, provocations which seemed shallow, and a comment on himself.

He hurried on, as if past the scene of some embarrassing accident.

Karen Gunston watched him go, preoccupied with her own troubles, resenting the attendance of the men around her more than she might have done had they not been police. That they were police, and that they were interested as much as she in the job of directing cameras, was obvious as soon as he looked. He waved to her, and she raised a hand in return, which then went to her hair, which straggled more than usual. She knew she looked exasperated, hot, and not at all beautiful.

When she saw Greenberg heading toward her, smiling in the most irritating manner, towing behind him a tall, fair-haired man who could only be English, she cursed under her breath. She was to be exhibited to the stranger by a former lover who would enjoy her discomfiture. Greenberg was close to laughing aloud.

"Karen—meet Dave Allardyce."

"Greenberg—the last thing I need is a hostess, or a pimp! What the hell do you want?"

"Sweet girl—say hello to the nice man." Ben Greenberg, tie loose, shirt-sleeves rolled up and linen jacket across one arm, started laughing. Karen Gunston was aware how hot she felt, how untidy she looked—the Englishman's appraising look made her aware, and regretful. And she was irritated by the fact that she wanted to look her best. Allardyce held out his hand. She found herself wiping one hand on her cream skirt before shaking his, like a garage mechanic.

"Hot, isn't it?" Allardyce remarked, loosening his own tie, putting his hands on his hips. "Ben, my boy—I think we all need a cool drink."

Greenberg seemed amused, as if a stranger observing them, then he nodded.

"You getting hassled?" he said to Karen. She nodded her head vehemently. "So's he," Greenberg added, indicating Allardyce. "But—that's because you and Davie and a lot of other working stiffs are all here under cover—" Something darkened Allardyce's features for an instant. "No bona fides, like Ben Greenberg, sportswriter."

"Yeah—you thought Moscow was on the moon till you got out here. Foreign affairs—what does it mean to you? Egyptian cathouses?"

"The lady definitely is for burning," Greenberg explained to Allardyce. "Come, Miss America—let's get on the outside of a sweetener."

Greenberg walked off, and Karen looked up at Allardyce.

"You're a stereotype, right? Archetypal Englishman—that's why they sent you."

"I did go to all the right schools, yes," Allardyce replied, offering his arm. Karen took it, throwing her hair away from her forehead with a toss of her head, which also seemed to imply he had no proprietorial rights.

"Are you being hassled?" she asked as they followed Greenberg.

"Yes—are you?"

"Yes. Yes, we are. I have two guys with me all the time—an *assistant director*, one of them is called. He couldn't assist my ass. He has one eye, that's why they employ him—the eye sees what they want him to see. And I have to use his eye as a camera."

"What is the other one for? Man, not eye."

"He helps carry things—carry things off in the direction of Dzerzhinsky Street if you step out of line. Oh, and he translates for me, sometimes. What he thinks I should know—you understand?" Allardyce smiled, nodded.

"I have the feeling of being followed most of the time."

"*Followed* I don't mind being. It's standing between two towers of B.O. I mind."

Allardyce laughed. Then he caught sight of the passenger of the Zil sedan that had followed him out to Cheremetievo from the press center on Komsomolski Avenue. And the code word *Burgoyne* popped into the front of his mind like something in neon. His laughter must have died too suddenly, for when he turned his head he found Karen Gunston studying him curiously, her head slightly on one side.

"You got trouble?"

"No," he replied, and wondered whether he was convincing her.

Leonov was in his office in Moscow Center when Dmitri, his sergeant, brought him the news. Leonov looked up from a chart he had constructed weeks before, tracing the complex links between information purportedly leaked—checked against the full transcripts of the SALT II meetings—and the members of the Ministry staff who wpuld have had access to most, or all, of it. It was all so tenuous, so much more wearing and tedious than asking someone questions in a naked room under a bright light. Extracting secrets from deductions, from hints and implications concerning a series of discussions more than a year before, was all but impossible. He was thankful for the interruption, immediately alert when he saw the suppressed excitement in Dmitri's manner.

"We've got him," he said, proffering a monochrome picture to which was attached a single typed sheet. "This one," he added unnecessarily.

Leonov looked at the photograph—two men taken in a busy Moscow street, snow falling, heads bending together as cigarettes were lit, or information exchanged. No, it wasn't Moscow. He looked at the back of the snapshot. Vienna, he was guessing, but then he recollected the strange clock that appeared at one edge of the picture at the same time as he read the legend—PRAGUE, DECEMBER, 1979.

Leonid Vassilich Levin. An unimportant Ministry courier who delivered diplomatic bags to most of the countries of the Warsaw Pact. A mere baggage animal. Identified in the photograph as having made contact—on at least one occasion—with a known CIA operative. Prague, December, 1979.

There was no way Levin could be the double agent. At best, he was a courier, a pickup. And it was with a certain admirable irony that the CIA appeared to have suborned someone who traveled officially as a Defense Ministry courier to produce a courier for their double. If it was true. They'd been watching Levin for six months, and he hadn't gone near a CIA man, or the embassy on Tchaikovsky Street or any of the safe houses the KGB knew about. They'd been on the point of giving up on him, making the dubious assumption that Levin hadn't been bought, had asked too much—

"What do you mean, *got* him? Arrested—?" Dmitri shook his head. Leonov noticed another picture in his other hand, until that moment concealed behind his back. Dmitri grinned.

"Taken two weeks ago—just come through from Warsaw in the usual way. They were still keeping an eye on Levin, on our orders. Bloody good job."

It was Levin, on a park bench on a sunny day, eating sandwiches and taking no notice of the man at the other end of the park bench. Leonov compared the two snapshots. It could be the same man—

He was prepared to grasp at the straw. It *was* the same man.

"You've checked the ident on the other man?"

"The same man. He transferred from Prague to Warsaw three months ago. Careless of the Americans to use the same man twice."

Leonov wanted to suppress his excitement in facts—so that when he was convinced, he could revel in their good fortune.

"We still have no link with our double."

"I agree, sir. But it's the right Ministry, and if they've closed down this end of the network, then they'd need someone like Levin to get the stuff out of the Soviet Union to somewhere *quieter*."

"It's one way they might do it, yes—" Leonov was studying the two photographs, nodding his head intently at the progress of some inward dialogue. The Americans, protecting their source, had suborned Levin and kept him on ice until the investigation he was leading pressed hard and they were forced to close down the operation in Moscow, move the handover as far away as Prague or Warsaw or Bucharest or Berlin.

There was only one way to find out—ask Levin. He looked up at Dmitri.

"Assemble the team—we'll take him now. No mess-up this time. I'll come myself."

"Sir," Dmitri responded, as if insulted.

"Well done, Dmitri," Leonov offered by way of conciliation. "Well done."

Dmitri grinned.

"The team's ready when you are, Captain."

There were three of them—only two of any importance, since the third man was Vladimir, his coach, hovering at the edges of the room, in the shadows thrown by the lamps, as if witnessing a distressing scene. Federenko watched his face as a screen onto which were thrown reliefs of his own feelings. The other two were officials from the High Performance Unit of the Soviet Olympic Committee, the people responsible for overseeing the development of elite sportsmen, organizing him, just as they had sat on committees to organize schedules of training, accommodation, timetables, diets, gym time, competition for the Russian athletes. Organizing him out of a medal. They were the people who dictated policy, determined procedures, forecast goals, for top sportsmen and -women. One of them was from Georgia, the other from Uzbekistan, but both of them were Moscow men by adoption.

Tretsov the Byelorussian, the good boy at 5000, the unimaginative, consistent plodder, was to win the race. Carefully, but only careful of precision, not of his feelings, they explained the strategy of the race. Tretsov, during the past twelve months, had put in consistently better times than he—Federenko had no idea whether it was true—Tretsov had won the Olympic Trials, with himself a poor second, almost beaten by a student, a Latvian at that; Tretsov was the good dog, the puppet they were destroying as they made it.

Federenko knew that Tretsov's specialized training had been developed after their plan for the race. And he was the kind of runner who could successfully fulfill the plan. So the coaches had decided on a time that would be necessary to win—amended perhaps in the light of Irvine's world record, so that the training would have intensified, and all of it would have been geared to producing that time in the Olympic Final. The development of pace judgment would have been foremost. He had a vision of Tretsov, like a robot or a dog on a treadmill, running every thousand meters of the Final at exactly the same pace, waiting for his teammate to burn the others out. In training, he was running endless 400s, 800s, 1500s, all at the required pace so that judgment became automatic; altitude training to build up the blood condition; surrounded by doctors for daily medical analysis—even changing the blood just before a race or training like the Finn, Viren, had done in Montreal—they wouldn't have missed that trick; and the special psychological preparation, which might even have included mild hypnosis, instilling the superiority, the mental toughness to absorb a lowly position in a race and stick to the strategy, ignoring the tactics of all the other runners.

Poor bloody Tretsov. Federenko shivered. Offered the prize, he had submitted—as he might have done himself. Had he been more orthodox, more *reliable*, the offer might have been his.

"Tretsov will *just* qualify for the Final, Arkady—" The

emphasis on his first name by the Georgian was like an obscene caress, touching his skin. He rubbed his forearm as if washing it. "You, on the other hand, will win as easily as possible."

They did not seem to regard his silence throughout as sullen, or insolent. It was what they required of him—lack of dissent. And he knew he would not dissent—the paint in that room, the sofa he sat on, the television, the small Moskvich in the garage block behind the apartments—all told him that he would keep silent, that he would be casting them aside if he opened his mouth. He was struck dumb by the materialism he had taken as if his right, and which was now threatened. Insidious, he realized—for fish in the refrigerator, for emulsion paint, for a strip of carpet in the hall, for the red vest like his own credit card; for them, he would accept, accept—

"In the Final, you will be one of the favorites—a dark horse suddenly, a threat to them all." Still the Georgian speaking in the thick, clogged accent as if he were speaking through phlegm. "You will set out at a pace that makes the world record there for the taking—you understand?" Something seemed to be required of him at that point; eventually, he realized he must nod. He saw Vladimir moving, reflected in the TV screen. He nodded. "Good. The field will not dare to let you get out of touch—mm?" He nodded more quickly this time. "You will stretch them, while Tretsov hangs on, running entirely his own race. You *break* the field—" He noticed how big, gnarled the Georgian's hands were. "When they are broken, Tretsov sprints past the pieces, and wins. Simple." Then the deep-set eyes stared at him, as if anticipating an objection. The Georgian nodded. "Good. Now that everything is—*settled*, we are much happier. You, too, Arkady Federenko, will be happier now. Now that you *know*."

When they had gone, he understood that it could be made to work. He had run few races—but competition didn't matter if he was to run to a plan like this. He had been trained—his own *special training*—to run a fast two miles, burning up almost everything and everybody. In an Olympic Final, no one could afford to assume he would burn himself out before the end. They would have to keep in touch, stretch out.

He clenched his fists, beat them on his knees, and felt the tears pricking behind his shut lids. He wanted to damage something. He picked up the veneered coffee table, in one hand, and stood there, threatening the television set. The color set.

And he put down the coffee table, very precisely, in its indentations in the carpet. Saw what he was doing, and crossed to the window, swung it open, and leaned out, as if desperate for air. It was cool, stars bright above the sodium lamps, the noise of a car, probably their car driving away.

He looked down and saw the white globe of Vladimir's face, under a streetlamp, staring up at him like a drunk confused by a vaguely recognized apartment block. Hate, frustration, the sense of time-serving, arse-licking self-abasement, all concentrated on Vladimir. The warder.

"There's one thing wrong with their fucking plan, Vladimir!" he yelled down at him, the noise bouncing back from the pavement and walls. "Tretsov couldn't beat Irvine over 5000 given two laps' start!"

The echoes died away, and he was acutely aware of the silence. Then of Vladimir's reply, dropped like stones into the pool of that silence.

"They're taking care of that."

Levin lived in an apartment block in the northern suburbs, a pink granite lump to house workers and minor officials near the permanent site of the Exhibition of Economic Achievements in Sokolniki Park. When the driver parked the Zil, Leonov got out swiftly, urgently, followed by Dmitri and Ilya. The rest of the team, in a second car and under Georgi's authority, would wait outside the building, covering all the exits. A classic, quiet lift. Leonov nodded to Georgi, who ordered his men to position themselves. Across from the block of flats there was a subdued, hazy light from the dance hall and theater in the park. Leonov glanced up at the windows of the block, most of them lit, and counted his way up to the fifteenth floor.

"That one, third along," Dmitri said at his side.

"Let's go. Ilya, keep in the background, and stay quiet." He looked at the young man, whose hand came guiltily out of his jacket, leaving the gun in place in its shoulder holster. Leonov nodded. "Softly, softly," he said.

They entered the foyer of the block, and Dmitri paraded the red KGB ID card before the janitor, who had been warned to expect them. He was deferential, but more fellow-conspiratorial, since he was himself a KGB "unofficial," like a great many of the janitors, cleaners, concierges, and desk clerks in the city.

"Fifteenth floor," he said unnecessarily. "Apartment fifteen-oh-six."

"Make my men outside a cup of tea," Leonov said, getting into the elevator that the janitor had summoned as soon as he heard the cars arrive. The janitor nodded. He didn't like the way the captain looked at him like an unpleasant reality, but he certainly would not reveal his feelings. Except that when the door closed he tossed his head defiantly.

Leonov watched the buttons as the elevator began to move, then studied the lights above the door as it moved slowly, audibly upward. When he spoke, it was as if to himself.

"If he answers the door, we'll be the janitor. And *listen* carefully. The doors on these flats are like paper—I should know, I used to live in one." He smiled, but that, too, was directed inward, and the corners of his mouth pulled down as if the smile threatened to become a quite different expression. "If there are *any* strange noises—" He looked at the two men with him for the first time since getting in the elevator. "Like tearing paper or guns being cocked and the rest of it—" They grinned. "Kick in the door and we'll have him away before he can protest his innocence."

Fifteenth floor. The elevator door opened jerkily, unsettling Leonov as he thought of the maintenance the elevator must need, reminded of the slight, nagging fear that had stayed since boyhood of being trapped in an elevator. The elevators had worked better when the apartments were newer, when he and his late wife had lived there, when they first married.

Apartment 1506. A plain, mustard-painted door with a letter box that was pitted with rust and dull with never having been polished. Leonov snapped awake, knocked on the door. Then he listened, very carefully. They'd heard two lesbians arguing like man and wife in the opposite apartment to theirs, in the old days—and then realized that all the visitors of those two women had been women. An absence of men—

Listen. An argument just like one of their own—

The noise—after the silence when the TV went off—of a curtain being drawn aside. Beside him, Dmitri and Ilya were likewise bent to the door. It made Leonov smile, then frown with concentration.

The silence seemed to last for minutes after that, and the tension transmitted itself from Leonov, who was certain, to Dmitri, who was suspicious, then to Ilya, who merely imitated his superiors and did not reach into the room, picturing Levin in the silence.

"What's he—?" Dmitri began. Leonov waved him to silence. He rang the doorbell again. Then he listened as footsteps came down the narrow passageway he could clearly visualize behind the door, paused, then turned and hurried away. Leonov, leaning almost off balance to hear, waited. A bedroom door—? Kitchen light?

Then he heard a scrape, visualized everything immediately, the hand on the window latch, the kind of window—he must have been looking for the key to the French windows, out onto the balcony, couldn't find it—*it* was *the noise of a key!*

He stepped back, kicked violently at the door, and spilled into the hallway, stumbling on a loose rug there, slipping to one knee, calling out, "Stop him—the *window!*"

Someone jumped over him, cannoned off one wall of the passage, blocking the light from the living room. Dmitri passed him then as he got to his feet, and Leonov was filled with sudden foreboding, visualizing eager young Ilya, and Levin on the balcony. . . .

"Shoot him in the *leg*—!" he called as the Makarov Ilya had drawn exploded once, a deafening noise in the little room, the narrow passageway, loud enough to suggest a piece of artillery that could vaporize Levin. Deafened, Leonov ran into the living room, and the scene was a sudden tableau about which he could do nothing, which was complete.

The one main, barely furnished room. Levin had collapsed back onto the sofa, his hand still gripping the handle of the French window onto the balcony. The orange-dappled darkness of Sokolniki Park was behind his head, partly obscured by the starburst hole in the window where the bullet had exited, and the bloody mess that surrounded the hole, obscuring the view like a thin curtain.

Levin's body moved on the sofa, the hand letting go of the French window. The ruined face was exposed, where the 9mm bullet had emerged just below the right eye. Then the body continued to sag sideways, and the vision was gone, the back of the head just exhibiting a trickle of red, a slight mussing of the hair near the neck.

Leonov looked instead through the half-open doorway onto the balcony where the lights of the dance hall in the park were reflected in an ornamental lake. He felt a sense of loss out of all proportion to what had happened, a community of loss in which Levin and his dead wife died together. Perhaps just the familiarity of the surroundings—

He shook his head. Ilya, his face white and reflecting the churning of his stomach at the sight of what he had done to Levin, was trying feebly to return the Makarov to its holster, as if it was the gun that had offended, led him to this state.

"You—fucking idiot!" Leonov roared, breath and voice coming at last, anger welling up. "He can't tell us anything with the back of his head open and his face on the windowpane, can he?" Ilya seemed to turn more pale at the imagery, averted his eyes from the sofa as if he anticipated more sudden, revealing movement from the corpse. He'd never killed anyone before, he wanted his captain's sympathy, not rage. "Why didn't you shoot him in the leg, you stupid, stupid bugger!"

Leonov turned to look at Levin's body.

"Sir—sorry, sorry, I—"

"Get out—get downstairs and wait!"

He heard the door of the apartment close, hurried footsteps. Then Dmitri was making the futile checks of the body, and looking up at him. Leonov saw the hanging shadow of an old man.

"The boy panicked—you remember the first time you pointed a gun in anger. It's got—"

"All right, all right—it's got a life of its own, you don't aim, I know all that smart crap! But our one good lead—stumbled on by us blind men—is dead. Killed by that stupid graduate kid who still needs his nose wiped!"

Leonov had stopped looking at the body, but everywhere his eyes darted, he saw the familiar. The contours of the first years of his marriage. It caused acute discomfort, a tight sensation around his chest which added to his blind, unreasoning anger with Ilya, even with the corpse. He was uncomfortably full of memories rich as good food and drink, a five-course experience of lost years and a lost wife which bloated him with useless regrets and angers that added to the strange poignancy with which he received Levin's demise.

"Anyway—how much did he know? The name of his CIA contact—?" Dmitri offered, mollifying him. "He wouldn't know the source, and there'd be cutouts between him and anyone close. Or a dead-letter box. He wouldn't have known."

"O.K., O.K.—maybe you're right. But you'll eat anything when you're starving. And we're starving, Dmitri. We've got nothing."

"Look, Gennadi—" Dmitri used his first name sometimes, not often. It was permitted—now it was further mollification. "We know a lot. What we know has caused them to close down. Here, we've closed something recent and new. We're pressing, squeezing—" He moved one hand into a fist. "And the pips might come spurting out of the orange any day now. The Americans will have to protect—or *lift*, their source."

Leonov, aware again of the professional life, said, "You think the double's made a distress call?"

"The double's been drowning, not waving, for a while now, I think. But the Americans want the source to hang on—for the defense budget resolutions. That's got to be the prize. If we go on squeezing—"

Dmitri's face was hopeful, almost pleading, his hand a tight fist. Leonov nodded.

"Then July's the optimum—now that the meetings are about to begin. And with the network cut off from the source, then the source has to take out the information—or will use it to bargain a way out—?"

"I think so. Under cover of the Games."

"Maximum smoke—yes, I agree with that, Dmitri. Yes, I agree. Which means we have to press harder than ever—"

"And there'll be a case officer coming in, maybe a salesman, as we thought. Gennadi—we've got them, *because* Ilya killed Levin. The Americans will *have* to get the source out now, because the source will demand safety as the price of the information."

"The double's put in a *stronger* position—?" He looked at Levin, then laughed, an abrupt barking sound. "You're right—dammit, you're right! The double's cut off, screaming for help, and holding back supplies until there's a deal—" His hand, too, had become a fist. "Then we *have* to identify the case officer when he comes in, and any other personnel! The Americans can *help* us trap our double!"

CHAPTER 6

A rest area on the main highway from Dnepropetrovsk to Donetsk, 230 miles southeast of Kiev. It was shielded from the road, the noise and weight of passage of the iron ore and coal trucks that used the highway incessantly, and overlooked the Volchya from an outcrop, so that the barges on the river and the railway that snaked beside it both seemed toylike, pretty. The tension of the journey in the vegetable truck had worn away at Zenaida's confidence, had—she noticed in the driving mirror—blanched and drawn her features so that she looked thinner, undernourished. They were still hours from Donetsk, in the industrial heartland of the Ukraine, and now Shubin wanted to make love—she used the euphemism quite consciously for what they did together, as a disguise, a veil over her own enjoyment of what was simply his taste for her body, his wish to subordinate through sex.

There was no tenderness. The sacks of potatoes and cabbages provided a comfortable enough bed—if that was what she could call the half-upright support they gave her. The ludicrous aspect of the whole thing never occurred to her. In Shubin she sensed an excitement that had little to do with her, most to do with Donetsk and the bomb he was going to collect from the ordnance factory and his friend Belousov. But he used her as an escape valve, or perhaps danger heightened his sexual need. She did not know, and did not care. She leaned her head back, staring at the blue sky, aware of the noises of setting up tables, brewing tea, and eating that came from the family in the ancient car that had pulled off the highway just after they had climbed into the back of the truck, and at which she giggled and he had appeared annoyed—with her. She felt his beard rasp against her breasts, her stomach—he had opened the jeans she wore, down to her pubic hair; he kissed her infrequently, just rubbed his face, his body against her like an animal.

She could never decide whether she enjoyed the degradation that seemed attached to their copulation—she did not *want* it to be enjoyable because it was degrading, using her—or whether because it was with him, Shubin, and the closest she could get to him was when he was in her, that only then was she in some sort of communion with him.

She felt her jeans pulled roughly below her knees, tried to spread her thighs as much as she could, proffering, felt him move his hand between her legs urgently, as if trying to hurt—then he was in her, and she leaned farther back as he seemed to straighten, so that they were touching only at the groin—as if they wanted nothing else to do with each other—and he pushed into her, increasing the rhythm, accelerating. She stared at the sky, her hand in her mouth, teeth biting the soft web between thumb and forefinger because this, this was what made her want to call out, moan as if begging for endearments, while he thrust in an uncomplicated, inexpressive silence, as if determined she should have nothing from him but the semen. He never cared, never asked, whether there was any climax for her. Then he shuddered—that one moment when he submitted, was drawn completely into his ejaculation—and before the moment in which she climaxed, he pressed down on her, finished, and already becoming indifferent.

She dared not stroke his back, under the shirt, touch his neck with her mouth—he disliked it, would pull away from her. She lay still as a mattress, waiting for his rough breathing in her ear to quieten.

They climbed out of the back of the truck, to be greeted by surprise and almost instant realization and disgust. Zenaida, cheeks tinged with pink, was aware of the instant, as if in slow motion, in which the fat woman's features changed from conventional greeting-smile to suspicious contempt. She seemed to stare at Zenaida's groin, and at Shubin's, as if they had stained their jeans. A fat woman in a shapeless dress out of which she threatened to boil and erupt if she moved. Shubin put his arm around Zenaida, not for comfort but for suggestive insult to the fat woman, then they climbed back in the cab. The bald little husband, tiredly playing with bats and a ball on a length of elastic with two intent children—Zenaida realized she had heard the thocking noise as a rhythm in herself and Shubin—stared after them. Zenaida thought he envied them their freedom, their escape in a vegetable truck more than he envied Shubin his sexual indulgence.

Shubin pulled back onto the Donetsk highway, still withdrawn into himself, silent. Zenaida glanced at him once, saw the bottom lip jutting, the beard like a stiff brush, the eyes emptily concentrating. She wished she could dislike him, even hate him, because such an emotion would suggest superiority. She tried, for a long time, to generate a distance between them of *her* making, but it was as if the copulation had left her too weak.

The cab smelled of diesel, and, as tension began to extend again from the tight little knot in her stomach, it began to make her feel sick. She could not ask him to stop—anyway, he wouldn't. The fumes seeped into her, like an emanation from the industrial landscape into which they now passed, as if into another country. Pit wheels, slag heaps, low blocks of rolling mills flung on the scene, as if someone had once built a tower there, and someone else had demolished it, leaving these heaps and slabs and spiky, wheeled towers. When they saw the Volchya, its color seemed to have changed, too.

There was one check by a patrol car, which Shubin seemed to regard carelessly, confidently. The policeman checked their transit papers, the ID cards that Shubin had had forged somewhere, or even had passed back to him from the student organization in Munich, were desultorily inspected—the policeman seemed more interested in the fresh vegetables. Zenaida felt her stomach surge, again and again, as if it would never settle, as the policeman slowly selected half a dozen cabbages. Shubin stood beside the cab of the truck, exchanging a mock housewife-and-shopkeeper dialogue with him. Zenaida tried one smile at the driver of the patrol car, sensed its wan inadequacy, and concentrated on the fingers of black chimneys and cooling towers ahead of them which like graffiti marked Donetsk.

When the patrol car pulled away, Shubin climbed back in the cab, spat out of the window, and put the truck into gear. There had been no comment of any kind that he had a woman in the cab. The forged ID card described Zenaida as a driver's mate.

Then they were into the suburbs of Donetsk, and she had to read the street names, the map on her knees.

"You O.K.?" he asked finally, when she made a mistake. There was only a hint of irritation in the voice, and perhaps a touch of concern.

"Yes, yes," she replied too eagerly, snatching at the vestigial compassion he seemed to express. "Sorry—just the fumes." He nodded. "Next left," she added ingratiatingly.

The builders' yard they wanted was in the northern suburb of Donetsk, where the suburbs of the neighboring town of Makeyevka had crept to some soiled marriage with those of Donetsk. The postwar regiments of identical houses and terraces and apartment blocks seemed to be trying to disguise the blatant industrialism of the Donets basin. New light industry on scrubby, weedy plots, or next to holes in the ground where companion factories would be erected, attempted also to lighten the griminess of the scene. Zenaida was thankful it wasn't raining. Yet the sun seemed determined to expose the shabbiness of the place—slag heaps in the middle distance, the low block of a brush factory, the art nouveau of a scrap heap. Then they penetrated the old village that formed the heart of the suburb, and older, narrower streets the Nazis hadn't destroyed and Stalin hadn't pulled down. Oppressed by recent grime, leaning drunkenly toward each other across narrow cobble streams, nevertheless the houses and terraces belied the industrial scenery.

She relaxed for a few moments—Shubin knew the way—and then was brought to immediate, tense alertness by the slamming of the gates of the builders' yard behind them as soon as they drove through. An announcement of urgency, and the dreams of the previous night came back to her.

A big hand slapped over her own as it rested shakingly on the door of the cab—she jumped, startled, and looked down into Pyotr's smiling face. He winked, seemed to see into her head, know what to say.

"Hello, beautiful lady."

"Rubbish," she replied, but something tight and growing in her chest dissipated as she laughed shakily. Pyotr opened the door, bowed, waved her down from the cab. Shubin was already down, talking to an older man—Aram whose parents had come from Armenia. Aram was angry. She rested her head briefly against Pyotr's chest, sensing she was encouraging where she had no right to, but was momentarily grateful for his amused devotion.

"You're late, Feodor Yelisavich—*bloody* late!"

Shubin raised his hands to shrug the words away.

"All right, Aram—"

"It's not fucking all right, Shubin! We're late already. This is supposed to be a normal oxygen delivery—they're expecting it. It should have been made three hours ago." Aram rumbled his complaints, the indigestion of tension. "And another thing—this truck—" He tossed his head, waggled his finger over his shoulder to indicate the parked truck. "This truck has to be back at its depot tonight. And I don't mean tomorrow morning, or the day after—tonight!"

"It will be, it will be—" Shubin was relaxed, confident, even arrogant. "The factory is half an hour away, the working day has a couple of hours to go—it will take less than an hour in the factory—stop worrying!" Only on the last words was there an emphasis of threat.

"You said lunchtime—" Aram began to grumble, a lesser noise like a dog whose tether has been forcibly demonstrated. He looked instead across at Zenaida and Pyotr. "Why bring the tart?" he said crudely, as if to reassert himself against Shubin.

"Cover."

"She stays here—me or Pyotr goes with you."

"Sure."

Zenaida realized that Shubin had intended to leave her at the builders' yard from the beginning; she was angry, and relieved. She moved away from Pyotr as if she no longer needed his support or his arm around her shoulders. She glanced at his face. It seemed still to be amused—certainly not hurt.

"You'd better get changed—you want something to eat?"

"A drink," Shubin said. He looked at Zenaida and Pyotr, and seemed amused by something. "You come with me, Aram—Pyotr can wait here with Zenaida." It was as if he expected some expression of gratitude from the young man. Then he grinned, without warmth, and turned on his heel, making for the offices that leaned red-bricked and dilapidated over the truck full of oxygen cylinders.

Rudolf Ivanovich Belousov paused in the long, starkly lit corridor, head cocked like a dog listening. Then he turned the key in the lock of the plain flush door, and slipped inside. He switched on the light, a single weak, naked bulb, crossed the narrow cell and, bending before untidily heaped cardboard boxes below a dusty row of metal shelves, he pulled aside a worn out tarpaulin.

The cylinders—four of them—lay in a neat row like the still, chrysalis stage of some insect's development. He rolled the first to him, and carefully inspected—sight and touch—the wax-filled seams that stretched the whole length of the cylinder. He knew where they were, but because there had been no further shrinkage, neither eye nor thumb could discover them. The dull green paint—a medical color—hid the wax that held in place the substituted panels in the cylinder.

He inspected the other three cylinders quickly and expertly, with the same satisfactory result.

He stood up, the backs of his knees already tight from crouching. From a mildewed cardboard box on the shelf at waist level, he took four valves. They were, even under careful inspection, identical to those found on oxygen cylinders for industrial or medical use. Except that the gauges, before fitting, indicated full contents and pressure.

He took from the pocket of his white coat four thick gaskets, fitted one to the base thread of one of the valves. With a soft cloth, he wiped a short protrusion on the underside of the valve, and a matching recess in the top of the first cylinder. Both had a film of shining copper.

Only when the gasket was removed could the device be armed. His own little sophistication, to prevent some heavy-handed oaf turning the valve too far, too early.

He performed exactly the same series of movements, finishing with the fitting of the dummy gauges to the cylinder, three more times. Until all four cylinders nestled in innocence beneath the tarpaulin.

Then he eased himself back into the dingy corridor. His little devices were awaiting collection by Shubin. Lying there in the dark—

Shubin spent minutes checking the delivery notes, the transit papers, the new ID cards. When he seemed satisfied, he swung up into the cab of the delivery truck, alongside the silent, impatient Aram, started the engine, and without looking either at Zenaida or Pyotr, pulled out of the yard. Zenaida read, for the hundredth time, the legend DONETSK OXYGEN SUPPLIES on the side and tailgate of the truck, before Pyotr shut the gates behind it. Then, suddenly, the yard was quiet again, and she was alone with Pyotr, and despite his company she was beginning to worry again.

Shubin halted the delivery truck at the gates of the Makeyevka Ordnance Factory, and stared up as if looking at prison gates. Electrified wire along the top of the gates, along the wall which must have been twenty feet high. The regularity of the brickwork stretched away down the street on either side of them. The ordnance factory was old—immediate postwar—and out of date except in one area of production, the one which interested Shubin. A judas gate opened in the main gate, and a uniformed security man, armed, stepped suspiciously out into the street like an agoraphobic being pushed from behind.

"Papers."

Shubin handed them over, sensing the tension in Aram beside him, sensing in himself only the confidence he needed, only the *belief*—the contempt for the pea-brained guard trying to appear thorough in his examination of the dockets and ID cards. Too long, and they're just staring at the ink and paper. He knew that. He rested his hand on the door of the cab, close to the peaked cap of the guard. Ridiculously, he wanted to knock it askew, and laugh in the man's pompous, stupid face. Then the guard looked up at him, and the papers were handed back. He ducked back through the judas gate, the noise of bolts—no electric locks—and then the big gates began to swing open. Shubin looked at Aram, and winked.

"Here we go, Aram Feodorich—into the lion's den." Aram's face was tight, unmoving with the effort of appearing calm, in control. Better than Zenaida, Shubin thought—just.

The ordnance factory was like five or six old schools dumped together behind the brick walls. The simile of the prison receded in Shubin's mind. Going through the gate, turning the wheel to follow the signs to DELIVERIES, dispelled any menace. Shubin was fully into the role he was playing—he had oxygen cylinders, they were expecting a delivery, he had the right papers.

"Simple," he muttered.

"What—?" Aram snapped, as if startled.

"Hang on to your bowels," Shubin smirked, turning a corner past a dusty, cracked window—*hospital*, he thought. A broken-down hospital. Aram's hand on the door handle was white, as if he had been ordered to jump from the moving truck. "Balls," he muttered, and this time Aram heard him, but sensed the object of his comment, and stayed silent.

He pulled up beside a porch, its sign reading ALL DELIVERIES HERE. ENLIST THE AID OF A SECURITY GUARD BEFORE UNLOADING. All the inadequate security of the place seemed concentrated in that notice, and the fact that there was no one about, though the guards must have heard the truck draw up. This was a smaller brick building, almost a guardhouse or shed, behind which stretched another brick perspective of factory buildings. They manufactured small-arms cartridges, grenades, mines, some HE, and what he wanted, the FAE device, designated OX/370 (anticivilian) by the High Command and the Ministry of Defense (Weapons Development). A nasty little toy developed at the Kharkov Research

Establishment and contracted for limited production for experimental purposes to the Donetsk Area, Makeyevka Factory. The jargon ran through his thoughts like an anesthetic, reducing the weapon he sought and the tension he could not entirely resist. Block C-3 was responsible for production and storage. They were parked in front of B-6.

Shubin breathed deeply, once, and opened the door of the cab.

"Wait," he said, and climbed down. Aram watched him walk with a casual, lazy jauntiness toward the door of the guardroom.

The guardroom was a counter, behind which one man could squeeze with just a little effort, then a blank chipboard wall behind which he could hear a television set, and the pop of a beer can being opened. There was a bell. What was there to be secure about? FAE. What to be secure against? *Do pobachenya*. But then, they didn't know about *Do pobachenya*, so who could blame them. The last time so much as a bullet was stolen, it was probably for a souvenir for some kid—unless you counted the extra rounds any quartermaster would expect added to what was on his docket. He pressed the bell.

The chipboard wall shuddered slightly as the door was opened, and a bored security guard appeared, appeased by the overalls Shubin wore and the dockets in his hand. He was still chewing a sandwich—the remainder of it was in his hand—and he took the papers, flicked through them one-handed, then sniffed and wiped his nose with the back of the hand that held the remains of the sandwich. He handed the papers back. Shubin felt a shiver beginning in his left leg as he stood there, and erased any trace of self-contempt from his features.

"You want C-3," the guard said.

"Any chance of a hand—full load?" Shubin said lightly.

The guard bent and looked through the window toward the truck, and Aram.

"You've got a mate with you—piss off. You can afford to stroll round here just when you like—" The guard looked at his watch. "Then you can unload the bloody stuff yourself!" he said, and turned back into the room behind the chipboard, demonstratively biting on the sandwich. Shubin shook his head at the retreating back, and left the cramped little office. Outside, he smiled, keeping his face toward the truck. They were so stupid it was a shame to do it to them. Generations of the backward breeding the subnormal, just to produce the security guards at the ordnance factory. Genetic conspiracy to assist *Do pobachenya*. It was a nice idea.

"All right?"

"Of course. Thick as cowpats, all of them." He started the engine, turned down the alleyway between two brick, windowed walls. "They're not expecting us—how do you think Belousov managed to make an FAE bomb just for us except by having to be overseen by these cretins? Half of the stupid buggers can't read the dockets!" He laughed.

Belousov was waiting for them outside block C-3. Two men in overalls lounged against the pillars of the main entrance, idly watching the truck's approach, while Belousov, in a white lab coat, studied his watch.

"Time?" Shubin said.

"Four twenty-six."

"Thirty minutes, no longer. Otherwise the chess grand master on the gate is going to wonder where we are." He wrenched on the handbrake, switched off the ignition.

"There's a bloke I don't know—" Aram began.

"Where?"

"One of those two—" He pointed through the windshield at the two lounging men.

"Shit! Keep your hand down! You're sure?"

"Of course I'm sure—that's Ghekh, but the other one I don't know—"

Shubin turned on him, impatient of the solution, even though Belousov was down the steps from the concrete unloading bay, almost at the cab.

"If you've buggered it up—" Then Belousov was alongside looking up, his face mobile with relief, and complaint.

"You're late," he began.

Shubin snapped down at him, "Who's the little stranger among us?"

"Bulgakov is ill—phoned in this morning—"

"Why couldn't you leave it with just *one* man to help?"

"Look, I don't draw up the rosters for porters—!" Belousov's crumpled, tired face—he had always looked ten years his own senior, even in college—was flushed, angry rather than frightened.

Shubin reluctantly surrendered to him. "It'll still work—as long as you're careful."

"If he spots anything, makes one move—I'll break his neck, and leave you to find a place for the body." Belousov backed away from the door, and Shubin climbed down. He looked up at the two immobile porters who had not even lowered the tailgate of the truck, not even put out their cigarettes. "Are you kind gentlemen going to give us a hand unloading this stuff?"

The man Aram did not know appeared less reluctant than the bribed Ghekh, who puffed twice more at his cigarette, then ground it out, watching the other porter let down the tailgate. It thudded against the floor of the bay. Then Ghekh wheeled a trolley forward.

"Aram—get on with it," Shubin whispered. "For God's sake, keep an eye on him—chat to him, distract him, tell him I've got the runs—anything! Anything, understand?" Aram nodded. The eyes did not flinch. Yes, better than Zenaida.

"Come on," Belousov snapped at his side.

Shubin nodded, strolled to the rear of the truck, behind Aram, then said in a loud voice, "I'll see you—got caught short again."

Aram, alert, grumbled back at him, "Your dose of the runs will last about half an hour, I suppose, then miraculously clear up!" Ghekh laughed, and the other porter, hefting a cylinder onto a trolley, smiled, the strain making it appear as a red-faced grimace.

Shubin walked off as if careful of every betraying step, while Belousov, appearing irate, guided him toward the main doors of C-3.

As soon as they were inside, and looking down from the ground-level gantry which stretched around the huge, basement bowl of the factory floor, Shubin said, "It's finished—you're sure?"

"Yes, thank God. I wouldn't have sent the message for you to collect—"

"Yes, yes, Rudolf Ivanovich—I appreciate that. What do you want me to say—to thank you in the name of the group, hand you an illuminated scroll—?"

"Not from you, Shubin—that would be the last hypocrisy. We all work willingly for the cause, which is—what is the cause, by the way?" There was an almost hysterical relief about Belousov's careless manner as they clattered along the walkway, looking down on the assembly lines, the pieces and functions that became gleaming shells at the far end of the block. The FAE section of the block, where Belousov worked, was guarded at the far end. Shubin could see the soldier or KGB man in uniform, Kalashnikov, over his shoulder, before a steel door like the door of a great safe, wheel and combination dial, the lot.

"What's the matter with you?"

"Do you know—do you even begin to comprehend—what the last few months have been like here?"

Shubin paused. He sensed what was required. "I'm sorry, Rudolf. I'm sorry. No, I don't even begin to realize—you're quite right—"

"It hasn't been *so* bad—" Belousov responded, and they walked on, the fussy, white-coated little man in the lead.

"We don't have to come back this way—?"

"Of course not!"

Belousov ducked through a door, and Shubin followed. They were in a narrow corridor, and Shubin could see the sign TWALYET. Belousov glanced again at his watch, and hurried ahead of Shubin, left, then right, passing blank doors on either side, the dust relatively undisturbed on the concrete floor, even growing more noticeable. Storerooms, probably unused for years—

Belousov halted, fished in his pocket, and produced a key. He opened an unmarked door, and beckoned Shubin inside. Only when the door was closed did he switch on the naked bulb suspended from the ceiling.

"Is this where you—?"

"Don't be stupid, Shubin."

The two men seemed crowded against the door. Belousov went down on one knee and rummaged beneath what appeared to be stored, rotting tarpaulin. He pulled this away, grunting with effort.

"Give me a hand here, Shubin!" he snapped.

Together, the two men rolled out from beneath the shadow of the lowest shelf four cylinders, much like oxygen cylinders except that they—

"Smaller, you see?" Belousov remarked. "I couldn't place them with the empties for loading." Shubin nodded, absently, stroking the smoothness of one of the cylinders. "The detonators are built in —only way I could disguise them. And it had to be two groups of two for the specified area—" He looked at Shubin then, his eyes bright, almost moist, behind the spectacles. Shubin could not comprehend, or guess, what he was supposed to reply. He merely nodded.

"Yes—"

Belousov seemed to give up the effort.

"Carrying them the back way through here won't matter—but be careful when you get outside—and I can't be seen carrying one—"

"Then get a bloody trolley, and I can take them all at once!"

The two men stared at each other, the smaller man diminished in his sense of what he had done, at what expense of nerve and time and belief. Belousov had limited the horizons of his imagination

during the months he had worked secretly on four FAE devices—
but now as he stared into Shubin's uncompassionate face, he began
to see again the moral nature of what he had done.

"I—" Shubin's eyes, burning. "Yes. Wait here."

When he was gone, Shubin settled into a sitting position on the
floor, looking at the cylinders. He stroked one gently, patted it,
fondled it, head back, eyes closed. Belousov found him like that, saw
him come instantly awake, eyes battening on Belousov's face,
hands. Then he relaxed, the hand coming away from the cylinders.

"Got it?"

"Yes."

"Where are the operating instructions?"

Belousov sighed.

He removed an envelope from his breast pocket. "In here.
Three slides, numbered in order. All you need is a viewer or a
projector." He passed them to Shubin. "I don't want to hear from
you again, Shubin!" It was sudden, an outburst.

"You decided that while you were looking for the trolley—uh?"
Shubin was grinning contemptuously. "Want to begin to forget now,
eh, Rudolf Ivanovich?"

"You're a bloodless bastard, Shubin—you always were."

"Forget it. Help me put these on the trolley—"

The effort forced both of them to rest until their pulses faded,
sweat dried under the arms, across their backs. Then, Belousov
leading the way, Shubin in overalls pushing the trolley, they
followed a twisting, narrow series of corridors and walkways until
Belousov pushed open a side door, and they emerged onto the
loading bay thirty yards from the delivery truck. Belousov motioned him to wait, then waved him out. Only Aram could be seen.

"Hurry—!"

Shubin trundled the trolley, with what seemed now magnified
racket, to the truck, and gesturing to Aram, began to unload the
cylinders.

"Quickly, quickly, you fat slob—!" They heaved the first
cylinder over the back of the truck, rolling it toward the cab. Then
the second—lift, *lift*, up, stepping backward, be careful, you fat
bugger, be careful—down, *down*, roll—use your boot! Then the
third, and the fourth of them, the sweat in his eyes, his heartbeat
racing out of control. Finally, he was breathless, grunting with
effort.

"How—how much more—?"

Aram waved his hand, bent double, catching his breath.

"Last load, so I'm told—"

"I'll—get down—*Christ!* You watch the other man."

The truck had been badly, sloppily loaded, presumably by intent on Ghekh's part, laziness prompting the other man. Shubin strolled to the back of the bay, near the doors, while Belousov stood indecisively, nervously, near the tailgate.

Ghekh and the other man came out through the main doors, with four empty cylinders on the trolley. Ghekh watched Belousov's face, Shubin saw the tiny nod of his head, then Ghekh turned and saw Shubin.

"Giving your ass a rest?" he asked. The other man snickered.

"For a minute or so."

They began to roll the empty cylinders onto the truck. A noise like some circus drumroll. One—drumroll . . . Two—drumroll, clatter . . . Three—drumroll—

"Comrade Assistant Director—" the other man began, and every one of the others could see the direction of his fixed gaze. "Those cylinders—" He walked forward—one step, two onto the back of the truck, closer. He was moving more quickly, it seemed to Shubin, than was possible, while Shubin's own legs seemed to refuse to function, and Aram was standing with his mouth wide open, Ghekh was still half-bent with dropping the cylinder, and Belousov was as still and empty as one of the cylinders. Move— *move*—!

And he saw the man bend, try to lift—turn, face narrowing in suspicion before he was halfway across the loading bay—then reach inside his overalls, left-hand side, under the armpit—

"Jesus Christ! He's the fucking KGB man—!"

His hand came out, fist clenched round something—and Shubin, released at last from the glutinous element through which he seemed to have been moving, was on the back of the truck and bending, heaving at the last empty cylinder, arms cradling, up, every muscle used in the desperate lunge.

The man in overalls was caught across the chest—it *was* a gun coming out from a shoulder holster—and went back against the other empties, spilling them around him. Shubin jumped one that rolled toward him, bent for another while the man's face registered something hurting at the back of his head—then Shubin raised the empty over his head, both arms stretched, and down across the man's skull. A noise of bone, no cry or words, and the breath expelled in the moment of silence after the empty cylinder had finished rolling.

Shubin turned to Belousov, rage, fear still unspent.

"You stupid fucking shit! You used the *KGB man* to load the truck—and you didn't even know who he was!"

Aram's face began to register fear—Ghekh seemed unable to uncurl from his bending position, hands on knees in exhaustion. Belousov waved a feeble hand, and his mouth kept opening and closing, but never voicing the explanations flashing in his mind.

A hooter sounded like an alarm.

Five o'clock.

"Bloody five o'clock! They'll be coming off shift—!" shouted Ghekh, waking up.

"What about the body?" Aram, moving to him.

"Get it under the cylinders—quick, do it!" He ignored them then, went to Belousov, who flinched as if struck. "Nothing—you know *nothing*! Understand? Nothing." And, because the residue of extremity surged up again, "You stupid bloody fool!"

"All right—he's hidden." Aram, out of breath.

"You know nothing, Ghekh." Ghekh nodded. "Right—get away from here, the pair of you. Aram—let's go!" He stared at Belousov, as if lost for words or finding too many things to say. Then he nodded, jumped off the tailgate while Aram closed it, and ran round to the cab. The engine was started, the brake off as Aram climbed in, slammed his door.

"Oh, Jesus, Jesus—!" Aram muttered.

"Shut up. Shut up! All we have to do is get through the gates—now just shut up—"

Shubin glanced once in the mirror, saw Belousov like a castaway still on the loading bay, then they turned a corner and the little blob of white was out of sight.

Then the gate was in front of them, and they were just ahead of a troop of overalled men and women heading for the gates, which were wide. Shubin began to slow, but the pea-brained guard waved him on, and turned his back. Aram collapsed with relief back into his seat as they pulled out onto the road.

"What do we do with the body?"

"Dump it—it doesn't matter. It doesn't change anything!"

It doesn't matter—it doesn't change anything. His mind kept repeating the ideas, like a litany, a formula encapsulating a faith—a faith he seemed to be scrabbling to hold on to—all the way back to the builders' yard.

Leonov, eyes gritty with lack of sleep and mesmerized by the camera's viewpoint, his ears sensitive to the chatter of the slide cartridges, the whir of the endless footage of the projector, was angry with his team. Very angry.

White splashing black and quick numbers on the wall of his office as a film ran out—clucking of the loose end of celluloid against the projector case—

"Lights!" he bellowed. He was angry, but he was in control, using and exaggerating his emotions into a performance. Good lads, enthusiastic but inexperienced—a result of the policy of placing the university-trained top echelon in sensitive and important departments right from the beginning. So, just sometimes, he had to be their Senior Sergeant rather than their Captain.

The lights flicked on, scratchy neon, stuttering, then blooming. He prepared his face for revelation. He could tell by their reactions that they were nervous, both of them. Ilya and Oleg. One dark-haired and Lithuanian, the other a Georgian. He had shown them that last film twice, just in the hope—

"Well—you've bloody well missed him, then?"

Ilya—who had shot Levin in the apartment the other night, but had recovered after just shadows under the eyes for a day or two, and an unwillingness to meet other people's eyes—was suitably startled, chagrined.

"Who, sir?" Oleg was more in control, suspecting a feint.

"Who?" He opened a buff file, shuffled and spread the prints like a cardsharp. "That one," he said, tapping the photograph he had placed uppermost. "Recognize that face from the last film?" He glowered at them then, dyspeptic, disappointed. "You're not looking for someone with cauliflower ears and a broken nose. This one—name?"

Both young men glanced at one another, then back at him. They were going to guess, but they were trying to make it as safe a guess as possible.

"You should have seen this face in the files—you have been studying the files, I take it." Embarrassment. "One of you goes to the files, while the other lines up for dinner for two in the Center canteen?" Blushes. He almost wanted to laugh, but continued to administer their salutary medicine. "Sloppy, bloody sloppy! Don't let it happen again." He looked at the photograph once, then continued. "This man's name is Burfield, John D. Burfield, alias, alias, alias, et cetera. Covert Action Staff, CIA."

Collapse of two young parties, he thought. Shamefaced huddling on their chairs, into themselves.

"But, sir—" Oleg said.

"Yes, yes—don't finesse me, sonny. He may be a blind—even if you didn't see him—but he is a case officer who is known to us. There may be another—which is why you have to go back to the files, both of you, and for as long as it takes, and check and check until you find one other person. The agent already in place. There has to be one. There's a *salesman* somewhere, who will make contact, who will be operated by the case officer. Find him as well!"

David Allardyce sat on the edge of the bed in the small, spartanly furnished room in the Intourist Hotel he shared with Greenberg, staring at the small pile of materials that signified his presence in Moscow, his official existence, and the surface that he understood only as a frightening, transparent lie.

Keys. Wallet. Press card. Visa, passport. Accreditation from Intourist, from the Soviet Olympic authorities, from his newspaper, from the KGB masquerading as the Olympic Security Office, his booklet of travel warrants, his passes to get in and out of the village, his day-to-day tickets for the press box, his right-of-access docket to an interpreter, his stapled application blanks—self-carbonating, three copies—for whenever he wished to interview a Soviet competitor, his metro tickets, reusable for not more than five journeys of not more than three kilometers, his plastic-coated press badge, bearing his identification and picture, for entry to all Olympic sites (*This must be worn at all times*, it reminded him in five languages).

A heap on his desk. When he had emptied his pockets, it had been with no specific purport, but now he realized there had been a motive. Something to do with self-preservation; something to do with a need to remind himself of his official purpose, with the overt life not the covert trap in which he had been placed by Maulle and the smooth men in Secret Intelligence Service.

You're the salesman, David, Maulle had said. *You knock on the source's door, and sell the source the goods we have to offer.*

The heap of papers on the bedside cabinet, just a stretch away from him, next to the pack of cigarettes and the Dunhill lighter, as if placed for some topical advertisement for the tobacco company, were heavy as a threat, fragile as a thread. His life—his mask. He was out of condition for the work, and writhed still under the blackmail unspoken but evident in the tone of every voice in Queen Anne's Gate who had spoken to him—every word of the briefing down at the "summer house" in Wiltshire. *Do it, or we screw up the rest of your life*— even after you've told us to fuck off, you'll do it.

Yes. Oh, yes, yes. Even at Crystal Palace, in the moment Pete Lydall had qualified and he had left Maulle's side, he had known he would do it.

Burgoyne.

Why the hell did he have to *know* the source?

The telephone rang. He had to snatch at his left hand with his right to block the automatic response. Each telephone for accredited press use had an outside line, not an extension number—which was a simple illusion, as Greenberg had remarked. They were bugging everything, including the toilet pan. Greenberg had suggested some interesting and unusual feces that they might like to take away and inspect. Nerves made the silly laughter bubble in his chest like indigestion.

Two, three, four times. Five, five—

Four.

The case officer was in place. The code had announced it.

Four rings, David—that'll mean the case officer operating you will have arrived, and be in place. Contact can be expected within a reasonable time. Thus spake Maulle.

He looked at the silly, ineffectual heap of documentation that was intended to keep check on him, and which he had to use to stay in deep cover. His own life, his job, was his deep cover, what a bloody laugh, so that he could play silly buggers with the KGB as if the covert part SIS had grafted on was the real him, the important part—and all the papers and cards and badges appeared insubstantial, unreal.

He reached for the cigarettes and the lighter, wanting to sweep the papers to the floor, but afraid to do so. Bad luck, evil eye, walking under a ladder.

He coughed on the unaccustomedly acrid smoke.

Irena Witlocka arrived with the Polish team at Cheremetievo, via Aeroflot Tupolev, her coach beside her—coach become keeper—clinging to one idea; that the CIA would take notice when Martin Gutierrez asked them to help her, to reunite them.

She was now beyond being able to look at that dream

dispassionately or objectively. Since the flat rejection of her appeal for help—they claimed Martin had shown a distinct disinclination to discuss the matter with them—she had lived in an approximation to anesthesia. Pouring the water of final training on the rock of doubts, she felt like a lump at the bottom of her stomach. Inside the training, not looking out. Tight as her track suit around her. Jumping into sleep as quickly as exhaustion could allow her, avoiding half-waking images, ignoring the growing sense of the physical, the tiny betraying sense that it might only have been sex, that she was hung up on copulating with a skinny American. She wanted him—she loved him. She did not want to test the ideas.

"Smile—you're happy," Grachikov snapped at her side. When she looked at him, her depression deepened. He could even order her to do that. All of them could.

The flashbulbs, bright as betrayals, mostly from Soviet press-men, hurt her eyes. She tried to smile.

PART TWO

SKIRMISH

CHAPTER 7

The open, paved plaza at the center of the Olympic Village complex, the fountain's spray feathered into a peacock's tail. A giant chessboard at one corner, black and cream and a Spanish fencer and a Bulgarian weight lifter with giant croupiers' batons, moving the pieces. Competitors arranged as if for a still life, and Irena Witlocka aware of Gutierrez before he saw, and avoided, her.

"Irena—"

"Martin."

Gutierrez had tried, and succeeded, in avoiding her for two days—at frequent moments finding himself ridiculous, *diminished*, by his furtiveness. Now, looking at the girl, poised on the edge of emotion like a swimmer about to plunge—the image brought Peggy to mind, muscled, strong, in contrast to this lean, stringy girl—he was not certain that avoidance had been the wrong policy.

He was determined to grab at the incident, squeeze and finish it there.

"How you been keeping, Irena? Long time, no see." The words more clipped than usual, colloquial American English she might have difficulty with, language just another barrier.

"Oh, I am well." She wasn't, but she wasn't put off by his lack of warmth. "Can we talk?"

"Sure. What about?" Blunt. He was observing himself minutely now, assessing the effect of each word. She seemed determined not to understand, to be insensitive to tones, nuances.

"You—know that I applied to your embassy in Warsaw?" She sat on a bench that was vacant. Gutierrez reluctantly settled beside her, stretching out his legs, head resting on his chest as if he were studying his open sandals.

"Yeah. I know that."

"They spoke to you?" She seemed uncertain, reluctant to probe, but in ignorance. He decided on a lie.

"No—I heard from a friend—in the State Department. But the spooks never came near me."

"Spooks?" She knew the answer, and he let it go.

"You unhappy, Irena?" He wished he had not spoken the words

as soon as they were out. He glanced at the red knees of her track suit pressed virginally tight together. "You got it made in Poland—number one this year. A medal—?" Blunt jocularity, the reunion of mere acquaintances.

"Oh, Martin—!" Something with the force of a wind seemed to seize and shake her frame, and Gutierrez was frightened by it. He could not look at her. Something similar to the anger he had felt like transmitted electricity in his father's shrunken old body that hot day in the orchard. Passions he wanted no part of.

"Look, Irena—" he said, out of control for a moment, no coolness. "It's over, uh?" Drawing the words into a minimal statement which would seem more final. "A good time, yes—maybe better than that. But—over."

He looked into her face, then. Heavy lower lip, trembling just visibly. Dark eyes, hard as chips of coal, but glistening. The untidy, wiry hair.

"I see," she said. She seemed to be assessing him, but looking into herself at the same time.

"Look, I'm sorry—" The words popped onto his tongue, unbidden, unconsidered. Something about the way in which she did not give in, did not fall apart, reached him. Her face was a mirror in which he was not distorted—just sharpened, unflatteringly. He got up suddenly, as if cramped. "See you around, uh?" he said, walking off without looking back, away from her.

He was suddenly in a race, and understood that he was.

Allardyce parked the Lada which had been made available to him in the principal parking lot outside the twenty-foot-high electrified fence behind which the Olympic Village huddled for security. He knew it would be searched while he and Karen Gunston were in the village. No vehicles were allowed through the fence, except the escorted delivery vans which were checked at their depots, then escorted all the way—a duty KGB man in each cab—and checked again at the main gate.

Already, he knew, the cameras would be swinging to identify them. His press ID was clipped to the pocket of his linen jacket. Karen's disk to her skirt pocket. He watched her study the paraphernalia of the red-and-white barriers that would herd them slowly toward the guards at the main gate—her nose wrinkled in appreciation and dislike. He felt a sudden need to escape from something, to be distracted—with her.

Ten minutes later, they were inside, on the main thoroughfare of the village. She had been largely silent in the car after he had picked her up from the hostel at the Lenin University, and now she asked him, bluntly and as if he were a guide, "Tell me—color the village for me." It was a demand.

"Ah, there you have me. I never did qualify for the British team after the time of dormitories and self-service canteens. My colour is a little faded."

Karen waved her arms about.

"I'm having a hell of a time trying to get a camera in here. Pity. I can feel it—you know that?"

"The atmosphere? Largely imagination, my dear—but, there is something." They passed the empty high-rise building waiting for the Russian team—empty balconies, closed windows, only a guard on the door. To Allardyce, there was an uncomfortable impingement of something very real, oppressive, on his senses. "Except for Colditz there, of course."

Allardyce nodded in the direction of the Russian block.

"Colditz?" she said. "Oh, yes—the prison camp." Then she smiled. "You were there, right?"

"A hit—I do confess as much," Allardyce replied, hand on his heart.

"Twelve thousand people—it's like a town."

"No, it's like a collection of extremely individual egos, in egg boxes."

"Don't let the Soviet Olympic Committee hear you—David."

"I mean no particular village. They're all the same. Like seven eggs packed into a box for six—even eight or nine. Hard-boiled, too."

"Are you always so cynical?"

"Don't let the bright colours, local or otherwise, dazzle you, ma'am. You've met your runner, Gutierrez, for instance—Ben's pet lion."

"A jerk."

"Perhaps. But he's a jerk because he's a complete egotist. One hundred and ten percent a competitor. If he gets near a rostrum and a victory ceremony, he might not even hear the anthem. All he'll care about is the fact he won, *he's* the greatest."

"Are you anti-American?"

"No. We have one just like him, in the same event. We have one just like him in every event. Maybe—just maybe, in the Soviet team, and in the Eastern bloc—where sport has become the opium of the masses instead of religion—there's some sense of being part of a team, and doing it all for Mother Russia, or for the DDR or Rumania or Poland. Any way you care to look at it, there's an inequality of opportunity. Even Americans are jealous of the top coaches, scientists, doctors, and administrators all working together behind the Iron Curtain to produce the best athletes. Even your college system is hit-or-miss by comparison with the way they try to produce success over here. Maybe they even breed in patriotism? I don't know. Elsewhere, it's done by men and women, individually, for themselves. To prove to the world—not to belong, but to mark them off from everyone else."

Karen stopped, standing hands on hips, the noise of a transistor blaring out oppressive rock music from an open window on the fourth floor of the Swedish block.

"You mean it, don't you?"

"I most certainly do."

"You were like that?"

"I was. Never good enough to indulge it to my satisfaction—but, yes. I was only there to win."

"What do they *do* here?"

"Before the Games—before their event?"

"Yes."

"It's a mixture of waiting, boredom, tension, anticipation, distractions, sexual tensions—played against the background of a sea of faces and track suits, and a dozen languages every few square yards. They play chess, swap badges, swim, eat, take photographs, watch girls, watch men, take saunas, watch films, listen to music, play table tennis and pool, write home to Mum—and talk to promoters about their fees for the big meets after the Games—oh, and they train." Allardyce smiled. "An answer to your question?"

"Will you do an item for me—maybe with Ben, one or two others? Maybe we can get a Russian to argue about the individual and the national side of it?"

"Delighted. I thought my best speech had just gone to waste—I thought you'd never ask. Dinner, by the way?"

"You know a little place?"

"No. But I'm sure Intourist does. Dinner?"

"O.K."

The routine checkpoints for travelers by road to and from Moscow are sited on the massive ring road that completely encircles the city and its suburbs, built between 1960 and 1962. At each intersection with a major or minor road leading to the city, there is a checkpoint manned by members of the KGB Border Guard, the military section of the Committee for State Security. Only some of the most major roads, such as those to Minsk, or Leningrad, or to Yaroslavl or Tula, are open to visitors to the Soviet Union, provided they have obtained the prior permission of Intourist, and the requisite travel documents. In other circumstances, no visitor is allowed to travel more than forty kilometers from the center of Moscow.

Similarly, citizens of the Soviet Union not resident in Moscow or working there, but requiring to visit the city, must obtain the necessary travel permits and warrants. This rule had not been waived by the security service during the weeks of the XXII Olympiad.

Shubin possessed forged ID papers; the others in the group, being less of a focus of official attention, were traveling under their own papers. All of them had sufficient reason to be in Moscow—tickets for the Games.

"Just play it nice and easy," Shubin said over his shoulder into the back of the minibus in which they had traveled from Kiev, staying at campsites in Gomel, Bryansk, and Kaluga on their leisurely journey. "It's a hurdle we can sail over." Slowly, casually, he turned into the narrowing lane of orange-and-white bollards leading to the barrier and the intersection with the ring road. There were two other cars and a truck in front of them. "Just stay relaxed—turn on the radio. And *not* something orthodox. You're students—they expect to hear Western pop, even if it will make them frown." He laughed. "And put that rag down," he said to Kostya, who was studiously pretending to read the Kiev edition of *Komsomolskaya Pravda*. "You wouldn't read that bullshit at home."

Kostya grinned, childlike, and stuffed the Communist youth newspaper into the door pocket. He glanced at the crumbs in his nails when he withdrew his hand. Shubin pulled the minibus forward as the truck was waved on, its warrants in order.

"Shubin—" Zenaida began from the rear of the minibus.

"Don't call me that!"

"Feodor—*darling*—" the girl corrected herself with heavy irony. "How far after this?"

"Half an hour, no more."

"What's the name of the campsite?"

"*Serebryany Bor*—'silver wood.' Uncle Feodor has it all arranged. There's even swimming. So, enjoy."

He edged the minibus forward. Only one car between them and the KGB guard with his Kalashnikov over his shoulder. The sun glinted off the glass of the guardroom on the verge, hiding the faces that must also be watching from inside. One car between the KGB and the four FAE cylinders manufactured by Belousov, now hidden in a specially adapted compartment beneath the floor of the bus. And the HE device rolled up inside one of the tents. Shubin felt the adrenaline begin to run, the tingle in his fingertips, up his arms, the small tightness in his chest. Come on, come on—

Not because he was anxious, but because he welcomed the challenge, the bluff required, the proximity of possible discovery. Like spitting in their faces.

A guard at his window, another at the rear door, staring up at the faces looking down at him. A silly little tableau that Shubin could almost register through his shoulder blades as he met the gaze of the guard who took his papers. The man was bored, hot, dusty from cars and trucks pulling away from the checkpoint.

"Nice day," Shubin ventured.

"O.K., all out." The guard at the back. The door opened, then the stutter of footsteps down the two steps to the ground. Kostya next to him climbed out of the passenger door

"Your camping permit, comrade?"

"Oh, sorry—" Defeat, bureaucratic frustration as he passed over the folder of self-carbonating sheets already completed in Kiev by Intourist.

"*Serebryany Bor*, eh? Don't piss in the swimming pools, uh? I take my family out there regularly." There was an amusement. "Bloody pop music," the guard grumbled, listening nevertheless to the noise of Abba pumped from German transmitters. Then he looked down the length of the bus. "Finished, Josef?"

"Yes. Only a gang of sponging students—and with tickets for the athletics, no less."

Sudden, real envy.

"Any for sale?"

"Sorry," Shubin replied. "My aged mother sold herself to the factory inspectors to get them."

"Cheeky sod." The guard tossed his head. "O.K., you lot. Back in the van, and piss off."

Shubin burst out laughing, as did most of the others, as they pulled away from the barrier which lifted brief and small as a loophole in a solid wall, but his laughter was deeper, more fierce, above which theirs trilled like that of children who know no better, who merely echo.

They passed under the great span of the ring road, heard the rumble of traffic above as they might have heard the noises of a fairground machine, turning endlessly, populated by wooden horses. Then sunlight again, and more laughter, as Shubin branched off the Vernadsky Prospekt, following a signpost to Kuntsevo.

When they had stopped giggling with relief, he said, clearly and precisely, "If we had a control in Kiev, we'd need to send a signal. Agent in place. We're in!"

Someone—Yakov or Ferenc—cheered. A child's enthusiasm. Shubin shook his head, relaxing into the recollection that he had killed a man.

The telephone went on ringing, there in the upstairs room in Kiev that he could picture so clearly, clearly enough to see his mother, overcoming sciatica and hypochondria to answer it. It rang too long for Zenaida to be there. He despised the little tickle of panic he could feel round his heart.

"Mother—?" he blurted as the telephone was answered.

A querulous, blameful voice repeated the number slowly, oblivious of his remark.

"Mother! It's Arkady."

"Arkady—how are you? I'm bearing up myself. The people downstairs give me no peace—"

"Mother—where's Zenushka?"

"Always playing their radio, too loud—"

"Mother, listen to me! Where is Zenushka?"

"What—?"

He tried another, less direct tack, but something that might register with the mercenary side of her nature.

"What happened to the tickets I sent—?" He had an image of the policeman, Kazantsev, handing them over in an envelope, and he wondering whether the fact that they were already addressed had some significance for him. "Did you get the tickets for the Olympic Games?"

"Yes, yes—he was jealous, so *jealous*, he was—!" Poor, long-suffering Fedukhin, he deserved a medal for putting up with her. He wished he had instructed Zenaida to give the tickets he had originally supplied to Fedukhin—just as a gesture.

"When are you coming to Moscow—?" More importantly, "When is Zenaida coming to Moscow? She can stay here with me. When?"

A silence—he wondered whether it was fear, worry, puzzlement.

"She left two days ago, Arkady—in a minibus, crowded in with the others—"

"What? Who was with her?"

"Him." For a moment, he imagined Fedukhin, knew at the same moment that he was deluding himself. "Shubin. Arkady, you must do something about Shubin—he's no good for Zenushka—"

"She—she's coming to the Games? She has the tickets with her?"

Silence, then, "Yes. She took the envelope."

"Very well. Then I will be seeing her soon."

"Is something the matter, Arkady—?"

"No, Mother—nothing. Take care of yourself. Good-bye, Mother."

Federenko put down the telephone, then sat staring at it, as if it radiated malevolence, or foreboding. Why was Zenaida with Shubin, in Moscow? Shubin didn't like—*despised*—sport of all and every kind. Why?

The questions clicked in his head, numbers of a combination he could not find, the safe remaining locked to him.

She liked to stand in front of him, arranging his clothes. Had it been winter, she would be tucking his scarf into his overcoat, checking his galoshes or fur-lined boots, just as she did the children. He waited patiently until his tie was straightened, dandruff or ash brushed from the lapels of his suit—saw the wince of facial muscles, the slight tremor in her hand, as she brushed near the sleeve, felt the hard shape of the Makarov in its holster under his armpit. She resented, after all these years, his bringing that into their home.

"Am I presentable now, Tina?" he asked, smiling down on her, a little dark woman fussing round his huge bulk. She patted his chest with both hands.

"A good thing you're not going for a job—you wouldn't get it," she observed, studying him, seeing once more the way he threatened his clothes. He was big, and clumsy, and a bear—she felt a hot lump in her throat begin to choke her. She had never, never gotten used to his absences. It wasn't even the danger he might be in—just the absence itself, the stupid dependent blankness she felt when alone in a place without him.

"Ah—if I get the sack, then we never eat again!"

"You—you take care, mm? Just because the world is full of people smaller than you, you never take care." She saw he was mouthing the formula with her. "You mock—go on."

He locked her in his arms then, kissing her, lifting her off her feet, bending his head, making her short of breath. He was always gentle, but never understood how strong he was. When he put her down, she felt tiny, and flushed, and untidied. He slapped her bottom.

"What about the tickets—?" She blurted out, as he opened the door onto the landing. He grinned. She was, as usual, just prolonging the conversation, postponing departure.

"Pity you can't take your mother!"

"You make sure she stays in Kiev—selfish pig."

"You want another beating?"

"Please."

"Don't be decadent—we're puritan Soviets. Take the kids, anyway. They'll enjoy it. And don't buy them an American flag to wave. That sort of publicity I can do without!"

Then he was gone, clattering down the stairs because he was always impatient of elevators. And she leaned against the closed door, a heaviness in the pit of her stomach, and the fear beginning. Yes, it was fear this time. He was going to investigate the death of a KGB man at an ordnance factory. Clever, clever Oleg Kazantsev, who knew terrorists and explosives better than anyone else. Why did *he* have to be so clever? Nothing missing, they said. Except the KGB man, whose body they had found half-hidden in a trash can outside Donetsk. She thought of the children playing who had found it, and thought of the possibility that her own children might have experienced something like that—

All Oleg did was laugh at her fears, but she could not escape them.

No one had arranged it. It had happened with the lassitude of coincidence but adopted the appearance of inevitability, fate. It began with Lydall and Holmrath the German agreeing to a bout of checkers on the giant board of paving tiles. Lifting off the remaining chess pieces, substituting the easier checkers, as if moving the sawed sections of a trunk. By the time they had made their opening moves, Gutierrez was there, and Jorgensen the Norwegian. Diderot, at first wandering past, appearing abstracted, drifted over minutes after Gutierrez. Irvine was last—perhaps he had seen the little knot of competitors gathering from the balcony of his apartment in the Australian building. But he was there, bare-chested, in shorts and bare feet. A towel—presumably he had just come from the pool—draped over his shoulder, his hair untidily damp.

Something like a bullfight, maybe even a gunfight, might have been the occasion. Many of them had run against one another on previous occasions, were on first-name terms. They belonged to the same event, possessed the same prowess, were the favored runners in their event. There were other 5000-meter men there, the little Italian, a second American Gutierrez ignored, a Japanese, a Greek; but they were the outsiders, relaxed, an audience to the favorites.

They were all there except the Russians, who were moving into the village the following day—all? Lydall, watching them between moves, leaning on his hooked pole, counted them off. The rivals. All of them except Jorgensen, who had no current form whatever, had done faster times that season than he. All?

Then he saw Ochengwe, the black face an expressionless mask, the eyes, however, darting from side to side, as if seeking out some bolt-hole. Lydall pitied Ochengwe in a selfless moment. The murder of his family had been headline news when it happened. It had paralyzed, or cauterized, something in Ochengwe. He looked hunted and beaten.

At the moment, Lydall's observation of him became professional, detached. Ochengwe was beaten already. He was here for the sake of appearances, or just because he needed a change of environment. Or because Amin Dada said go there, and he didn't, couldn't, say no. Something in Lydall breathed in relief, just as another part of him, a spectator spotting the selfish animal on a lower ledge in his mind, despised the calculation.

But the others were doing it, too. He could tell. Gutierrez affected indifference—maybe he was indifferent—but Diderot, Holmrath on the other side of the board, Irvine—Irvine especially, so that Lydall knew he had been worried about the Ugandan—all of them had scented defeat, picked out the emanation of collapse of the will, decay of purpose. Amin's soldiers had shot a hole through Uganda's single Gold Medal hope.

Few words were exchanged for a long time. Lydall felt he was being assessed even as he played—chess, of course, would have been the game. Were they chess players, they would have been weighing each other up, outpsyching each other. It might have gone on for hours.

"You making it to the disco, you guys?" Gutierrez said eventually, not because he had broken but because he considered talk might establish his superiority. "Or is it early to bed? Some of you guys must be getting too old for this kind of thing—uh?"

"Punk," Lydall muttered loud enough for him to hear. Then he looked up, grinning. "So, I'm to watch out for you on the bends, mm?"

"Keep your eyes facing front—you'll see me."

"Behind me, Pete—he'll be the little one behind me," Irvine remarked, hands on hips next to Gutierrez, a head taller, better-muscled, an advertisement for the Australian climate. Gutierrez looked up and down his torso, and shrugged.

"Any more offers?" Lydall commented. He avoided looking at the silent Ochengwe.

"You could all fall down, or pull muscles, maybe," Diderot said, smiling. Each of them was aware of the improvement in Diderot's form over the three weeks before his arrival with the French team. He might have left it late, but not too late. "Or the cuisine might get you," he added.

"Are you playing, or psyching?" Holmrath inquired, pointing with his pole at the board, which appeared sparsely populated with Lydall's pieces. "Crown that one."

Lydall hefted a checker onto Holmrath's piece at his feet, reflecting that each of them there—now with the exception of Ochengwe, perhaps—was a guaranteed, mint-condition finalist; and not one of them had an Olympic medal. A new board, a new set of pieces. They were all hungry for the first three places—some of them because they were young, and unbeatable, some of them because they had everything still to prove—and himself because he had this one last chance to make a mark, to fulfill what early promise he had shown. *A man of promise for too long.* Who had said that to him, about him? Joan, probably.

He avoided that subject, a mental portcullis descending with a decisiveness he could almost hear.

"Don't forget the Russians," he remarked, his back to them.

"Hey—" Irvine. "I hear Federenko's a dummy. That right?"

"Dummy. What's dummy?" Gutierrez, intrigued as he was meant to be.

"You worked that out, Ken—or have you heard?" Lydall asked, turning on him, jabbing toward him with the pole.

"O.K.—I worked it out. Just a couple of pisspot races, and the big silence in the press. Either he's a winner, or he's going to play dummy for the other bloke—Tretsov."

"That's interesting," Diderot said. "We watch him in the heats, uh?"

"It doesn't make any difference," Lydall observed. "If he goes off like a rocket in the final, then we all have to go after him—you, too, Ken. We're in a straitjacket, a rat's maze. We have to do what's laid down."

They began to discuss the Russians, then. Lydall turned away, to find the game almost lost. He glanced once at the silent African, shook his head, and considered Federenko. Dummy or not, he was another runner he had to beat—someone else he could see, in his dreams, out ahead of him, leaving him trailing badly by the middle of the race.

The telephone rang six times, then stopped. The glass of the booth was becoming fogged with tension. There was a woman waiting to use the telephone, displeased at having to wait for someone who appeared not to be using the telephone at all, and about to rap on the glass with her kopecks. Look at the directory—look at it.

Flicking the pages, eyes not straying from the Bakelite.

Abruptly starting to ring again, the woman outside puzzled, then annoyed. Four, five, six—it had begun as if it had started ringing somewhere else, inaudible until the cycle had begun. Six. Pick it up.

"*Burgoyne.*" Not a question, a fact.

"Yes."

"You are secure?"

"For the moment—I have to go soon." Someone else had joined the woman outside, and she was explaining to the man in the sports shirt—who evidently did not speak Russian—that she had been kept waiting. Arms gesticulating, the man becoming embarrassed.

"Very well. First contact with the *salesman,* repeat salesman, will be at the reception on Opening Day. Opening Day. You are briefed." Another fact. The buzz of the telephone as the connection was cut off.

Listen, listen. No clicks, safe phone.

The case officer had made contact. The salesman would follow up with details.

The air, though hot outside the booth, seemed sweet, fresh. The woman's face was malevolent as she pushed past into the booth. The man smiled apologetically, though he hardly knew why.

Kazantsev studied the face of the chief security officer at the ordnance factory—the whole investigation, which had turned up not a single clue or indication, coming down to reading a man's professionalism, his conscientiousness in the muscles of his face.

"You're certain this inventory is complete? That no single item is missing from this factory?"

"As you can see, Comrade Lieutenant—" There was puzzlement at the power Kazantsev seemed to exude from his huge frame. "We can account for every grenade, every bomb—every magazine and box of shells." Kazantsev scrutinized the face for a long time, then looked down at the sheets, neatly typed, that provided a current inventory of factory production.

"I know," he admitted, aware of the man's conviction that he had overlooked nothing, and certain that he wasn't lying. "It is very complete." He moved his hand to another, thinner wad of typed sheets, columns of coded numbers, tapped it, his huge, splayed hand covering most of the top page. "And—the FAE devices—each one accounted for. I did that myself. Again." The security chief merely nodded.

"One of them would have been a fine prize to come away with," he commented.

"And worth killing a KGB officer for. But there isn't one missing."

Kazantsev was frustrated, felt his time was being wasted. Something repelled him from involvement in the mystery—perhaps something as unimportant as the approaching Games. He had tickets, and time off. Instead, he was sitting in a borrowed office in filthy Donetsk—and it was raining outside when it wasn't a hot, dusty smell in one's nose—faced with an insoluble contradiction. A man murdered, head bashed in, and the body hidden, but nothing missing.

"Are we tackling the wrong end of it?" he asked. "Thinking there had to be a motive, that the KGB man was a prelude to something else. If this was another sort of factory, then we might assume he had been killed because he'd stumbled on some fiddle, a bit of petty theft, wrong papers. It's happened before. Could it have happened here?"

"It might have. He was an officious—*conscientious* officer." The security man corrected himself hurriedly.

"I understand."

The telephone rang, and the security man picked it up, listened, then handed it to Kazantsev. "My man you sent to the oxygen company."

"Yes?"

"Nothing to report, sir. The driver who delivered the cylinders at about four-thirty remembers two men doing the unloading, and another man in a white coat in charge of the delivery. He identified the picture of our man straightaway—said the pose improved him—" The picture had been taken with a flash, after the head had been cleaned up in the morgue.

"Callous bastard."

"He remembers the two men wheeling off the empty trolley, then he drove back to the depot here."

"O.K. Report in, type it up."

He put down the telephone.

"Nothing?"

"Nothing. Perfectly ordinary delivery. The man was killed after five, then." Kazantsev sat back in his borrowed chair, swiveled it—it creaked badly—and considered. "He was a mess, mm?"

"Who—Officer Druzhin?" Kazantsev nodded. "Yes, he was. I had a job recognizing him before they cleaned him up. Whole side of his head, face—nasty."

"If I showed you a picture—something fell on his head, from a great height. The pathologist's report states, possibly a very heavy object brought down with a great deal of force—" He shuffled through the files on his desk, turning up the postmortem report. He flicked through the pages. "Yes—something cylindrical, possibly, but very large in diameter, it suggests." Kazantsev suddenly lost all speculative interest in the XXII Olympiad.

"If I showed you a picture of a dead man, one who had had his head bashed in—and you'd seen him unloading oxygen cylinders when last alive—would you recognize him?"

"I might."

"You might—after a good look. But—but if you knew you were going to have to recognize a *dead* man and that he would look dead, then that's the face you'd pick—wouldn't you?"

"I might." The older man was puzzled. Kazantsev splayed his hands over the files and sheets on the desk, as if absorbing their information through his fingertips, or trying to prevent his conclusions from escaping back into the files.

In the USSR, you killed KGB officers occasionally, for a variety of reasons. In an ordnance factory, you killed a KGB officer for—? The whole bloody country was an arsenal, and there were lots of people with a missionary need for explosives, cartridges, weapons. From the Far East to the Polish border, little men were running around loose who wanted to make a bang in life, blow the chips off their shoulders, satisfy their kinks. Did it mean anything in this case?

"But only if you knew the man you had to identify was dead. No, no—it doesn't work. If you did recognize him you'd probably say you didn't. More innocent that way. Hell—" Kazantsev rubbed his chin with one huge hand. "I don't like the *coincidence* of the probable time of death and the oxygen wagon. And the kind of dent in Druzhin's head—" He stared at the ceiling, feeling himself come to life, galvanized. Not by any sense of urgency, but by the fact that he now had all the information before him. It was something he had observed in himself on many previous occasions. Stasis, cowlike dullness while the pieces were being assembled, just waiting—then, when the last pieces were before him—the whole jigsaw, jumbled—he began to unfreeze, and his brain began to reason. Especially if the last piece was negative, like the report from the oxygen company.

"Let's see. Why not have a forensic done on the oxygen truck, on the cylinders at the oxygen company—?"

"All of them?"

"Yes, all of them—and quickly. Meanwhile, I'll have a word with the other porter, what's his name—?"

"Ghekh."

"Yes—wheel him in. Maybe we'll find out who else was around. A chap in a white coat—lab, technical staff—?" The security man was puzzled. "Sorry. There was a third man—so the truck driver says. I wonder who he was?"

"Twice round the Mausoleum, once round the Kremlin," Lydall offered, stretching in his seat as the Intourist circular tour of the city arrived before the walls of the Kremlin, and the driver offered his papers for inspection. Behind the bus was the huge, garish bulk of St. Basil's Cathedral at the southern end of Red Square, onion and pineapple minarets, great patterned reliefs like highly decorated dinner plates stacked as if on shelves around the central towers. Ahead, Lydall could see past the bobbing heads of his traveling companions—many of them from Cuba, or from black Africa—the Spassky Gate, the main entrance to the Kremlin from the square.

"You are allowed to enter the Kremlin Theater and the Congress Building, also the three main cathedrals and the Armory. Please observe the limits indicated by the white lines, and follow all instructions you may be given by the guards." The skinny, blonde guide's voice over the bus microphone was as thin and sharp as her face. "And please stay together as a party."

She held on to the rail as the bus pulled forward under and through the Spassky Gate.

"Directly in front of you you will see the Kremlin Theater—" There was no attempt to translate into any language other than English. "Beyond that, Ivan the Great's belfry, which is eighty-two meters high, and you will see it against the background of the three most beautiful cathedrals in the Kremlin. Beside the belfry you will see the Emperor, the heaviest bell in the world, which is six meters in height and weighs nearly two hundred and eleven thousand kilograms."

Lydall, appalled at the barbaric world the Kremlin walls had hidden, the Kremlin towers had foretold, tried vaguely to convert the metric measurements and weight to imperial, failed, and gave up.

"We will be descending from the vehicle—" There were only moments when the woman's excellent English became stilted and textbook. "In Cathedral Square. Please remain near the vehicle until we are joined by our official Kremlin guide."

For some reason that startled him, Lydall was relieved that the woman would not be giving them the tour—but might be more relaxed, open to conversation. He was aware that, unbeautiful though she was, he had been studying her carefully, repeatedly, during their guided bus tour. And he did not know why, unless it was the sense of defeat that seemed almost imperceptibly to leak through her facade of efficiency and assurance. Realizing, as he probed, that there was some unacknowledged affinity between them, he abandoned the scrutiny of himself and the woman, disliking the possibilities any such affinity suggested.

Two hundred tons—the bloody bell weighs two hundred tons, he told himself, some part of his mind having continued with the sum. The bell, monolithic, a fragment of it on the ground beside it like an abandoned infant or embryo for an even larger bell, slid past the window of the bus. Then they were in Cathedral Square, and the bus began to bump on the uneven paving as it idled to parking space alongside a dozen other tour buses.

Gilt domes, bulbous roofs, belfries. Faith and indifference pressed down around them as they stepped off the bus. The Cubans and the Africans—one or two Americans clicking steadily, remorselessly with Japanese cameras and telephoto lenses—seemed not so much stunned as uprooted, put down again on another planet. While their ancestors tended disease-ridden cattle, or grew maize, or were sold into slavery—at the other end of the world the architects of Russia were jumbling together dozens of different styles and creeds like children's blocks, then making cathedrals of them.

Lydall found himself standing next to the guide—Natalia; she had introduced herself when she had boarded the bus. She wasn't beautiful, but something affected him like an odorless gas; not the standard Intourist uniform, not the dragged-back hair or the pale thin face with minimal makeup. Something in the dark eyes, something that looked like bruises on the retinas.

"Terrifying," he said, loud enough for her to hear. She was watching a self-important little man in a peaked cap and with a clipboard striding toward them as they hovered by the bus.

"I beg your pardon?"

"Terrifying," he repeated. Nine domes, he noticed, looking ahead of him, seeing that his glance disconcerted her. Cathedral of the Annunciation. "How could anybody believe in Christ in the middle of this lot?"

"We don't," she observed. "You think it ugly?"

"Overpowering—oppressive, like St. Basil's. Is that right, Ivan the Terrible had the architects' eyes put out so they could never build another one?"

"So the story goes. Oppressive—" She looked around. "Yes."

The pompous little man arrived, clipboard held before his chest like a shield or badge, and fussily checked the list of passengers. Then he marshaled them into a line—Lydall allowed himself the amused luxury of becoming one of the recalcitrant, eager children he shepherded to the public swimming pool in such a line, every Thursday afternoon. As the line moved off, he saw Ochengwe. He hadn't even realized the man was on the bus until that moment. The Ugandan was dressed much as he must have dressed for his job—open-necked white shirt, khaki shorts. He seemed out of place with the other Africans, many of whom wore their traditional costumes like declarations of independence, or assumptions of a communal identity. Ochengwe was halfway—to where? Not Cathedral Square.

What struck Lydall most forcibly was the isolation of the figure, as if it emanated from him. So forceful was the impression that Lydall knew he could not approach the man or speak to him. The sight of him—he was tempted to use the word "vision"—as they snaked in a crooked line toward the Cathedral of the Archangel Michael disturbed and saddened Lydall, who was surprised by the ease of sympathy he felt, unemotional as he had made himself. Ochengwe was a lost man—he couldn't even go along for the trip, like many of the people on the bus tour. Enjoy, enjoy. There was no hint of enjoyment. He was truly an alien in an alien culture.

Cathedral of the Archangel, Cathedral of the Annunciation, Cathedral of the Dormition, Cathedral of the Deposition of the Virgin's Robe—the guide's English was a blunter instrument, awkward and stilted, and Lydall soon tired of concentration. Chapels, sacristies, Renaissance windows, altars, bishops' stalls, frescoes, iconostases, and the tombs of the czars from Ivan Kalita to Peter the Great—all becoming a shimmering curtain of impressions, stirred by the breeze of his indifference. He began to tell himself he really ought not to have come on a bus trip; but the kids in his class would want to know—if they hadn't already been on a Thomson seven-day tour to Moscow and Leningrad—so he had come. Forgetting his camera anyway in his halfheartedness. He would have to buy some slides instead.

Perhaps the kids would settle for stories about the Russians who had approached him, offering four times the going rate for a currency swap—or four times the price for any jeans he might have, ten times the price for a track suit top.

The Intourist girl was alongside him. He caught sight of Ochengwe staring up at an icon of the Virgin of Vladimir, as if attempting to make sense of it or communicate with it. There was an intensity about his face, as if it had been honed to sharp angles and edges. By the set of the mouth, and the way the muscles of his neck stood out, it might even have been that he was a child, forcing tears that would no longer come—straining to evacuate a prayer. Lydall turned to the girl.

"Can I buy some slides—of all this—?" He waved his hand airily round the vast, musty gloom of the Cathedral of the Dormition. "I forgot my camera—" he added lamely, grinning.

"Yes, you can."

"Where—or is that a state secret?"

She seemed shocked, as if at lewdness. Then she smiled, almost unwillingly. "In the tourist shop, not here. I will show you—"

"Now?" he invited.

She glanced at the pompous little guide, his face reddened with concentration on a foreign tongue—he had probably learned it in the Cold War fifties, when it belonged to the potential enemy, so he had botched it, sabotaging capitalism in yet another way. Lydall smiled at his thought, then the girl said, "Come."

They came out of the west door, into the hot sunlight, into the crowds of tourists—a busload of Japanese debouched on the other side of the square, and he heard a voice that might have been Yorkshire admitting wonder.

"I'm a teacher," he admitted. "The kids—the pupils—always like to see where I've been. Censored version, of course." He watched her face, careful of disapproval. She smiled. She was still pale and skinny, but her eyes didn't seem bruised. Her hands were naked of rings.

"Do you like teaching?"

"Not a lot—it's the only thing I can do, really. Apart from running."

She nodded sagely, as if he had said something profound that required careful thought.

"I began as a teacher, also, but I prefer this job. Not so tiring. Though I would like the longer holidays—my daughter."

"You're married—?"

"Divorced." She looked up at him quizzically. "That answers another of your questions, of course?"

He grinned, bumping into a small, wiry old lady with a baseball cap to protect her from the sun, and a Nikon camera slung between her shrunken breasts.

"Sorry—"

"Just be careful, sonny." She winked. "If the Russian girl won't play ball, I could stand being treated to dinner." And she went off, cackling.

Lydall looked at Natalia. "It shows?"

The girl nodded. "It shows."

"Well, then—?"

"This evening I would be unable to get a babysitter. Therefore, either we make an arrangement for another day—or you must eat with me and my daughter at home." She was, he realized, being deliberately blunt, businesslike. He was being ridiculed, and being informed that this was a business arrangement with a strict limitation of lease, and that such arrangements had been made before, and would be made again, after his temporary occupation.

Lydall felt like a somnambulist awakening—he had moved without thought, almost, to this point of proposal. But before a word had been spoken, a single piece of protocol observed, he found the situation unavoidably sexual, yet also aseptic and clinical, and was strangely disappointed.

"Yes," he said. "That—would be nice. Be careful, mind. I have to watch my diet."

"I will read a book, find something suitable," she remarked.

The telephone was ringing, needling down into his after-dinner nap—taken because there was nothing else he wanted to do in Donetsk—and Kazantsev's hand fumbled across the top of the bedside cabinet, smothering the instrument, then lifting it.

"Yes."

"A call from Moscow, Comrade Kazantsev." It was the KGB man on the hotel desk.

"Switch to scramble, then."

"Very well—go ahead, Moscow."

Using his feet and back, Kazantsev climbed up the headboard to a sitting position. He ran a hand through his hair, yawned, looked at his watch.

"Oleg—is that you?"

"Sir." It was Puchkov, his superior. His father figure.

"Oleg—we want you back in Moscow straightaway."

"Sir—things *are* beginning to move down here. I'm making headway—"

"No need. We know what was taken—a bomb. *Pravda* and *Izvestia* had letters today—and every major newspaper in Europe and the United States—telegrams or letters. And the broadcasting companies. Every one of them posted in Munich. We're presuming it's one of the émigré groups—probably our Ukrainian friends—"

"Sir, will you explain, please? There's nothing missing here."

"There has to be, Oleg. Some Ukrainian group that calls itself *Do pobachenya*—understand?—has threatened a 'major target' in the city of Moscow during the Olympic Games. All hell has broken loose here, officials climbing all over the department—"

"Sir—Colonel Puchkov. Sir, there's nothing missing from here—no HE, no FAE device. I'm certain of it. The KGB man was killed for a good reason, but I haven't found it yet. Your group could have got HE anywhere."

"Oleg, don't argue. Upstairs wants you back to lead the bomb squad when the balloon goes up. Get the first train tomorrow morning. That's an order."

The connection, broken, buzzed in his ear. He took away the receiver, rubbed his ear as if it had been stung. He was angry with Moscow, indifferent to the crank letters received by *Pravda* and the evening newspaper.

And certain that there was some hidden, indissoluble connection between the death of a KGB man in the Donets basin and a bomb threat in Moscow. A connection as tangible, and fragile, as the railway line between the two cities.

CHAPTER 8

There was a newsstand in the Olympic Village, selling the national dailies of some fifty countries. Perhaps only one newspaper from the smaller nations, with fewer competitors. Newspapers not to be taken out of the village compound, certainly not to be resold to Soviet citizens.

François Diderot had no interest in doing any of those things—merely a pressing, squeamish desire to hide the page of yesterday's *Le Monde* to which he had turned, tear it out, wrinkle it into a gray ball of newsprint. He stood in the cool morning light, arms akimbo as he studied the item on an inside back page. Insufficient information for it yet to have become front-page headlines.

Reports of documents bearing the athlete's signature—or what purports to be his signature—have been made to this newspaper— evidence exists of an advertising deal with Dumas-Quenelle— jeopardy—possible ban—official inquiry—full investigation—real chance of a medal on recent form—

He felt sick, as he sometimes did after a grueling run, at the beginning of a hard training schedule, short of breath and weak as the consequences suggested themselves luridly to his imagination—so luridly that he thought the approaching French team manager, evidently looking for him, might have been some illusion, a projection of his fears. Going back, going back, he seemed to be saying to himself, over and over again. But he was unsure whether he meant the desire to go back to a point in time before he had signed the contract, or whether he simply envisaged the likelihood of being sent home, expelled from the French team and the race.

"Diderot—they want to see you, right away." *Diderot*. Not François, pampered favorite, darling of the team. Diderot. "Right away, the French committee rooms." And he hurried away, an ex-shot-putter running to steroid fat now. Steroids. He wanted to laugh at the mockery it all suddenly seemed.

The Comité National Olympique et Sportif Français had the power to ruin everything. Even the damned contract, which would be reneged upon by Dumas-Quenelle if he was expelled from the French team. A good advert—

He threw the paper into the wire wastebasket on its tripod just in front of the shop, and tried to straighten his body, square his shoulders, thought how it must resemble someone ascending to the kiss of Madame, and walked away as casually as he could.

On the front page of *Le Monde*, crumpled in the basket, was an item splashing the bomb threat from a "dissident group," and reports of rumors of an incursion into Ugandan territory by Tanzanian troops, supported by aircraft.

The main press center for the XXII Olympiad was sited in the new Novosti Press Agency building on Zubovsky Prospekt, a section of the Sadovaya ring road near the Crimean Bridge over the Moskva. Six stories high, it contained all the necessary press services—an auditorium to seat five hundred, three thousand press booths and duplicating machines, information rooms, post office, bank branch, telephones, teletype, restaurants and cafés, transmission rooms and studios, a medical center, and a computer to issue up-to-date competition reports and entrant lists.

The main auditorium was equipped with headphones for instantaneous translation into five languages for the five hundred pressmen it could hold. As the senior press liaison officer faced the room, the rows of banked seats, the expectant faces, the frame of headphones around many of them, he almost began to count the occupants. It was his task to placate the press, to turn harmlessly aside their questions relating to the letters to *Pravda* and *Izvestia*, neither of which had been published but had been passed direct to the antiterrorist section of the Second Chief Directorate of the KGB, but which had also unfortunately been sent to the major newspapers and TV networks in Europe and the United States, and to the major wire services which would ensure its circulation in every country which had sent competitors to Moscow, or whose tourists and spectators were beginning to arrive. The letters had been posted in Munich. Federal authorities, including the security service, the BFV, assumed that they were the responsibility of one of many Ukrainian émigré groups in the city.

None of the journalists possessed the full text or a copy of the letter. There had been a major disruption of the telephone service from the press center the previous evening, and the engineers were still working on it, and only a few of the press corps had received information from their agencies or newspapers, and a demand for fuller information.

Allardyce was well aware—perhaps a little more so than many of his more bona fide colleagues, including Ben Greenberg—of the diplomatic and governmental games being played as they sat in the main auditorium of the press center, waiting for the press liaison officer to finish mopping his wide forehead and begin his placatory, sanitized, anesthetic speech. He was amused as well as intrigued by the possible reality. With a more uncomfortably close understanding of the KGB than most of those around him—and a present fear of them—he found it harder to believe in *Do pobachenya* than the others. To him, they were little more than a news story, something specifically designed for print.

His foreign editor had spoken to him for almost half a minute before the connection had been broken. Then all the phones had gone dead, including the public call boxes nearby on the Zubovsky and Lenin Prospekts—a sufficient deterrent to most of his press colleagues, who suspected the deliberate rather than accidental nature of the fault, and its probable source.

The press officer was on his feet now, and the auditorium, already uncomfortably hot, was silent almost at once.

"Ladies and gentlemen of the world's press—" Allardyce looked sideways at Karen Gunston, who was frowning in concentration, probably considering the press officer's face through an imagined camera. Sanitized, Allardyce knew. They weren't going to learn anything. "You have a right to know—to have your questions answered. I have here a prepared statement—" Some theatrical groans from the back of the room. "A prepared statement that assures all of you—and those of your fellow countrymen who will be in Moscow during the next two weeks—that there is no danger, that the messages your newspapers may have received are the work of a lunatic, but *harmless*, fringe group that seeks to embarrass the government of the Soviet Union during this most hospitable and public season—"

Allardyce grabbed Karen's hand.

"Come on—you're not going to learn anything here." He stood up, and she looked quizzically at him for a moment, then also rose. They squeezed past a row of knees to the door.

"Tomorrow's opening ceremony of the Twenty-second Olympiad will go ahead as planned. There is nothing to be feared from the empty threats of a few—"

The words faded behind them as the doors sighed shut.

Allardyce was still holding her hand, fingers cool to the touch, and she had not removed it. Suddenly, she swung his arm like an eager child.

"Buy me an ice cream soda, Uncle David?"

"Certainly, my dear." Allardyce smiled, then said softly, "It is going to happen, you know."

"What—we're going to get blown up?"

"Inflated, perhaps—"

"Seriously—is there anything to this? You're a foreign desk man."

They had walked into the candy shop in the foyer of the press center. Allardyce, in his more than adequate Russian, ordered her ice cream, then another for himself. Karen studied him, as if listening to something in his accent, or trying to learn something of what lay beneath his bland surface.

"*Do pobachenya?*" he said thoughtfully. "I've never heard of them before—which may not necessarily mean anything. It's Ukrainian, I know that. It means 'good-bye.' "

"Sick joke?" She licked at the ice cream cone, curling her tongue round the blob of peppermint ice. She found Allardyce studying the way she ate, her mouth. He was staring almost obsessively, uncomfortably.

"I don't know. The KGB have had a lot of trouble with Ukrainian nationalists over the years—ever since the war, even before that. The Ukrainians don't like central government, and they don't like Russians."

She waited for him to say more, but he seemed to return to the intent study of her mouth, until she felt distinctly uncomfortable. She ate the ice cream as quickly as she could, then wiped her mouth.

"I have to work. See you."

Allardyce watched her go out of the glass doors into the bright noon sunlight of the Zubovsky Prospekt, looking somehow insubstantial on the other side of the doors, bleached by the sunlight as she put on her sunglasses and turned right, looking for a taxi to take her to the Ostankino, the radio and television HQ for the Games. Allardyce regretted not being able to take the girl, or the seduction of the girl, in a more serious spirit.

He had an image of himself in tennis shorts and a sweater, entering onstage through open French windows, ready with his immortal line. But it was the wrong stage, a different play. In this one, the only reply was not a love song on the piano, but the rattle of gunfire. In this play, people were killing one another.

He felt fatuous, futile, and knew that the sense of his futility would grow steadily during the rest of the day and the approaching night. He looked at his watch. Perhaps thirty-two hours to the time of his contact with *Burgoyne*.

"He's been what—?"

Leonov was angry. Anna stirred in the big bed, saw the bulk of his shoulders as he sat on the edge of the bed, the bedside lamp haloing the fine hair across his shoulders and forearms. She smiled, undisturbed by his angry tone. He was a remarkably hairy individual, Gennadi Leonov. She touched his spine with her fingertips, stroking softly downward into the small of his back. She watched his skin shiver with pleasure, then he waved his free hand to stop her, angry dismissal.

"You wait there—I'll be there right away. No, don't do *anything*, for God's sake! There've been too many fingers in this pie already."

He rattled the receiver back onto its rest, sat staring at it for a moment, then turned to look at her. She saw his immediate awareness of her body, saw the eyes habitually begin their study of her neck, shoulders, breasts, stomach. A little boy, greedy and eager and worshipping. She put the image aside, as if it suggested transitoriness, or lack of depth, which would be disloyal.

"In spite of your art appreciation you're going out, I take it?"

Leonov smiled.

"Yes. I am going out." The return of anger excluded her, canceled her presence in the room. "Don't worry about the kids. They won't wake."

"It's not them I worry about—they're used to my being here by now. It's you. What's happened to make you angry?"

He hesitated for only a moment. "Two days ago, we identified a CIA case officer—" Her face had gone narrow with concentration. "The information was duly circulated, with a Hands Off notice. Some stupid bastard has just arrested the man, and put in a request for his immediate extradition as an undesirable. *Undesirable?* I want him so badly, I can feel it!"

"Why—why have they expelled him?"

"Publicity. Playing the old game—look what the naughty Americans are doing under cover of the innocent Twenty-second Olympiad. It makes me sick—we're after a double, this man could have been his contact—and some bright boy screws it up!"

He got up, dressed quickly, she watching him intently all the time. When he was ready, he said, "Look, I don't know how long I'll be—I may not be back by the time—"

"Remember, Gennadi. No excuses. I want you at the Opening Day ceremony this afternoon—and don't try to get out of it. This is a fortnight you are going to devote to me, remember?"

He bent and kissed her—hand suddenly touching her breast, cupping it, withdrawing again as if it were hot, or he had soiled it. She took his hand, stretching up in bed, kissing him with a sudden fervency, as if after a long absence, or in anticipation of it.

"Don't tread on too many toes, mm?"

"Kicking backsides is more in my line," he replied. He paused at the door, then went out, smiling. She heard him look in the other bedroom, to check on his children. Then the front door of the flat shut softly, and she was alone.

It was a long, restless time before she fell asleep again.

By nine in the morning—the Opening Day of the Games, Saturday, the nineteenth of July—Leonov was face to face with a Senior Assistant to the Deputy Chairman of the KGB responsible for the Second Chief Directorate, for whose first department Leonov worked. To reach the spacious office on the sixth floor of the Center in Dzerzhinsky Street had taken five hours, and angry exchanges with eight senior officers. And his anger had still not burned itself out, or learned a more cautious approach.

"Comrade Senior Assistant," he said with heavy sarcasm, "I do not care about a paper war, publicity battles. I am interested in traitors and I am pursuing one at the moment. One you and the Deputy Chairman were very worried about only last week—so worried that you reemphasized the express need to cut off the source of information as soon as possible."

"You have not done it, Leonov." Hands coming together, forming a knuckled lump in front of the square, expressionless face. Tiny black points of eyes.

"I am pursuing my investigations—in the Defense Ministry. I am not being helped by the desire of people in this Directorate to make propaganda victories." Leonov was standing before the huge desk. He had not been invited to sit down; every so often the Senior Assistant seemed to regret the way in which he had allowed Leonov to loom in front of him, regret that he had to raise his gaze to look at Leonov's face. Leonov, aware of his growing anger and abiding sense of challenged superiority, was nevertheless reckless.

"The man Burfield has been removed to the American Embassy. He will be escorted onto a plane for New York this evening."

"That will spoil his Olympic holiday, I suppose. Dammit, *sir*—I needed to talk to him!"

"That is no longer possible. I suggest you return to your investigations. In any case—" The admission of weakness now; Leonov was more angry than ever. "He can now do no more damage."

"Somebody will try to get our traitor out—if not Burfield, then someone we don't know. We're in the dark again."

"This interview is over, Leonov. Return to your duties."

Leonov raised his hands at his sides, then slapped them against his thighs. The little dark eyes opposite him narrowed even further. Now he would be committing professional suicide. He nodded.

"Thank you for sparing me your time," Leonov said in a tight voice, and turned and left the room.

Outside, past the guards at the main entrance to the barrackslike building that dominated Dzerzhinsky Square, and behind which was hidden the Lubyanka complex, the sun was already hot and high, the pavements crowded with tourists. Guards moved among the nearest ones, informing them that photographs were forbidden in the square—Americans, British, other Europeans, heads stuffed with the identification of the Center that stemmed from dozens of novels.

The crowds moved in front of Leonov like a sea. One of them, *any* one of them, might be the contact, the salesman with his rescue kit, coming for the unidentified traitor.

Shrugging his shoulders, he went down the steps to the pavement. If he spent the rest of the morning at the Ministry, sniffing around, it might lead somewhere. Besides, he could take Anna to lunch earlier. Before—he sighed—they went to the infernal Opening Day ceremony, just to please her.

"Then you can't let anyone in until after one o'clock!" Oleg Kazantsev was yelling into the telephone, hot and exasperated in his little office almost under the roof of the Center, overlooking the main courtyard of the Lubyanka from its one narrow window. He had the window open, but some clown had jammed the radiator open, years before, and because the central heating was always on in the Chairman's rooms and those of the Deputy Chairmen, he got the full effects all through the summer—every summer. "I don't give a bear's ballocks what the press of the rest of the world make of it—don't let them in, either!"

Novikov's voice squeaked at the other end of the line. As Chairman of the Soviet Olympic Organizing Committee, he was the target man for grouses and grumbles and public gaffes. No wonder he protested about the main stadium being taken over by a KGB team on the morning of the Opening Day.

"Comrade Novikov—go and watch the last runners carrying the Olympic flame, will you? The lucky lad should be on the outskirts of the city by now." Pause, squeak, squeak, protest without weight, exercise of the vocal chords. "I repeat, Comrade Novikov, this is now a matter for the Committee for State Security. No, we have taken care of that. The airborne cameras are all Soviet—there won't be any embarrassing pictures of my men searching the main stadium for a bomb—" Squeak, squeak, a grumble of acceptance. "One o'clock. Then you can let them in."

Kazantsev put down the telephone. Poor sod, worried stiff, but not enough to consider the results of a *real* bomb. For him, it was all on paper, all a matter of PR. Kazantsev mopped his forehead, inspected his shirt for patches of damp, and cursed the central heating.

Opening Day, and the central Lenin Stadium—what a target. One hundred thousand people, the majority of them foreigners with suspicious governments.

Do pobachenya. Unholy good-bye. More like fuck off, he thought. The Ukrainians, his own lot—bloody fools, even if it were only a publicity stunt; no one would forgive it, excuse it. It was almost impossible that anyone had smuggled anything into the stadium, but he had to be sure. Priority number one: check everyone that moves, everything that doesn't. His teams had been at it for thirty-six hours already, and they needed until one to be as certain as they could be.

Well, he'd given it to them. God help them if they found anything. Good-bye.

There was no point, he considered a few minutes later, in sitting in his chair, melting. He might as well be at the stadium.

Aerial shot, from a camera helicopter. Courtesy of Soviet television, with the accents, languages of fifty, a hundred countries with hundreds of millions of viewers, dubbed onto the silent shots.

Zoom. A runner in red vest and white shorts, arm aloft, the torch streaming smoke back behind him. Down the wide thoroughfare, making a round trip of the motorway ring, then the inner Sadovaya, for the sake of spectacle and all the Muscovites who didn't have tickets. Extracting the last ounce of publicity, harmless, plastering-over Olympic publicity.

Shubin watched with contempt. Glancing occasionally out of the dirty windows of the dispatch office of the deserted warehouse tucked away off Kirov Street. Only he and Zenaida had come in from the campsite, in the minibus, to store the FAE cylinders until he required them. The HE device they had brought, too. It amused him to think of the panic that must be going on, totally unreported, in anticipation of a move by *Do pobachenya* on Opening Day. A fool's mate, had they really tried it. Premature ejaculation, leaving them spent and dissatisfied. They had only begun.

And Zenaida was out now, posting some more letters typed on a machine they had destroyed before leaving Kiev, letters that mocked the KGB, warned the Politburo. One to Andropov, one to the First Secretary, one to Novikov. She would post them in the box nearest Dzerzhinsky Street, just to give them two fingers. No point in their Munich contacts telling the European newspapers again—the cameras were what he required. A couple of notes for the press center, and the Ostankino, when the time was right—but not just yet.

Shubin leaned back in the hard chair in the dispatch office, staring at the portable TV. The helicopter camera was cruising above the motorway, which was empty of traffic on the inside lanes. The runner and his torch. It had come from Kiev and the Ukraine to Moscow. It was appropriate, symbolic. Setting light to something, inaugurating—

There was an override on the TV coverage—everyone knew that. Not just the normal Olympic override where the vast majority of the cameras were operated by technicians of the host country— NBC, CKR, the BBC, and other European networks had a small number of cameras in Moscow, Tallinn, and the other Olympic centers—but the hand that could pull out the plug, which no one was supposed to talk about but of which everyone was aware. It rankled like an itch or a splinter beneath professional skin—anything interesting, and the lights might go out.

Karen Gunston smiled at Ben Greenberg through the glass that separated producers and directors from commentators. Ben was doing a color piece around the turgid commentary of her network's regular man, a nonathlete and dedicated jogger, who was stretching the material by turning more and more frequently to Greenberg for reminiscence and padding. Karen looked at her watch. Another hour before the first teams entered the stadium—undelayed, despite that the crowds had been kept out of the stadium until one o'clock, without explanation but with copious apology from Mr. Novikov over the public address system. No good digging—she understood that. Lunchtime viewers in Europe, early morning audiences in New York, late night birds in California—they didn't want rumors, just spectacle.

She studied the bank of monitors—the Soviet cameras showing the track, the crowd, the athletes disembarking in their uniforms from the buses that had brought them from the village to the assembly point, where they would wait, bored and hot and uncomfortable in blazers and flannels, until given the signal to march.

A huge publicity vehicle, because hundreds of millions *wanted* a stage show, an opening ceremony that was colorful, pompous, and harmless. Some of the competitors, she knew well enough by now, disliked, even hated, Opening Day. She listened to Greenberg through her headphones, talking over shots of the first teams assembled behind the main stadium, on the warm-up track and the park around it. The Russians were prominently in place, to attention, trying to win respect where they might not raise too many laughs, evoke affection.

". . . you're all keyed up for the competition, muscles tuned, nerves uptight—and you have to get out of your strip, into a jacket and pants and a tight tie, get on a bus and come miles from the village, then stand around until the first teams get moving at three. I tell you—women athletes *don't* like Opening Day ceremonies!" Chuckle from the link man. "It'll take maybe eighty, ninety minutes for all the teams to march through, before the flame arrives. But—the people at home want to see *their* boys and girls, so you got to do it."

"Tell the viewers back home, Ben—what do you think about down there while you're waiting?"

Karen smiled encouragingly at Greenberg again—making laughing faces, waving her arms. He nodded, turned away to his own monitor.

"Most of the time your mind is on the instructions you're getting from the team management. How to line up. You know the

British do it smallest at the front, biggest at the back? And we do it the opposite way around—the last little girl has all the weight lifters and shot-putters breathing down her neck, and she's just hoping the flies don't make those bulls stampede!"

"We'll watch out for that, Ben!"

Greenberg turned again, and she gave him the thumbs-up.

"O.K., let's see if we can pick out some expression on all those faces down there—" And she nudged the cameras into close-ups of British, Russian, American, African faces. Some of them she picked out—Gutierrez, looking disgruntled, rebellious, his collar threatening to asphyxiate him; Lydall was that, the British contender? Silent, as if he were carved, hands in front of him as if clasping his genitals; in the sea of black faces, no chance of picking out Ochengwe and reminding people of his tragedy. The Russians—she'd been allowed an interview with a couple of gymnasts the day before—but they were dull stuff, just kids.

"O.K.—let's feed in some crowd faces, too."

The crowd—face after face eating, yawning, shadowed under the official suncaps and shades, or newspapers and handkerchiefs. The camera picked out nationalities just as surely as out on the warm-up track; most of the colors dominated by blue, as always seemed to be the case in any crowd in shirt-sleeves. Impassive Russian faces—eager, too—made up, bored, gossiping European faces. Image crowding on image, spectators indistinguishable except by dress from the competitors for a long moment and a community suggested to the world by satellite picture.

Karen cut in the aerial picture of the torchbearer, almost completing the run around the Sadovaya ring road, breaking the illusion, making her reflect that it was nothing but monitor hypnosis.

Anna seemed absorbed, drawn into the scene in a way he could never be. The seats were good, as they should have been for a senior member of the Secretariat of the CPSU—she had obtained the tickets, not he, not trusting his enthusiasm and perhaps considering she had more pull than he did.

"Satisfied?" he said, smiling, wanting to hold her hand, nervous as a boy at touching her, except where her arm rested against his sleeve.

"Marvelous—isn't it?" She looked at him quizzically.

"You're just a big kid, you know that?"

"And you're an old woman." She poked out her tongue at him, and he leaned back in his seat and laughed.

"All right—for you, I'll enjoy."

"Thank you, kind sir." She nodded her head.

"Just let me relieve myself of some of that rough Georgian wine, and I'll be more in keeping with your festive mood."

"You *are* crude."

He shrugged, smiling, and stood up, looking at his watch.

"I've got another ten minutes before they start marching in."

He walked down the aisle, toward the exit from their block of seats. As he turned to go down the next flight, to the gallery behind the grandstand, his head about to disappear, she caught sight of someone she recognized—standing with his hands on his hips, staring up sightlessly, head moving slowly from side to side, as if he were looking for someone, or perhaps just assessing the mood of the crowd. The press box, a great sheet of glass with rows of heads behind it, was a dozen rows behind the seat she occupied. He would, if that were his destination, pass quite close.

David Allardyce. She shivered, as if cold.

"No, boss—it's O.K.—nothing's going to happen."

Kazantsev rubbed his nose.

"You're *sure*—I mean, really sure?"

"Whatever this mob is up to, they haven't got a bomb in this stadium today."

Kazantsev looked at his watch.

"And they haven't brought it in since one o'clock?"

"We're certain."

"I need a drink—something long and cold. Then I'm going to sit with my wife and kids." He began to walk away, then turned. "If they haven't got this place down as a target—then what the hell *do* they want?"

The signal. Karen saw heads turn at the sound of a whistle. The Greek team was ready to move off, traditionally first as the founding nation of the ancient and the modern Olympiad, and nearest the main tunnel into the stadium. The commentator was injecting sudden urgency into his voice, grating on her through the headphones. Afghanistan, Albania—straightening ties, robes, flannels, skirts. Coming to attention, despite cynicism, commercialism, rivalry, lack of patriotism, presence of supreme egotism.

"Let's take the runner again, ground shots." she said to her director. "Let's have a little more cutting, uh?"

Two teams so big the cameras seemed to have stopped their ceaseless, caressing movements across the face of the stadium. Volume of sound unprecedented that afternoon, even for the huge DDR contingent, or the Cubans—the United States preceding the USSR. Home and away—the Americans greeted with charter-flight visitors blasé about spectacle, and the Russians by a crowd still feeling its way into hosting the Olympiad, rubbing shoulders with the rest of the world in one huge, windless bowl.

Two juggernauts, two parades of force, hats off, eyes right, passing beneath the box reserved for diplomatic and political visitors. The Politburo—almost entire—standing as if on the balcony of the Lenin Mausoleum, but without their overcoats, still unsmiling. The sound welling up round them as if it threatened to sweep them away, or was their orchestration of some basic and profound feeling.

Shubin smiled to himself as he watched the two largest teams in the Games settle into their allocated positions on the field. The noise, the *solidity*, of the scene, the close-ups of the unsmiling leaders, the washing camera movements over the specks and blobs of color that formed the capacity crowd, defined an enemy he could at last see, localize. And, contained in one general shot of the stadium, from a helicopter, on twenty inches of screen, it seemed capable of being overturned, defeated—wiped out. He knew as he watched that he could do it—it would be done.

The runner, heading down the Vernadsky Prospekt, torch aloft, the crowds thicker now, hands clapping and cheering in a constant accompaniment. Passing—the ground-level cameras on top of the state television vans show this impressively—the Lenin-Lomonossov University, rising away from the wide thoroughfare, sprawling on the Lenin Heights. Heading for the bridge across the Moskva, and the Luzhniki complex.

A windless, hot afternoon, the temperature in the middle of the stadium in the eighties. A hundred commentators in scores of languages, responsive to their monitors, record their lack of envy of the torchbearer, who looks hot and weary.

Five thousand Russian children, dressed in red-and-white mock-peasant costumes, garlands in their hair, dance around the laned track, which is browner than in reality on a television screen, welcoming the athletes of 125 nations. The voice of the huge orchestra that accompanies them seems shallow and mild in the bowl of the stadium, and the voices of the children, drilled and coached to utter unison, are high and almost lost, the words incomprehensible.

When they have finished, they form a fragile link chain around the track, enclosing the teams. The crowd is silent, the orchestra dramatically still. One Soviet athlete steps forward to take the Olympic oath on behalf of the others. Photographers stalk him, half-crouched, as he makes his way to a dais below the gleaming bowl prepared for the Olympic flame.

Only the television audience hears noise, gabble, or watches movement imposed upon the eyes by hundreds of producers and directors. The athletes are still, the crowd silent.

Then the runner. As if he has lit some gas in the air, or brushwood at his feet, a noise like gathering fire can be heard while he is still in the tunnel. Then he appears, and the noise deafens him, almost jolts him in midstride. He, entering that open cathedral dedicated to something, at that moment senses an inspiration, recollects a past occasion, *believes* for a short while.

The noise crashes down on him from all sides as he laps the track, and he is aware of the clicks of the closest cameras like the noises of persistent insects, of the faces of children sliding past him, and the thousands of competitors who have broken ranks and rushed to the trackside, all of them with identical smiles, some with tears.

The steps—too many of them, it almost seems, sliding together in a smooth carpet, until he begins to ascend, then he watches only his own feet and the step ahead of the one he touches, with whichever foot. He is hunched, the torch leaning slightly, but all that interests him is that he must not stumble, spoil the effect. He, too, has moved into the occasion, aware that he is a broadcaster before he is anything else.

Turn, breathe easily, *easily*—arm outstretched, holding the torch steady, lowering it. Sudden silence as if the assembled crowd waited for some mystical blessing. He can hear the hiss of the gas that will be turned off a fortnight from that moment. He winces, afraid of fire since a child, and there is a soft *whoomp* as the gas ignites, and the crowd roars at something achieved, some certainty in things, as the Olympic flame rises, wavers, spreads, straightens.

The Russian athlete to take the Olympic oath was Viktor Alexeivich Tretsov, competitor in the 5000 meters. More than anything else, that privilege convinced Federenko that there was no way in which he would gain a medal in his race. He was beaten already—Tretsov was a *favorite*, and his favoritism had nothing to do with form, odds, or journalists. Tretsov had been chosen. He listened to the man's adequate English.

"In the name of all competitors I promise that we will take part in these Olympic Games respecting and abiding by the rules which govern them, in the true spirit of sportsmanship, for the glory of sport and the honor of our teams."

Then, in Russian, the voice stronger, more confident. In both languages, Federenko resented it.

Gutierrez letting the words pass over him, unacknowledged.

Ochengwe with a blank face. Diderot aware only that the Opening Day ceremony might be his final appearance at the XXII Olympiad.

Lydall, head slightly bowed, as if taking some more private oath.

Holmrath visibly affected by the moment; Jorgensen glum by habit, and realization.

Irvine erect, eyes front, alert as an animal aware that its victim cannot escape it. Confident.

Irena Witlocka crying, silent as to the cause of her tears.

At all Olympic Games—and those held in Moscow were no exception to this rule—each country's track and field team is allocated a specific training site. Here, one of the hundreds of stadiums subordinate to the Lenin-Luzhniki complex which littered the city. However, this rigorously stated rule rarely applies in fact, since athletes use the training track of their own choice. Some athletes seek out those tracks where spectators, photographers, and rival coaches are thickest; some prefer quieter tracks; some sites are less windy than others; and some athletes seek out the psychological warfare that arises from competitors in the same event training at the same time, on the same track. The evening of the Opening Day, early enough for the floodlights not to be in use at the Central Sports Palace of the Soviet Army, on the other side of the Leningradsky Prospekt from the expanded Dynamo complex, site of the football, handball, hockey, and shooting events. Officially allocated to the British team, after a fortnight of use it was one of the locations used most frequently by the middle distance runners of most countries—together with the main warm-up track alongside the Lenin Stadium.

Lydall, running into the long shadow of the grandstand, moved out of the slanting sunlight which caused him to screw up his eyes. Irvine was watching, and Gutierrez. The Russians were still training in relative secrecy at the Hippodrome, near the Byelorussian railway terminal, but the others, Lydall knew, would be gathering there with their coaches, some journalists, and a contingent of the Soviet coaches whose only job it was to assess the competition offered to Russian athletes in various events.

Lydall had had to accept, from the first few days, that he was being used as a kind of yardstick, almost as if he were of an older generation, and laying down parental guidelines for the others. Or—a more bitter realization—they had decided that he would be the watershed either side of which would fall the medalists and the nonmedalists. To qualify for the Final, be as good as Lydall. He found himself cast in a role and achieving a kind of *average* performance which he despised, which was often no more than an extended warm-up. His coach, not an official team coach but nevertheless able to get into his training sessions every day, was irritated with him—and perhaps had given him up, accepted that to make the Games was sufficient, all that could be expected—

He slowed opposite Harry, jogged another lap, then stood in front of his coach.

"Harry—fuck this." Harry's eyes narrowed. "Irvine's here—so is the Yank—"

"The Frog's around somewhere—and plenty of Russian coaches with watches—" added Harry, seeming to sense something in his runner. Pete Lydall with a tight-drawn face, eyes screwed up. He nodded. "All right—do three thousand, and we'll time each lap for speed. You sure you—" Lydall nodded. "O.K., son. Get to it."

Irvine had stripped off, was doing his warm-up laps. Gutierrez was talking to the Polish girl, again. Holmrath was jogging, having done the lightest session in front of the others—he'd perhaps done his time trial—Harry hadn't been there, so Lydall didn't know the result. The stone-faced blokes with the stopwatches—two apiece—seemed attracted by Irvine, but, strangely, more by himself.

Seven and a half laps of the Soviet Army Sports Palace track. Each one a segment on the face of a watch, each one a sweep of the second hand.

He was feeling good. The first time he passed Irvine, there was a nod and a brief grin from the Australian, while he continued with his warm-up. He didn't flow like Ochengwe, but none of them had seen the Ugandan do anything other than the briefest and most desultory sessions, despite the anger and temperament of his coach and the team management. Lydall rounded the bend, dismissing the Ugandan and the returning image of the man before the icon of the Virgin of Vladimir, dismissing the images of Natalia that bobbed unbidden in his consciousness at the same moment. He was unaware that she was watching him from the back of the grandstand.

Gutierrez waved at him, fist clenched, a gesture of support or derision Lydall could not say before he turned back to Irena.

Three laps, and moving into another gear. Gutierrez watched Lydall with the indifferent face of a bored spectator, while his mind took the time trial to pieces, like the innards of one of the watches being used on the Englishman. Something was pushing the man, something at stake down there—not the result of a quarrel with his coach, or dissatisfaction, it seemed to Gutierrez. He was surprised that the Englishman could suddenly notch up his performance by an effort of will, outside a race, with no runner helping or competing.

He turned his attention reluctantly to the girl beside him. It was becoming messy, he told himself. Being made to feel responsible for her, involved. The girl wanted out—maybe he wanted the girl, here and now, but no way could he picture them together after that fortnight or three weeks, back home. He was inside something that had built walls round him—but he knew where the door was.

If he didn't want the girl, then he shouldn't have been in her room the previous day and he shouldn't have noticed as he entered her the tears standing in her eyes or the dumb *grateful* look as he reached a climax. He should have darkened the room before they began anything on the bed. He'd breezed in easy in mind—Peggy's taking up with an Italian notwithstanding—ready for a workout and the girl had made it a five-act tragedy. Somehow, she'd had the capacity—maybe the cunning—to show him an unflattering picture of himself. And he didn't like that.

Something he didn't welcome had happened, and at the moment he was refusing to acknowledge it, give it credence. He kept his body slightly apart from her as they leaned together on the rail, while he watched Lydall moving strongly into his last lap and a half.'

"Fifty-nine!" Harry's words were left behind, the outstretched hand holding the stopwatch, the free hand pointing at the face of the watch.

I knew it, Lydall told himself. I knew it was. Irvine had stopped jogging, was standing, hands on hips at the side of the track, watching him. Diderot was up in the stand, with Holmrath and Jorgensen. Gutierrez was observing him. He stretched out down the back straight, and there was none of the leadenness of Crystal Palace, and none of the pressing, cramping sense of having to do it, of perhaps failing. He could go like this for the rest of the time trial, increase his speed a little. Just a lap left. It was easy—

He slowed down, imperceptibly at first, then visibly. Harry was looking gloomily at the watch as he came down the home straight, onto the bend. As he passed him, Lydall winked. Harry was mouthing sixty-three, but then he realized and acted up, prancing with the stopwatch, running alongside as if exhorting or complaining, being left behind.

Lydall completed the last lap like a tired man. Irvine, face sharp with suspicion, walked past him as he bent double, hands clasping his knees, Harry leaning over him, face an angry red. Irvine slapped him on the back, perhaps with irony in the touch.

"I must get my thigh strapped," he murmured, loud enough for Lydall to hear. Lydall grinned, his breathing slowing to normal.

"How do you feel, son?" Harry asked.

"Bloody good, Harry. I feel great." Lydall stood up, and winked again.

Then he saw Gutierrez, high up on the terrace, hands above his head, applauding ironically. He knew, and so did Irvine.

"Twenty percent are very sure—they're believers," Harry said. "Now, warm down with a couple of laps jogging. You can look as tired as you like."

Allardyce had spent most of the afternoon before the Opening Day ceremony talking to officials of the Ugandan and Tanzanian teams, later while the teams filed into the stadium to a Reuter's man who knew southern Africa as well as he did himself. Other journalists were interested, but most of them didn't have the political background Allardyce had acquired, and many others of them could adopt no other attitude to Uganda and Amin than one of head-tossing contempt or derisory laughter. The terrorist threat—which had come to nothing—and the political wrangling were sidelines to be followed only by the most persistent or the most cranky. The rags picked up the sexual gossip—gay athletes seemed to be a cause célèbre for the moment—and the heavies discussed the competition ahead.

Amin had sent a telegram. That much Allardyce knew before he arrived at the Soviet Olympic Committee's reception for officials and the world's sporting press at the Yunost Hotel at the entrance to the Lenin Stadium complex in Luzhniki Park. Members of the Politburo, the Council of Ministers, the Presidium, and the Secretariat were also present, though the Soviet First Secretary—rumored to be tired after the Opening Day ceremony—would be absent.

Amin had sent a telegram. Its contents remained unrevealed to Allardyce by the tight-lipped, uncooperative Ugandan officials he tried to question before the buffet was served. The Tanzanian delegation, every one of them, remained in another exclusive, tight-knit group in another part of the huge reception room, patently ignoring the Ugandans, politely refusing to comment to the press.

Greenberg was spectacularly uninterested in anything but the food and drink, and even Karen Gunston seemed indifferent to the potential squabble of two of the more prominent African nations at the Games. The Third World was small change, Allardyce supposed, to two journalists from a nation expecting to gain between thirty and forty Gold Medals, and maybe sixty others. Allardyce began to wonder, as he nagged at the two circles of intense, private conversation, flitting between them like some innocuous insect, whether he wasn't so much seeking a story as distracting himself from his forthcoming contact with *Burgoyne*. It was easier to concentrate on his journalism, anyway, than it would have been trying to make preseduction small talk with Karen Gunston.

He noticed, as the evening went on, how senior Soviet officials of the Olympic Organizing Committee tried to infiltrate the two groups of Africans, then noticed one or two members of the International Olympic Committee introduced into heated conversations with the team managements. Mr. Novikov fluttered hesitantly between the two groups. Looking around him, Allardyce realized how few of the pressmen present seemed aware, or interested, in what appeared to be building. The Chief of Protocol of the IOC, the Director of the General Secretariat, some Africans Allardyce took to be diplomats rather than team management, Killanin himself, President of the IOC, all talking with the Ugandan team management, then, ten minutes later, with Novikov and the Russians, later again with the Tanzanians. The Tanzanians acted with the stiff rectitude of the irreproachable. The Ugandans appeared increasingly unhappy.

Allardyce crossed, easing through the crowded center of the room, to Giulio Malagressi, Italian member of the IOC and someone he had known at Oxford when Malagressi was a visiting Fellow.

"Giulio—what's happening?"

"David—!" Malagressi embraced him, careful of his champagne glass and his cigarette in its ebony holder. He was smiling broadly, his gray hair whiter than the last time they had met, his stomach more ample, his eyes as warm as ever.

"Oh—the business, mm?" He gestured toward the Ugandan delegation. Novikov was waving his arms, talking persuasively. "I was congratulating the IOC on behaving unsuspiciously. But you are, of course, a foreign correspondent, not one of the swilling sportswriters."

"So—what's happened? The telegram was a recall, wasn't it?"

"I think so—" He turned his head, his eye caught by the movement of the African diplomats toward the doors, in the company of Killanin, the Chief of Protocol, Novikov, and the Director of the General Secretariat. Allardyce recognized the Ugandan Ambassador among the party. "David—we'll talk. When something has been settled—mm?"

"Now, Giulio. Please." Malagressi nodded reluctantly. "Amin has recalled the Ugandan team—right?" Malagressi nodded. "Why? These border incursions haven't happened, have they?"

"You would know more about it than I do, David—"

"I've been checking, as much as I can, all day. Tanzanian regulars are supposed to have crossed the border with Uganda, supported by aircraft. Just like 1978. To the aid of some coup that the President had just uncovered. As far as I can find out—the putting down of the coup is real enough, but not the Tanzanian invasion. That's been *invented* by Amin—"

"That is my understanding, also. It is unfortunate, but President Amin of Uganda appears determined to recall his athletes.

Unless the IOC expels Tanzania from the Games. Frankly, I admit that it has me baffled. There is, of course, no possibility that the Tanzanians will be expelled. Now, David, if you'll excuse me—"

Malagressi walked away toward a group of IOC officials still in conversation with Soviet Olympic Committee members, while the Ugandans, still more despondent, made a pathetic little group near the laden tables.

It was another twenty minutes before the group led by Killanin reappeared. Allardyce could tell by Killanin's expression that whatever suggestions had been made, they had not been accepted. The Ugandan ambassador spoke briefly to the Ugandan team officials, and then they made their reluctant way to the doors in a tight little group, gathered together as if for safety in numbers.

As they made it apparent they were leaving, a number of pressmen began to take a serious interest. Allardyce shook his head as Malagressi gave him a thumbs-down signal from across the room. It had been as simple, as unobtrusive, as that. A few black men left a hotel reception, and dozens of athletes found four years' preparation all for nothing, and each faced a bleak moment of futility. And the Games suffered a little more from the crushing weight of national interests, political gambits, and committee-room contests.

Amin, for some twisted reason, had wanted to quarrel again with Tanzania on his southern borders. Perhaps only to distract the world from yet another bloodletting in his own backyard. The reason did not matter, the fact had been accomplished.

"David—!" The woman was at his elbow. He recognized the voice immediately, recognized its artificiality, its assumed pleasure overriding the deeper nervousness, even fear.

"Anna—how lovely to see you." He opened his arms, they kissed each other Russian fashion as they embraced. He held her at arm's length, as if admiring her. "How are you?"

"Fine, David—fine. May I introduce *Captain* Gennadi Leonov, my companion." The tall man standing behind her nodded stiffly, heels almost clicking together in frigid politeness. Allardyce was warned by the rank, his breath taken away by the coolness the woman displayed making contact in the company of a man who undoubtedly belonged to the KGB—and who was undoubtedly her lover, by the way he studied Allardyce as a possible rival or former lover.

"Captain Leonov—"

"Call him Gennadi—he doesn't like to be formal." She rubbed her head lightly against Leonov's sleeve, which seemed to instantly placate him. Allardyce smiled as innocently as he could as he confirmed that the woman and Leonov were lovers, and in love. It was a huge effort to betray nothing but benignity in his face. He looked at his empty glass, wishing for a drink. Anna sipped the last of her champagne. "Gennadi—get me another drink, please."

"Sure—you too, Mr. Allardyce?"

"Thanks."

Leonov, assured by the woman's touch, moved off without reluctance. Allardyce watched his retreating back.

"David—it is you, isn't it? My contact. It's the sort of thing they would find amusing." She observed the fact without rancor, merely as an item of information. Allardyce nodded.

"Yes—I'm the contact." He wanted to refer to Leonov, could not find the words.

"Yes," she said softly. "Gennadi and I are lovers—I love him. And he is assigned to the tracking down of the double agent in the Defense Ministry—" She studied his face carefully. "Be careful of your features, David. They don't seem under control."

"I'm sorry. How close is—he?"

"Too close. Will they get me out?"

"Yes."

"When?"

"Maybe ten days' time—no longer than that."

"What about the man, Burfield? He's been expelled."

"How did you—?" he began, then realized. "No, he was the blind. The case officer is in Moscow, making the arrangements."

"Gennadi is coming back," she remarked with a bright smile, as if talking of something lighter. "Where next?"

"First day of the athletics. We can meet by accident, at the stadium."

"Good. And—thank you, David." Leonov arrived, handed them their drinks. "Thank you, Gennadi. David has just been congratulating me on the tickets I seem to have acquired—"

"Don't bother to congratulate me," Leonov observed with mock sourness. "I shall have to spend most of each day sitting beside her—"

Allardyce felt that his answering smile was very strained, very artificial.

The girl was speaking in Polish as she moved beneath him. Gutierrez did not understand, but received only the sense that the girl was begging, pleading—then losing herself as she approached a climax, seemed to be calling out a single word over and over which was not a name, probably simply "Yes! Yes!" Her long fingers were pushing down on his back, his buttocks, as if aiding his thrusts. His mouth was near her, yet he could not allow himself to speak, do anything but breathe more and more urgently, the wiry dark hair against his cheek and neck. He felt her long legs move up, encircle his waist, the girl suddenly more open to him, and yet he felt confined, trapped by the eroticism of it. He even had a sense of her assertion of self, of sexual confidence, that he had never found in her before.

Then he climaxed, sensed that she wanted him to continue, her legs squeezing, her pelvis still moving. He did so until her breath escaped in a long shudder, then he felt her relax under him, her thighs losing their fierce grip on his body. He could hear her breath in his ear, feel her lips pecking against his neck as if reluctant to admit the act was finished. It irritated him far less than usual, so much so that he rested against her for a time, until he could feel his heart rate come down, and her breathing become still. When he moved aside, she reached for his shoulders in a tiny preventive movement but, as if sensing he might resent the restraint, relaxed again.

He did not want a smoke—they were still stashed inside an old training shoe, in the locker in his quarters—even though there was no sharp sense of the usual satisfaction of a sex trip, the satisfaction of a good workout, a successful performance. He found himself wanting to know what she had been feeling, thinking, as they made love. What was happening behind that tight-squeezed face with the strangely abandoned look while it was just below his own? He remembered staring into it as if trying to decipher more than her words.

He sensed she wanted to talk, but was afraid of giving some kind of offense, overstepping a boundary that he had made. He reached for her hand, felt the eagerness of her grasp, the long fingers curling round his in a compulsive, clenching action. He slightly regretted the offer of contact. Nevertheless, he turned to look at her, took in, in the darkened room, the flattened breasts, the slim body, the black tuft of pubic hair, the long legs. But he was more impelled to study her face as she lay staring at the ceiling.

"Thanks," he said hoarsely, clearing his throat. She did not look at him. "Good—uh?" It was as if he had cooked something for her, or bought a present. Gratitude on her behalf was expected. She seemed to resent his breaking the silence. Then, suddenly, he wanted to know. "Why, Irena? Why me?" And in his head the conversation began to arrange itself coolly. He ascribed dubious motives to her together with a lack of self-awareness, and cast himself in the role of passport and visa.

She looked at him, scanning his face so intently she might have been reading his mind.

"Why you?" Bracing herself for some confession, her eyes retreating suddenly, then some conviction that a moment of importance had arrived. "You mean—do I wish for the California sunshine and—Disneyland?" She raised herself, disengaging her grip on his hand. "That's what you think?"

He wanted to avoid the pitiless view of himself that her fumbled words presented. He shook his head. Leaning above him, resting on one elbow, her breasts cradled in her arms, she was erotic yet distant and superior. In control of herself and the situation.

"Well?" he answered. "You want out, girl—that's right?"

"Of course I want *out!*" It was as if he had descended from wisdom to banality and she was disappointed in him. "What do you think my life is like to want to stay?" He perceived the gulf that divided their separate circumstances. He felt he had taken a great many things for granted. "I am too honest for you, Martin?"

"No—you want America?"

"I want you."

He put his hands behind his head and stared at the ceiling, aware that she was still resting on her elbow, unmoving as an artist's model at the corner of eyesight, troubling the mind's eye.

"Why me, Irena—?" he said finally in a voice that could not now recapture the coolness of the first question. Suddenly, he had to be upright in the bed, at no disadvantage. He sat up. "Why me? We knew each other for a couple of weeks, for Christ's sake—!"

She registered no acceptance of his remark or tone. Brevity excused nothing, explained nothing away.

"Yes—and absence makes the heart fonder, also," she remarked. "I know that. I have spent a year dreaming about you. Do you know what the dreams of a Polish athlete can be, the first time she knows a man?"

Again, he felt helpless, felt that her remarks possessed the irresistible wisdom of an adult.

"I don't see—"

"You don't—how could you?" He sensed her urgency, as if she

were fighting for something and already into the last round of the contest. He felt chastened to silence while she searched for the words, her eyes seeking them as if they might be scattered crumbs on the sheets. She brushed her hand on the space of sheet between their bodies, as if simply to give force to the image that came to his mind. Then she looked at him again with the same disconcerting intensity.

"Of course I want freedom—I have had glimpses of it, when I have traveled with the Polish team. Don't you understand the—the *power* of shop windows in your country, in England—?" Her hands were willing him to understand her, conducting her emotions, summoning them to the aid of her awkward, stilted English. She murmured quickly and softly in Polish, seemed impatient, then said, "To see through a small hole what lies on the other side of a wall— Yes. And—perhaps, perhaps you are the, the *visa* for me. *I* think I love you. When we—are together like this I don't want anyone else. I don't want anyone else to touch me like you have touched me. How can I *know* if it is real, this love I say I have for you?"

She seemed at a loss. Gutierrez was ashamed, pierced by something that might have been remorse, even love. Sensing the duplicity of his emotions, their uninterpretable ambiguity, he was slapped by her honesty.

"I—what do you want me to say to that? You just told me I might just be your ticket out, what am I supposed to say to that?" He touched her face, gently. "God, baby—you make my life such a *mess*—!" She flinched, he rubbed her cheek again with rougher cameraderie, reassurance. "I'm simple, maybe. I mean—I keep things simple. I like life in little packs. Things come to me—" He was clasping his raised knees now, staring to where the curtains moved in a slight breeze and let in the sodium flare of lamps. "They come like training, you know? A girl, another girl—" She winced, but he did not see. "For a week, a few bouts—just like a workout. Nothing interrupts—" He turned to her. "Maybe I'm not prepared for you or anyone like you, girl." He huddled into himself for a long time then, suddenly silent. Eventually, as the girl was beginning to feel cold, and rubbed her arms and legs, he shrugged. "But—you're here, right?" She nodded, the former assurance now replaced by timidity. "O.K., you're here, and maybe—just maybe—you're different. All I know is—sure as hell I can't ignore you anymore!"

Floodlights on in the Young Pioneer Stadium on the Leningradsky Prospekt. Winston Ochengwe had the small stadium to himself, except for a couple of Ugandan hurdlers, and some Rumanian field athletes, high jumpers, a couple of triple jumpers, one from the men's decathlon who preferred to limber up and practice away from the rest of their team. Ochengwe paid them little attention, and they largely ignored him, as if he were a local jogging. There were no spectators, no watches.

His body was lethargic, as if the blood moved in his veins like mud. His chest was a hollow space that automatically filled with, exhaled the air to no purpose. Trots, a couple of slow laps, jog again—exercises. Even the team coach, with whom he had had little to do before coming to Moscow, had given up on him, unable by bribery, cajolement, or threats to improve his training form.

And Ochengwe never reflected on what was happening to him, except that sometimes, in waking dreams, he relived those moments in M'seka after he crested the last rise and saw the armored car and the running troops. It was as if he had done something then, sustained some injury, that prevented him from further training and competition.

Two slowish laps, trying to put something into it, but not trying very hard. Jogging another two laps. Then two more, without a watch, no sense of time, no attempt to measure in his mind what he was doing. It wasn't even a session he was doing—nothing like what the others in his event had to be doing now. He had even entered this stadium, maybe an hour before, shamefaced at showing the security guard his pass, apologizing for his masquerade as a competitor.

One of the assistant managers arrived just before midnight. He seemed to come reluctantly, with an important task to perform, but one which gave him no pleasure. He called over Ochengwe and the two hurdlers from Kampala, the man and woman who always trained together. They were native Ugandans, not immigrant Tutsi like himself.

The official explained. The girl, without a moment of pause or reflection, burst into tears. Perhaps she saw everything in a single moment, waste, danger, futility, anger she could not display, rebelliousness she would need to hide. The man put his arm round her shoulder, nodding. Then the official looked at Ochengwe.

"Sorry, man." He did not seem to be, not when talking to Ochengwe. He had been more genuinely apologetic toward the other two. Ochengwe had disappointed, would have been a nothing when it came to the 5000—

Ochengwe shook his head. The assistant manager seemed surprised.

"Get your things together, uh?" he suggested to all three of them. "We got a plane to catch."

"No."

Simply that. He had not designed the moment, or even sought it. No choice seemed to have been presented to his forebrain, about which he ought to consciously decide. But the word was there, between them now like something alive and dangerous.

"What you mean 'no,' man?"

"No—just no. All I mean is—no. To everything you say."

"Hey, mister. This is Presidential, you understand? You saying 'no'—crazy, uh?" He invited the others to join him in mocking laughter. The girl looked up at Ochengwe, tried to smile, but was also afraid for him. The man seemed sheepish. Joseph, his name was. Ochengwe remembered it, suddenly, as if it were important to do so. Again, he shook his head.

"I am not going home," he said carefully and distinctly, as precisely as he might have repeated a lesson from the nuns when he first learned a language other than his own.

Before there was any reply, he walked away, ignoring the call to get ready, come back, don't be stupid, and the little impotent threats that followed. He took off his track suit and stood, hands on hips, breathing deeply and regularly. He was committed now. He could not go back. It did not matter. Ideas precise as the words he had used to the assistant manager.

He did not need a watch. He would know.

First lap, fifty-eight. Second lap, fifty-eight. Third lap, fifty-nine. Fourth lap, fifty-three.

All the time he was running, the two hurdlers and the assistant manager watched him in silence. When he slowed down after the fourth lap, and jogged on a little, letting the heartbeat come back down, the breathing settle, the body draw back from what it had been doing, its pride in doing it—he heard a single pair of hands, clapping. He turned his head. It was the girl, Elizabeth.

She waved as she disappeared into the tunnel. Then he was alone in the Young Pioneer Stadium, under the floodlights.

They knocked on the door of his room, which he shared with three other Australians, a sprinter, a rower, and a swimmer, all of whom he knew well enough for them not to drive him out of his mind with a fortnight of their company. They were most polite when they broached the subject, they were quietly insistent, apologetic as he dressed, and reassuring when he referred to the Australian team management and the Australian Olympic Federation.

But he was accused—they had the man in custody, who had confessed to the deal—of selling two pairs of denims, at a black market price, to a known black marketer. He had requested to be paid in U.S. dollars which he could take with him after the Games. He knew, of course, that rubles could not be exported.

Yes, he did have two pairs of denims missing. He'd reported the fact—what was all this—?

All the way to KGB headquarters, in the back of the Volga sedan, Kenneth Irvine could not believe that it was happening to him. He could not even begin to take the incident seriously.

CHAPTER 9

Thursday, the twenty-fourth of July, the first day of athletics at the Lenin Stadium. The right occasion, François Diderot had time to think, for the little drama on the track to be played out—the two figures in blue track suits, the white letters CCCP on the back of each. Tretsov and Federenko, kept in the dark like bulbs, hidden behind a curtain until now. They must be good—they're here to impress, he thought. Something in him wanted to grin, and there was a tightness in his chest as if he were responding to the challenge they represented. Then he turned back to Loriot, who was wearing the Givenchy sunglasses and a pale blue Dormieul suit, jacket over the shoulders. His hands were in his pockets as he lounged against a barrier rail, apparently enjoying the sunshine. Down on the track, Ochengwe continued his limbering-up exercises, and Lydall watched the two Russians as if they were a species of unpredictable wild animal. Diderot saw that much even as he turned his gaze back to Loriot.

"François—it's serious." A smile, mechanical and unreassuring. "I won't disguise that from you. People—people at the top—are worried. Publicity could do us a lot of harm. It *is* doing us harm. Most of the newspapers behave as if we—*seduced* you?" Again, the smile.

"Tell me, Loriot—what is happening in Paris? The company is admitting nothing, right?"

"So far, that seems to be the case."

Ochengwe, jogging a few laps, passed beneath them in his orange national track suit— Strange, Diderot thought, distracted, that he was still wearing that. The black man flowed round the far bend. Lydall was talking to his coach. Diderot saw Holmrath and Jorgensen arriving together. Gutierrez was absent. The Army Sports Palace track was on the point of being returned to the British team by the 5000 men. For the next four days, their training would become more secretive again, solitary.

"Are they going to go on denying it?" he blurted, suddenly very afraid again. They had to keep quiet. He had a sense that he was disallowed from being down on the track, from running with the others, which was all he wanted to do.

The Russians were going to run a tandem training session—to impress or mislead, he wondered. Officials, coaches—there seemed to be more of them, suddenly, all of them ostentatious with stopwatches, spreading out round the track. The black man seemed not to notice them, increasing his speed as he began his series of repetition runs. A lonely man, living alone in the Ugandan block in the village until someone asked him to bunk in with them in the British quarters. Was it Lydall? Emerging every day just to practice and train, then going back to his room. They said he just sat on the bed, staring at the floor, or at the hands clenched in his lap.

But, Mother of God, on the track he looked good.

Diderot tried to shake his mind free of the clinging burrs of other people's lives, other subsidiary matters. He was fighting for his own survival.

"François—we're not going to ditch you now." Affable grin. No deeper than the capped teeth. "We can't afford to have this whole thing blow up in our faces, any more than you can. The newspapers have no proof, however hard a time they may be giving us—there will be no copies of the contract made. That is safe." He touched Diderot lightly on the forearm, as if to transmit sincerity through the contact, like a current. "France-Allemagne Sporting can't afford a scandal like this. Don't worry. Just so long as you keep your mouth shut, and you run in that race—" Meaningful pause, tapping of the fingers in emphasis on Diderot's track suit. "But without the medal, without the *glory* that would surround you, there is no contract. Understand?"

Then, quite quickly, he was gone, leaving Diderot staring down at the track. Red vests, white shorts, an orange track suit, and British high hurdlers practicing over on the other side of the stadium. Diderot watched a huge shot-putter, bearded and fierce-looking, go into the throw. The whole scene appeared without meaning for him, or as if robbed of color. Loriot had given him the warning—unless you're in, we're out. And the French officials were meeting the day of the heats to make a final decision.

One scrap of proof, one big payment by one newspaper for one photocopy of one contract—a thin chain still to be forged—and he was out. He'd denied everything, and they could prove nothing. They might go chicken, and kick him out anyway, but he didn't think so.

So far, the IOC seemed content to leave the matter in French hands. But they would want to be lily-white, and be seen to be.

Lydall, watching carefully, his own repetitions completed and Harry satisfied, the leg holding up better than ever, wondered how genuine the whole thing was. He understood why the wraps were being taken off the two Russians, and why they were training in tandem. But were they supposed to be genuine, or not? Ochengwe, doing six fast laps before going back to the jog, seemed oblivious of the two Russians, though Holmrath and Jorgensen—and Diderot up on the terraces—were intent connoisseurs assessing precious objects they might have to bid for, farmers assessing the meat on display.

No, it wasn't genuine. Harry had the watch on them—just as the Russians and the Americans had had the watches on him, on Diderot, on the others, for the last fortnight. Droves of officials, especially Russians, with no other purpose than endlessly to clock times, compare day-by-day improvement, look out for injuries, lack of motivation, a tailing from a too-early peak—

Lydall grinned as Tretsov and Federenko, like Siamese twins, hip to hip, passed him onto the bend. Too rigid, too regimented. Sometimes in Eastern European teams, the two runners in a middle distance event might work in harness—one the breaker, one to win the race. Here they were acting like mirror images, two robots repeating the same time for each lap, exactly.

They had warmed up, then gone into what Lydall could only describe as a routine. This was an audition, and a bluff. Someone had worked out exactly what time they should both do for their 3000-meter time trial, on public display, to impress and worry the competition—without giving anything away except the impression that they both had plenty left in reserve.

Lydall shook his head, trying to distinguish the two. Clockwork regularity. He could tell nothing about condition, tactics, favoritism, rivalry. It was an impressive display piece, and it wasn't meant to be anything more than that.

They passed him again, for the last time, with a stutter of watches from Russian officials every forty yards. One more lap. Jorgensen and Holmrath were limbering up, waiting until the display was over before they began any serious repetition work. And himself, glad to have finished. Ochengwe taking no notice, and Diderot hanging back, as if shy.

A fast last lap. They came up to pass Ochengwe, still in his track suit, who was in an outside lane, making room for them. The black man seemed to watch them pass, in irritating tandem, but Lydall was too far away to see any expression on his face.

Then, as the two Russians went into the last bend, Ochengwe seemed to kick into another gear, lengthening his stride, flowing faster round the outside, almost with the stretch of a 200-meter man, leaning into the bend. Lydall had always wondered—he began to grin and couldn't disguise it—whether Ochengwe was really interested in competition, rather than simply in running. Was he a *winner*? Into the last straight, the two Russians doll-like and inseparable, the big black man on the outside, nearest the stand, coming level with them.

Tretsov saw him, wondered, did nothing. Federenko caught the bright track suit, seemed to kick suddenly and instinctively, and then dropped back into stride with Tretsov outside him.

Then Ochengwe dropped his pace, shortened his stride, and all three runners crossed the finish line together. Ochengwe ran on as the other two slowed, as if wanting to hurry into their track suits. As he passed Lydall, he grinned. It was the first time Lydall had ever seen him smile since he arrived in Moscow.

"Winnie—you're a bastard," he said, laughing. Ochengwe, still grinning, jogged on round the track. Already, surrounded by officials and coaches angry at Ochengwe's piece of gamesmanship, the two Russians were in their track suits, warming down before being taken away—

Yes, taken away. They had been put in the shop window, with their performance figures on a neatly printed card, then they were being taken out again, point made. A little publicity exercise; a little piece of psychological warfare.

He wished Gutierrez and Irvine had been there to see it. When he thought of Irvine, his face twisted into a grimace, and he didn't find the Russian charade funny any longer.

Kenneth Irvine knew they had gotten to him. The bus taking him to the warm-up track at the Luzhniki complex was full of team officials, members of the Australian Olympic Federation, a couple of people from the IOC and another two or three from the Soviet Olympic Committee, as well as the security men who were purportedly present to keep the press and spectators from bothering him while he trained. And all he wanted was to be alone. In a silence where he would hear none of these buzzing voices, where people would not be able to ask after his welfare and his fitness and apologize and reassure and commiserate. His head was burning and aching with questions, with sleeplessness, with the irritating, sapping bee stings of denial after denial after denial.

He had long given up the idea that he was living inside someone else's nightmare, that he was the victim of some grotesque mistake. The routine imposed upon him by the KGB made him think in its terms. He was allowed to return to the village every evening, he was given the meals appropriate to his diet whenever he asked for them, and cosseted by the apologetic questioning. Every morning there was a new session of questions—then he was allowed to train, and to talk to the officials who now surrounded him, however much he wished to shun them—then he was taken back for more questions until the evening. It had been going on for four days, and it now seemed that the whole world wanted to talk to him, study him, reassure him.

There was no way in which the questioning would stop, or could be stopped. The IOC, the AOF, the team management—all of them had blustered, protested, lodged complaints, threatened action, consulted lawyers, embassy officials. To little purpose. He was accused of having sold two pairs of denims to a known black marketer. There were photographs, and one of the men in them might have been him, all the way to the long fair hair and the casual clothes. The KGB were determined, with his *assistance*, to put the black market ring in prison where they belonged. There were other competitors—some from Eastern Europe, a couple of Americans, some Africans—who'd been similarly *compromised*, he wasn't the only one.

He'd been told the Australian newspapers were full of it, that the ambassador was lodging daily protests, that lawyers were being flown in, that they'd soon have him out—but it hadn't ended yet. He was allowed a respite from the questions to run in his 10,000 heat at five in the afternoon, the climax of the first day of the athletics program. The KGB were apologetic, even wished him good fortune—and would be waiting for him after the race with *a few more questions—*

How did you meet this man? Where did he approach you? Who was with him?

I don't know, for Christ's sake—then, more calmly, *I have never met this man before in my life. That isn't me in the pictures, there's been a mistake.*

The man has implicated you, Mr. Irvine—he is known to us, he has described your meetings—you asked for dollars, U.S. dollars, or Swiss francs, he claims. He quarreled with you about the price, asked for other items, team shirts, training shoes, that kind of thing—

There's nothing to be afraid of—

It's all a mistake.

They'd gotten to him. The edge of something sharp and polished had been dulled. Now, as he was ushered down the steps of the bus where it was parked next to the warm-up track, and he saw the few dozen spectators, he suddenly felt naked, under a bright, unceasing light. Psychologically, he wasn't right. He wasn't keyed up, fine-tuned. The training sessions had become mere respites between the bouts of questioning, and not the *center* of things, his reason for being in Moscow at all.

Officials shepherded him to the warm-up track, he winced at the flash of cameras, the chatter of shutters, the comet's tail of spectators dragged behind him in the wake of the officials. Even his coach, Bill, had no separate and important reality for him.

And then he was on the track, warming up with a few laps of jogging before stripping off his track suit, aware of spectators almost holding their collective breath as if they expected to see scars or bruises. He went into a fast repetition.

Stale, sour. Like a morning taste in his mouth, or an old affair in his mind. Repetition, round and round like a rat in a maze, a dog on a treadmill. Bill, arms waving, hurrying him on, a semaphore signaling the coach's distress and perhaps his own.

Physically he was all right. No cramps, no stiffness, no weariness. Psychologically, worn. The dregs of enthusiasm, no sense of a killing, of invisible competitors at his shoulders or in front of him. Just a man running round and round an empty track watched by a lot of silent people.

He wanted to wave his arms, shout at them, get them to make a noise, not study him, but *enjoy* him. Bill's face looked worried and edgy as he passed him, his voice coming from behind and fading as he tried to comment on the times he was doing.

Jogging again—but after half a lap he couldn't stand the futility of it, and he speeded up again. Bill looked puzzled, even more worried.

Allardyce watched Irvine complete his repetition work, put his track suit back on, climb onto the bus, shepherded by the team officials, studied by the crowd of morning spectators, and shook his head as the bus pulled away, back to the village. A man four races away from two Gold Medals—a distance of perhaps . . .

A distance he might not make.

"Looks shaken up, uh?" Ben Greenberg was at his elbow, just as Allardyce's reflections turned to the personal, began to anticipate the questions. *What is the name of your case officer?* Dunkley. *What are the arrangements?* I'm to hold her hand until the escape route is prepared. *What is the route?* Passenger flight to London, then a diplomatic flight to Washington. *When?* He didn't know when— Dunkley hadn't told him. *You just hold her hand until we're ready, Dave—just do that.*

"What?" he said to Greenberg.

"Irvine—the kid looks shaken."

"Yes."

"The IOC ought to have gotten the charges dropped by now."

"You should care, Ben. Unless this pressure actually has the effect on Irvine of getting rid of the boredom and frustration of waiting for his events, your boy has a better chance than ever."

"True—but would you want to be him—four days of questions, questions? For two pair of denims I wouldn't thank you for as a gift?"

"No," Allardyce said. "No, I wouldn't like that—"

What is the name of your case officer—

That afternoon, he had to instruct Anna on what the CIA required from her before she was lifted out. A last look round the house she was leaving, picking up the last few scraps of information she could—

The idea filled him with disgust.

Irena Witlocka had forty-eight hours before the qualifying rounds of the high jump. That morning, she had begun dropping the inside shoulder—the most common, silly mistake of the jumper striving to beat the two-meter barrier. It was more difficult to drop the shoulder with the Fosbury jump rather than the straddle, but she was doing it.

Grachikov was angry, as he usually was. She got it right—four jumps with correct approach and takeoff, and no dropped shoulder. All except the double arm shift which she had been experimenting with that season, and which still came right only most of the time. She was keyed up, of course, but not in the right way. It wasn't even that Martin Gutierrez was watching her practice session from a bench twenty yards away, but that he had told her just before she began her session that he had approached the embassy, that he had argued with them, that they were not about to see things his way. Later, maybe—

She looked at him as she balanced herself, relaxed before yet another approach run. He was watching her intently as she swayed her balance slightly from leg to leg, poised to begin the run-up. He was smiling, seemed content, earnestly interested.

Could she believe him, believe in him? Did he mean to go on with it, get her out, take her with him?

She wanted to believe it—so much she wanted to.

She began her curving run, fairly late after an initial straight movement. Ten strides, a fast but relaxed approach, takeoff from the leg farthest from the bar after the slight side step on the last stride; plant the takeoff foot toward the bar, drive upward—drive *both* arms—lead the movement with the inside arm, high shoulder, head and shoulders across the bar, lift the hips, leave the legs behind—*now* straighten the legs, knees up to the chest, arms stretching—

The bar, caught by her right heel, clattered and fell as she landed on the foam bed on her shoulders, bounced, saw the evil face Grachikov was making, and wanted to laugh with nerves.

"Concentrate!" he yelled at her as she lay there.

She stood up, saw Gutierrez still looking at her, studying her, it seemed, as if weighing her worth, the trouble he ought to take on her behalf. He grinned again. She returned his smile, then it faded on her lips as she saw the two men dressed in vile-patterned summer shirts and light slacks, with dark glasses and cameras. She knew they were not tourists. Seeing the direction of her gaze, Gutierrez turned his head.

"Come on, come on!" Grachikov bawled.

She waited until Gutierrez turned back to her. He was no longer smiling, but he nodded his head, as if for reassurance. She went back slowly to her spare training shoe which marked the start of her takeoff run.

Gutierrez watched her, and was aware of being watched, while bright little scraps of his conversation with a spook at the embassy winked in and out of his awareness. They didn't want to, but they hadn't said they wouldn't. Not right out. He was using what muscle he had to get her out, and they didn't like that but they didn't want to say no right away. He might be able to fix it.

He wasn't sure she was worth it, or whether it was merely the opposition of the spooks that drove him on, the energy of a challenged ego. But he was into it now, and he wouldn't let her go without a fight.

But he had to make an effort not to turn his head again, to look at the two men with the cameras whose pose as tourists was all too studied to be real. And he shivered, only slightly, only once—but shivered.

It was as if he had heard one of the men behind him say to the other, "You agree there will be an—*incident?*"

"Yes. She's got him interested again."

"You'll support my recommendation then?"

"Makes sense. We don't want publicity like that."

"Good. We'll increase surveillance, too. It might overload this fragile little relationship—nothing might happen. Scare him off with the attention we pay him—?"

"Suits me."

The *Serebryany Bor* Park, that part of it turned into a temporary campsite for visitors to Moscow during the fortnight of the Olympic Games. Oleg Kazantsev himself, because he was bored with paperwork and staying in his hot little office, was leading his team checking the bona fides of the occupants of the hundreds of tents and campers.

He had warned his team. Tread very softly with any foreigners, especially Americans and British. Look for Ukrainians, especially students—make sure the papers they carry are genuine, and anything slightly suspicious give them a chit and get the stuff back to the lab—and look for Europeans who might have some Russian connection, some Ukrainian ancestry.

It was a stupid piece of methodology, he considered, but there was no alternative more likely to bring success. They had pulled in Ukrainians suspected in the past of dissident activities, however harmless, and were running them through the mangle, but it was leading nowhere, giving the impression only that the *Do pobachenya* mob had no ancestry, were mint-new and unidentifiable. Students, then, most likely, was his reasoning. Hotheads—but perhaps sufficiently organized to have some entrée to an ordnance factory—just to steal nothing.

An FAE device had the right kind of appeal to a terrorist— almost as much as a nuclear device, and easier to handle and trigger. An antipersonnel weapon that made Kazantsev less than usually objective about explosives. But there wasn't one missing.

Belousov, who had supervised the loading of the oxygen truck, was certain that nothing was taken other than empty oxygen cylinders—and convinced that the driver and his mate were genuine, even though he had not recognized them. But Kazantsev knew the men had not been genuine, there were blood traces on one of the cylinders and in the truck, and fingerprints that did not match those of the regular driver in the cab. The KGB man had been killed in the back of the truck, and not for nothing.

But the manager of the oxygen company had told them nothing in Donetsk, and perhaps he knew nothing. And Belousov and the other man at the factory, Ghekh, seemed to know nothing.

Could they be like this little group? Just bloody kids, arsing around, smirking as they waited to be questioned. He stood with his hands on his hips as if trying intentionally to loom over them, make them sense his full height, full power. A bright orange tent, a smaller blue one. Both fairly new. He almost smiled as he tried to work out the sleeping arrangements. Six of them—two girls, four boys. None of them much over twenty.

"O.K., let's have your papers." He emphasized his own Ukrainian accent, telling himself that you never know, it might soften them up a bit. He squatted down on the rug one of the girls was lying on, dark glasses hiding her eyes, bikini straps pulled down to her forearms so the tan would be even on her shoulders. A slim little body, of which she was quite aware, so much so that he wanted to laugh. Two of the boys were impressed by her coolness, by what they supposed was his interest. They wanted to see him disconcerted, embarrassed. Maybe the girl would take off the bikini bodice—?

He winked at one of his assistants, who was studying the girl.

"Zenaida Federenka," he said matter-of-factly, looking at her papers, checking the date of arrival stamped on the travel visa. The girl seemed bored with the whole thing. Kazantsev looked beyond the tents to the dappled light falling on a minibus from the sun shining through a clump of silver birches. Kiev license plate, but an old vehicle. Probably hired.

"You the driver?" he asked casually.

"We take turns," she replied, taking off her dark glasses and sitting up.

"All six of you?"

"Except Lyudmila—" She nodded to the other girl, in a skinny sweater and slacks, who bobbed her head, kept her eyes down. "And Yakov—they can't drive." The girl was confident, Kazantsev thought. Skimpily dressed, aware he was KGB, but as much at ease as if she had been at home, reclining fully dressed and in the presence of a friend.

He was assailed by the normality of it—by their youth, their apparent innocence. The checkered football, the bats and the ball on a length of elastic, the shorts and sweat shirts, the books and magazines strewn about on the grass and the blankets. Normal. He knew that a policeman in London or New York or Rome or Belfast might have looked at this group more suspiciously, more shrewdly. But in those places they had terrorists who were children or students, and they were driven by precedent to question, to understand. They raced against time—but did he?

"Here for the Games, I suppose? You are his sister, aren't you?"

Someone—he wasn't quick enough to see who—drew in breath sharply, as if jabbed painfully in the ribs. The girl kept her stare level, forgetting she ought to be surprised.

"Who—Arkady? Yes. How did you know?"

"Sports fan—I met him recently. He mentioned you."

"I see—" Did she?

"Where's Shubin?"

Now they were on edge. He had tilted the machine, signs were beginning to light up; he was scoring. But only a little, a dribble of points.

"Shubin? You mean Feodor Yelisavich Shubin?"

"Yes. Isn't he with you?"

A moment when they all hovered on the brink of something, the sunlight not so bright, or so bright it washed the color out of the scene. Then one of the boys, as he handed his papers back to Kazantsev's assistant, offered, "He doesn't like sports. He didn't come, didn't bother to get time off work—"

"You are—?" Kazantsev said sharply.

"Kostya—"

"O.K., Kostya. You know Shubin—you do, Zenaida. What about the rest of you?"

The admissions were slow in coming, as if they were communicating by telepathy, reaching a silent consensus.

"We all know him," Zenaida said at last. "To some degree or other. No doubt you do, too." There was an edge of contempt.

"Oh, yes. We know him."

"You're still hounding him—" It was a reluctant accusation; the girl was not held back by nerves, but almost by indifference. It was a brilliant little deception—he was certain it had to be a deception. Was Shubin in Moscow? He would have to check with Kiev.

"No tickets for today?" He asked it with studied lightness.

"We sold them," she said bluntly, as if she knew they had come originally from him, and wished to insult his gift. "To some Americans—for the *face value.*"

He laughed.

"I'm not interested in the black market, dear. I'm interested in terrorists."

Lyudmila smiled, but the boy Ferenc laughed out loud. Perhaps an escape of nerves. They all seemed stiffer, as if some electricity had affected their muscles, bunched them. Kazantsev wondered what, precisely, he held in that small group around him.

"We're terrorists?" Zenaida mocked him.

"I shouldn't think so. I'd be more suspicious if Shubin was here with you."

"He's not a terrorist—"

He stood up quickly, taking them by surprise.

"*Do pobachenya,*" he said, and watched each face in the moment after the words. "Good-bye."

"*Do pobachenya,*" the girl said with an assumed indifference. But the electricity was there, in all of them, and more evident.

As he walked away, he said to his assistant, "Alexei—I want that little lot watched—*all* the time. Everywhere they go."

"You think—?"

"Maybe—maybe not. But I want them watched."

Gennadi Leonov was distracted almost against his will, certainly against all sense of his own dignity, self-respect. It was a creeping, uncertain, pathetic thing to do, to request the file on David Allardyce from Central Records. There was one, of course, for the two years Allardyce had spent in Moscow as a foreign correspondent.

He was checking because he was tormented—yes, he admitted it much as he might have expected one of his children to have admitted bed-wetting or theft of his loose change—tormented by jealousy. He believed, hatefully, that Anna and David Allardyce had been lovers. He knew he was wasting time—tried to redirect his attention back to the files and reports already on his desk. But he knew that he had begun his desultory reexamination of them only to try to put Allardyce's file out of his mind.

Three suspects, he told himself. Concentrate—three suspects, in the Defense Ministry. Only those three could have access to the kind and range of material they knew had been leaked over a period of four years.

Four, four—

Inadmissible. People, not years. No, only years.

The fourth possibility was Anna Akhmerovna, his mistress. As a senior member of the Secretariat—like two other suspects—she had access, opportunity.

He despised the watery indigestion he felt when he contemplated the idea, the flushes of heat that rose up in his chest to his face and neck. A competent, calm, rational officer—

The information being leaked had dried up. The source was protecting itself, retreating into its corner again. It also meant that help was near, that the double agent would be lifted from Moscow in the immediate future.

He had to turn to Anna as suspect lover; otherwise, he could not dismiss the idea of her as potential traitor. He began to read Allardyce's file, looking once or twice at his gold watch as he read the duplicated sheets—the time slipping toward three in the afternoon, and he already late to meet her at the stadium.

That much time off from her work, he observed, snatching at the calm, the innocence it suggested. She had arranged a considerable part of her annual leave to coincide with the Olympics.

Innocence, innocence—

He continued reading. Not much—some brushes with the KGB surveillance teams watching dissidents, numerous refused travel visa requests, some intercepted and censored articles; the usual run of stuff from a foreign correspondent in Moscow for more than a couple of months, and working for a Western newspaper of reactionary political color. He moved on from Known Activities to Known Associates, swallowing anticipation like a hard lump in his throat.

He scanned the list of other journalists, embassy officials—including suspected SIS agents—to the subsection headed Natives. A large number of names—he scanned again, as if searching for his name among winners of a fortune, or among proscribed individuals.

Akhmerovna, Anna Borisovna.

There it was. He glanced at his watch, now as a distraction—a fully blown image of her in that grandstand seat, watching the, the . . . heats of the 800, he remembered; then he read on.

The encapsulation of something he had read so many times

before. The social round enjoyed by senior civil servants in Moscow—embassy lunches, cocktail parties, weekends at one of the dacha parks around Moscow, the kind of thing he had read so many times before, he repeated to himself, as if disinfecting any evocation roused by the dry jargon of the report summary. They had met on numerous occasions—Anna, he read with trepidation, had been warned not to become personally involved with the man. As if weakened with relief, he sat back in his chair as he read that their meetings had seriously lessened in number, gradually disappeared, over the following months.

He closed the file as if he felt some moral system in which he devoutly believed had been vindicated—a noise of folded card coming together.

He looked at his watch. He must go to see her now—he had promised.

Tidy the desk, just by habit. Allardyce file to one side, innocuous, harmless, unimportant. The others, including hers, gathered up, together with surveillance digests, prognoses, diagnoses, everything—

The words came into his mind unbidden, clear as a printed notice or a painted sign.

Prognosis, June, 1976. Allardyce is in a position to be a courier for an intelligence service. Likelihood assessed at Beta Minus.

Quite high, quite probable, he told himself.

Diagnosis, December, 1976. Allardyce's activities do not provide sufficient opportunity. No concentration on contacts or material to support Prognosis of June this year. Downgraded to Gamma Minus.

He was, in all probability, not an agent but a genuine press reporter.

February, 1977. Downgraded to Delta.

All of it from that part of the file he had skimmed. But the words had stuck. During the months when Allardyce and Anna had met with greatest frequency—always on *social* occasions, he reminded himself—Allardyce had been graded Beta Minus, which was high.

Gennadi Leonov went out of his office in Moscow to take a taxi to the Lenin Stadium, more troubled than in that fearful moment when he had opened David Allardyce's file.

"Ahhh!" Ben Greenberg exclaimed, winking, exhaling noisily, patting his chest with both hands. "Smell that wintergreen!" Allardyce, standing with him at the top of the flight of stone steps leading up from the exit tunnel to the press box, smiled, watching the back of Anna's blonde head following the last of the heats for the 800 meters. An East German strolling in first, another third, split · by an African. Something of an inevitability about the result, in a slowish time, which did not seem to discourage Greenberg.

"I'm not sure I really like athletics anymore," Allardyce observed.

"You can say that after four days of rowing, basketball, boxing—" He was ticking off the sports, like offenses, on the fingers of one hand. "Cycling, shooting, swimming, wrestling— You want me to go on, uh?" Allardyce shook his head, smiling. "Man, I am full up to *here* with gymnastics!"

"Your newspaper sent the right man—obviously."

"They should have sent a pocket calculator, 'cause all they want right now is the medal count!"

"And the good old U.S. of A. didn't score in the Greco-Roman wrestling, mm?"

"I shall conduct a witch-hunt into that lamentable failure on my return home," Greenberg said stuffily, assuming pomposity. "Screw it. You never ran for your country—uh, Dave?" Allardyce shook his head, watching the competitors assemble for the start of the 20-kilometer walk. Strange, unathletic-looking, tougher than most competitors, and unfeted.

"No. I always ran for David Allardyce—until I got fed up with seeing other vests in front of me rather than the tape."

They were silent for a moment, sharing some common past. Then Greenberg said, "If you're going to talk to the lady, why not do it before we have to work?" Greenberg was surprised at the depth of shock his remark seemed to have elicited from Allardyce. He could have sworn the Englishman blanched at it. Greenberg nodded down toward the blonde head. "She's been looking up here, a lot of times, that old *acquaintance* of yours—I shouldn't let Karen know, if I were you. She has designs on you—and she won't like them thwarted." He studied Allardyce shrewdly. "Anything wrong, Dave?"

"No, nothing. Yes—I have to have a word with her. You're quite right—I'll get it over with before the ten thousand heats—" He waggled his hand in farewell, and headed down the steps toward Anna's seat. Beyond him, almost unremarked by the noisy capacity crowd, the walkers assembled in the late afternoon heat—skinny men, often short, in string vests and knotted handkerchiefs or peaked caps. Greenberg grinned at them, remembering the way he had once been challenged by a walker, way back in college, and the crippling *stroll* he had been put through, then he turned his attention back to Allardyce, watching him sit down next to the woman.

Greenberg shook his head.

"Take care, Dave—" he said softly. "Her boyfriend is in the KGB."

The walkers lined up, and the identical sudden coming to attention, the snap and electricity of adrenaline was in their frames. A medal—20 kilometers around the streets of Moscow, and it would belong to any one of them.

Gun. A surge through the large field of walkers, as if a wind had caught every vest, rippling them, then the robotic yet loose stride, and the fat huddle of people at the start spreading and elongating already as they began their initial circuit of the stadium before leaving it temporarily empty before the 10,000 heats.

Greenberg, considering the earnest conversation that Allardyce had immediately fallen into with the Russian woman, and thinking of her KGB lover, considered the mess Martin Gutierrez was getting into over a Polish high jumper. He shook his head. The kid ought to realize there was no chance—the spooks wouldn't get the girl out just to please him.

The walkers streaming out of the stadium, a crowd leaving. Already there were competitors dropped meters behind, with 19.6 kilometers to go.

Allardyce watched the last walkers leaving the stadium, felt the noise level of the stadium increase, like the rustling of one huge paper bag full of sandwiches, as he talked to Anna. For some reason, or reasons, he didn't want to look at her.

"It's what they want, Anna—I'm sorry, but that's the way it was put to me. Those *four areas of interest*, the case officer said." His face twisted in disgust, and Anna felt grateful for the sympathy such a look implied. "When you assure me that you have the necessary information, then I can outline the plan to you—" He looked at her then, suddenly, and she, seeing the boyish good looks, the unlined features, the fair hair, thought him inadequate for the task they had given him. She felt much stronger, much older, than he. "They haven't told me the actual details, just in case I tell you."

"Don't worry, David." She placed a cool, slim hand on his,

resting it there lightly for a moment. "I can obtain microfilm of those estimates when they are duplicated for circulation on Friday. They always intended to learn as much as possible on the defense budget allocations for next year before they let me come over—" She was smiling in a hard, humorless manner, staring down at the empty track, the officials looking like so many worker bees deserted by their ruler, and making abortive, scrabbling searches through the empty hive. She added, "I can't take a duplicate, you see. It has to be a clumsy, old-fashioned camera job. The machine that duplicates material for any Politburo or Chiefs of Staff meeting records every copy made, and you can't fool it—"

"Christ, Anna—I'm sorry. Sorry about the bloody mess that's being made of the whole thing!" She saw that his face was quite wild, and she had a momentary fear of him, and the possible weak link he might prove, should anyone suspect. Gennadi should not meet David Allardyce again, she decided.

"Don't worry, David. It is almost over now. I will get them their precious material—" She smiled, patted his hand.

A noise from the crowd, quite distinct, an urgent buzz of comment akin to fifty thousand pieces of identical gossip. Allardyce looked down at the track. Green track suit trousers, gold top. Australia. Irvine. Everyone knew that Irvine had been "helping the police with their inquiries." Perhaps they expected him to look broken, weak, unable to stand, bruised—? Allardyce sickened of an interest he could regard as nothing other than voyeuristic and gratuitous; and something that pressed upon him a sense of his own *detachment* from Anna Akhmerovna. He was little more than a spectator of her drama.

He suddenly envied Leonov, at the same moment he felt deeply afraid for the woman next to him.

"You go back to the press box, David. I'll see you when I have the information—" Her face went stiff, unsubtle with suppressed anger. "And, when I have it, I shall scream to be gotten out—"

He stood up, nodded—the gun, suddenly, startling him. He hadn't even noticed the athletes lining up for the first heat of the 10,000. They were crowding into the first bend as he looked down. He nodded to Anna again, then went quickly back up the steps toward the press box.

Leonov, coming into that block of the stand at that moment, recognized his retreating back, and his face darkened with rage. Then Anna saw him, and he waved, taking great care that he should not look in Allardyce's direction again.

Anna was puzzled at the intense way he looked at her face, as if studying it for some sketch he might make, before he sat down.

Irvine knew he was running it wrong, that he was going to go on running it wrong. He understood why. A hundred thousand people in the stadium had all become members of the KGB, assessing what they had done to him, how the last four days had affected his form.

He should not have been leading by the end of the fifth lap, with twenty still to go. Even if the pace was not particularly fast. He had no control over a challenged ego that pumped the adrenaline through his system; he was like some small animal in a laboratory experiment, massively injected with a stimulant, frantically burning off excess energy.

It was a good-to-average field, but the 10,000 was an event he could win easily. No one wanted to take the lead—he didn't himself, but was compelled to do it—and no one wanted to lose touch with him. He looked over his shoulder. A Finn, two East Germans, and a New Zealander bunched five meters back, then a straggle of runners who would drop away with each successive lap, then another, ordinary bunch making no impression on the race, no contribution to it—a British runner back there, a new boy whose Final might come next time around.

It would be so easy to let go now—four slightly faster laps, stretching everything out.

He was afraid of the thought, as if some circuit had fused in a flash of light, the sharp ozone smell. Rationality disappearing.

"He looks good—but dangerous."

"To himself, you mean?"

"That's just what I mean. The last three laps he picked up, and I really wonder whether he knows he's doing it." Greenberg rubbed his nose with thumb and forefinger. Allardyce scribbled, cigarette in the corner of his mouth as if he was trying to readopt the comfortable role of being nothing more than a journalist.

"That's the thirteenth—plenty of running left in Kenny," remarked a Sydney newspaperman from farther back in the press box. Allardyce presumed the chauvinism was to disguise the same nagging doubts felt by himself and Greenberg and perhaps most of the senior pressmen.

"It's quickening up—when there's no need," Greenberg whispered conspiratorially. "He could blow it." Allardyce nodded, studying Irvine down the straight below them through his field glasses. Irvine's face was that of a robot; he was obeying some command he could not dispute, and the crowd, buzzing faintly through the glass like so many insects, was doing that to him; the continual mutter had even reached the pressmen, making them appear cramped and uncomfortable, or bored or nervous. Buzz, buzz—what's happening down there?

Irvine was thirty meters up on the better East German and the Finn, with eleven laps left.

There was no sense of tiredness, of energy draining away. Rather, he knew that he had lost his sense of perspective. Always, in a race, there was a narrowing of awareness, a growth of concentration so that *this* race, and each segment of it, was the most important thing in the world. But never before, in the Commonwealth Games in '78 or the biggest meets in America, had he lost his sense of strategy, a strategy that extended beyond each step, each lap, each race to the goal of a series or a season. He had always had that.

Now, he could not see the Final of the 10,000, then the heats and the Final of the 5000 as part of this race, an extension of what he was doing in the twenty-eight minutes of this race. It wasn't a race. It was an exhibition.

The loss of perspective was a sapping blow to his psyche, to the entity he regarded himself as being when he ran. Like the buildup of lactic acid in mental muscles.

Lap eighteen. Seven more—to *what?* He felt something would end for him when he crossed the line. And he knew that they would come again, with their questions, with their oppressive presence in his life, as soon as he had finished the race.

He looked over his shoulder. East German, Finn, African again in touch, and the Spaniard bobbing away just behind them. They were all going to qualify.

He ran on, alone in something that was no longer a race.

"You can't keep a good man down!" the Sydney pressman exclaimed from behind them.

"Too true," came an Australian rejoinder. They had fallen in, Allardyce knew, looking at Greenberg, with Irvine's fiction down there, with the assertion of self, the recovery of identity that the race had become.

The Australians in the press box were looking at their watches every lap now, with five laps to go. They were cocky to hide their doubts, their reservations. Kenny Irvine was the best in the world, and he was bringing home the bacon. Question not.

"Poor bastard," Greenberg murmured.

"How so?"

"He's blown it. He'll win this—he might win the Final. But no way is he right for both Golds. The five thousand—he's giving it away with every lap."

Shubin, who had no interest in sport, found himself becoming obsessively interested in events in the Lenin Stadium. He sat for most of the day in the dispatch office of the warehouse off Kirov Street, watching the athletics. The others might have sold their tickets for the first day in an act of superstition, and pretended to indifference—but he found himself fascinated. Especially, he found the roving shots of the crowd, the splashes of color with blue predominating, plucked at his attention, made a small physical excitement in his limbs and chest.

He had commandeered a color TV from a Ukrainian in Moscow who wanted to contribute, but not much and without danger. Somehow, he needed the color images more than the monochrome of the other set, needed the vivacity, the solidity of color, especially for the glimpses, sweeps of color from the stands and the terraces.

Zenaida had telephoned him from the campsite as soon as the KGB had left, and before, in all probability, they set up good surveillance. He would not go back to the campsite now, and they would have to be instructed as to how to lose their tails when the moment came for them to move into Moscow itself.

Thinking about them—dragging his attention away from the hypnotic color images—they ought to move out at once. In a moment, he would ring them, get them away from surveillance, even if it declared their hand.

In the first aid box screwed to the wall of the dispatch office was the HE bomb that was their prelude, their drumroll before the big one. And the letters were in the old bureau that tottered against the same wall, beneath the first aid box. He had chosen their storage deliberately—the apparent harmlessness of the hiding places an irony he could savor.

Best irony of all. *Do pobachenya* itself. Untraceable, undetectable, because it had no ancestry of dissent, no history of activity. The children thought it was in the idealistic mold of the *Banderovtsy*, or the Ukrainian Helsinki group, most of whom were doing hard labor or in exile. But *Do pobachenya* was him—Shubin, with printers' ink from an underground press still under his fingernails, hands still callused from banner waving. No one could take *Do pobachenya* seriously, especially if they thought it was him behind it all.

We haven't made a sound, he told himself. Yet.

At the end of the race, which the Australian was going to win easily, he would ring Zenaida—someone would be standing by one of the public telephones, waiting for his twice-hourly safety call—and get them out of *Serebryany Bor* and into Moscow.

The Final of the 10,000 meters was on Saturday, the Russian commentator told him as Irvine began his last lap.

Saturday it was, then, Shubin decided.

The grouped officials, the finish line, the tape, all wobbling in his vision. Now he had thrown down such a declaration, he had to crown it—stride home easily down the last straight.

He didn't want to. He didn't want the race to finish, because then the questions would start again, and he would go back into small rooms full of people.

He was close to the Olympic record, and the second man—the East German—had to be a hundred meters or more back. The crowd, sensing some kind of vindication, something settled that was before in doubt, stood to him all the way to the tape.

Arms up, breast through the tape, slowing, jogging on, he felt as if he had hold of nothing, had embraced emptiness, as he slowed to a walk.

Anna Borisovna Akhmerovna blew smoke at the ceiling and tapped one foot with slight impatience on the office carpet while her secretary completed the last pages of the *Estimates for 1980–1981 Concerning the Fiscal Requirement for the Defense of the Soviet Union*. The abstracts, the prognostications, the requirements, the pleas and demands and the strategic studies all came down to a bundle of double-spaced sheets—no carbon—which would be photocopied and locked away, ready for distribution at the first meeting between the Politburo, the Main Military Council, and the representatives of the General Staff on Monday. A basis for discussion, for appropriation, and for policy.

She listened to the absence of noise from the corridor outside her office. Most of the clerical and secretarial staff had already gone home—Friday evening—and many senior officials had left for their dachas and weekend places, rushing out of the city as the business class did in New York to their second homes. The cleaners were on the ground floor, working their way up through the building preceded by security men who checked that desks were clear, files locked, shredders inaccessible, wastepaper bins unbetraying.

The single copy of the defense estimates would be copied as soon as typed—on the Japanese machine on the fifth floor—then locked in the principal Ministry strong room over the weekend, guarded and impregnable. If she was going to copy the principal sections of the estimates, then it would have to be done somewhere on the journey between her office and the fifth floor and the copier—or before they went into the strong room. She had an idea, but, at that moment, as she pretended the impatience of being kept late at work, she was more concerned with remembering the numbers of those pages she had to photograph.

Her secretary sat back, and rubbed her eyes, then her back. She had been typing continuously for the last four and a half hours, beginning as soon as the estimates were brought to the office by the Minister's senior aide. She sighed aloud, then yawned.

"Go on, Svetlana—get your coat on and go home to that husband of yours."

The girl smiled, stood up after taking the last sheet from the IBM typewriter, and shuffled the sheets into an orderly pile. She put on her jacket, picked up her handbag, and turned at the door.

"See you on Monday."

"You won't, my dear—I'm going to the Games."

"Lucky devil." Svetlana went out, closing the door behind her.

Anna calmed herself, reached down by her chair for her capacious shoulder bag, and then crossed to the secretary's desk. The sheets were in reverse order, just as Svetlana had laid them down from the typewriter. Anna looked at her watch.

Five fifty-eight. The senior aide would ring at any moment, to check on progress as he had done every half hour. She would be summoned to take the estimates up to his office, and accompany him during the copying operation, before he handed the material over to the security guard for safekeeping. She took the small camera with its steadying handle for one-hand operation from her bag. Atop its slim, matchbox shape was a tiny electronic flashgun. She photographed the last page of the estimates, shuffled it aside, did the next after pressing the wind-on trigger in the handle of the camera. Click—another page of clipped, precise, authoritarian conclusions from the General Staff and the Minister. Then another, and a fourth.

The telephone rang. Hastily, she picked it up.

"Anna? Alex. I don't hear the typewriter—all finished?"

"Yes, Alex—I'll bring them up at once. Just let me slip them into the impressive leather folder—" She laughed easily, without sign of effort, and complimented herself on her performance.

"O.K., Anna. I'll be glad to get away—I have a *promising* dinner date—" Alex was always attempting to convince her that his private life was overloaded with beautiful, attainable women and she had long ago ceased to consider the motives behind his revelations. "Oh, by the way—Vassily, my new assistant, is hanging about the building somewhere. I think he wants to drop in on you to escort the stuff up here—keen lad."

"Does he?" Anna said, observing the performance of her voice minutely. "Well, I won't wait for him—see you."

She listened. Nothing. Vassily, she was certain, was one of Leonov's men. Recently promoted into the Ministry, and military rather than Secretariat—in itself not unusual—he had, for Anna at least, the unmistakable aura of a policeman. Was he expecting to catch someone—now?

She looked at the camera, as if caught by a spotlight, then down at the sheet under her other hand. Her damp fingertips had left slight indentations on the paper. Vassily would wait somewhere—if he was what she thought him—until he saw Svetlana leave, then he would give her sufficient time to incriminate herself, then come in. He couldn't know, of course, and Gennadi Leonov wouldn't have ordered any special or specific watch on her. It was the estimates they'd be watching—

Click, shuffle, click. The meat, the final shape of the research and development funding, proposed and likely. *Four areas of interest*, Allardyce had said. Research and Development, Strategic Rocket Forces, Airborne Forces, and Submarine Armament Capacity (Increase/Alterations). Pages, pages—?

The numbers escaped her for just a moment, but it was

sufficient to cause her to begin perspiring, and to make her hand shake. She was keeping an animal at bay with nothing more than a nail file. She cocked her head, listening to the corridor again. She heard, distantly, the billowing noise as a vacuum cleaner started up on the floor below. The routine security check which preceded the cleaners would be there at any moment—as would Vassily, without doubt—

Pages 17–19, 5 and 6, 8–11, 22–24. She could remember them. And when they walked in, she would be standing over Svetlana's desk, a camera in one hand, and it would all be worth nothing except a long time in the Lubyanka—with trips to Moscow Center across an enclosed courtyard—before they put her down like a rabid animal.

What could she do—what? How could she *disguise* what she was doing—?

Hurriedly, she shuffled the remaining pages onto the floor, pushed them half under Svetlana's desk, then stooped by them, listening again. The noise of the cleaner would disguise any other sounds until the door opened. She flicked over three pages, found 22, and photographed it. She could feel the heat of the flashgun close to her face under the desk there—page, page 23, as she shuffled through, where was page 24, or 19? She couldn't find them, and began spreading out the sheets to take as many as possible because it was 6:01 now, and she should be on her way and where was 17, 17—?

Six oh-one. She realized the stupidity, the teetering figure on the edge of panic that she had become. And wrinkled her nose in disgust. Part of it, part of the whole thing, was her coolness under pressure, the game-playing, poker-table quality of the whole secret life. So—

She selected page 8 carefully, smiling. She would show this one to Allardyce, as a proof of what she had, and be damned to the rest of it. She had done enough, there was sufficient information in Langley and the Pentagon to program the satellites, make the right informed diplomatic inquiries, or mount the right penetration operations—

Page 8.

The door handle, turning. Her finger was slow, so slow, to depress the trigger, the electronic flashgun's light seemed to elongate in time, linger on the retina like an old-fashioned flashbulb, flash powder—

"Is that you, Vassily?" she called, putting the camera into her shoulder bag as she spoke, observing the timbre of her voice and knowing that her position behind the desk would disguise any nerves. "I've dropped the bloody papers all over the floor!"

The door closed. Footsteps hurrying muffled across the carpet, military boots coming round the desk—not Vassily, an older face, one of the security men.

"Sorry, Comrade Akhmerovna—what did you say?"

"Stay away!" she snapped. "I'll pick them up—you're not cleared for this stuff!"

The security man stepped back while Anna shuffled the papers, stood up, put them back on the desk. Anna looked up at the guard.

"Don't let anyone in until I tell you—*anyone*, understand?"

"Comrade," he murmured, and left the room. She sat down for a moment, wanted to laugh, was tempted to take more pictures since she had effectively barred Vassily from the room, then saw herself as a puppetlike figure, arms jerking, legs flung out, as if the strings that moved her were being cruelly, fiendishly tugged by a child. The image was quite clear, and pressed upon her.

She swiftly sorted the papers into order, placed them in the folder, and went to the door. The guard was outside, and Vassily was coming down the corridor. He seemed to approve her precaution of placing someone outside the door.

CHAPTER 10

Lydall, stroking the woman's angular body as if to smooth some of its angles and planes, or flatten the small breasts further, smiled at the idea that morning sex was just that in order to fit into his training schedule. Not that Harry wouldn't have forbidden it altogether, had he known about it. Puritanism and dedication in a deadly combination, which made Lydall broaden the smile that had begun by being for her, at her. Natalia had accepted her role, subordinated her erotic life to the demands of his schedule, just as she only cooked the kind of meal he prescribed for himself. Best of all, she didn't seem to worry about the caretaker of her block of flats, who she described as a "casual" for the KGB, like most of his kind.

She kept her eyes closed as if asleep. But her hip moved slightly against his hand, and her mouth pouted slightly when he stroked the flat of her stomach, above the pale thin pubic hair. She was pale, almost anemic, with light freckles across her narrow shoulders, and blue veins close to the surface of the white skin of her arms and breasts.

He was beginning to become involved with her, and the restless need to understand himself and his motives that often came to him when he ran, and in his job, seemed stilled, absent. He was afloat, these moments like a narrow raft which drifted.

He lay back, hands behind his head, and stared at the patch of damp in one corner of the room. The rain outside somehow chilled the room, made the patch seem bigger, as if the water threatened the ceiling above the bed. He pulled the sheet up over both of them, sensing a community, however fugitive, from the fact of their being covered by the same bedclothes, closed in, bound up together. He drifted into a light doze, thinking of training in the wet—Moscow and Barnsley linked together for some reason in his mind, for the first time.

Ten o'clock. Irena Witlocka huddled in her red track suit with its white-striped sleeves, the rain running down her neck from the wiry hair which held it like a bush, then spilled it as she shuffled her body, waiting for the qualifying rounds of the high jump to begin in a two-thirds empty stadium. The heats of the hurdles would begin in half an hour, then the 400 and 200 heats before lunch. The stadium would fill up for those. For the qualifying of the women's high jump and the women's pentathlon long jump, there wasn't the following.

She was sitting next to a West German girl, favored for a medal, and on her other side was the American number one, who might just make the Final. The qualifying height was one meter eighty. More difficult in the wet, despite the tartan track which was as good as any she had used as a takeoff surface.

A time without coaches, without officials, without the silent watchers who were now anonymous in the stands or watching Martin as he trained. She breathed deeply, got up, and walked, tugging her *cagoule* over her head, to take her first jump at one meter seventy-five. Just a warm-up.

Knots. Her stomach was suddenly in knots, swift as the coiling of a snake. She dropped the soaking blue *cagoule*, then slipped off the track suit.

She failed at the first attempt, to the surprise of most of her rivals.

"You *have* to find them." Kazantsev was briefing his team in one of the basement briefing rooms at the Center, and they all seemed so bloody young and keen and wet behind the ears to him; or a sleepless night had made him older. It was a simple, flat statement, carefully drained of all histrionics, all drama.

Though it was dramatic, even desperate. The disappearance of the group of kids—like the kids in front of him—from the campsite before he had time to install a proper surveillance team meant they were running from him. He had panicked Zenaida Federenka and her little team. And their flight told him that Shubin was in Moscow—Kiev couldn't find him, anyway—just as surely as if he'd seen him.

"It has to be today, or tomorrow. You do not have any time left of your own—all of it is borrowed. They're here for some very serious reason, not just for fun. They have to be stopped—*dead*."

He let his hand fall through the air, edge on, until it rested on the table behind which he was standing to address them. A casual movement; the size of his hand alone suggested an imperative.

He studied their faces. These were the bright boys—there

were two girls, he corrected himself, two of the best question-and-answer operators he had seen—graduates of the Lenin-Lomonossov University and the KGB training schools, professionals. He had no doubt of their abilities, their dedication. But somehow they were inured against a proper realization of what might happen, like children playing on the edge of a frozen pond, with no conception of their potential danger. They had been coddled, rewarded by the system to the point where their privileged places deep inside the Soviet state gave them a sense of the immortality all children possess—especially when skating on thin ice. They were KGB, this was Moscow: nothing could happen, nothing really *serious*—

He tried again.

"I know you think I'm a Ukrainian clod, and the next best thing to a primitive tribesman—" Smirks, one or two slight flushes of pink. "But at the risk of boring you, let me remind you that it wouldn't be the first time that we Ukrainians have tried to blow the shit out of you Russians—" He grinned. "This group, *Do pobachenya*, have something nasty up their sleeves. Your job is to rip the guts out of the Ukrainian underground in Moscow, and find the disappearing students." One man put his hand up. Kazantsev waved it aside. "I don't care how rough you have to get—smash the presses if it gives you a thrill, roust Ukrainian whores and black marketers, bully the dissidents—somebody knows where they are. *Make somebody tell!*"

When they had been dismissed, turned out onto the rainy Moscow streets, Kazantsev took the lift to his office, and rang Donetsk. Already he was contemplating suggesting to Puchkov that he return there—that the key, whatever it was, lay in the ordnance factory and the theft that was not a theft. He instructed Donetsk to pull in Belousov and the man Ghekh for more questions, then made an appointment to see Puchkov in the afternoon.

Then he stared moodily, for a long time, out of the foggy window, down into the courtyard of the Lubyanka, which was empty and gleamed in the rain like the gray, polished shell of a snail.

Eleven of them had achieved the qualifying height set for the Final, and the number, as with all Olympic jumping finals, was made up to twelve competitors, this time by the addition of a French girl who had struggled with the rain and her takeoff and trailing leg—she was a straddle jumper—all morning. Irena, once she had knocked off the bar on her first jump, only did it once more all the way to the qualifying height. Something in her settled, perhaps the dust of nerves settling after the swift passage of emotions, and she was able to concentrate, able to assess and weigh the emerging rivals. German, Canadian, Russian, a British girl, a Rumanian—

She had room, now that she was inside the competition, to know that a medal was hers. She would not define, even to herself, which one. But one of them, certainly.

She would be jumping in the Final when Martin was running in the first heat of the 5000. That made her shiver, and the little warm compact place she had become—a case for a medal—dissipated, and she became aware of herself in the context of her secret life again.

It was still raining. She thought, with a certain sense of futility, that she might have her hair washed and set at the village hairdressing salon, before the evening. The evening might bring Martin, or take her to Martin's room.

Anna met Allardyce in the Café Praga on the Arbat. She was almost certain she had not been followed from her apartment, and was more concerned that Allardyce should be similarly sure. At least he had taken the precaution of finding a table toward the rear of the café, where the light from the rainy windows seemed hardly to penetrate and the table lamps seemed to shed a secretive, inadequate light. She hung her sodden raincoat and umbrella on a stand, and took the seat opposite him. The café was full, mostly with visitors to Moscow. He nodded to her almost imperceptibly, and she was relieved to see that he attached a suitable importance to the meeting, presented a definite professionalism.

Allardyce remained an enigma to her, a casual lover for whom she now had nothing more than a vague, affectionate regard and little respect; she wondered what motivated Allardyce, wondered whether he knew himself. There were suggestions about him— glances, or momentary emotions—that indicated depths, hinted even at an ennui beneath his blandness which she felt it safer to avoid, and which he seemed careful to ignore. There was little to make him a *dependable* agent or contact or courier or salesman. Today seemed a good day.

"I wasn't followed. I won't ask about you," he said lightly. "Coffee?"

"Please," she said, concentrating on disguising any accent in her English. "That would be nice," she added by way of experiment.

He summoned the waiter—Allardyce being an expert in such

matters, as in seduction, she observed with acid amusement—and when her coffee had arrived, he said, "Filthy day. Did you get too wet?"

"No." She sensed his reluctance to proceed with business, and became irritated by it. There was no one close enough to eavesdrop on a conversation at normal volume. "I have the proof of my good offices with me," she prompted.

"Good, good—"

"Just one frame."

"One?" He paused, the cup almost at his mouth. He was puzzled. "Only one?" He seemed sorry, and afraid for her.

"One is all they are getting—until we're on the plane to Washington." She sipped the dark coffee, in command of the conversation as she had known she would be, exercising a new *control* of the situation that pleased her, which she enjoyed as some indulgence of taste or emotion long suppressed. "You see, David, I don't trust them anymore. They will see from the frame number that I have a lot of material besides, but they will not acquire it unless I get out—on schedule."

She watched Allardyce change sides, the concern become amusement in his eyes. He nodded, smiling.

"Oh, yes—I like that." The waiter passed the table. Allardyce sipped his coffee, then offered her a cigarette. She leaned forward for it to be lit. He said, "You are a remarkable woman, Anna—he's a lucky man."

"Who—?" she asked, a catch in her throat, her brusque, calm manner caught on some thorn. "Lucky I shall be leaving him behind, you mean?"

"Sorry," he murmured. "Give it to me, then. I'll persuade our masters that you are adamant, and that you have all the correct stuff because I've seen the rest of the film—" She knew he was almost certain the CIA was being shortchanged, but he did not concern himself. Except for a tinge of enjoyment. Unlike her, he'd been blackmailed, his future made suddenly uncertain and cloud-hidden, and he didn't mind his masters being cheated.

"Thanks." She fished in her bag, brought out an envelope that was stamped and addressed. "Under the ten-kopeck stamp, of course. Page eight, as a foretaste."

"An aperitif—I'm sure it's appetising—" Then his tone changed as he saw that the hand she extended to pass the envelope was shaking. "What is it?"

"Collapse of stout party," she said, fighting to control her lip, which was quivering. Her eyes, likewise, appeared moist. "I'll be all right."

"They're shits to a man," he said, pressing her hand, pocketing the envelope. The surreptitiousness of the action caused his concern to appear hollow.

"I got—into it by myself. I offered my services for money, like any tart." She was in control of herself again, Allardyce observed. A carapace had regrown.

"You didn't do it for the money." He looked into his empty cup. "More coffee—something stronger?"

She shook her head.

"I got into it through fear—yes, you're right. I asked for money—a lot of money—because idealists always get taken for a longer ride than the greedy. Strictly cash deals, evidence of deposits made in a numbered account—I even have pictures of the home they're going to provide for me." She smiled bitterly. "It—yes, it's all nasty, like stepping in dog's mess on the pavement," she continued acidly. "Just tell them, David—tell them there will be no more delays, no more prevarication—either they get me out, or they get no more than that one page!"

Allardyce nodded.

"I'll tell them."

"Only that—don't describe the stupid woman who almost cried and who did everything because she was afraid that the next war was about to start when she began her secret life." She stubbed out her cigarette. "Don't ever tell them that."

Nobody wanted to stop, to talk to CKR-TV, whether Russian, American, or any other nationality. The beating rain—it was sweeping across Red Square in great gray wintry curtains by four in the afternoon, an hour before the 10,000 meters Final—was driving visitors to shelter in museums and art galleries, where they would stare moodily, dripping wet onto block floors or strips of faded carpet, into glass cases or up at icons and paintings, asking themselves endlessly when the rain would stop. Muscovites had taken to overcoats and plastic raincoats and galoshes and umbrellas and pretended they did not speak delaying English as they hurried past, bent as if with the weight of the rain.

Karen Gunston was dressed to combat the weather, but nothing in her nature prevented her from being bored, frustrated, angry, and cold. Thrusting her microphone under forty or fifty noses, and getting perhaps two or three minutes of usable film—to the camera crew's damp irritation which warmed itself at the small flame of her growing discomfiture—was not something she enjoyed, or was prepared to continue indefinitely.

If she was honest with herself—and as the water ran off her umbrella just in front of her face, she was prepared to be honest—she was bored with the Olympic Games. Of course, the permit to film street interviews had been granted before she arrived in Moscow; but she had taken it up, with its incumbent security man, who did not seem to mind the wet, and its agreement to censorship if necessary, only because the days of competition, seven now, had worn away any enthusiasm she might have been able to pretend in order to be CKR's lady at the Games.

She looked at her watch. Four-twenty. Al, her director, and the rest of the CKR personnel would be at the Lenin Stadium, or picking up film action from the basketball or the weight lifting or the swimming—a couple of poor slobs were out at the rowing, getting drowned on a mobile unit. But most of them were in the dry, and doubtless laughing into their beards and beer at her idea of "local color."

An American—the cancerous tumor of a camera beneath his plastic raincoat, summer shoes and splashed light slacks. She moved forward, and Jerry held the umbrella over her.

"Sir—could you give CKR Los Angeles a little of your time—?"

Because it was so wet, perhaps she allowed herself to be deterred by the evil look on his broad, lined face, by the disgust and anger at the weather that she saw in the eyes beneath the broad-brimmed hat. His wife seemed attracted by the camera, but he dragged her away in silence.

"Jesus," she whispered.

"Hey, Karen, can we give up on this—?" Larry was shining and wet in his *cagoule*, the camera bobbing on his shoulder like a settling rooster.

"Screw it!" she snapped.

The line of people in front of the Lenin Mausoleum was smaller than usual—a few straggling faithful and the more stubborn or inured of the tourists. But at least they were a captive sample of humanity.

"Hey, Ivan the Terrible—" she called, addressing the security man whose English was excellent and who seemed not to resent the soubriquet. "Can we move along the line of the faithful over there—?" She pointed at the Mausoleum, red granite more inhospitable than ever under the gray cloud and washed by the rain, and to the damp little line of people snaking into its open mouth.

"Of course," he said, grinning, apparently dry beneath his huge umbrella.

"O.K., team—let's get over there. And try and generate a little enthusiasm, uh?"

There was a concerted silence.

Federenko was living at his flat, not in the village. The Soviet Organizing Committee had made the gesture of housing the Russian team in the Olympic Village, but turned a blind eye if any of their competitors preferred residence outside its enclosing fence. All competitors from other countries, of course, had no choice in the matter—unlike Montreal where many athletes chose to live outside the village compound, in hotels and motels, even the homes of relatives and friends.

Kazantsev had saved himself a wasted journey to the village by checking the flat first. He had come by taxi, but had stopped the driver a couple of blocks away from Federenko's flat, so that he could walk, get soaked, and thereby add physical substance to the anger he wished to impress upon the athlete. He had no doubt that Federenko was innocent of any involvement—even any knowledge—of *Do pobachenya*; but he might know where Zenaida was, or where she might be.

He didn't sit down, deliberately, for some time, preferring the impression he made dripping rainwater on the carpet, and bulking in the room, threatening its compactness. He moved in sudden, jerking movements, and his voice was studied and harsh.

"Listen to me, Arkady Timofeyich—" He used the man's patronymic in ironic familiarity, to isolate him from his sister and make him side with the policeman who wanted only to help. "We know she has something to do with this dissident group—I call them only dissidents at the moment—not *terrorists*." He let the word affect Federenko before he went on. The young man seemed to emerge from some self-centered awareness, as if Kazantsev had clicked his fingers before someone in a mild hypnotic trance. "But—I think they mean business. I don't know what business, but something very nasty—maybe a bombing—" Pause for effect, watch the young man's eyes widen, mouth open to protest. "Yes, maybe. They disappeared, as I said, as soon as we got close to them.

Shubin came with them to Moscow, with false papers, and now they've all gone under cover. No one connected with them used any of the tickets I gave you to send. So—I panicked them." His voice was sharper, breaking the narrative thread. "Where are they?"

"I don't know—"

Kazantsev sat opposite him, probably marking the easy chair with his wet raincoat, which he could smell in the warmth of the flat as it dried out.

"You know her. Think, man—! Has she got friends in Moscow, any links you know of?"

Federenko frowned conscientiously. Kazantsev could see the fear, the very real concern. But he sensed ignorance also, and perhaps the self-delusion that Federenko had sustained until then. Zenaida was O.K., nothing would happen, nothing come of her relationship with Shubin—

"Shubin is a madman—a nut," Kazantsev offered persuasively. "He's capable of anything."

"I warned her—" Federenko began.

"Where could she be? What about Shubin's contacts here?" Kazantsev knew he had more idea than Federenko, but he asked nevertheless.

"I—Christ, Lieutenant, I don't know anything—!" The self-deceit becoming self-criticism, so that Kazantsev would have to prompt him again, bully him into remaining attentive to his priorities.

The telephone rang. Federenko appeared startled, then, as he glanced at Kazantsev, secretive and afraid.

"Pick it up."

"Yes—yes, Arkady Federenko," he remembered to say. Then, even before Federenko spoke again, even though he could hear only the tinniest whisper from the receiver, Kazantsev knew from the way Federenko's mouth dropped open and he looked at him that it was Zenaida—"*Zenushka*—!" Protective diminutive—there was no way he could stop himself calling her name, even though Kazantsev was leaning toward him as if to snatch the telephone.

"Keep talking," he whispered fiercely, demanding cooperation.

"Zenushka—the police—have been here, looking for you—" Kazantsev nodded, partly with relief. Federenko was a good boy—training, privilege, protective fear for his sister, inherited fear of authority, all combined to make him cooperate. For a time—

Kazantsev stood up, and Federenko flinched as if threatened.

Kazantsev waved his hands, mimicked that he should keep talking, pointed to the door, made a dialing gesture. Federenko nodded, nodded—

Kazantsev ran to the stairs, bullocked down the first half-flight, frightening a cleaner, bounced off the wall, took the next half-flight, raincoat flying behind him, the next flight, down, turn, down, turn, as if the block of apartments was endlessly high.

Telephone in the entry—free. He dialed the Center, his heart pounding, his breath coming in great heaves, his mouth filled with phlegm he found difficult to swallow.

"Trace—quick! Fuck who it is—it's Kazantsev, you idiot! Trace an incoming on Moscow—" He paused, visualizing the number on the receiver, then gave it. "Got that? Get moving—it's the girl ringing her brother—"

The caretaker of the apartment block had come out of his office, and was staring at the stranger. Kazantsev put down the telephone, stared up at the half-erased scrawl of felt-pen graffiti—*Dynamo*, and *Fuck the KGB*, to which another hand had appended *and Leonid's old mother*. He laughed, perhaps out of relief, perhaps anxiety, perhaps just an exhalation of breath louder than the others.

The caretaker had his hands on his hips, but was already recognizing the authority, the assuredness that meant KGB. Kazantsev gave him a two-fingered salute as he began to ascend the stairs again, and the caretaker heard him yell "And Leonid's old mother!" as he began running again.

Zenaida looked around her secretively as she spoke to her brother. She could see nothing through the fog of her nerves on the cold glass chilled by the rainsqualls across Red Square. She was uptight, she knew—perhaps that was why she had left the patient line and made this telephone call to Arkady. Not for comfort, but just so she could let off some steam, watch the nerves dispel, cloud the glass of the phone booth.

"Listen to me, Arkady—it doesn't matter about the KGB. They don't know where I am. No one does. They can't do anything—"

His voice at the other end, something strange about it, but perhaps only his fear for her strangling the words.

"Zenushka—please, Zenushka! They know about you—they know *who* you are—! They'll find you, eventually."

"It doesn't matter—" she began.

"It does, Zenushka. What will happen to you—what will happen to *us*?"

"Zenushka is dead, Arkady—can't you understand that? A long time ago. You can't pretend to yourself any longer—" She realized that she was shouting, but it was as if the opaque glass protected and muffled her. She felt her stomach settle, the pluck of uncertainty at her heart and her eyelid slowly disappearing. "You can sit there, Arkady, and take what they care to hand out—but not me. Not anymore. Shubin is right—you're spineless, you're a spineless *toady!*" That hurt her, cost her an effort, a catch in the breath which followed. But she persisted. "*Do pobachenya* will make an impact—a big bang—" She wanted to giggle at the unintended pun. "A bang the whole world will hear! The Soviets are going to regret they ever held the Olympics in Moscow!"

"Zenaida—for Christ's sake, Zenaida—! Listen to me!" He, too, was shouting, as if they were on opposite sides of a chasm, and could hardly hear each other, could not reach each other. "Don't be a fool, don't *do* anything—!"

"Just sit and be crapped on? Like you. Good-bye, Arkady—*Do pobachenya.*"

"No—!"

She slammed the phone down on that last squeal, and stood up straight in the booth, as if unbending from a great weight. As she opened the door and went out into the sweeping rain, she felt very calm, very certain.

Kazantsev appeared in the doorway of Federenko's lounge, a huge, threatening shadow. It was as if he saw his sister close to the policeman, in some obscene embrace, or with her arm twisted up behind her back—a tiny, vulnerable figure. Federenko still had the receiver in his hand, held perhaps a foot from his cheek.

"Well?" was all he could say, his breath wheezing.

Federenko shook his head, then put down the receiver even as Kazantsev moved forward to take it.

"She rang off—" The posture of the athlete's form, slumped in the chair, informed Kazantsev that he had not warned her; he was stunned, nevertheless, by what he had heard.

"Hello—trace?" Kazantsev dialed the Center in a flurry of fingers, trying to calm his breathing. "Who's that? Maxim—any luck?" He paused, nodding his head to the voice Federenko could not hear. "Shit! Nothing—?" Pause. "O.K., not your fault." He put down the receiver. Looming over Federenko. "What did she have to say, your kid sister?"

"Strange—" Federenko observed, then returned to some inward contemplation.

"Did she say where she was—what it was they intended doing?" Federenko shook his head. "How did she sound?"

"Excited—I can't think of anything else, just the *excitement* in her—" Suddenly he seemed startled awake. "She didn't say—but it must be *now!*"

"How do you know?"

"She was trying to—cut herself off from me. Working herself up to something—"

"And you don't know what?"

"No."

"*Shit—!*"

Irvine felt his stomach lurch, as if he were drunk or bloated with unpalatable food. Jogging back and forth, like most of his rivals, waiting to be called to the start, he was acutely and fearfully aware of his physical condition. The adrenaline was like an injection to make him vomit. He had no perspective now, only a consuming, growing fear that he would not win this race. The noise of the crowd, their tension and excitement, came to him like a nauseous odor or a growing claustrophobia.

Small rooms, full of people. A crush like the beginning of a middle distance race. *This race*, he told himself. In four years' time, he would be too old, there would be others faster, better. He had to win it.

Ten thousand meters. Twenty-five laps. A little more than six miles.

His mind picked at the rivals—the East German and the Finn from his own heat, a Kenyan and a New Zealander from the second one. But as his eyes swept, as if shifty or unwilling, over the assembled field, each of them became a rival, and he no longer knew how to run the race. He had not had time to think. Whenever they left him alone, he only wanted his head to go quiet and his mind blank, to close his eyes and hear the silence.

He was sweating like a nervous colt. Prancing aimlessly, continually startled, waiting for the whistle.

From the press box, Allardyce and Greenberg watched the fair hair become more lank as the rain soaked Irvine, as if they were watching some litmus of his condition. The track was pooled with water along the straight below them, and the conditions were against a fast time.

"He looks terrible," Allardyce confirmed, putting down his field glasses.

"Poor bastard looks beaten already," Greenberg retorted. The Australians in the press contingent were silent, their nerves as palpable as those of the runners. "You know they'll drop all charges tonight—uh?"

"How do you know?"

"Just a guess—"

"You mean—"

"I don't mean a thing. But Irvine won't win this race, never mind the five. He's blown. The publicity the cops have got out of it is bad already—if they keep it up, then no one will believe Irvine's anything but a martyr."

Allardyce nodded.

"Poor sod. You really don't think he'll make it?"

Greenberg shook his head. Below them, the runners bunched at the start, prompted by the whistle. Allardyce picked up his glasses again, watched the drenched starter with his plastic raincoat over his blazer and flannels, his trilby hat pouring water as he moved his head, raising his arm, then he looked again at Irvine. The others looked like drowning rats; Irvine had already drowned. The unhealthiness of his appearance struck Allardyce—white face, hair plastered down the sides of his face, held off his brow with a check-ered headband, gold vest hanging limply on a frame that in its half-bent posture appeared thin and consumptive.

"Poor sod," he said again.

Puff of smoke, report of the gun. A surge into the first bend like the rush at sale time when the doors first open, everyone wanting the one fur coat—elbows, legs, body thrust to be out of the bunch, on the inside.

Irvine was twelfth as they stretched a little more into the first back straight, the Finn leading.

Zenaida looked at her watch, prompted by the changing of the guard, which happened every hour. Five. Only the two immobile sentries outside of course, the ones for show, not the security men inside that checked the bags and the cameras. She hated the arrogant stamp of the men coming on duty, the goose step of the two who were relieved. They marched, looked, as if there was no rain or that it had not dared make them wet.

The American woman with the film crew was working her way along the line of visitors, Russian and foreign, and Zenaida kept breaking into a nervous, amused smile at the thought of being interviewed by her.

Not that she would, or could, say anything. But she relished, like a child's secret or comforter, the hope that the film camera would still be there in another hour, having recorded everything that happened in Red Square. It would be that extra, irrefutable witness.

They were almost at the bronze doors, standing on the first of the ascending steps. Yakov had the bomb under his raincoat, the work of a few moments to arm it. She pictured the panic they would cause. It was like someone leaning against a solid structure which suddenly reveals its cardboard pretense, and wobbles, threatens to collapse.

The rush hour just beginning in Red Square—fleets of taxis, the hundreds of buses already beginning to be washed into the place as if by a tide, to logjam by 5:30. And the Mausoleum open later than its habitual four o'clock closing because of the number of visitors to Moscow during the Olympics—

Even forming the word deliberately, she observed that there was no immediate flicker or image of Arkady, her brother. She had to consciously attend to the idea of him before he would come. That was a satisfaction.

In through the doors, taking the steps to the left, down to the chilly vault where the remains of V. I. Lenin lay, garishly illuminated like a circus sideshow or a pop spectacular. Shuffle, shuffle, down each of the porphyry steps, the smell of damp clothes like the smell of a recently opened tomb.

The guards searched the hand luggage, looked at the cameras, and warned that photographs must not be taken—as if they feared too many exposures, too many slides and prints, might extract what remained of reality in the mummified corpse. Zenaida looked at Yakov as the guard handed back her shoulder bag, and smiled—a damp, nervous little smile.

Shubin had shown them the place the previous day, on a map. Kostya had checked it out visually. A bend in the staircase on the other side of the vault, whereby visitors ascended. A shadowy corner where it would not be seen for just long enough. Yakov had practiced arming the bomb blindfold, by touch alone. He could do it under his raincoat, then release the webbing holding it to his chest, lower it to the floor—almost without pausing. If she stood behind him, twisted her ankle, and had to stop, no one would see. They had practiced, practiced in the warehouse, the empty space echoing to Shubin's bullying until they got it right. Perfect.

Shuffle, shuffle—

Last step. No one was allowed to stop in the vault. Yakov, suddenly grinning at her, took off his woolen hat, which was heavy with rain, and moved in front of her. He put the hat in his pocket, then both hands into the pockets. She could see no movement beneath the coat.

Four guards. She wanted to spit at them, even spit at the glass of the box in which the corpse stared at the ceiling, or at the harsh lighting, in disdain and indifference. *Just like life,* Shubin had joked. She remembered it now, realizing as she pushed down the rebellious humor that it was caused by nerves. Kostya, who was by now phoning Shubin, having been posted outside the windows of GUM on the other side of the square ready to observe their disappearance into the Mausoleum, had added, *Is he stuffed, or just preserved?* They had all laughed the laughter of relief, of rising nerves, at that.

One guard at each corner of the glass box, outside the railing. Even now V. I. Lenin had no real contact with his people, Zenaida observed. They simply filed past—

Out of the vault, onto the first step. Which one—? Fifth. Three, four—she stumbled, cried out as if she had twisted her ankle. Someone muttered in irritation, but then an arm held hers, which startled her, but she saw it was an American, heard him ask, "You all right, young lady?" She nodded. "Steps are kind of slippery—uh? You know what material they are, by any chance?" She shook her head, wanting to laugh. She rubbed her ankle. "You O.K. now?" She tested her weight. Someone pushed past them, giving her an evil look from under his wet cap. She wanted to poke out her tongue, because Yakov had already gone. He had done it.

"Thank you," she said, smiling. She walked gingerly a couple of steps, turned back, and smiled again. "Thank you very much."

She could hardly see the slim knapsack, pressed against the wall of the niche into which Yakov had lowered it, then shunted it with his foot.

It might be spotted, she thought as she reached the doors again, and saw Yakov waiting for her. It would depend on timing—

An identifiable noise—a telephone ringing down in the vault.

Then, as she linked arms with Yakov and they headed across the square, threading through the thickening traffic, to pick up Kostya, she heard an alarm bell ringing, as if someone had robbed Lenin's tomb.

Shubin cut the call from Kostya, and immediately dialed the number of Moscow Center, a number not at all secret in the Soviet Union. He was grinning as he waited for the connection, and preening himself for the little conversation that would ensue. The children had done well—now he had to raise the alarm before someone innocent—and therefore stupid with bombs—found the knapsack and what it contained.

"Antiterrorist Squad, please," he asked just as he might have asked for any extension number in any office. A bluster of curiosity, denial, suspicion. Shubin chose his moment, then he said, "Perhaps if you haven't done it already, you should try to trace this call. It is not a hoax. There is a bomb in the Lenin Mausoleum at this moment, timed to explode in thirty minutes. Just pass the message on, will you? *Do pobachenya.*"

He put down the receiver, threw back his head, and laughed, helplessly, triumphantly.

Lap five. Two groups of runners had established themselves, with the New Zealander seemingly stranded between them, the Finn and the East German leading the first group of five, and Irvine at the back of the second group of six, fifty meters down on the Finn as he splashed through the shallow trough of water that had formed despite the tartan track and its excellent drainage on the straight below the grandstand and the press box. Allardyce felt depressed by the sight of Irvine, head hanging, water splashing his legs a dirty brown, his position in the field immobile and unchanging, except that it suggested a gradual slipping back toward the straggling bunch gradually losing touch.

"Come on, Kenny," moaned an Australian voice behind Allardyce, who looked at Greenberg as an adult with superior knowledge of events might look at another adult, confident of greater experience than the child who had spoken.

"He's knackered," offered a British pressman from a safe distance, already preparing his copy on Irvine's collapse, and the possible KGB responsibility for his lack of form.

"Wait and see," the Australian offered glumly, as if defending a belief he had renounced but for which he retained a sentimental affection.

"Christ, how can you kid yourself—?" the Englishman remarked but abandoned the comment, perhaps aware of its rancor.

Irvine was on the back straight, a curtain of rain between him and Allardyce's view through the foggy window of the press box. Dropping back on lap six, at that point a quarter through the race, where the crowd, where the hundreds of millions of television viewers, where the press, where his coach—would all begin to accept that he would never make up lost ground, lost time.

Allardyce's depression seemed to deepen. He distracted his gaze to the unfamiliarly empty seat where Anna usually sat. And realized that perhaps his edginess, his mood, arose from that, rather than from what increasingly appeared like Irvine's failure.

Kazantsev turned at the head of the stairs as Federenko called him. He had heard the telephone ring, and had almost turned back in the hope that it might be the man's sister again—but Federenko simply said, "Your office—" His face expressed urgency, carried the stamp of someone's panic, and Kazantsev feared the worst.

"Yes?"

"Oleg?" It was Puchkov. For a moment, Kazantsev wondered if the man was annoyed at their broken appointment for five. "Get down here straightaway—there's a bomb in the Mausoleum. We're evacuating now—"

"What type?"

"We don't know—I've got everyone out of there—it's murder in the square—the traffic—"

"I'll meet you there."

He slammed down the telephone, and looked once at Federenko.

"What is—?"

"Your little sister and her playmates have just left a bomb in the Lenin Mausoleum. Supposed to be a joke, is it?"

He did not wait for a reply, but ran from the flat, hurtling down the stairs, through the foyer, out into the rain to hail a taxi.

Lap nine. The New Zealander had slipped back into the second bunch, which now numbered only four. Irvine was still in touch with it, deaf to the siren call of the stragglers, now a third of a lap behind. The Finn and the East German were still alternating the lead in the first group, and forty meters up on the second group. The time was slow—nothing to do with the weather, only with the tactics of the race. And everyone knew that Irvine was beaten, not even among the medal chances. Even at the slow pace, he was making no impression.

There are 150,000 private cars in the Moscow metropolitan area, and 25,000 taxis, while 700 buses or trolleybuses serve the Marx Prospekt on the other side of the Kremlin every peak hour, and perhaps two-thirds of that number pass through Red Square. There are sufficient passengers for three hundred metro trains an hour during the peak at the three main stations around Red Square.

As Kazantsev arrived, running down 25th of October Street into the square, flashing his ID card to any policeman who challenged him, weaving and doglegging through the congealed traffic, it seemed that the three main streets—October, Kuibyshev, and Razin—had spilled all the traffic of the city into Red Square. Between St. Basil's and the Historical Museum, the Kremlin walls and GUM, there seemed nothing but a dense undergrowth of vehicles from within which the animal calls of horns sounded in a cacophony—above which could be heard the pleading of sirens as police, ambulance, and fire services tried to force their way toward the Mausoleum.

Rain, flashing lights on top of vehicles, crowds gathering with police frantically trying to keep them back behind hasty trailing ropes and red-and-white barriers. Everything conspiring with *Do pobachenya*, the children, the dangerous children.

Kazantsev felt a panic, a sense of being too late, even as he eased through the last of the crowd, halted like a tide a hundred meters from the Mausoleum. The strangest thing was the absence of the two sentries either side of the open bronze doors.

Puchkov was standing beside a bomb squad pickup, the microphone for the loudspeaker on its roof, in his hand. He looked old and wet and not in control. Beside him, three of Kazantsev's team were donning antiblast visors, chest and thigh padding, and their throat mikes.

"Oleg!" Relief was evident in Puchkov's voice. Kazantsev saw the smiles, welcoming and nervous both, as he appeared. A sudden feeling of desperation and inadequacy appalled him. Kids, playing with bombs—the terrorists and the antiterrorists. None of them has seen a body blown apart, except pictures from Belfast or Rome. None of them knew—

The noise all around them was like a cry of protest, their experience was inadequate, futile.

Kazantsev stooped, picked up a chest shield, webbing dangling, from the rear of the pickup. Puchkov's hand was on his arm immediately.

"What kind of bomb?"

"We don't know. Just a knapsack, wedged into a niche on the steps up from the vault—that's all we know."

"Then it isn't—?"

Puchkov shook his head.

"We're pretty sure it isn't—unless the knapsack is a blind. It's not likely—"

"O.K.—let's get on with it."

Puchkov looked at Kazantsev. The hand on his sleeve was now a restraint.

"No, Oleg—the team's going in without you. The boys are ready."

Kazantsev looked at the three pale faces, the antiblast visors held in the crook of each arm like a knight's helmet. He turned Puchkov away from them, and whispered fiercely, "I have to go in—it's my job."

Puchkov seemed flustered, disturbed—but impelled, too.

"No, Oleg. I know there are risks—but with an FAE device *possibly* in the city—" He nodded. "You know it's possible one was stolen, and unaccounted for since. If that's the case, *you* have to be alive to do it. If anyone is going to get hurt in there—" He tossed his head toward the Mausoleum fifty yards away. "It isn't going to be you. And that is an order."

An ambulance siren, trying to bluster through the traffic jam, sounded portentous and keening to Kazantsev.

Lap thirteen. No injection of pace from the leading group, who seemed to have succumbed to the constant brainwashing of the conditions. The race was something to be endured, something to be gotten through. Totally unlike an Olympic Final, so that even the crowd was muted in its reception; reaction and response almost absent.

And most of them hadn't noticed that Irvine was leading the

second group, and that the gap had narrowed again to just over thirty meters.

The three young men waved from the doors of the Mausoleum.

"Testing, testing," Kazantsev said mechanically into the microphone. "Number off, you clowns—"

"One here."

"Two, chief."

"And three."

"Good. Now, just stay cool—and keep up the running commentary. I want to mark this as a test."

One of them laughed. Looking up, he saw them disappear into the doorway, three padded tire men with black visors covering their faces, packs on their backs making their figures even more grotesque. He had tried—dismally, he considered—to keep the mood light, to prevent them realizing why he wasn't with them.

"Steps now—"

"At least we're in the dry."

He could almost hear the echoing cold of the interior, certainly hear their repeated, rasping breaths in the empty space. He could see them taking each step gingerly. Just boys, clever, trained children.

Puchkov had walked off to supervise crowd control, handing over command of the operation to him. As if he had expended all his will and nerve just keeping Kazantsev out of the Mausoleum.

"What's happening?" he snapped, regretting the tone instantly.

"We're on the spot—sir." A stiff, angry tone, as if he were nursemaiding.

"O.K. Describe it."

"Knapsack's open at the top—someone smuggled it in under his coat by the look of the webbing."

"Good. Can you see the mechanism?"

"No—going to lift back the flap—now." Pause, and Kazantsev listened across the fifty yards with one ear, to the earphone with the other.

"That's it—that's got his pajamas off—" He'd remembered a joke about surgeons. No good telling him not to be stupid, forget the levity. It was keeping them calm.

"What can you see?"

"There's a booby trap, chief. Time clock for the detonator—but a trip on it as well—"

"Can you dismantle it—the trip?" He wanted to ask them to describe it in detail, so that he could coach them, but knew he must not.

"Let's have a look. It looks like—yes, it is."

"What?"

"Another wire, a much thinner one. Disconnect the clock, and you haven't disconnected anything—"

"Can you bring it out?"

"Better to do it here—in the dry—" Another chuckle. "Old Vladimir Ilyich will have to put up with it—" Then, "Go and see if the old bugger's still asleep, eh?" Laughter, faint over the mikes, echoing. He had to say it now.

"Describe it to me—in detail!"

Lap seventeen. The closing second group now perhaps twenty-five meters adrift of the leading four, having swallowed a second East German. Irvine had put in four moderately quicker laps, taking the second group with him and burning nobody off, but catching up with the leading group, where no one—as if they were in a separate race where only one of them could fail to win a medal—would stretch out and try to lose the others. And they could not act in sufficient concert to move farther ahead of the pursuing group.

Irvine thanked his gods for being able to comprehend the race at last, as if he had escaped from some mental straitjacket. The point for him had come in the twelfth lap—when he had wanted to throw back his head and bay at the gray, pouring clouds, stand in the middle of the track, and scream out everything that had happened to him, until he was purged of it.

Instead, something had taken hold of the sagging will, snapped fingers to the straying, dulled brain, and made it attend. Now the tiredness in his body was the result of effort in the race, not the leaden futility invested in it before. He had shrugged something off, and now he knew he was going to win.

Like a litany, he chanted to himself in each breath through gritted teeth.

Fuck the KGB, fuck the KGB—fuck the East German, fuck the Finn, fuck the Kenyan—

Hate, however forced and artificial, was a good substitute for sound psychological preparation. At least, as they began lap eighteen, it seemed to be.

Karen Gunston was at his elbow almost before he realized it. When Kazantsev saw her, heard her words, saw the microphone thrust at him, he was furious.

"American lady—I don't have the time," he said levelly, not even wondering why she was allowed inside the barriers, and with the film crew. Then he saw Puchkov behind her, his face explaining, his eyes glancing to the sky. Someone higher up had decided that this whole thing would be a propaganda triumph for the KGB and the Soviet Union. There was no way in which the incident could be hushed up, or played down—too many foreign witnesses, which was presumably what the dangerous children wanted—so the foreign film crew were permitted to film, to interview—

"Go away, lady. I'm busy. Talk to my chief." He turned his back on her. Of course the film would be censored appropriately. The cynicism behind it apalled him.

"Right, listen carefully. You have to remove the second battery, the one feeding the trip. Where is it?"

"Under the main part of the bomb."

"Can you cut into the bag, get at it then? One wire would be enough." He rubbed his face. "What time have you?"

"About ten minutes—ten minutes and fourteen seconds, to be precise."

"O.K.—cut open the bag."

"He must have carried this like a baby—"

"He did."

"Right—beginning to cut the bag open now."

Lap nineteen. Twenty meters, and Irvine knew they were closing. And behind him, his chasing group had begun to straggle out, lose contact with him. He was suspended, alone and the focus of the world's attention, between the two groups. *That* enticed him, drove him now. Everyone in the world hung on what he was doing, whether he would make it.

He splashed down the straight again, with five laps left, and he could hear the swelling murmur of the crowd. Not because the race was three-quarters done, but because of what he was doing.

"Yes, that's it. Simple twist in the wire down here."
"Make sure of that."
"Yes, chief—yes, that's what the bugger did—twisted them together when he switched on the clock. Careful—!"
"What's happening?"
"Boris almost tipped the whole thing over, securing it. Clumsy sod."
"Take it easy—"
"Right, here we go—" The silence went on forever, the rain pouring down on his bare head, running down his neck, the crowd caught in a cone of silence, as if they had been warned of the approach of some climax in the drama. Even the sirens and horns seemed to have stopped.
"O.K.—"
"What?"
"Simple. Twist, untwist. Just a delay—"
"Right. Get that thing out of there and into the sealed van—"
Kazantsev looked at the squat olive green shape of the lead-lined truck in which the bomb would now be placed.
"Don't worry, boss—I can get the clock disconnected now. It's a quick job—"
"Get out of there. That's an order."
"Only needs a couple of minutes—"
A short silence, Kazantsev about to lose his temper, then another voice, perhaps that of Boris.
"Fuck—there's an egg timer behind the bomb—!"
"Get out of there, now!" Kazantsev heard himself scream.

Three laps to go, and he was fighting the track, the rain, the tiredness spreading through his legs, up from his calves to his thighs—and fighting to hang on to the three runners left in front of him who had at last sensed and seen his approach, seen their medals threatened. The crowd's noise—the roar of a sea—spurred them now, enclosed them as before it had been entirely for him. The crowd sensed a close finish, a dimension of excitement lacking before, and had become unprejudiced again.

Into the bend, and ten meters down. The Finn looking tired, the East German stronger, moving a meter or two up, the Kenyan third, but closing on the Finn—everyone else out of it.

Was he out of it? The distance to the Kenyan seemed too great as the black man moved to the Finn's shoulder. Go for the Finn, and he would be in a medal spot. Go for the kill—

Two timing devices, a clock that could be seen, attract due attention, and an egg timer—running on something as short as twenty minutes, hidden behind the bomb case, with the obvious trip device, to absorb them and challenge expertise. Someone very clever had thought very carefully about it. Someone who wanted blood, not just an ad for the world to see. He intended killing. It was the whole object—

"Get out—get out—!" He was running—the stretched lead of the mike jerked it from his hand, the headphone pulled off his head, clattered behind him against the pickup. He was running the fifty yards, the only thing moving in Red Square, still shouting. "Get out—get out!"

He thought he saw a padded, ridiculous tire man in the doorway of the Mausoleum, outlined against the sudden flare of light from inside.

Then the noise.

The bell. Irvine was in the Bronze position, and the crowd was roaring like a swelling choir, or a bombardment. Constant, stunning noise coming back off the grandstand, off every concrete surface in the stadium. The Kenyan, then the East German, then himself, for a moment floundering before the bell just in front of the tiring Finn but picked up by the bell, like a hand propelling him forward. A large blanket would cover the runners, their heads twitching their faces in his direction. Onto the bend, still in line, one behind the other, each of them having only the energy left for one attempt to break clear, and suffering a loss of nerve to use it. Not yet, not yet—

Great organ swell of the crowd, almost like a cry of disappointment that their positions remained the same. Three hundred meters. Irvine waited, because he had to wait, because he had less left, he suspected, than the Kenyan, who seemed mesmerized by his

Silver position. Two-fifty, and no one moving into another gear, even this late. All three of them accelerating slowly, like a film winding up to its proper speed. Nearing the bend, the last one—

Irvine kicked—and as if he were trying to start a motorcycle, his body's engine seemed to stutter without catching—then he began to move up on the Kenyan, who seemed to have no finish, or no will to finish—

Silver, Silver—

Kick. Stutter. Almost life, as he came out of the bend into the straight, into the wall of sound that seemed to restrain, and the rain a grasping thing, the wet track clinging, deadening limbs—

Then nothing but the noise. Everything blanked out, and he unsure whether he was level with the East German or not— uncertain whether there really was nobody ahead of him. Just the body running, the awareness like a child afraid to look.

He stumbled across the tape two yards up on the Silver Medalist, the East German, six yards ahead of the Kenyan in the Bronze position. He collapsed on the track, and they hovered over him, with the oxygen mask close to his head, just in case.

After a long time, he opened his eyes, and his ears. What he had thought was the roaring of the rain was the cheering of the crowd.

Silence. The moment of silence before the appalled communal identity dissipated. Kazantsev came out of the Mausoleum, tears in his eyes, mostly from the smoke, remembering most vividly how the bend of the staircase had flung the main force of the explosion back on two of his team, who were in pieces—no longer identifiable forms, let alone individuals—and had by that same twist prevented serious damage to the vault and the sarcophagus. The glass had shattered, there were shards of it in the clothing, in the mummified hands and face of V. I. Lenin, but no more damage than that.

The third member of his team was concussed. He had been nearest the doors and had obeyed Kazantsev's scream to get out. The other two had not.

He saw a KGB man confiscating the American camera equipment and the cans of film. The American woman in her scarlet plastic raincoat was arguing violently. The incident, he realized, would not have happened. All reports other than those of Tass would be described as exaggerated.

Two of his men were dead. Someone had wanted to prove they could kill—easily, in the middle of Moscow, opposite the walls of the Kremlin.

Do pobachenya—he was certain of it now, without evidence—had an FAE device in Moscow that could kill thousands. And he knew, with a sickening certainty, that they meant to use it.

PART THREE

HEAT

CHAPTER 11

Four-thirty on Sunday morning. Oleg Kazantsev stood on the Kotelnicheskaia Quay, just below the Oustinski Bridge, watching something that belied both his mood and the events of Saturday—the innocence of small high clouds turning pink as the sun rose. He had walked there from the Center, via Solyanka Street, avoiding Red Square. The Lenin Mausoleum was closed to the public for "minor repairs."

Valentina, he knew, would have lain awake all night, ever since his telephone call to say he would not be home. He was ashamed now of the motives that had impelled him to upset her, keep her wakeful, a residue of rage and frustration that had succeeded shock and grief. If he couldn't rest, then neither should others.

The Center had been shocked by the deaths of two of the bomb squad. But—the incident was played down. It was steamrollered out of shape and proportion and significance by the massive inertia and complacency of the Committee for State Security. Or perhaps it was just closing its basilisk eyes, not liking what it saw—KGB guts over the floor, KGB brains spattered on the walls.

All the time—even down here in the silence that was almost complete since the cleaning cart had passed out of hearing and a derelict had sunk back into stupor—all the time it came back to Shubin.

The face. On his office wall. They had looked at him in Photography when he asked for a blow-up of the face—just *one* copy. When it had been delivered, he had pinned it to his office wall, and sat staring at it, as if at an icon. He had sat between that face and the window overlooking the Lubyanka, for hours. Until it began to get light, and he thought the air might be fresher outside.

It did not seem to be.

Lenin on terror and its proper uses, he thought, as the Moskva became glassy with the first slanting sunlight, and the towers and minarets of the Kremlin were tipped with gold farther along the river. Terror for terror's sake. That was what *Do pobachenya* believed—and practiced. There was nothing else—there would be no demands, nothing except the threat, the *execution*. Rock the boat, the ship of state, hole it below the waterline—whatever the image, there was no object beyond that, no trade envisaged—

No way it could be prevented, or forestalled.

He knew, with a certainty that made his frame quiver, and his stomach lurch, that an FAE device was somehow missing from the ordnance factory in Donetsk, and was now in Moscow. A nasty, dirty weapon—a terror weapon. In the right conditions, it could kill thousands. He imagined, with a fresh shudder, what might have happened had one been detonated in Red Square amid the hooting traffic, just before his men went into the Mausoleum—

He knew he would have to return to Donetsk. It was stupid, even fanatical, to believe that the KGB would turn up the group in the next twenty-four or forty-eight hours, even with the extra men now assigned. The answer had to be in that dusty, hot-aired ordnance factory, behind its high brick walls.

Someone, someone had—*what?*

He felt suddenly galvanized, as if an itch or mild electric stimulation possessed his whole skin. After the hours of listless moping—as he now saw them—he had a course of action and a journey to begin.

His mood had lightened, and the sense of loss seemed evanescent. The Kremlin was now bathed in golden light.

Kenneth Irvine lay on his bed, staring up at the ceiling, undisturbed by the snoring of one of his teammates, or the movement of the net curtains in the fresh little breeze that had sprung up just after dawn. Nothing disturbed him; but he was unable to sleep, unable for very long to close his eyes, because when he did it all came back.

All charges have been dropped. Please accept our profound apologies.

And so forth, and so on. Those mockeries had run round and round his head, along with everything else, all night. He was naked because at first he had thought himself too hot to sleep, and on top of the bedclothes because he had felt hotter as soon as he removed his pajamas. The exhaustion was a palpable physical sensation, heavy in his arms and legs, his rib cage a weight on his lungs.

All charges dropped. Profound apologies.

The tears he had wanted to shed when they told him that, in the Australian Olympic Federation offices in the village when he returned from the medal ceremony, and in front of the gaggle of officials, had not been tears of relief, but tears of anger and weariness, as if he were struggling toward something which had been suddenly snatched out of his reach. A child reaching for chocolate, and an alert parent who had removed it to a higher shelf in the kitchen. He winced at the slaps on the back, the study of his face by sharp, questioning eyes.

Then he had been alone in his room, after the party the team had thrown, champagne and gallons of beer and very little to eat, and after the press conference for the 10,000 medalists, and the various TV interviews—they'd raised the issue of his incarceration, and he had refused to talk about it, to any of them—a cone of silence around him.

The Gold Medal for the 10,000 meters of the XXII Olympiad of modern times was in his bedside locker, where he might have kept a paperback he was reading. Even that had been spoiled, so that he had wanted to hide it because it turned a spotlight upon him.

He did not want to read the Australian papers when they arrived, did not want to go out where the eyes were, the smiles of envy and congratulation. He had no resources left, as if he had experienced a relationship rather than a competition, the end of an affair, leaving him emotionally and spiritually spent and tired.

An empty, blaring anthem, hollow cheers. He had stumbled with more than weariness stepping down off the plinth after the ceremony.

He could not bear the idea, like bedclothes on burned skin, of the necessary training later that day for the heats of the 5000.

David Allardyce, standing at the window of his room, staring down at the first traffic of the morning, could not regard his comparative failure in the opening sexual bout with Karen Gunston with his habitual lightness of mood. It was as if he had lost the capacity to smile or be humored by events.

The girl was asleep, half-covered by a sheet, her auburn hair covering most of her face. One arm was flung out over the edge of the bed, pointing at the door as if bidding him leave, an unsuccessful acolyte. He had wanted her, tried to enter the closed, narrow perceptions of sexual arousal, but even as he browsed his mouth against her flattened breasts and stomach and pubic hair he had sensed another person in the darkened room. Anna.

It wasn't Anna's body—that was too long ago, and only a single occasion, so that it could not substitute for the skin and curling hair he tasted. But Anna's presence, lying beside them as a great book might lie on a coffee table, catching his eyes each time he turned the pages of the sad and dirty little paperback he had chosen to read. Anna, in danger—his responsibility, his fault.

He had assisted in her recruitment, creating the mess her spying had now become, and now had been called back to clean up. And he hated it, and was frightened of it as of an experience he knew himself incapable of entering or sustaining.

He had a half-erection because he wanted to urinate, and for no other reason. The little breeze was chilly, the black Volga sedan more chilling. Down there, parked where it could observe the main entrance to the hotel.

Someone had decided he was worth putting under surveillance. And he knew it had to be Leonov.

If it was his evident jealousy, and not professional suspicion—? Even that idea could not lighten his mood.

The girl stirred in the bed, turning onto her stomach as she had done while they made love, turning to present her buttocks, her hand reaching behind her to guide his entry. The touch of her long fingers shaking off a torpor that had assailed him, making him ejaculate at once, hardly inside her—

He drew on his cigarette, trying to dismiss the image of her buttocks, her mask of frozen superiority when he next looked at her, her hunching into pretended sleep almost at once.

A black KGB tail car. Allardyce's image for that Sunday morning.

Arkady Federenko had made a decision. He had to find Zenushka, and that day, if possible. Before the KGB found her.

Whatever the radio and TV had said—he had gone back to his flat the previous night, as if by being alone when he listened to the bulletins he could keep their messages secret—he knew who was behind it. Shubin, Shubin—

The name acted on him like a blow, making him weak in the legs so that he wanted to sit down immediately after he recited it. Shubin. Making breakfast—pickled herring, black bread—the name affected his appetite, rousing gastric juices as if he were trying to digest his own hatred.

Zenushka in bed with Shubin, entered by him, subordinated— willing to do anything for him, even to—

Hesitation, a mental stumble, quick excuses. But she had, she *had*. . . . Two members of the bomb squad were dead. He'd heard that from gossip at the training track, among the coaches. Someone had seen the bodies carried out. Still the radio and TV had played down the story, talking of a hoax, a minor explosion, the work of a harmless madman—

The Games are on, so forget.

He waited for more than a minute while the tepidity gathered during the night flowed into the basin and away, washed in cold water, and tried to rouse himself to freshness. He had narrowed his perspective to Ukrainians he knew in Moscow. They might know where she was, might have seen her or spoken to her. A distant cousin—he had his address—one or two college friends, a couple of girls from her college who had started teaching that year. Hopeless and futile, but he had no alternative.

He went down in the elevator, through the foyer, and out into Rusakovskaya Street. The distant cousin worked in the Dynamo electrical plant, in the still-named "Lenin suburb," the most industrialized district of the city. It lay beyond the oldest monastery in Moscow, the Novospassky, on the western bank of the river as it curved away southward beyond the confluence with the drainage canal. He lived in the largest block of flats in Moscow, seven hundred apartments in all, overlooking the Moskva where the Kotelnicheskaia and Yauza Quays met. If Federenko hurried, he might still be at home, before taking his family to one of the parks of culture and rest in the company of millions of Muscovites.

He was not aware of the tail car, or of the man in a summer shirt and light slacks who detached himself from the entrance to an adjoining block of apartments, and followed him, at a distance of perhaps fifty yards, all the way to the Komsomolskaia station.

"Get moving, then. Don't lose him—" Kazantsev had seen, from the passenger seat of the Zil, the hunched shoulders and swift gait of Federenko, had felt him emanating a purpose. He was in touch with the tail by walkie-talkie—built into the dummy camera the pretend-tourist was using with great frequency—and when the man reported himself fifty yards beyond, in Komsomolskaia Square, with Federenko crossing to the entrance of the metro station, Kazantsev had felt an urgent impatience.

"Sir."

Kazantsev flicked a switch on the dashboard receiver.

"All units—don't lose Federenko. One of you must get on the train with him."

The static humming like a wasp in the car. Kazantsev looked at his driver, and nodded. The Zil pulled away from the curb, down Rusakovskaya Street toward Komsomolskaia Square.

"He's in the ticket line—lucky he hasn't got change, by the look of it—"

Kazantsev cradled the microphone to his cheek.

"Close up on him—don't lose him when he gets down below."

Traffic lights at the entry to the square. The oriental facades of the three main railway stations and the metro station. The driver was aware of one of Kazantsev's huge hands opening and closing on his knee. Menacing.

Kazantsev had explained to Puchkov, submitted his request to return to Donetsk—and had been refused. At the moment when he had explained his conviction that an FAE device was in the city, he had seen the older man's eyes sharpen, heard the excuse to keep him in Moscow. If such a device was discovered, he would be needed. As he had pointed out, the bomb was here, not in Donetsk.

So the frustration, the impotent fury, of a silent breakfast in the Center canteen, and the surveillance car outside Federenko's apartment.

The traffic lights changed.

"Pull off the underpass. I'm going in—"

The driver pulled into a taxi-stand parking space, winked at the taxi driver whose face from the next cab challenged his right to be there, and Kazantsev got out, microphone still in hand. The taxi driver, in the act of opening the door of his cab, saw the mike and the curling lead, and shut his door again.

"Where is he?"

"Looks like he's going down to the Circle."

"Keep up close—I'm coming down."

"Sir."

He dropped the mike through the open window of the Zil, onto the seat. The driver was already reading the previous evening's copy of *Sovetsky Sport*.

Kazantsev crossed the largely pedestrianized square toward the entrance to the metro station surmounted by its pointed dome as if he had a vital train to catch. He sensed he was only sublimating the importance he attached to getting back to Donetsk, and trying to disguise from himself any sense of wasting time—but it was a sensible precaution to watch the girl's brother. He had left his apartment in an urgent, purposeful manner, without his kit bag. He wasn't going training for Monday's heats.

The girl had rung him—they had had her on the end of a thin line for a moment, just before she planted the bomb. She *must* have planted it, even though the guards, quite naturally, did not remember her.

Through the barrier, the five-kopeck coin in the slot, the arm almost catching him in the back so preoccupied was he, and down the escalator to the Circle, the metro line that ran like a subterranean ditch just outside the Sadovaya motorway ring around the city center.

He hurried now, as if he had heard something ahead of him. Two, three steps at a time, squeezing his bulk past the tourists and Muscovites—knocking the map from someone's hand, mumbling an apology—down past the frescoes, the bronze busts in niches, toward the mosaic on the floor at the bottom of the escalator. The victories of the Russian people. They were all there, in fresco or mosaic, and the heads of the famous in bronze. Like catching a tube train in the middle of a museum. The War against the Fascists—1917, 1812.

He skipped off the running last steps of the escalator, unamused by any parallel or foreboding, and the idea of victory and defeat.

One FAE bomb, and every innocent, stupid, ordinary bugger and his mother in the Komsomolskaia metro station would be—

The Circle platform was crowded, and he searched immediately not for Federenko but for the distinctively patterned shirt of his own man. Yes. He squeezed through the waiting passengers toward him, and realized that he passed directly behind Federenko in doing so, almost nudging him. He was studying a Circle station chart as if he had never had occasion to use the metro before. It was an image that suggested to Kazantsev the futility of expecting a hick from Kiev—a runner—to find *Do pobachenya* for them.

"I'll take it," he said without thinking when he reached the tail. The man looked as if he might be about to argue. "Yes, I know he knows me—I'll keep out of sight. You get back to the car, and give me the camera."

The tail unslung the dummy camera, and passed it over. Then he moved away with a nod, heard the distant sigh of an approaching train, and began to quicken his progress through the stirring crowd to be back at the car before Kazantsev left the station.

Kazantsev watched Federenko as eagerly as he might have watched his wife as she moved around their apartment. Federenko was frowning with thought—or the effort to resist thought. He seemed possessed of purpose, but not with any sense of action. Kazantsev, as the train sighed in, and the doors opened and he was moved forward by the crowd, wondered where he was heading.

Federenko knew they had to be tailing him and it would be stupid to be unaware of it. But he swept his gaze only perfunctorily over the faces around him, as if turning his head back repeatedly to some small screen just in front of his eyes on which some gripping, inescapable drama was being played out.

He had narrowed everything down to the short metro journey to his cousin. Everything down to the anxiety that he might have gone out, be away from home. That small but blooming anxiety was a shade under which he could shelter from larger concerns.

His body felt heavy, as it sometimes did after a long layoff from running with a pulled muscle or strained hamstring, unfit, somnolent.

He was shunted onto the train by the pressure of the people behind him, found a seat, looking round swiftly, inexpertly, as soon as he was seated, not seeing Kazantsev enter the next carriage. He looked out of the window, as if expecting the sudden sight of a tailing policeman, abandoned on the platform. Only a cleaner with a broom. The train rushed into the tunnel.

Kourskaia—Taganskaia—Pavoletskaia. Tourists trying to do as their Berlitz guides suggested and read off the first three letters of the Cyrillic station names, alighted with a sense of adventure or doubt. Federenko was still seated with his back to Kazantsev, the KGB man enjoying his undetected presence and the small routines of surveillance.

Federenko was standing at the door as the train slowed into the Pavoletskaia station. Kazantsev, straphanging near his own door, stepped onto the platform and strolled toward the escalator behind the younger man.

They came up into the narrow, busy Volovaya Street, lined with apartment houses, crowded with shoppers and tourists. He memorized carefully Federenko's build, color of T-shirt, denims as he crossed the station foyer, then crossed to the other side of the street, dropping back almost fifty yards, as they walked toward the Krasnoklnlinski Bridge which cut across the southern tip of the island between the river and the drainage canal. There was a slight breeze coming off the river. Kazantsev bumped against an American party photographing the east and south of the Kremlin from the middle of the bridge, lost sight of Federenko for a moment in a huddle of print frocks and long-haired students, then saw him detach himself—he might have been recognized by them, even known them, but it wasn't a contact—and move on.

Kazantsev stopped, held the camera to his eye, spoke into it.

"Krasnoklnlinski Bridge—river end. Federenko's just turned onto the Kotelnicheskaia Quay. Looks as if he knows where he's going."

A tinny little voice as he pressed the shutter release and held it for Receive.

"We're crossing Karl Marx and Chkalovskaia now."

Kazantsev released the shutter.

"Pick me up at the Oustinski. Out."

He hurried then, Federenko a hundred yards ahead. He could see him below the bridge, apparently strolling, but still with something purposeful in his movement. A man heading for a specific destination.

Federenko studied the lists of names of the apartment occupants, in alphabetical order, numbers and floor opposite, for a long time, as if deciphering some complex hieroglyph. Something had shut down inside him, some motive force—as if his legs or will had given out. Then he crossed the huge foyer to the row of doors of the ten elevators that served the vast block of apartments. Suddenly, he no longer wanted his cousin to be at home, as if he understood that the man knew Zenushka's whereabouts, and would tell him—and then he would be left with an imperative to act that he could not put aside.

He pressed each of the summons buttons, watched each arrow light up, then waited. He was almost fretfully nervous, and he could feel a cold perspiration across his back, as if an opened door had let a cold wind into the foyer.

A bell sounded, a high tinkling noise like a tiny gong, and a fat woman almost knocked him down as she struggled out with two camping chairs and a picnic basket bound with straps. She was looking behind her, into the elevator, ushering out a brood of small, tubby children whose eyes went straight to Federenko's denims and

T-shirt in envy and admiration. The woman looked him up and down with a more appraising, more resentful eye. He almost didn't recognize his cousin's wife, so much weight had she put on since they had last met in Kiev.

"Nina—?"

She seemed surprised—then aware, so that she put down the basket, dropped the chairs more carelessly, and embraced him, her lipstick imprinted on both cheeks in a moment.

"Arkady—!"

Kazantsev stopped halfway through the revolving glass doors into the foyer when he saw Federenko greeted by the fat woman who had come out of the elevator. He went back down the steps, still able to see into the foyer, see the woman in animated conversation with Federenko, see the elevator doors close, the floor indicators light up one by one as the elevator went back up. Then he raised the camera, focused on the river panorama, and pressed the shutter release once, and released it.

"I'm at Stalin's Folly—pick me up. Federenko's made contact with the Gorgon."

He switched off before they could ask for a translation, and tried to look around him unconcernedly, a small excitement catching at his breath. Something, something—

Anything *real*?

Federenko thought so, he told himself. He and the woman and the sulky kids had been joined by a little man with thin hair struggling with footballs and picnic chairs. Federenko, drawing him aside, the woman puzzled—

The Zil drew up fifty yards down the street, and the tail in the distinctive shirt got out. Kazantsev waved, and he leaned on the roof of the car.

Kazantsev ducked his head round, saw Federenko voluble and demonstrative, the little man shrugging then silently thoughtful, then apparently struck by an idea—

Kazantsev went down the remainder of the steps quickly, and across the street to the Zil. When he reached it, he turned back, watching Federenko emerge from the flats and head away from them back the way he had come. Then the family emerged, the little man laden, the fat woman struggling against gravity and the hampering chairs and basket. The children trooped down the steps in a sullen line.

"Pick up the Gorgon and her old man—I'm going after Federenko. When you find out what *he* found out—call me!"

The Olympic Village had a Sunday morning appearance about it. The newsstands were busy, the piazzas and walks almost deserted. Radios sounded from open windows in dozens of apartment blocks. Peter Lydall, coming back from a training run begun soon after dawn, showing his pass before he could get through the complex of barriers leading to the main gate, paused to absorb the sudden, even unexpected ordinariness of the scene. After the checks, the armed guards, the high fence, this was suddenly like some new town development on the outskirts of London or Leeds.

What he wanted now was a shower, to change, read a paper if possible in the refectory while he had breakfast, and then go into Moscow for lunch with Natalia and the little girl. Yes, he decided, allowing the deception of the bright sunlight and the hardly stirring village, he did want that—that ordinariness. Just as he wanted that Sunday to be over, and Monday's clock to slide round to three-thirty in the afternoon.

The first heat. *His* heat.

He dressed with a careful casualness after his shower. Cotton shirt, striped, short-sleeved, and the pair of denims he usually wore only at home, never for any visit or occasion, however small. It was calculation, retention of that mood of deceptive ordinariness that had met him as he came through the main gate. He was lunching at home.

He had eggs, steak, toast, fruit juice, and coffee in the refectory—an annex to one of the main restaurants of the village, where only breakfasts were served, and which pandered to the more solitary or reticent of the competitors. Nevertheless, Gutierrez was there, with the Polish girl—deep in a whispered conversation that stuttered and almost died when he carried his tray in, then began again in fierce, indecipherable whispers. Lydall watched them surreptitiously from behind the airmail edition of *The Observer*, flown in overnight to Cheremetievo, assessing the degree of feeling on each part, sampling the intimacy they seemed to have achieved. Measuring it against himself and Natalia.

"But they follow me everywhere now, Martin—!" the girl suddenly burst out audibly. Gutierrez looked swiftly in his direction, and Lydall attended conspicuously to his newspaper. He sensed something he could only describe as desperation in the girl's voice, the noise of something snapping with tension, and he did not want to hear any more because the ordinariness in which he had been basking had been shuffled aside and what he had heard had seemed somehow foreboding.

"Keep your voice down, Irena, for Christ's sake!" Gutierrez pleaded as he turned back to the girl. Her face was like a light that hurt his eyes. She was pale and drawn, and there were dark smudges under her eyes.

"Martin—you don't understand what it's like," she pleaded, her eyes flickering in the direction of the now studiously reading Lydall. Gutierrez's eyes flickered over the wall, insect-alighting on grilles, light fittings, surfaces. Only for a second, perhaps. Then he was drawn into the situation again; there was no mocking or frightened awareness of himself any longer, only reaction.

"All right, Irena. I'm trying, for God's sake. Just take it easy for a little longer, baby—" He was aware of stopping the gesture of taking her hand, for a moment; but it was merely the sense of danger that prompted it, not reluctance of another kind. If there was a watcher, the scene had to be as casual as possible. "Just try to play it casual—cool. Now, we get up, and we walk out of here, arms around each other, but smiling—uh?" He grinned at her, squeezing her hand.

The girl nodded. She sniffed, loudly.

As they went out, Gutierrez looked back at Lydall for a moment, as if anticipating mockery. Lydall's head was still behind his newspaper. He looked—unencumbered, to Gutierrez, who felt a pluck of reluctance. Then he squeezed the girl's hand again, and followed her out.

Kazantsev yawned—nothing slow or satisfied, as if sitting back from his desk having compiled a successful report; more the yawn of nerves and frustration and utter boredom. Once the first one emerged, he could not stop them, and knew he must look like someone drowning, fighting for his breath.

He was outside the post office on Kirov Street, with Komsomol-skaia Square just ahead of him—the starting point of his ridiculous pursuit of Federenko. Driven all day by the illusion of the man's slightly bent head, slightly hunched shoulders, purposeful walk. Obsessive behavior by Federenko—and by himself. Grasping at straws.

A main shopping street—tourists packing the pavements, or heading now for the three stations and the metro in the square. Hot, breathless, dusty—gasoline fumes from taxis and buses, the sharp, thundery ozone smells from the trolleybuses. Kazantsev felt his body at last demanding attention—food, a bath, sleep.

Ridiculous. All day he had followed Federenko, and his men had followed the pair of them—he talking into a camera like an idiot, his men dashing into apartments, houses, shops, basements, cafés, to question the people Federenko had talked to.

And nothing.

Federenko was inside now, talking to a Ukrainian who worked as a postal clerk. Looking for a name, an address—sure, Federenko was obsessive about his sister, but he didn't know where she was, any more than the KGB did. And that truth was now slowly being admitted to prominence in Kazantsev's tired head. A jackass image, a laughing hyena, echoed in his imagination.

Federenko came out, and Kazantsev turned away. The young man went down the steps with the same purposeful walk, head slightly forward, shoulders slightly bunched. Kazantsev groaned, and signaled his men in the Zil parked a little distance from the bottom of the post office steps. When they reached him, he took them to the glass doors, and pointed out the clerk Federenko had questioned. Then he waited, watching Federenko head farther down Kirov Street, toward the crowded Sadovaya and Komsomolskaia Square. It was becoming difficult, already, to keep him in view. He yawned, made as if to move—

Federenko had gone. He could no longer see him. There—just there—? No. Crossing the street? Bus stop? No, no—

"Shit," he muttered, yawning again. "Shit!" A woman stared at him, offended, as she passed him on the steps.

Calculation—plan? He could not believe it. Where was he?

He looked round. A bright shirt, and his man, running.

"What is it?" He felt he was coming awake. "You've got something? I've lost sight—"

"The clerk—we've had him in a couple of times—nothing proven, just for questioning about Ukrainian presses—"

"Yes—?" Kazantsev was praying.

"He's admitted to knowing Shubin—!" The young man's face was flushed, excited.

"Bring him in!"

Kazantsev looked down Kirov Street. He was certain that

Federenko had disappeared deliberately. He had learned something—an address, something, from the postal clerk—

And, very soon, they would know it also.

Federenko tried the handle on the little judas door set in the flaking, rotting doors of the warehouse just off Kirov Street, a narrow little strip that served mainly as an access road for the shops and was little else but warehouses, unloading bays, tenement storehouses—many of them crumbling, glassless, and derelict. It was the address he had been reluctantly given. He had had to threaten Boris the little postal clerk with the KGB if he didn't tell—

He had begun to do that, to threaten the Ukrainians he talked to if they didn't help him. None of them had been able to, until a woman who worked as a waitress in a Ukrainian restaurant told him about Boris whom she lived with and who had had a visitor—a couple of times in the past week—whose description matched Shubin. And on one occasion there had been a girl with him, much like Zenushka.

He rattled the judas door. Dark green paint flaked off. He rattled it again, as if the flimsy rottenness of the door suggested his superiority, his invulnerability. And anger prompted him to dismiss any danger from Shubin.

All the frustration, the weariness, of the day's search had left him, as if he had showered after a training run. He was refreshed with this rusty handle, this door hiding an empty warehouse.

It had once belonged to a sausage-making company.

"Zenushka!" he bellowed, as if he had caught her at some forbidden game, parental. "Zenushka!"

Boris the clerk had supplied newspapers and food to Shubin over the last two days, when the man had not ventured out on a single occasion. He had dropped them off on his way home from the post office. Presumably the whole lot of them were crouching behind this door, afraid now to go out.

The prod in the back cut off his contempt, just as it was about to find voice. He looked round, startled, and saw Shubin's bearded face, eyes wild with rage—and a gun that he used to prod again, then a third time.

"Open up!" he called. "It's that arse-licking brother of yours!" Prod again, harder. Federenko's breath whistled between his teeth. "You are a stupid fucker, Arkady—!" he whispered, and Federenko could see the white teeth in the black beard, the red wet lips.

The door opened, and Federenko was thrust inside. Zenaida

was standing just inside. A fair-haired boy had opened the door.

"Zenushka—!"

"Zenushka—" Shubin echoed, falsetto. "What are you doing here, Federenko?" in a loud voice, so that each of them would hear him, absorb the sense of authority. Or perhaps Shubin enjoyed the display, would begin to strut—

"I came for you, Zenushka—" Almost as a prince to his long-lost sister in poverty, or asleep for a hundred years. It sounded remarkably stupid; he heard his voice with Shubin's ears.

Shubin laughed, prodded him almost playfully with the gun.

Two others emerged from the shadows—sunlight spilling through a broken roof in a few places, in one spot catching the glass of a dispatch office toward the rear of the warehouse. Shubin and Zenaida, and the boy who had opened the door. Five—no, six, seven, with another coming out of shadows to his left.

"This is the group, is it, Shubin?" he said, suddenly finding a voice he could employ against Shubin. "You and six kids?"

Resentment on the young faces—one or two almost deferential; one thinking ahead, perhaps—what do we do with him?

Still Zenaida had said nothing.

"Arkady—" She seemed frozen, as if a stroke had set the muscles of her face in unalterable lines. "Arkady, why did you come here? What are you playing at, you bloody fool!"

The trigger. Now he could say the things she had to hear.

"You killed two people—you could have killed hundreds! What's happening to you? Are you mad?" He asked it almost as if he had seen her dribbling, or pulling wings from insects, or mutilating cloth; as if it might be in him, too. "Are you mad?" he said in a small, ineffectual voice.

Which seemed to reach her—the first outside view, the first reaction to what she had done, until Shubin laughed.

"The whole world's mad, Federenko—didn't you know?"

One or two smiles, the smirks of kids tasting flip cynicism that appeared no less than wisdom. Federenko saw them treat it seriously, and saw the witness of Shubin's hold over them. Even his sister was contemptuous, superior. The eyes, assessing, switched from introspection by Shubin's mockery.

"I know *you* are, Shubin." They were round him in a circle now, but only Shubin had a gun. Shubin was watching him, but expected no danger. He sensed that Federenko felt unthreatened. "You're as mad as a bloody starving wolf in the forests." He spoke at his sister, who stood with her hands on her hips, challenging him. "You killed two people—and you could have killed a lot more. Zenushka—do you understand what I'm saying? If they caught you, you'd be sentenced to death. You're a murderer—"

Shubin was agitated, moving around him, histrionic but living his role.

"You understand nothing, Federenko—nothing! You don't understand history, you don't understand Russia—you certainly don't understand the Ukraine." Federenko was aware that it was a performance, and that the audience was not himself. But he wondered as he observed Shubin whether the audience was the others or just Shubin himself.

"Millions of Ukrainians have died, Federenko—since 1917 and the Soviets—when the Fascists came they were *less* destructive than Stalin!" Teetering on incoherence, just retaining the force of arguments, not their structure. "*You* are a *Soviet!*" Prodding his chest with a finger, tempted to prod the belly with the gun, but retreating again. Hand waving. "You arse-lick, boot-lick, brown-nose your way up and over. Forgetting, being bought off—the Gulag archipelago is still out there, Ukrainians still disappear in the middle of the night, the KGB just goes on beating up demonstrators, imprisoning scientists and anyone who wants to be free to work, to think, to speak—"

Fist clenched, knuckles white around the gun butt.

"Anyone who doesn't want his mind bought or his soul ignored is locked up, exiled, sent to the camps or the mental hospitals—"

He paused, looking at Federenko. He was standing next to Zenaida and Federenko hated it, as if he could see some bacillus passing between them.

"And your answer is to bomb them into agreeing with you, is it?"

Shubin shook his head.

"No."

"You do it for kicks, then?"

Shubin was silent again. The warehouse seemed suddenly arid, empty, disused. The air hot and unchanged for years, but with no smell of the meat or fruit or machines that might once have been stored there. He sensed he had arrived at the heart of some matter, that each of Shubin's disciples awaited some wisdom, some revelation.

"No—we do it for the sake of the act itself. To destroy—to terrorize—"

It was his sister's voice. Zenushka had said the words. He

could not believe it. He shook his head, dismissing an illusion.

Someone's breath in a sharp gasp. Zenaida's eyes had not blinked once, did not blink once in the moments of silence after she had spoken.

He had to say something.

"Sick—" It might have been a muttered apology for his own condition. He cleared his throat. "You must come with me, Zenushka. I'm not leaving you with this lunatic—"

Again, on one or two of the faces, the evident question—what shall we do with him? And not now because he was well-known, even famous. Just because he was there, and a nuisance—an opponent.

Shubin was confident.

"Zenushka—" he mimicked. "Do you want to go with him?"

"No." As if rejecting a proffered dessert, or an umbrella.

"Zenushka—!"

"Leave, Arkady—leave *now!*"

He looked at her face. It was that same voice, the one that had changed so strangely, that he had heard just a minute ago.

"You can't stay with him—!"

"Go! Go now." She was sending him away. He did not know her at all; he was a stranger being dismissed, a lesser thing.

The eager children's faces looking to Shubin, expecting. The gun a focal point, not a theatrical prop.

"No—" Shubin said softly.

The gun came up. Again, an audible sigh.

"Yes—" Zenaida said levelly, looking at Federenko all the while. "Yes, Shubin. Arkady is leaving now."

Mouths opened into little round children's holes of disappointment, or something inviting sweets. Then Shubin's anger, and the gun wavering around Federenko's stomach.

"You stupid bitch! He can't be let out of here—!"

Zenaida turned to Shubin.

"He won't betray us. If he does he knows he will kill me." Her eyes moved back to Federenko; slaty surfaces, the color of a pool under heavy cloud. Shubin was quelled by her, would not kill him now. But his sister—? What was happening to her?

"We have guns, Arkady—and something much nastier besides. Do you understand? I shall die here, if you betray us to the KGB."

"Zenushka—!" Shubin grinning, as if he approved the subtle aroma of the moral dilemma, perfume over the corruption.

The children accepted. Federenko could see that he was

safe—despite the rage that twisted Shubin's face just for a moment, and the flicker of the gun to the horizontal, before he put it away. His words were not empty, but irrelevant.

"You'll kill your sister—understand?"

Zenaida nodded, said one word, "Go."

Federenko had lost her. She was diseased, changed entirely. Unrecognizable. Someone he had never known. He thought, for the merest instant, of his mother, shabby and sniveling in the corner of a dusty, darkened room. How could he make her understand—?

He stumbled through the judas door, and it shut behind him. There was no one in the narrow street.

He wiped the tears from his eyes as he made his way back toward Kirov Street.

CHAPTER 12

Boris the postal clerk broke a little after seven on Monday morning. Kazantsev, in the mood of a man witnessing some inescapable drama and not wishing to miss a moment of it, had taken only two short catnaps during the evening and night, and the time to make a fumbling, weary telephone call to Valentina. That apart, he had been with Boris and the two interrogators from the Second Directorate and Puchkov for fourteen hours.

It was less dramatic than the snapping of a dry twig—one sigh that threatened to become a yawn, the hands holding the head like a delicate gold egg, elbows propped on the rough table in the bare, smoky room; then the whisper—apparently, they always whispered when they betrayed—in which he told them where they would find *Do pobachenya.*

No bribes, no threats, just the ceaseless questions like a downpour leaching soil off a slope, leaving only the bare rock.

"He didn't have it. It's the isolation with most of them," one of the interrogators said outside the door, pulling his jacket over his shoulders, then lighting a cigarette. He looked at Kazantsev, and winked. "You look like I feel. Don't make any premature judgments—your ability to gauge things might be a little shot—"

Then he went off along the corridor, whistling. Puchkov came out of the room, and a guard slipped inside, closing the door. Boris would be removed to the Lubyanka for his breakfast and a sleep. Puchkov looked ancient, wizened—and afraid.

"Enough to make you think they've got a bomb?"

Kazantsev rubbed his eyes, then his cheeks, hearing the stubble rasp against his palms.

"Oh, yes—they've got something nasty in there."

"Softly, softly, then—"

"I'll send someone just to have a look-see. No waves—just pick out the warehouse, the exits, the surroundings—O.K.?"

"Do that. Tell them to keep out of sight."

Kazantsev headed for the off-duty room.

Winston Ochengwe, drawn in the second heat, was awake before six, and simply lay on the bed, hands behind his head, staring at the ceiling. Minutely, he examined his thoughts, aware principally of how his wife and son had become removed to the distance of spectators. They were, that morning, neither alive nor dead—simply outside him, contributing nothing. Nor had he time or effort to regret the impression. It was simply so. There would be a time later for them to come back, to repossess the rooms they habitually occupied in his thoughts. But now he was lightly anesthetized against pain, grief, fear, loneliness.

He lifted his head. Lydall, across the room from him under a single sheet, appeared to have passed an undisturbed night, the pillows still fat, the sheet almost unrumpled. He was lying on his side, one arm trailing to the floor, the other palm up under his head. Ochengwe smiled—and Lydall went away to the distance that rivals occupied in his thoughts. But now he was lightly anesthetized place, adopting its appointed significance. He was ready.

François Diderot, running through the park complex adjoining the Olympic Village, moving easily, relaxed. His face distorted not by effort but by a sense that what he was doing was a mockery, a child continuing its antics even as it hears parental footsteps approaching. Soon the slap, the light switched off, the toy taken away.

Silver birch trees, soft, springy turf. A man in a blue track suit, grim-faced, stride easy. François Diderot dreaded the morning papers, and the decisive meeting which might ban him from the competition.

Gutierrez had not slept well. Yet he could not blame the girl, or the watchers who pretended they were tourists at his previous day's training—and at her high jump practice. There was no division between them; both were threatened. A trick, then. Divert the nervous energy. *Feel* pent-up, caged in. That was the illusion. *Need* the race to run off the excess nervous energy

The spooks wouldn't play—they had other fish to fry, noses to keep clean in Moscow. The girl was watched, they said. We can't help you, boy.

Gutierrez had an idea. Greenberg and his newspaper—Karen Gunston and her TV. When they interviewed him next time around, perhaps later that day, he would make the point. Let a hundred million know about Irena. Everyone loved a Romeo-and-Juliet story, so he would give them one.

What would happen after he got her out? He did not think about it, pretended indifference to his motives and his feelings. She depended on him, completely.

Need the race. Feel pent-up.

He smiled in the semidarkness of the curtained room. It wasn't too hot a day. It was his race. He was a winner.

Federenko had narrowed thought to one loyalty—Zenushka. What had been done, what might be done—*what he was*—all encapsulated in the one slight form. He was required to make a decision. During the long sleepless night in his flat, he tried to make it; to tidy the glimpses into his personality, his life, and into those of Shubin and his sister, into a neat package, firmly tied.

During the long walk to Sokolniki Park, after dawn, the air fresh, dew on the grass wetting the training shoes and the bottoms of his denims, he came to an understanding with himself. Only Zenushka mattered. If he could believe that, then he was excused the scathing contempt for him that she and Shubin exhibited in the warehouse, and he would be able to anesthetize himself against the danger Shubin and the children represented—to Moscow, and to Zenushka. All he had to do, his only imperative, was to keep the knowledge of his sister's whereabouts secret from the police. Zenushka was an accomplice to murder, and she must be shielded.

He jogged a little then. Through the swishing grass, beneath the trees, down to the lake. He felt better, almost fresh.

Irvine, pacing his room without waking his roommates, measured the weariness in his legs, apprehended the absence of will. Hour after hour—while he waited for breakfast much as a woman who has been crying will not answer a ring at her doorbell until her face betrays nothing.

When he considered himself sufficiently composed, he would go across to the refectory, try to eat something. Then sit around, probably back in that room—try not to pace—until it was time to change, board the coach for the Lenin Stadium. Envisaging that was uncomfortable, too. Like agoraphobia, or oversensitivity to noise.

Irvine continued to pace the room until one of his roommates stirred—a rower whose competitions had ended the previous day—when he ducked into the bathroom and began the business of washing noisily, as if he had just awakened.

The warehouse off Kirov Street. The surveillance car was parked on the forecourt of a garage seventy or eighty yards away. Just a quick look—the driver lit a cigarette, sat back in the seat, while the other KGB man strolled as nonchalantly as he could toward the closed doors of the warehouse.

No danger. The innocence of peeling paint, of the muted noise of traffic on Kirov Street filtered to a hum, of the morning still fresh despite the dog mess and the oil stains and the smells of long-stored things. The sky above the street almost cloudless. Fortunately, he had no Olympic tickets for that day, since the Lieutenant would keep them on surveillance most of the day, until they worked out at the Center the best way—

The judas door opening. Surprise made his body adopt a betrayingly alert posture, hand reaching behind his back for the gun tucked into his waistband. A young man, almost a boy, coming out perhaps even to do some shopping—his hands were empty, and he moved with all the innocuousness of someone collecting milk bottles from a doorstep—saw him, catching identity from the stance adopted by the KGB man, the mouth opening slow as a snail, hand reaching back for the door handle just released—

"Hold it!" He knew he was making a mess of it, prompted by mental habits that had not adapted to this situation—he should have walked on past—the gun already out. "Hold it there!" Gun up to eye level, arms out stiffly in front of him, legs in a crouch. The boy stepped awkwardly backward, then seemed propelled forward, and there were two shots, one of them the KGB man's gun discharging into the concrete as Shubin shot him.

Ferenc, sprawling on the ground, was stunned by the noise and the suddenness of the violence. Shubin fired twice more at the inert body on the concrete, then bent and picked Ferenc up—dragging furiously at his arm as if to tear it free from something glutinous.

"Come on—come on! There's a fucking car parked up there, and another KGB man in a sweat!"

He pulled Ferenc back inside the warehouse, then slammed the door.

The driver of the surveillance car popped out of the door like a glove puppet the moment the shock left him, but he went no farther than two or three steps toward the dead body of his companion. There was no point, and his mind refused to countenance the incident except as something to report. Turning back to the car after the warehouse door had shut again, he fumbled the mike from beneath the dash, and pressed the transmit button.

His voice was strangely hoarse, breathless.

"Center—Center—come in!"

"Proper procedure—" the radio room began.

"Damn! Surveillance seven-four-Alpha—my partner's just been shot. The warehouse off Kirov Street—tell Kazantsev, the terrorists are going all the way!"

Kazantsev watched Puchkov's face become gray, as if at the reek of cordite rather than the report of a shooting. He clasped his big hands together in his lap, stilling them. Puchkov was holding the telephone, and Kazantsev watched the lip just above the bowl of the mouthpiece, seeing it brighten with a thin line of perspiration. Puchkov was being diminished by *Do pobachenya*, as if the barbarians were already in his back garden, having climbed all the fences—and he hadn't locked the back door.

Kazantsev took the receiver.

"Radio room—general alert—all vehicles in the area to converge, block off each end of that street."

Then he looked down at Puchkov, who seemed grateful, and still an ashen color. He'd got them in a box. Damn it.

"It's a siege. They'll go all the way," he said to Puchkov. "All the bloody way!"

Behind the warehouse was a small, dusty, odorous courtyard in which trash cans and boxes were stored, and where one or two of the shops in Kirov Street, which backed onto the courtyard in company with some of the warehouses, had outside toilet facilities. Shubin looked, with Zenaida and Yakov, from the upper floor of the warehouse through a cracked and grimy window down into the untidy, cramped sunlit space. A whistling man—no tune, no melody, no harmony, just noises—went into one of the lavatories and closed the wooden door. Shubin smiled.

He got up, went to the edge of the gallery, and looked down. They were trapped, those children's faces down there, looking up to him, looking to him. There was one way out, to be tailed by the surveillance car. Already, he thought he could hear the first distant sirens.

"Get him," he said, going back to the dirty window. "And the butcher's shop he came out of. The staff should all be there by now—" He looked at his watch, nodded. "I want hostages. We'll have to trade our way out."

Zenaida seemed to study his face for a long time. He knew he must show no fear, no doubt. She would be looking for that, and she was sharp. When she seemed satisfied, she nodded.

"Take Ferenc as well—and don't be long about it!"

He listened to them climb down the ladder, then open the door, choosing to watch them still from the window, standing above their level so that events became more easily part of a design. Hostages were the easiest thing of all, of course. Anyone would do. Even if you got a gaggle of mental defectives or cleaning women, you could trade them off for police officers, or officials—get all the way to Andropov and Brezhnev eventually—

It was an accident—Federenko would never have risked his sister's life by betraying them—but it was an accident he could turn to his advantage. It was almost time to part company with the children, take off this mask, and assume another one—

He heard a shot, then sirens, this time closer, and certainly real. He had an image of a butcher's cleaver being wielded, and winced at it. Perhaps—?

Then three men, white overalls already bloodstained, and two women, came out of the rear of the shop, one of them holding his arm, hanging limply in a red sleeve. Zenaida and Yakov behind them, giving orders—and Ferenc, his ego inflated, confidence up, booted the lavatory door open, and yelled. A frightened man emerged.

He heard the door downstairs slam shut, sensed the presence of the hostages in the warehouse. It satisfied him for the moment—six hostages to trade, to buy his passage out.

The sirens were close now, and winding down through the scale as the police cars stopped, blocking both exits from the street. Time to give orders—

"You got to eat something, girl—" Gutierrez, cereal and fruit juice and toast in front of him, watched Irena pick at some bread, shredding it into bird-sized mouthfuls, eating none of it.

The refectory was crowded—those who had finished competing or been knocked out or who still waited or who were in events that had no dietary restrictions like the shooting, eating as if the food would run out that day. Eating steadily through a remarkable choice of menu. The Africans especially eating themselves fat during the fortnight as they always did. Gutierrez had passed a remark like that to Ochengwe, who had smiled and shaken his head at the suggestion he put on some weight. And the French with their chefs, the Italians bringing in cases of wine, the weight lifters eating through mountains of food, the Africans eating best beefsteak for breakfast, lunch, and dinner—

He saw a Russian weight lifter and his groaning tray coming from the serving line, and wanted to draw her attention to him. But he knew she would not be amused. He was slightly irritated with her mood—selfishly because he had found the frame of mind he wanted for the morning, and unselfishly because her high jump final that afternoon would find her mentally unprepared. There was no time, no capacity, to talk her out of her mood. Grachikov, her coach, would not do it. But through the day he had to keep a sense of self, of self-containment, carry it into his heat with him.

"Stop picking at the damn bread, honey!" he snapped, then immediately took her hand, stilled it, as she looked up, the stains like bruises beneath her eyes. For a moment, he loved her, felt a tenderness almost alien to his experience—then cut if off, put it away for later when it would not interfere with his preparation for the race.

"Oh, Martin—!" Eyes brightening. She was close to useless tears.

He searched for a method of operation. Found it.

"Look, you have to jump well this afternoon. Just to give Grachikov the big two fingers—uh?" He smiled, cradling her hand as if it were wounded or sore. "That bastard has tried to ruin you, all the way down the line. Give it back to him. Spit in his eye, kick him in the groin—" She seemed to want to believe him. "After this afternoon, I promise. I promise we'll make plans. We—we'll be together—"

Like leaping into a strange element. Calculation, coaxing—but something he found he could say almost naturally at that moment. She nodded, sniffing back the tears, tossing the wiry hair, then brushing it back from her forehead. She had finished toying with the bread.

He saw Lydall, carrying a tray, sit at a nearby table. The Englishman seemed to take in the scene, and smile as a result.

Outpsyching, Gutierrez thought, and raised his hand and Irena's, in a victory clinch. Lydall nodded.

"There is no alternative, I am distressed to say, but to withdraw this athlete from his event this afternoon," declared the Chairman of the Comité National Olympique et Sportif Français, who had flown back to Moscow just that morning, having returned to Paris to personally investigate the allegations against Diderot the day they first appeared in the French press. The discussion—the French team manager had made it an argument, rancorous and heated and recriminatory—had been going on for more than an hour in the village offices occupied by the officials of the French Olympic team.

But there would be no vote. The Chairman voiced the opinion of the other Comité officials present, and the IOC had accepted the evidence that the Chairman had gathered in Paris, the most damning being photocopies—the manager could still smell the acrid, oily smell of the photocopier, he was certain—of the contracts signed by François Diderot with Dumas-Quenelle. The signature had been verified, and the company was not prepared to make a categorical denial of the documents. The team management, Diderot's coach—the athlete was waiting in another room for their decision, and had not been called into the meeting—had all argued that the decision should be postponed until after the heats, even after the Final.

The Chairman had replied, "We will not expose the Comité, or France, to the humiliation of having a French athlete stripped of a medal, should he win one. We had more than enough of that at Grenoble—"

And the remainder was hot air, arguing an increasingly untenable case. Eventually—

"Call Diderot in. We must tell him of the decision of the Comité and the team management while there are still some hours left before his race. Diderot—we are agreed, gentlemen—will be withdrawn from the French team, and sent home as soon as is convenient."

When he got outside the room, even outside the building, then outside the fence, he could let the tears prick, then run. He had been good in there, good enough—stiff face, unblinking eyes, a curt nod of acceptance, turn on his heel, exit. But not now. There was no one to see him as he sat on a bench under a birch tree in the mint-new park outside the fence. And if there was, he no longer cared.

When he looked up—still not looking outward, but his head having lifted from his chest—it was as if some part of his thoughts had taken external form, detached itself and become a manifestation. Loriot was there—Givenchy sunglasses now utterly sinister, suit immaculate, uncreasable. He blinked, the sunlight through the leaves strong and dazzling on his wet eyes. He wanted to wipe them, but did not want Loriot to see the gesture.

"It's all over then, François?" Loriot was idly turning his sunglasses in his hand now, swinging them by one arm. Diderot let himself be mesmerized. He could not look into Loriot's face. "I'm sorry it had to end this way—the company is sorry. But—"

Surely the man wouldn't actually say it, verbally get rid of him—? He knew he was finished with Dumas-Quenelle, that they had chucked him on the project scrap heap and would be recasting the central role of their campaign. Surely Loriot didn't *enjoy* the telling?

"Shut up," he said, still watching the swinging polarized sunglasses, his hands in his lap, his body leaning forward. The useless fitness—

"François—you have taken it badly—"

Diderot turned on him.

"Some pig in your employ, Loriot, told the newspapers, for *money*. It's all a manure heap, Loriot, the whole business." Loriot looked distastefully at him, as if offended by his presence. He also looked as if he wanted to get away as quickly and quietly as possible. Diderot had resolved he would cry out only once, that he would hide the swill and mess of his emotions after the one outburst. Loriot would do for an audience.

"You understand—mm? You pay me to advertise your crap, I take the money because I'm greedy, and some other greedy little bastard comes along and sells me out for what the rags will pay him to tell a juicy story. And now you come round to give me the brush-off, cancel the contract. I *know* the contract's canceled, you arrogant turd!" He wanted to hit Loriot, but he sensed that self-flagellation would be more just, and refrained. "It's my fault," he added, as if continuing his thought, "I know that. No one else is to blame—it's just all shit, the whole thing. The whole Olympic thing is just shit, and someone ought to blow the whole bloody thing into the clouds!"

He did not wait for Loriot to speak, to move, even to don his glasses. He walked away, bitterly amused, even as he choked on his emotions again which pressed up from his chest like vomit they were so palpable, that his body was walking. Something was making him *walk* away—not run, or jog, but just walk. Spectator, not competitor.

Loriot watched him for a time, until he had shrunk to unimportance in the distance under the trees. Then began to consider his alternative suggestion to the board of Dumas-Quenelle, which they had not, as yet, rejected. Two people—the girl Barseaux and Phillipe Modraine, two of France's rising young tennis stars. A joint campaign—?

They had blocked off both ends of the street—blankets draped right across the access, barriers beyond those, and signs that claimed that there was a danger of building collapse and the street was therefore closed. And police guards to keep out the curious. And all the shops closed on the block of Kirov Street that backed onto the courtyard behind the warehouse, and the warehouses still used also closed.

A little hot island inhabited by the KGB and the terrorist group known as *Do pobachenya*. Marksmen were stationed in the rear rooms of buildings that overlooked the warehouse, and in buildings opposite the front doors. The smell of gasoline from the garage, now deserted, in the hot air, and the silence.

There were no windows or doors of the warehouse overlooking the forecourt of the garage, and Kazantsev and Puchkov had set up their command post—a large trailer—there. Even with the windows of the trailer open, and the door wide, it was stifling in the tin box on wheels emblazoned with the Cyrillic letters KGB. The walls were boarded with cork panels, and one of the team was pinning a huge street map section to one wall. On another wall, architects' plans of the warehouse and its adjoining buildings hastily searched for and found. The plans dated from before 1917, and Kazantsev supposed they were lucky they had survived. He and Puchkov were pushing around, as if shuffling cards, aerial photographs taken by a KGB helicopter only an hour earlier. Their monochrome glossiness looked still wet.

Puchkov was smoking. He appeared to Kazantsev to be more relaxed. As head of the small Moscow Antiterrorist Squad at KGB Center, he was in overall command of the countermeasures.

Kazantsev, as his senior deputy, effectively ran the squad, as he had done for the last year. Both of them knew it, and neither of them resented the other. The Antiterrorist Squad, part of the Second Chief Directorate of the KGB, was considered by many of the senior officers of that Directorate to be a show department. It was wise to have such a squad, just in case, to allow everyone to sleep better at night—but it was small, meagerly staffed by inexperienced young men and one or two old stagers who had missed out on promotion, some transfers from the military, older men reaching pension age, or second-grade bomb experts. To have created a larger, better-staffed department would have been admitting to the existence of terrorists and the threat they might pose. The weight of internal security in the Second Directorate had always fallen on prevention, and the rooting out of dissidence—not on its having to be foiled when it had gained, however temporarily, the upper hand. Kazantsev, whose personal reputation with his superiors was high, had fought the inertia of hidebound attitudes for years without success.

For him, the blankets at the end of the street, the single cursory visit by a Deputy Chairman—much as if he had been on a kit inspection or a PR job—and the silence and the heat created and sustained the impression of shipwreck and an island. The authorities had drawn a veil over them, and were trying to forget what might be going on in and around Kirov Street. They were unprepared to accept the hypothesis that the terrorists might well possess an FAE device. Most of them wouldn't know what one was if he told them—

No word from Donetsk—nothing, nothing, nothing. Nothing bloody missing—!

Puchkov was tapping the photographs with a pencil, talking.

"Right—the radio check confirms they're bottled in. Each of these exits through other warehouses or shops is blocked off by marksmen on loan to us from that rather nasty department no one talks about—" A thin smile. Kazantsev nodded. "They're bottled up, and they'll have guessed they are. What will they do next? They don't answer the loudspeaker—"

Kazantsev screwed up his face, then proceeded to roll up his shirt-sleeves, a gesture that was not businesslike so much as a pause for thought.

"They won't have any demands—except to get out."

Puchkov raised an eyebrow.

"You're pulling that little-boy face, Oleg. Something worrying you—outside this little mess, naturally?"

Kazantsev leaned back in his canvas chair, hands stretching above his head, fingers curling and uncurling, as if unknotting a tangled ball of twine.

"The powers that be have decided this is an end game?" Puchkov hesitated, then nodded. "I thought so. I wondered why the nasties were so eager to lend us marksmen. Sweep this little lot under the carpet. No show trial, no long sentences to deter—just oblivion."

"Now don't get moral with me—"

"I'm not, Sergei. I just—I'm angry they don't understand. Angry they want to ignore it. We *know* they've got an FAE device, and it must be in there, we just can't prove it or work out how they got it! If that little lot goes up, even in there, they won't be able to hide the fact."

"Look—practicalities. Your strong point. What do we *do?*'

"Work on their weakness."

"Which is?"

"The need to get out of there. Shubin—from his file, and from talking to Federenko, I'm sure he wants a bigger audience than we're providing. So, he has to get out."

"The hostages?"

"If necessary—" Kazantsev drew one thick finger across his throat.

"Hell! What excuse do we offer the Special Investigations Department?"

"All right. We're hamstrung. It's a stalemate." He shrugged. "I agree—we're buggered."

Kolya, one of his juniors, stuck his head through the door of the trailer.

"Sir, they want to talk," he said.

"Demands—at last?" Puchkov asked.

"Maybe. Let's find out."

Two-fifteen. The Lenin Stadium packed to capacity—100,000 people who had just seen the qualifying finalists of the 110-meter hurdles for women posted on the electronic boards at each end of the stadium, to be replaced by the finalists in the women's long jump. While they waited for the semifinals of the men's high hurdles, they could direct their attention to the early stages of the men's hammer event, and the rivalry between the Russians and the East Germans and Rumanians, and the final of the women's long jump.

Irena, in track suit trousers and her red-and-white vest, was next to jump, drawn sixth of the twelve finalists in order of jumping. Something *had* happened to her nerves, to her stomach. Or perhaps only her mind. Four of the girls ahead of her had cleared the bar first time, but the Canadian had caught it with a trailing heel. That small, human incident was like water dashed at her. Rattle of the bar, the face of the girl as she bounced up out of the landing mattress, the applause for a Russian hammer throw at the other end of the stadium—her attention was narrowed, refined by them.

She stood up, removed her track suit trousers, strode to her run-up mark. What Gutierrez had failed to do for her she had done for herself; entered that small, enclosed, isolated egotism of the international athlete. She rocked slightly back and forth, testing her readiness, breathing regularly.

Beginning the run. The bar at 1.84 meters, which twelve years before would have won the Gold for anyone who jumped it in Mexico. Curving in, back on her heels for the last three strides, leaning away from the bar on the final stride, explosive lift, bent free leg swing, opposite arm drive, turn back to takeoff, hips up and extended, big arch of her body, hips over, hold the arch, *hold*— begin to lift head, *jackknife*, straighten legs—*relax*—

The bounce in the rubber, the bar still there above her. Up, arms up, listening for the noise from the Polish spectators— nationalism was allowed a place in the scheme of things the moment she finished the jump—big smile. A narrow little awareness, sharp as a blade.

They climbed out of the bus, and self-consciousness struck each of them with the ease and suddenness of putting on a garment of some shiny, garish material. It altered the posture of bodies, tilt of heads, caused them to strike poses, attitudes. Gutierrez was perhaps most energized by the crowd of spectators around the warm-up track next to the stadium. None of them, however, felt anything but superior to those who watched, or to their coaches who waited for them with final instructions, with sedative talk or exhortation, or to the fussy officials, as if waiting to docket and load beef, wanting tidiness and smoothness above everything.

Three o'clock.

Ochengwe jogging, warming slowly for the second heat. Irvine flapping arms, kicking legs, almost a parody of preparedness.

Lydall talking to his coach, nodding sagely, his face an expression-less mask. Gutierrez's smile becoming fixed, false as the adrenaline began surging. Holmrath relaxed, Jorgensen nervous, dispirited yet determined because there were no more excuses to be made, and he was glad in a way that the moment had come. Tretsov trotting past the Russian spectators, his face carefully devoid of plan or intelligence. Nonentity. Federenko, in the second heat, lounging against the barrier round the warm-up track, watching Tretsov with an obsessive attentiveness which parodied love.

Diderot, sitting in the bus, a spectator of the scene.

Kazantsev weighed Shubin, almost as if he might be measuring up to him in some physical contest. The man was shorter than him by a good six inches, but Kazantsev never considered bulk any longer, since most of the people he met were smaller than himself. He was slight—he might have said wasted—of frame, his black beard highlighting the fierce eyes, the red mouth. And the girl behind Shubin, the one in the bikini at *Serebryany Bor*, now appeared taller, stronger. Less feminine, and not because of the denims and the loose shirt—because of the Polish PM-63 submachine gun she held at her waist; even more, he suspected, because the situation had become extreme, and she was one of those who had suddenly found not fear in it but something like delight, joy.

Shubin was five yards from the judas door, the girl a few paces behind him and to his left. And the others had guns on the butchers.

Strangely, he could feel little sense of identification with the hostages, but thought of them in terms of their being snatched from their patient watch over the sausage machine, or from the cold store amid the hanging carcasses. And already, he knew, the hostages would have begun to slip into that mood where he was their enemy, because the safety of the terrorists would have become synonymous with their own safety.

Yes, he decided, the girl wanted to go all the way. Something blind and ecstatic lurking in her. Not with Shubin—? No, he was certain of that. Shubin had something about him, as if the man were looking over Kazantsev's shoulder, into a future he clearly envis-aged.

He could not tell—now that the guns had interfered, were omnipresent—whether there was a bomb. Was there something in there behind them whose scent, whose confidence, they still carried? He almost visibly shook his head, angered that he could not decipher that code.

"What do you want, Shubin?" he said when the silence had gone on a long time, broken only by the patrolling beat of a helicopter above them.

"Food, and something to drink." Shubin grinned, resting the automatic pistol across his folded arm. "Not drugged, of course."

"We don't have one that works that fast. You know that."

"Maybe. But we'll give it to the butchers first, naturally. We'd like the food fairly soon—" Still grinning. The confidence might indicate—? Kazantsev probed.

"When do we start to talk about terms?"

"For what?"

"Releasing the prisoners—"

"Our free passage, I suppose you mean?"

Kazantsev waved his arm very slowly around, behind him, taking in the street's perspective, the frozen attitudes of his men, the blankets stretched across the ends of the street.

"Just a piece of news, by the way. My superiors are determined to ignore what's going on here. They don't believe you have any *real* threat to offer—bar the lives of a few butchers. They want you cleaned off the pavement like so much dog turd." He raised his hands, palms out, defensively. "Not my decision. I'm just informing you how much of a standoff this is. They know you've killed three of my men—" He paused, valediction and effect. "But they don't think you're important, or effective. So—we'll wait it out."

Silence. The buzzing of the helicopter now quieter, overtaken by the buzzing of a fly round Kazantsev's head. He was careful not to brush it away. The girl seemed impatient with Shubin, or perhaps just impatient for action. She was dangerous—he might even have to tell the marksmen, if it all fell in on them, to get her first. A possible imperative—one burst with the PM-63 would take care of all the butchers.

"Six hostages isn't enough is what you're saying," Shubin observed. "You'll steamroller us anyway." Kazantsev nodded. "Then why don't you do it, mm?" Shubin grinned. "Oh, no—I believe they don't think we're important, the farts at the top of your tree and in the Kremlin. But they don't want us running around, or shooting butchers or getting shot, while there are all these visitors in Moscow. That wouldn't be politic. So, you have to keep us here. You won't do anything risky."

Kazantsev had not expected any other reply. It was a truism. "Where's the bomb, Shubin?"

"What bomb?"

A slight flicker—? He could not be sure, and the split second had passed. The girl's nerves, or reaction, seemed to go into the gun, which shifted slightly more into alignment on Kazantsev. And, no doubt, a marksman on the roof of the garage had shifted himself, realigned, tensed—

"You know which bomb—the FAE device. Shall I explain?"

"I understand—I'm an engineer, not a peasant."

"I know you have a device, Shubin. I don't know how, but I know. You won't get that out of here—and here it will do a minimum of damage." Shubin smiled—and Kazantsev did not understand it at first, then explained it to himself as a further denial. "Think about that. You'll immolate yourselves, and a couple of my people—bit of a damp squib, really."

He turned on his heel and walked away, satisfied that he had given Shubin a sufficient sense of his isolation, and a glimpse behind the curtain at the desolate perspective stretching ahead of him.

"Don't forget the food and drink," Shubin called, just as he ducked back through the judas door, and it slammed shut. Kazantsev wondered why he sounded so unconcerned, and hoped that the poison inherent in the situation would begin to work once the man had had time to think.

Four heats, seeded by computer on the fastest times by the competitors in the 5000 before the Games; the first and second in each heat automatically qualifying for the Final, and the six with the remaining fastest times also qualifying. Thus, Lydall would run in the first heat, cannon fodder in terms of his season's times in the heat Gutierrez was expected to win. A new Kenyan with some fast times in 1979, a South American with one good race in Europe—and the rest of the field.

Allardyce watched the track as the runners stripped off, jogged, and fidgeted—Gutierrez for a moment appeared to be watching the high jump and Irena Witlocka, then he looked up instead at the electronic scoreboard as the names unrolled, seemingly satisfied as his own appeared. Lydall intent, white-faced and thin, a stringy, untidy appearance, almost unathletic. Allardyce had seen him on the warm-up track, exchanged a few words. Lydall would qualify in this heat, unless his mental attitude was no more than bluff.

Even so, the crowd was watching Gutierrez. Greenberg, sitting next to Allardyce in shirt-sleeves, was fiddling with his ball-point, chewing some imaginary cud. Ready almost to race himself.

"He's not going to be another Prefontaine, is he?" Allardyce asked lightly.

"That isn't funny," Greenberg replied. Allardyce wondered at the personal commitment of a journalist to an athlete; saw that in Greenberg's case it was unconnected with copy or headlines. Greenberg really believed—Gutierrez was Greenberg's surrogate, his race in Rome played over, with a different result.

Allardyce continued studying the runners on the other side of the track through his field glasses, then swung them down, a sudden sliding view of the central field, then the brown and white of the home straight, then the crowd.

Finally Anna, sitting with Leonov below him. He had to talk to Anna—and he found he had no stomach for it. He was afraid even of briefing her; or perhaps guilty at the relief he felt would come when the job was done and the case officer took over. His tail had worried the CIA—they were making other plans. After today, he would be out of it.

He didn't like the feelings—

The gun, and perspective jumping as he adjusted the glasses. The field bunching, squirming, struggling into the first bend, as if the front-runners were being physically pulled back into the bunch. Black faces up front, including the Kenyan, with the Europeans and Gutierrez content to let the pack straggle out. He noticed that Greenberg was using field glasses, and knew they would be riveted on Gutierrez.

A floater—the boy was a floater, running like Viren and the other Finns, as if gravity were having no effect, as if his feet were hardly touching the track. Allardyce admitted that he looked a great runner—smoothness, balance, the essential quality.

Allardyce watched Lydall, near the back of the field, as they came down the straight past the finish, twelve laps to be run. Hunched up, determined, thin, and tough. He never looked as if he was fit, as if he had reserves, as if he could win a race. Allardyce, perhaps catching something from Greenberg, felt an identity with Lydall, and allowed the tug of nationalism at his feelings. The more favored British runner was in heat four and would be bound to qualify—

Therefore, he told himself, not nationalism; just for Peter Brian Lydall, whose problems were simple, whose drama was beginning. He turned to Greenberg, and grinned.

"Fast time?" he asked.

"No. Field's too weak for that—your boy and mine, they'll make it easy."

It wasn't easy. Lydall, by lap five, was uncomfortable with the pace of the race. He had been content to remain at the back of the bunched field for the first five laps, while thirty meters ahead the Africans juggled for position and each tried not to become, or be made to become, front-runner. Thus the pace had dropped disastrously. This would be the slowest heat, and Lydall would have to win it or come second in order to qualify.

He was angry, coldly angry with himself. It was his intention to hide in the field, giving away little of his style or tactics to Gutierrez and the others, or to the coaches watching in the stadium, and using a quick finish to put himself among the qualifiers in a fastish heat. Now, he couldn't do it; he would have to show his hand.

Lap six in sixty-two. Lap seven in sixty-three. Gutierrez was content to remain just ahead of him, understanding his urgency but not visibly challenging it. He was giving the impression that it was an easy race, taking nothing out of him. Lydall, gambling on his mental confidence, slowed the eighth lap to sixty-seven, putting himself back into the main bunch, behind the dithering front group of five still alternating the lead every lap or half-lap, obsessed by not having to make the pace.

Lap eight, and Lydall injected a sixty-one lap which put him on the shoulder of the leading group as they came into the home straight. Four laps left—and he wondered what Gutierrez would do.

There was no one, no one at all who would get between the two of them. Lydall was sure of it, even when the Kenyan seemed to lift his pace off the bend into the ninth lap. Then, when he ran the tenth in sixty dead, Lydall—and Gutierrez, because he glanced at the American's face and saw his concern—knew that the Kenyan had been prompted by the sense of Lydall's proximity and also perhaps by Gutierrez's consistent stroll, and the clock. Only two were going through from this heat—just maybe a third, but no more than that.

Gutierrez seemed to hesitate up the back straight of the eleventh, with six hundred meters of running left. Lydall ignored him, making the conscious transfer of target from him to the Kenyan twenty meters up. Gutierrez—and he shared the reluctance—seemed unwilling to reveal his full ability, as if showing it might dim its gloss.

Lydall kicked.

The crowd, seeing him detach himself from the leading group, which seemed instantly to straggle more thinly, sensed his pursuit of the Kenyan, knew the slowness of the time, and leaned forward as if to savor the unexpected drama.

The Kenyan, Lydall decided as they came down the home straight for the bell, knew what he had to do, but wasn't accelerating. Lydall looked behind him, saw Gutierrez seeming to make no effort. Perhaps the Kenyan would react to the bell as if it were a shove in the back—he stepped up, closing the gap to ten meters on the straight.

Bell. Don't look round on the bend, just listen for the others. White vest flapping on the Kenyan's narrow shoulders. Watch the stride—stretching—? The Kenyan wasn't stretching as he came off the bend into the last back straight. Two-fifty left. Lydall looked round. Gutierrez was struggling with the South American, who looked suddenly tired but was hanging on. An untried Finn, blond hair waving from side to side as he began to drop.

He kicked again to close the gap on the Kenyan, and halfway into the bend Gutierrez was at his shoulder, the Kenyan still two or three meters up, and aware of them. Lydall felt the bottom fall out of his stomach for a moment, and a chill wateriness in his legs. If two went through—?

Gutierrez flowed ahead of Lydall. Still the Kenyan had no extra kick—he could overhaul him slowly, step by step by step by—

The back straight. Level with the Kenyan, but making no more impression than that. Gutierrez three meters up, and holding it. He was no longer there, it was only the Kenyan who had to be beaten—

Something snapped awake. With fifty meters to go, Lydall inched past the Kenyan, and the crowd, impartially excited, roared its approval. Gutierrez holding, no, Lydall was gaining on him just slightly—he almost wished Gutierrez would pull him on with a faster sprint. The Kenyan's roaring breath clearly audible.

Tape. Gutierrez, hands above his head. Lydall two meters down on him, and two up on the Kenyan in third. A slow time.

Gutierrez trotted on. Lydall, almost sick with relief rather than effort, caught up with him.

"You stupid cunt," he said as they slowed down, the breath whistling through his teeth, a slight ring of spittle round his mouth. "You almost ruined it for both of us!"

Gutierrez shrugged, as if everything had been part of a larger plan, and he was satisfied.

CHAPTER 13

Martin was watching her, standing in his track suit, hair still damp and face flushed with the effort of his heat. She had had to shut her mind to it each time she jumped, and for as much of the rest of the time as she could, because it distracted her like no track event had ever done. Now he was through she could relax, and when he waved and everything was all right and he jogged away to watch the next heat, she could put him aside in her mind, and concentrate afresh and cleanly.

She was fourth—four of the finalists had completed their first three jumps and been placed ninth, tenth, eleventh, and twelfth. The first eight had earned another three jumps. She was fourth, with two failures at previous heights and having to go to a third jump before clearing the last height. The bar was at 1.90. She was one place from a medal, and her stomach was settled, her mental attitude right, her technique strong, consistent.

She began to know that she would win a medal.

Allardyce saw, suddenly, as he let his attention wander from the lineup for the second heat where attention would be focused on Ochengwe and the Russian, Federenko, that Anna was sitting next to an empty seat. He studied the crowd there, and the nearest exit, but saw no sign of Leonov. He had to speak to her now, and quickly.

Greenberg had left the press box to talk to Gutierrez. Allardyce slipped from his seat, threaded his way to the door, and went down the concrete steps to her seat.

It was as if she sensed his approach, for her head turned when he was still three rows away. She did not smile, merely seemed to nod and shift slightly in her seat as if to make room for him. It had surprised him that she had not been looking out for him, that she was so composed. As he sat down, he studied her face, while she said, "Gennadi was called away, back to the office. He is sorry—" Here she smiled, briefly. "To miss the races." Yes, she was confident, and her mouth firm, her eyes steady. He felt his own stomach settled by her air of confidence.

"We have time to talk, then," he said.

"Yes."

He leaned forward, and slightly toward her, as if savoring an intimacy with her, or making some obvious, adolescent approach. Then he plunged on with what he had to say.

"Look, I'm cut out. You'll be briefed by the case officer himself—"

Her face darkened, and she was evidently angry.

"Why do they persist in playing stupid games, David?" She was accusing the CIA, and him.

"Look, Anna—I'm sorry. I tried to argue with them, but the tail on me has panicked them. I'm simply to tell you how and when, and they'll do the rest."

"The tail on you?"

"Yes. They're following me about—nothing dramatic, but it's there."

"Gennadi," she said softly. Her brow creased, and he thought he saw her lip tremble. But her head was bent away from him, and he might have been mistaken. The gun startled her. She looked up, saw the runners across the track moving into the first bend of the second 5000 heat.

"What do you mean, Gennadi?" He felt impelled to persist.

"I don't know—that's what worries me. Either he suspects us of being lovers who might relight a fire—or he suspects you and me of being what we really are—"

"Christ."

"Exactly."

"His behavior to you—?"

"As always. He is in love with me."

"Could he deceive you?"

"I—don't think so." She looked around, as if expecting to see Leonov standing behind them, a threatening shadow. The runners passed beneath them down the home straight, with twelve laps to go.

"Then it's good we're not meeting again."

"Perhaps it is."

"How are their investigations progressing?"

"A little less intense than—" She seemed to realize what she had said, the conclusion that might be drawn, then added, "But no increase in covert investigation."

"You're followed?"

The runners, a string of colored vests with a red one leading, going off the bend into the back straight.

"No. Gennadi—perhaps he's keeping an eye on me himself?"

"Are your staff being followed?"

"No one has said—not recently."

"You could go to your dacha alone, without arousing undue suspicion?"

Her eyes widened in shock.

"They want to use my dacha? David—they're mad, careless children—!" She seemed very afraid now.

"It'll be all right—they'll take care. They assured me of that."

Her lips were pressed together, her chin set.

"Very well, when?"

"Tomorrow. Whenever you can. There'll be somebody there, waiting for you. Can you make tomorrow?"

"I shall have to." She smiled humorlessly. "Now, go back to your job, David—in case Gennadi returns."

He sensed himself as an actor, searching for an appropriate, even memorable, line on which to leave. Eventually, he simply nodded.

"Good-bye, Anna."

"Good-bye, David." She pointedly turned her attention to the track below them, and the runners coming down the straight, the crowd noisy with pleasure at the positive front-running of Arkady Federenko.

Leonov watched Allardyce through binoculars from the crowded terrace, as the runners passed beneath him. He was standing with Georgi, his sergeant, in the frame of one of the exits. When Allardyce paused, almost at the press box, and nodded to a man seated on the end of the row, Leonov caught his breath, went on looking, swung the glasses back and forth between Anna and the man—who got up and left, in the middle of the race.

"Him," Leonov snapped. "Passing her now, making for the exit."

"Got him."

"Photographs, full surveillance—now!"

When Georgi had gone scampering down the exit tunnel, his footsteps echoing and audible above the noises of the crowd, Leonov allowed himself to move beyond the narrow little excitement of having discovered Allardyce's case officer. And he felt a space

opening in his abdomen, as if vital organs were suddenly missing.
Anna Akhmerovna was his double agent.

Kazantsev was outlined by the sunlight in the open judas door, making him a perfect target. Shubin smiled inwardly, believing that it was bravado on the KGB man's part as he watched his juniors carry in the beer and sandwiches, moving gingerly, eyes everywhere, among the terrorists and the little white-coated group of hostages, who had begun to sink into that resentful stupor that followed fear, terror, hatred, tension. They seemed ungrateful for the food and drink.

Kazantsev, standing in the door, noted their condition as his eyes grew accustomed to the dusky interior of the warehouse. The men delivering the food, too, were chosen because of their training in psychology—which was why their heads turned repeatedly, taking in as much sensory information as they could in the few moments they were there.

The psychologists from the Center had arrived, to Kazantsev's intense resentment since they were even less experienced, practically, than he was himself.

Condition—lethargic but good, he concluded. A bunch of kids keeping going on notoriety for the present. It would be a long job, if they wanted to save the butchers. He looked at the little group, who now seemed to have decided communally that intense concentration on their sandwiches was the wisest course, and he had as little feeling for them as Shubin.

His men returned to the doorway. Kazantsev lowered the submachine gun slowly, stepped aside, and they came out. One of the terrorists slammed the door behind them. Kazantsev waved up at the marksmen on the roof opposite, and saw them relax.

As the door closed on the strip of sunlight, Shubin relaxed, too. He returned to his contemplation of the children, which made him more certain of his course, and of success, than the sight of Kazantsev's huge bulk in the doorway had done. He disturbed, like a child's nightmare of an enormous shadow cutting off the light. But contemplation of the children soothed him, made everything possible again.

He climbed the ladder to the upper gallery, taking his thoughts as secretively into a corner as a man might some jewel, being surrounded by thieves. He swigged at a bottle of beer. Zenaida watched him go, scrutinized him, and seemed to anticipate his solitary mood and so returned to eating. Shubin ate a ham sandwich, the bread thickly sliced and not very fresh.

It was almost time to begin his escape. It might take twelve hours, or twenty-four; it depended for its success on persuading the children that escape was an imperative. Blasting their way out.

Which would take time, but would succeed because the persuasion would hinge on the belief that the FAE devices were still in the compartment beneath the floor of the minibus. The children would risk everything to get them out of the trap. He, Shubin, simply had to keep his nerve, believe in the eventual outcome, and be able to act desperation sufficiently well to communicate it to them. Especially to the girl, who was cleverer than the others and knew him better.

He chewed on the thick bread, swallowed some more beer, watching the KGB men down in the courtyard below the grimy window being served with tea, smoking cigarettes, occasionally casting wary glances up toward the window.

If the girl believed, then the children would. And if they did—it really was *Do pobachenya*.

Fifth lap, almost halfway through the race. Federenko had done as he was bid and led throughout. The group behind him seemed satisfied to let him do the front-running, thinking him overconfident and not likely to last. It was a fast time and it looked good, a Russian vest leading the first group of runners by fifteen meters or more—dragging the Ugandan and the best Finn and the New Zealand number one behind him, forcing them to a pace they did not want, had not chosen. He had given them the dilemma, the fact that changed all their possible tactics. They had not expected in the heats a determined piece of front-running, from the first bend, this caricature of a man trying to qualify—someone who would burn himself out, someone they would catch with three, four laps still to go.

Past the finish, the crowd buzzing with admiration and perhaps with doubt. Burying the doubt in nationalism. For himself, he had no doubts as he went into the sixth lap. They might come later, if the legs got tired or he had to push the pace to maintain his lead, but not yet. He was full of running.

The concentration he required to run each lap at sixty-two or sixty-three squeezed to the back of his mind any and all of the things that had disturbed his sleep—Zenaida's face in the warehouse,

Shubin and the hot anger he aroused just by his physical appearance, by the jut of the black beard and the little burning coal lumps of his eyes. All that was gone, put aside as quickly and neatly as his track suit at the start of the heat. Perhaps, he realized briefly, not letting his concentration wander, he was showing them, too. The alternative. This way of self-assertion, of identity.

Sixty-three. The leading group had become detached eighteen meters back, and the also-rans were strung out halfway round the track by then.

Seventh lap, sixty-three. Eighth lap, sixty-two. The noise mounting like the heat of a midsummer morning, so that it was a physical presence around him, the tension striking off the track and the stadium like sunlight off brazen surfaces. And lifting him rather than dragging at his limbs. He could not remember when it had happened before. One hundred thousand people, almost every one of them willing him on and he picking up that emission like a broadcast of surging music. The noise took on an increasingly urgent rhythm through the ninth and tenth laps—he threw in another sixty-two on the tenth, with two laps left, stretching the group so that the Ugandan moved up on him, the Finn struggled to hold pace, and the New Zealander slipped four or five meters. The noise like the beat of his blood, lifting him.

The sense of drama increased—a more subterranean noise as the Ugandan closed on him through the eleventh so that he was six or seven meters down as Federenko went through the bell, and kicked at once into the bend instead of waiting until he came off it. A sigh transmuted to a roar as he moved away to ten meters, then slipped to five by the time they both hit the straight.

The last words, by a guilty-looking, shifty-eyed Vladimir. *You must make yourself favorite, after the American's performance.* But more than that now; those words were lost in the bellow of the crowd. Only his own words, his proven belief—this is the answer. This is what I do, Zenushka, better than anyone.

He kicked again, lengthening his stride, hearing the Ugandan almost at his shoulder as he went into the final bend. Nothing going muzzy, the noise sharp, almost solid. The body obeying the rhythm trained into it. The roar again as the Ugandan dropped another meter or two trying to come up on the outside. Blazered officials, trotting athletes—some Russians urging him on, national hero—

Forty meters, and stretching out, giving it everything, betraying his talent and tactics, making himself favorite. The Ugandan had probably looked over his shoulder, seen he was safe, slackened off. Federenko went through the tape six meters up on him, having led the race from start to finish.

Little change, no sudden collapse from inside himself, no silly weakness in his legs as he began his lap of honor, arms held aloft, everyone delighted, but the feeling as he acknowledged the cheering, the flags, becoming small and personal and satisfied. The moment of Russian-ness, of the red vest, gone and replaced by personal satisfaction.

The Ugandan was up with him, holding out his hand, which he shook. Then Ochengwe dropped back, letting the crowd have their hero.

When they told him the unofficial time, it was 2.4 seconds outside Irvine's world record, fifteen seconds better than Viren's Olympic record.

Irena Witlocka, at the end of the second heat, waiting for the noise of the lap of honor to die down before she took her second jump in the last series of three jumps, the bar at 1.95, two centimeters better than the Olympic record, which the Canadian girl had just broken and so had the Rumanian who followed her. At her own first attempt, she had dragged the bar off with her trailing leg. One ninety-five was going to break the last eight, drop the pieces either side of the medal watershed. She had to be on the right side.

Federenko was putting on his track suit, the crowd settling into the afterglow of participation. She rocked back and forth, then leaned forward into the quick approach run. Just right, each pace matching a mental image—back turned, explosive lift, slithering the upper body over the bar, kicking up the legs suddenly, as if jackknifing in a swimmer's fancy dive, and the body bouncing back up from the rubber almost too quickly, as if she had done the whole thing speeded up.

But the bar was still there. At 1.95. The crowd noise—she heard it then, and raised her arms, though the expression meant little beside the lump in her throat, hot and burning like grief.

The children, the silly wide-eyed children—

He clamped down on the refrain, running like a jingle through his head, as he looked at each of them in turn. Nothing must get in the way of the act he must put on, least of all any tinge of the contempt he felt for the rest of his group.

Pacing up and down, he was communicating his pretended distress to the others like a tiger he had seen in the Kiev Zoo had communicated its pent-up frustration in the cage to the adults and children who stood outside, looking in and eating ice cream. Restless pacing, repeated glances through the window, or at the minibus—pointless opening and closing of the door of the dispatch office; the inability to sit down for more than a few moments. Taunts at the butchers, and always the submachine gun carried openly and visibly.

They were jumpy now, his suggested mood adopted. Moving into this phase now, the silent confrontations with each of them, or with them all in quick succession. The girl was surprised, but not suspicious, he was certain; the others electrified, unsettled, trying to find images for themselves that would satisfy him, their eyes casting about on the floor as if they might pick up identities like pebbles on a beach.

And the hot dusk in the warehouse, and the silent, bovine hostages, contributed to the growing tension—as if a storm threatened.

Karen Gunston had joined Allardyce and Greenberg in the press box. Allardyce registered that he was now being regarded in much the same light as Greenberg; a superiority compounded of intolerant self-assuredness and sexual conquest. The image of the girl as a clichéd sexual conqueror of the other sex did not amuse Allardyce as it might have done; as Karen Gunston displayed her sexuality as something off limits to both men, he became increasingly uncomfortable and aroused, and tried to concentrate on the third heat of the 5000 with Irvine trailing badly behind Jorgensen and Holmrath, an East German and a Tanzanian.

The Russian pressmen, more than a hundred of them just to cover the track and field events, had delighted in Federenko's brilliant run—the African contingent had taken a quieter comfort in Ochengwe's having been at his shoulder until the last hundred meters. Greenberg had seemed abashed by Federenko's time, much faster than that of Gutierrez, while Allardyce himself came more and more to wonder what was happening to Irvine down on the track, especially as the Australians in the press box began to alter in mood, distancing themselves from Irvine's likely failure by pace making for the adverse comments that were beginning to be bandied about. Allardyce felt sorry for Irvine, the Gold Medal at 10,000 meters already forgotten.

Four laps to go and Irvine, an isolated, dogged figure more bunched up than usual in his running style, was adrift from the four leaders by more than thirty meters, showing no sign of having begun a sequence of faster laps to put him back in touch. There was an emanation of weariness, of mental fatigue, from him. The time was faster than the first heat, but a lot of runners from the savagely fast second heat would qualify on time. Irvine looked as if he might be out of it.

"There's something going on," Karen Gunston was saying. She was squeezed in discomforting proximity between the two men. Her thigh was deliberately hard against Allardyce.

"With you there always is," was Greenberg's comment. Allardyce watched the race, except for the mechanical, once-a-lap look down to Anna and the empty seat next to her. As he did it now, he was able satisfactorily to admire her, and in the same instant contrast the cheap bravery of sexual liberation that seemed to attend Karen.

"The problem is, how do I get a camera and crew down there?" She mused aloud, as if soliciting their help.

"You want to film it?"

"Benjamin—don't try to be clever, dear. It doesn't work."

"O.K., tell Uncle Ben all about it."

Irvine was on the back straight while the four beads strung together that composed the leaders went into the bend.

"Near Kirov Street—one of the guys told me, and I went down. Blankets strung across the ends of this side alley, police and some tough-looking men in badly fitting suits, barriers, the works. They say a building might fall in."

"And you don't believe it?"

"I've seen a setup like that before and I know my guns. That's a riot squad down there—snipers on the roofs, gas guns, everything—"

"A siege?"

Irvine was below them now, and perhaps, just perhaps, there was a little less between him and the leaders, maybe twenty meters, more likely twenty-five. Two laps left. Allardyce guessed rather than perceived that the leaders had accelerated down the home straight, and if Irvine was catching them—

He concentrated with even greater effort, Karen Gunston's

words now merely the irritation of her voice, without meaning.

"I think so."

"And you think—?"

"Right in one, Benjy—the people who sent the letters, and the bomb in the Mausoleum."

"Jesus—"

"Now, how the hell do I get down there with a camera?"

Irvine was perhaps twenty meters behind now—certainly no more than twenty. The pace of the race was picking up noticeably, so that it had to be the second fastest heat. He might just qualify—just.

"Anyone else know about this?"

"Who knows. There could've been a dozen applications to take cameras on the streets already."

"So, apply."

The bell. Jorgensen kicked almost immediately, and the Tanzanian went with him. Holmrath and the East German seemed content to wait around the bend, both of them looking back to assess Irvine, now eighteen meters behind, and stretching.

Into the straight. Something of the girl's conversation but more her thigh and its warmth impinged on Allardyce's concentration. He forced himself to watch events on the track, not even to look at Anna, who had been joined once more by Leonov, attentive as ever. The crowd's noise suddenly loud as someone opened the door of the air-conditioned press box, then cut off as the door closed. Irvine went into the bend, with Holmrath and the East German kicking for home. In front, Jorgensen was shoulder to shoulder with the stringy Tanzanian.

Irvine inched up on the two men in front of him, just as they seemed to overhaul the two leaders in slow motion. It was a moving tableau, the same order preserved among the participants, and the distances almost static between them so that it suggested something undramatic, almost lifeless. The crowd seemed to sense it as no position changed over the last lap, despite the efforts of the five leaders.

They finished in that order—Jorgensen, the Tanzanian, the East German, Holmrath, Irvine. Irvine collapsed on the side of the track the moment he crossed the line. And the officials hovered for a moment, then gave him oxygen. The stretcher onto which they loaded his exhausted body, the slow procession to the tunnel and the ambulance, seemed far more dramatic and intense than the end of the race.

Allardyce looked at Greenberg, who shook his head. Allardyce nodded in agreement. Karen Gunston caught his eye and, as if she were taking a moment out of a role she habitually played or was deliberately lightening her mood, she smiled at him. He nodded his acceptance.

"Pax sexualis," he said, and grinned. The effect was almost as relieving as the oxygen they had given Irvine; as if he had recaptured a former mood or self.

Kazantsev, tired of listening to the psychologists, had left the command trailer, and begun pacing the forecourt of the garage where it was parked. The hot bright evening—the rush-hour traffic increasingly audible through the blanket screen—disturbed him. He was certain it was not weariness, or nerves. It was something in the atmosphere, as palpable as the noise of the helicopter patrolling the area, something boiling up like a storm. He knew why he felt as he did—there had been no further demands, no threats, no defiance, no collapse of resolve. Nothing. They might have been surrounding an empty warehouse.

And he had begun to suspect that Shubin was playing a game whose moves he had worked out in advance—that there was something unreal about this siege, these terrorists. There was little conventionality of behavior, even the psychologists admitted that. They counseled sitting and waiting, even though they had begun to question the motives and reactions—or lack of them—of the terrorists.

There was no way out. He thought for an instant, almost laughing, that they might be tunneling their way through to Kirov Street. Shubin wasn't mad, not certifiably so—so what was he doing in there? Brooding over his navel?

Kazantsev began to recognize a dangerous frustration in himself, and tried to put it aside. He knew that he was entering a mood where, should someone order him to an all-out attack on the warehouse, regardless of the hostages, he might agree with them.

What was going *on* in there?

Tretsov had been drawn in the final heat so that his qualifying could be as quiet, and as borderline certain as possible. Diderot should have been the automatic qualifier from the heat. Along with the British number one and the fancied Belgian. The time for the heat proved to be the third fastest of the afternoon. The Belgian qualified, as did the Briton, and Tretsov, coming in an unspectacular third, two seconds inside the time necessary to qualify for the Final. He had gone through an intense experience, robotically following the lap rhythm that would allow him just to qualify, but in an unfancied position. When he crossed the line, he was still fresh, almost untested, with just the mental fogginess of so much concentration of an unrelieved, unchanging kind.

Gutierrez watched him walk away into the tunnel, puzzled by the race he had run, and more puzzled by the dark frown on Federenko's face. Federenko had worried him only in the sense that any challenge disturbed him—a prickling of excitement, a sweat in the palms of his hands, the adrenaline beginning to run, the stomach slightly hollow. But Tretsov disturbed him in a different way— because he knew no more about him at the end of the race than he had at the beginning.

He jogged away to watch the last stage of the women's high jump. Irena was third, and had already had one failure at her next height.

One official challenged his right to be there, trying to keep him away from the event. Gutierrez ignored him, walking past him, letting the protest fade behind him. It might take minutes before they got a ruling out of somebody, and formally ordered him to leave the long jump area.

The Canadian girl was going to win it—it was obvious. She had the bar at 1.99, and looked certain to assault the world record. The French girl had dropped to fifth, the Rumanian to fourth, Irena was third, and the Italian girl looked ready to take the Silver.

Irena came away from the bench, and took his hand immediately. "Sad?" he asked, struck by the look in her eyes.

"Yes—but only because I'm greedy. Bronze will do for me, Martin."

She turned to watch the Italian clear 1.99, then shook her head. "I won't make that," she said.

"You can, girl—"

"No. One ninety-eight is the—" She seemed to search for the word, flapping her arms as if to draw it into the current. "The absolute limit for me. I'm as good as that, but no better." She tapped her forehead. "Up here I'm one ninety-eight—" Now, she smiled at the idea. "I thought one ninety-eight, five up on the Olympic record, might have been good enough—and it is," she finished brightly. "But not for Gold."

She squeezed her hand in his, making it a little fist which he gently crushed for a moment, then released. As she went back, he could see her body adopt her mental concentration. He was surprised at her, felt as if he had learned something, or at least been talking to an adult—and he not yet grown up.

Two of the officials approached him as soon as she left him. He smiled, raised his hands, palms outward, and retreated to a distance, and continued to watch the event, until, half an hour later, the Italian girl had had three failures at two meters, Irena had dropped out at 1.99, and the Canadian girl attempted two meters, failed, but won the Gold on countback with fewest failures at any height.

Gutierrez watched the board as the medalists' names appeared, then the unsuccessful finalists, rolling like a waterfall of lights from the top of the huge electronic scoreboard. Irena waved to him as she went for a shower, hairdo, and makeup before the medal ceremony.

The Deputy Chairman under whose authority the antiterrorist squad, together with a number of other minor departments in the Second Chief Directorate, existed was displeased with the lack of progress. Handling him, Kazantsev felt he was trying to hold a coiling, dangerous snake while wearing slippery gloves. The man's mood kept rolling and sliding out of a firm grip, into the unexpected strike.

"There is no bomb." The statement, bald and not expecting challenge, silenced the command trailer so that the noises of the hot dusty evening became loud, and the buzz of a fly like a ripsaw.

"With respect, sir—" Kazantsev began, watching for the habit of command in the KGB—protect oneself at all costs. Though Kazantsev was aware of how the maxim applied to himself, he—like most junior officers in the security services—was conscious that it was the lifework of their seniors. In any situation, so the rules seemed to run, always find as a first priority the man who will be blamed for the failure, should it occur. Rule two, Kazantsev and men of his generation supposed, was that the man to be so blamed should, where possible, be encouraged to suggest the course of action, so that blame could be more easily attached.

And that was what Kazantsev knew might happen to him, especially when he heard what the Deputy Chairman considered to be a proven fact.

"With respect, sir—"

"I'm always suspicious of that kind of ingratiating statement." Humorless flinty eyes, a quick cunning that had sized up this junior so-called bomb expert, seen his assuredness and his sense of rank, knew the boy could be blamed, quite satisfactorily, for anything that went wrong.

The snake had wriggled in his hands, its head now pointing at him, fangs visible.

"O.K., sir—" Kazantsev countered with a disarming grin. "It's bullshit." Surprise—eyebrows moving. He added quickly, "Whoever is advising you, sir, has got it wrong."

Puchkov was behind the Deputy Chairman, pressing his hands down on the air, advising caution. Kazantsev watched the Deputy Chairman's face. He disliked the way in which he was forced to concentrate on the politics inherent in the situation, the thin scum of survival on his muddy pool, but he could not avoid doing so. If he had to play this game, then he would attempt to win it.

"You have proof, of course?"

"No, but I have experience, and I have talked to the terrorists."

"And—?" The Deputy Chairman was trying to rush him now.

"And Shubin, the leader of the group, smiles like the cat with the cream. He may have made a mistake by being caught in that rat hole, but he thinks he has an ace card."

The Deputy Chairman glanced at the thin-faced, bespectacled senior psychologist, as if to consult his opinion, then he turned back to Kazantsev, more intent on refuting him from the position of his own authority. Show no weakness—Kazantsev felt the snake writhing again.

"You have no proof. I have had expert analysts go over the material from the ordnance factory—and they have talked to Security there. There is no FAE device in that warehouse—there never was."

Kazantsev clamped his mouth shut, as if on an oath. Then he grinned again.

"Your analysts have just shunted the bureaucratic paperwork around, sir. The bomb in the Mausoleum was just a trial run. There's something bigger to follow—"

And then he saw how the snake had outwitted him. He almost felt its bite.

"Then our separate views leave no alternative. You will prepare a plan for a *successful* attack on the warehouse, to take place just before dawn." A slow, cunning smile; he forgave

Kazantsev his insolence because his stupidity had led them where the older man wished. "If there is no bomb, then these terrorists must be arrested, or killed. If there is, then the sooner that happens, the better. Eh?"

And Kazantsev, against his earlier mood, felt a reluctance to agree. As if Shubin had outwitted him, not this cunning old man looking out for his status and his pension and his dacha outside Moscow.

Kazantsev cursed to himself the cleverness that had led him into the trap.

There were two of them on the rostrum, the Gold Medalist and the Silver Medalist. As the first bars of the Canadian national anthem began, Gutierrez still could not believe what the loudspeakers had told the crowd.

"The Bronze Medal winner, Irena Witlocka of Poland, has been taken to the hospital, suffering from exhaustion. There is no cause for concern. She will be presented with her medal on a later occasion."

Repetition in four languages.

The anthem went on playing, and he still could not accept the information. It wasn't possible—it wasn't true.

Gutierrez felt very afraid, though as yet he failed to understand why that was his predominant reaction. Not concern, or worry, or the desire to be there—fear.

CHAPTER 14

Greenberg was like an anxious, indulgent parent. Allardyce, looking up from his copy as he tapped away on his portable, felt himself drawn into the conversation Greenberg was having with a wild-eyed, angry Gutierrez at the door of the press box. At first the intense whispering irritated him, then it became seductive, urgent. The pressmen nearest were attracted, then returned to deadlines.

Allardyce stood up—Gutierrez's eyes instantly challenged his interference, or nosiness—and moved to the door, closing it behind the three of them.

"Any help required?" he drawled, pleased with the irritation his tone caused the athlete.

"Butt out—"

"Shut up, kid," Greenberg warned, his hand on Gutierrez's arm. He turned to Allardyce. "The kid here is worried about Irena, the high jumper who didn't appear—?" Allardyce nodded. "He says there was nothing wrong with her half an hour earlier. She was fine—" He looked at Gutierrez for further confirmation.

"Who is this guy—?"

"Dave Allardyce—Marty Gutierrez. Now, shut up. If you want help, kid, we'll enlist Dave's. O.K.?" Gutierrez looked like a child who has handed over a bag of sweets to a special friend only to see them handed all round the class. But he nodded.

"Yeah—O.K." Then, like some change of TV channel, a smile, an extended hand which Allardyce shook. "Nice to meet you."

"How do you do? You've checked with medical officials?"

"No—I came straight to Ben here—" Greenberg pleased, Gutierrez somewhat shamefaced as if he had failed a simple test.

"O.K.—let's go and see them. I'll say I want to interview Miss Witlocka, and ask for the name of the hospital, and the other details—?"

Greenberg nodded.

"You ought to be glad this guy's on your side, Marty. Watch him operate—" He grinned, and Allardyce nodded a small bow. He caught sight of Anna Akhmerovna leaving the stadium with Leonov and saw his mood and actions as a specious charade—then led the way down from the back of the grandstand, to ground level and the medical center.

Allardyce was frowned upon as a member of the press by the doctor in charge of the medical center. Gutierrez, still in his United States track suit, seemed subject to a barely concealed hostility as he hung back in the doorway with Greenberg. And Allardyce was aware, in the well-lit, aseptic atmosphere of stretchers, oxygen cylinders, beds, and gleaming equipment, of the presence of a security man, although he was dressed in a white coat. His presence dominated the conversation, even though his head rarely moved from the medicine cabinet, which he appeared to be tidying, and he said nothing. He seemed like a censor in the wings of some experimental theater, ready to move in and stop the conversation at any moment.

"But, Doctor—Miss Witlocka has competed on a number of occasions in England. She is regarded with almost as much affection as her countrywoman Szewinska. My readers will be concerned to learn of her *illness*—you must give me some details—"

"I am sorry. Not for release to the press—" He made the word sound like a diagnosis of something terminal. Allardyce wanted to laugh, at the same moment as he perceived that there was a tension between the doctor and the security man, a ban enforced.

"I see. Then perhaps you could give me the name of the hospital where she has been taken? I will get in touch with her there."

Flicker of the head of the security man; a tight, intense little cameo Allardyce felt the three of them were playing in front of Gutierrez and Greenberg, the impatient audience. The doctor smiled blandly, moving to usher Allardyce back to the door.

"I'm sorry. There have a—been a lot of inquiries, but Miss Witlocka—" The indifference, the lack of interest, in the voice struck Allardyce. "She is not to be disturbed. There will be a bulletin in due course, after she—"

"Recovers?"

The doctor, who had paused, even stumbled over the poorly memorized lines, swallowed, then nodded effusively.

"Yes, yes—when she is recovered, then no doubt you will be able to interview her. Now, if you please—"

Polite, stiff, formal, white—the room, the doctor, the conversation. Then Gutierrez.

"Where in hell is she, you crud—?" Bulling through the door, past Greenberg, who seemed content to let him go. Allardyce was irritated for a brief moment by the intrusion of American bluntness, then switched his attention to the security man, observing his reactions. Gutierrez had the doctor by the lapels, seeming larger than his thin frame might normally suggest. "What's the matter with Irena, uh?" Walking the doctor backward. "Where the hell is she?"

Allardyce had seen sufficient. He pulled Gutierrez roughly away, feeling the muscles in the thin arms, the resistance to his interference.

"Ben—get your rude friend out of here, please—" And they bundled the protesting Gutierrez through the door of the medical center. Allardyce looked back once before the frosted glass cut off his view. The doctor was engaged in protest with the security man. "Calm down!" he hissed at Gutierrez as the American began to offer his opinions of Allardyce.

"What was it?" asked Greenberg, unblinded by anger.

"I just saved you from more than embarrassment, sonny," Allardyce said levelly. "I let you interfere in your delicate colonial way because I wanted to find out something. The man at the cabinet—he had a gun. And I think he might have been prepared to use it on you, if only to the extent of bending the barrel over your head—"

Gutierrez was all attention, even though groggy with the plenitude of emotions aroused by the little scene.

"Hell, what's going on, Dave?" Greenberg asked, also un-blinded by anger.

"I don't know, Ben, but it isn't nervous exhaustion." He looked at Gutierrez, and murmured, "Montague and Capulet in there seem concerned to keep you and your mistress apart."

"What do we do?"

"Start ringing the hospitals—all the hospitals."

The children were falling to pieces, like beautiful, glittering ersatz ornaments. Yakov was biting the skin at the edges of his finger-nails, obsessively, as if he were much younger and watching some celluloid procession of horrors; Ferenc and Kostya in a whispered, endless conversation over by the doors where they were on guard; Ilya up at the window at the rear, stared down into the courtyard, knowing the bullies were waiting outside for him; Lyudmila moved nervous as a cat in role reversal and being stalked; Zenaida— Zenaida, Shubin accepted his observations, was different. A danger-ous brightness in her eyes, which stared at middle distances, even at the hostages, for longer and longer periods, her tongue working at the corners of her mouth as if she was sensible of little sores there. Shubin could almost see a spittle of self-destruction on her lower lip.

It was growing dark outside. Inside the warehouse it was a close, lightless black, except for a square of dull orange from the rear window that looked out over the Kirov Street shops. Perhaps the darkness calmed them. It had made the hostages—the whispering little rodent family bundled up in one back corner—adopt a hibernating silence. The children, too, seemed reassured. There had not yet been sufficient darkness to rub at their last composure, scratch the nerves raw.

They had no attitudes to terrorism, Shubin decided, reaffirming old analyses. Glamour, incipient sense of failure or anonymity, frustration, hero worship; except Zenaida, who wouldn't let him have her anymore and had seemed to find something moving in the darkness of the warehouse to which she felt more akin—had taken as her lover. Shubin—though he scarcely admitted it—was frightened of her now, even as he realized that she could not have emerged from her chrysalis more satisfactorily for his purposes.

Kamikaze.

Oh, yes, she was that all right. Reduction of people to targets, cathartic bloodletting, power of the weapon, desire to inflict, self-expression through sadism—she had it all, and he had hardly suspected it when he gathered *Do pobachenya* around him.

For the children had always been expendable.

Shubin got up from where he had hunched in pretended rest, and crossed to where the girl was sitting on an upright chair in the darkness behind the glass of the dispatch office. His shoes creaked on the three steps up, and he could see her white teeth grinning as his hand touched the door handle, and he knew—yes, there it was, a dull gleaming sliver below her face—that the submachine gun was pointed at his stomach. She was in the bunker back there in the dispatch office. They would have to cross the killing ground to get to her. Shubin almost admired her.

He sat down on the other side of the desk, and she motioned him, with the gun, impatiently, to another seat that was out of her line of fire. He moved.

"We have to break out, you know that?" he said softly, almost insinuatingly, into the darkness. The last pale glimmer from the grimy window was fading on the concrete outside the glass box. He could make out her head, her shoulder, the gun, her crossed legs.

She might have been posing for a picture. He did not want her—the adrenaline would not come in that way now, he was calculating too much for that—but he felt almost a tenderness for her. It was without guilt, or responsibility; perhaps the recognition of an akin-ness with the girl.

"Yes. When?"

He drew in his breath sharply, stifled the exhalation in case it might betray him. It was that easy, that simple. All the time, he had only to ask, to say. Like an unconfessed passion that was amply reciprocated.

"We have to get the cylinders out—" He felt impelled to continue with the argument he had rehearsed so carefully. "The cause is—"

Her words hissed, like something writhing and venomous on the darkened floor between them.

"Don't give me a speech, Shubin. We both know why we're here, and what has to be done. Don't give me any bull, just the details. How, and when?"

A short silence in which he stared at her intently, as if he could see her expression clearly and minutely.

"An hour before dawn—I think they'll make their move just about dawn, so we should forestall them—"

"Yes," she said, a superior officer approving an aide's suggestion. "I think they'll try to take us out. O.K., Shubin—how?"

"Use the minibus. Ram our way through. We can do it—" Again, the sense of submitting suggestions to a superior.

"We'd have to turn left out of here—that's the weaker barrier."

"Yes, the two cars." He was almost eager now, hiding in the details like an enemy in a thicket. "We can shoulder one of them aside, if Yakov drives the bus. If we're all firing, on all sides, creating panic. If we get bogged down—"

"We can move the cars—if we can get that far." She seemed impatient of his reservations, qualifications. She wanted the violence of the action, its brutal suddenness. He had her. "What about the devices?" she added suddenly. "They won't explode?"

"No."

"Good. They'd be a waste, here."

"I'll tell the others."

"What about the butchers?" He wondered at her tone. It seemed purring.

"They can be left."

"Mm."

Shubin moved out of the dispatch office. It was minutes before satisfaction overcame the emotions her last remarks had evoked.

Kazantsev and Puchkov stood leaning against the two pumps on the garage forecourt. Puchkov was smoking in defiance of the signs above their heads. The sweet smell of the gasoline still lingered. When he had finished the cigarette he flicked it, in open defiance of good sense, away in an arc toward the command trailer, ghostly white in the darkness. Kazantsev watched it like a comet falling.

"What's the time?" Puchkov asked, yawning.

Kazantsev studied his watch, its face close to his bent head. "Nearly eleven."

"God, this is boring." Puchkov yawned again.

"Chief, why not take a nap? Nothing is going to happen for hours yet."

"You'll put that in writing?"

"No, but I'm reasonably sure." Kazantsev grinned in the darkness. Was he sure? Almost? Would the deadweight of the hours and the abiding sense of a dead end, rat hole of a trap oppress the kids in there, take them away from Shubin whatever he said or did, into innocence and fear and wanting to be let off because they hadn't really done anything very bad—?

Were they really kids? Fifteen-year-old kids stabbed old women for their purses, stole, cheated, beat up, swindled, extorted—eleven and twelve, some of the gang members. Was there enough *hopelessness* in the situation to paralyze them?

"Those things won't explode—you're certain?" Puchkov intruded another uncomfortable reality.

"I'm pretty certain he won't have armed them—not yet and not here."

"Tell me, Oleg—this is the idlest speculation, you understand—are there *any* certainties?"

"No, I don't think there are."

"Some of these men are going to get killed, Oleg."

"That is a certainty."

Natalia was leaving Moscow. She had been transferred to Odessa, to Intourist's office there. She had waited until after dinner, and after they had made love, before she told him. She told him in the dark, and he did not reach out to switch on the light, and she was grateful for that privacy for her wet eyes. He was silent for a long time, then he asked when she would be leaving and whether they were making her go and was it his fault, and would she be all right?

And she began to understand him—and understand the wife who had left. She was hurt, because she had all but lost control of the situation in the two weeks she had known him and had committed herself, just a little, a toe, maybe a leg in the water and ready to jump—

Yes, of course they had told her to go. She didn't know why and she was afraid to ask and she could not ignore the promotion whatever their reason for giving it. But him—he had talked *round* it, only round it—

Lydall lay in the darkness, staring at the ceiling which he could just see as a glimmer in the curtained light from the street. He deliberately did not touch her, even though the memory of their lovemaking was intense, his erection still present, a sensuous ache from the weight of her coming down on him, sliding from the bed's edge as he knelt to receive her weight. The small buttocks in his hands, the breasts against his face—

But it was fading, the erection becoming a need to urinate. She was going. Fact. Unalterable: accepted. He did not like, for a moment, the part of him that made it easy, but the self-loathing passed as most of his moments of personal insight did, and to be almost forgotten on waking the next morning. He was not a man who habitually lay awake, probing his abscesses or rotten teeth with an inquiring tongue.

His mind—he could not prevent it, it was compulsive—was already reaching forward, across sixty-five hours, to the final of the 5000 meters of the XXII Olympiad. He was already beginning to run the race in his mind.

"Nothing—she's not in any hospital in the directory!" Greenberg was infuriated. His Russian was primitive, and many of the people he had spoken to seemed either reluctant or bloody-minded in their ability to speak English. They were sitting in the press box, hearing the noises from the press bar above it, each of them using the telephone provided for their use during the Games while Gutierrez sat behind them, angry, silent, perhaps growingly afraid.

Allardyce nodded, murmured his thanks—*pozhalusta* from the hospital Reception—and put down the telephone. He nodded in confirmation of Greenberg's comment.

"We heard from that guy she was bundled into an ambulance, man!" Gutierrez burst out. Both men turned toward him as if he had interrupted some conventional ritual with an outburst of religious frenzy. As if he divined their mood, he added, "For you guys, it's just a game, maybe a story—uh?" Gutierrez's hands were bunched on his thighs, his body strained and set, the veins standing like cords on his forearms. Allardyce was cut by the remark, not simply recognizing its truth but sensing the inadequacy in dealing with a more desperate situation—Anna's—which had driven him to adopt the cause of Irena Witlocka. He returned the challenge.

"How interested are you in this girl?"

Gutierrez went as stiff as if he had been slapped. The eyes burned, but flickered with some reflective process.

"I'm worried about her. Is that enough for you?"

"Perhaps it is. Now, why has she disappeared? Ben—your theory?"

Greenberg was staring down from the lit press box—their reflections looking back at them from the glass—onto the bowl of darkness the stadium had become, the floodlights around the perimeter like an adornment to the blackness. He seemed to be concentrating on the security guard with his Alsatian on a chain, moving slowly round the perimeter of the field. A submachine gun was slung over his shoulder.

"My theory?" He turned to Gutierrez. "She wants out, right?" Gutierrez nodded. "She tried it in the States, last year?" Again the nod, as if Gutierrez was being asked to confess to minor offenses. "That's it, then. She wants to go, and they don't want her to. She'll be back in Warsaw or wherever anytime now."

"That's a theory? A little—"

"Unlikely? Too hawkish for you?" Greenberg was belligerent. "Maybe. But you're not a sportswriter, Dave. You haven't seen the *assistant managers* they send abroad with teams. Jesus, it's like Hitler's bodyguard most of the time. They don't let them give interviews, they stick together, sealed off from contamination, herded around. Man, you know what it's like!"

"She's been hassled ever since she tried it—" Gutierrez was attempting conciliation. "They've been watching her and me ever since we met here." He appeared almost ashamed of his feeling for the girl, like admitting to a weakness. Allardyce ignored the cold, appraising part of himself.

"All right. Ben and I will try to find her—I don't know how, and perhaps we can't do it. But we'll try."

He held out his hand, and Gutierrez took it after a moment's reluctance.

"Thanks."

Karen Gunston was standing in a darkened shop doorway, a hundred yards farther along Kirov Street from the barriers and the blankets and the smoking policemen. Her Nikkormat camera fitted with an infrared lens, her body tense and wary with remaining still, with the seeping nerves that she could not ignore. And the overriding frustration of knowing she could go no nearer, that she would eventually have to give up the stupid idea and walk away.

The conviction that the terrorists had been cornered in that narrow street cut off from the rest of Moscow, the excitement of the ego as she pictured the exclusivity of any material she obtained, both had faded into a self-ridicule that exacerbated the tension she felt. She could see Allardyce, even Ben Greenberg—even her TV crew laughing at her—*Karen Gunston, fearless cub reporter*.

Quite ridiculous.

She shifted her weight from one foot to the other, and felt the onset of a mild cramp. The regular Moscow police patrols did not penetrate this far down Kirov Street, because of the security surrounding whatever was happening a hundred yards away. In that she was lucky, avoiding them in the late evening rush hour away from the pleasures of the city center, amidst the window-shoppers and the few drunks, then waiting until—

Christ, until when? It had to be two, maybe three o'clock by now.

Quite ridiculous.

"Anything?"

"Nothing, Lieutenant."

The KGB marksman, on loan from Department V of the Second Chief Directorate—Kazantsev's "nasties"—shifted his body on the airbed on which he was lying, his Dragunov sniper's rifle with the personalized stock and trigger resting on sandbags to steady his aim, the night sight gathering the hard starlight over the roofs of Kirov Street.

Kazantsev, kneeling beside him, looked over the edge of the flat shop roof, down into the smelly, close courtyard behind the warehouse. A square of grimy window. Blank brick walls. A small wooden door through which the gas-operated rifle could pump its ten 7.62 rounds as through soft cheese. A terror weapon. Effective stopping range 800 meters, muzzle velocity 2,725 feet per second.

"When you get the flare, put half the magazine through the window, the rest through the door." The marksman nodded. Kazantsev looked at his watch. "Forty minutes. Unless you receive an update."

Kazantsev walked to the edge of the roof overlooking Kirov Street. No sign as yet of the BTR-40 scout car, on its way from Moscow Garrison, with which they would batter down the main doors of the warehouse, behind which they would go in yelling for the hostages to lie down and shooting anything that moved.

Something you can learn from the West—always something. Coca-Cola, American tobacco, Italian suits. And how they storm terrorists in Holland and airport buildings in Entebbe. Not, he thought with a disrespectful smile, that the KGB would ever admit to learning anything from Zionists.

There were no regrets now, no hesitation. He had convinced himself of the appropriateness, the effectiveness, of this assault.

A sequence of images, growing to a single point of view as the first noises and lights come. A sniper, bored and tired, rubbing the eye sockets that have acquired an ache from the night glasses; the door of the warehouse, opening a little; Kazantsev drumming his big fingers on the collapsible table in the command trailer, and staring at Puchkov; Karen Gunston shrugging awake in the doorway on Kirov Street, straining to listen and hearing only the silence.

Shubin stood by the door, his hand resting lightly against the rough wood. Yakov's white face was visible behind the glass of the windshield; Zenaida was professionally checking the Polish submachine gun, seated next to him; Ferenc was standing near Shubin, with the remainder of the children in the back of the bus, ready to knock out the windows, open fire. The dim white stains of the butchers' coats and aprons at the back of the warehouse where they were bound and gagged.

Three grenades—RG-42s—like green tins of fruit on wooden sticks; Shubin with one in each hand, Ferenc with the third.

Shubin breathed in deeply. The children were committed, they had even accepted the ploy of the grenades, and his apparent heroism in making a solitary escape after he had thrown them, opening fire with the submachine gun slung behind his back as a further distraction. He held up his hand, and saw Yakov wave in acknowledgment. He looked at Ferenc as intensely as if he were placing him under hypnosis.

Then they leaned against the doors together, which opened noisily—the door on Shubin's side scraped gratingly on the concrete—and Yakov fired the engine, overrevving at once, letting the brake off, squeal of tires, jerk and almost stall, then coming at them.

The first bullet tore a long white splinter from the door near Shubin's cheek, but he had already flung the first grenade by that time. The minibus charged past him, shielding him for a moment as he poised, then threw the second grenade before the first one exploded on the garage forecourt, twenty or thirty feet from the command trailer which he could see in the starlight as a ghostly white tent.

Back door of the minibus flapping open, Kostya's hand reaching for Ferenc as he began to run. His grenade exploded ahead of the bus, illuminating the police car blocking off the street. The grenade had not destroyed the car, but it had been lifted, shunted by the blast, its windows shattered, the fragmentation effect of the grenade ripping its bodywork as a knife might work on muslin..

Shubin's grenade exploded, another flare of orange, the thud of fragments into the command trailer, the roof of the forecourt canopy, then the second grenade, farther back, nearer the pumps. Shubin had no idea whether he could shatter the concrete of the forecourt and breach the underground tanks, but the panic was all he required.

Yes—a dull concussion, then a sheet of flame reaching forty feet up and boiling out under the canopy, seeming to envelop the command trailer as one of the pumps was skewed off its perch, and breached.

Shubin ducked back inside the warehouse. Everything was satisfactory.

Yakov headed straight for one policeman, his arm hanging limply like an empty sleeve, then jerked the bus away as if restrained by some moral force. Zenaida, window down, squeezed two shots into the white, pained face. Bullets coming through the flimsy bodywork, 7.62 and 9mm as the snipers on the roofs and the police from the end of the street, hidden by the blankets and the corner which turned into another alley, opened fire. Concentrated fire.

Zenaida heard screaming, and was unsure whether it was from

outside or inside. Then a hand fell almost gothically on her shoulder, and she recognized the garnet ring Lyudmila always wore. She pushed the arm aside, and heard the reptilian slither of the bleeding body as it slid to the floor of the minibus.

Yakov, heading for the small gap—a policeman trying to move the damaged car to narrow it—she opened fire, shot him, and he tumbled into the car as if she had pushed him from behind. The minibus scraped against the wall of another warehouse, bounced, making an excellent target in the light of the burning garage and the starlight. Yakov winced beside her, she saw the hand nearest her covered with blood like water he might have poured from a jug, washing himself—but he held on, sliding, edging the van toward the gap. The two policemen ahead of them, as if filling the gap with their fragile bodies, bent in the firing position, hands stiffly out—the windshield emptying into her lap, the pluck of a bullet at her ear and then being unable to see because something sticky and black filled her eye. She cursed, wiping at it with her sleeve, switched to automatic, and squeezed the trigger. Like a conjuring trick, she emptied the gap between the hood of the car and the wall.

She had no time for feeling, for nothing more than instinct. She was aware of how empty her thoughts were, except to keep her bowels clenched in case she was hit—that thought remaining all the seconds of the breakout, that she did not want to evacuate her bowels when and if she died. And to react, react—sweeping the submachine gun from side to side, like a garden hose, the garden hose she and Arkady had played with in the strip of garden that summer when they had heard that their father would not be coming home again and no more beatings and unkindness to Mama—no, she told herself almost primly, no, release the trigger, don't waste ammunition—

A dull, crumping concussion, the vision turning yellow, then orange, then white, and the submachine gun expending its last rounds toward the sky—flecks of fire in her eyes, but she could see the stars, cold and hard, she was sure of it. But the minibus rearing like a wild horse on its rear wheels, sliding the people behind her— who did not cry out or make any noise—toward the door at the back, dice in a box.

The engine squealing, wheels racing just under her feet, as she leaned tiredly sideways. The sensation of clenching her bowels had disappeared, and she was worried about it, though she did not understand that the impact of the bullet across her temple, and the two sniper's shots down through the roof of the minibus which had both struck her at the moment the grenade had slewed and lifted the vehicle, had caused her already to evacuate, just as her nose and mouth were running blood she could not taste or smell.

She felt the submachine gun slip away, felt her mind begin to spin as she was floundering, then falling a great way—her last conscious impressions adopting the disorientation of the minibus collapsing onto its side.

Kazantsev knew he had to keep going—not in a direction, not necessarily with physical movement, though that assisted, but simply to survive the numbing shock of the explosions, the sheet of flame, the smoke and noise.

Wiping the blood from two cuts on his face—flying glass when the command trailer's windows went, fortunately the explosions so close, so much force the glass had almost disintegrated—he stumbled away from the trailer, leaving Puchkov sitting rigid with shock. Forcing his legs to move, making the mind focus on Shubin, the one narrow image. He could see the minibus, and knew they would never make it—saw it rear up, turn over, sliding two bodies out of the back in grotesque comedy, knew they would all be dead from the grenades—frag radius twenty-five meters, and nasty—or from the snipers they had chosen to ignore, attempted to outrun. Men asleep would have had enough time, enough light—

And he knew Shubin would not be in that minibus, but somewhere else, trying to get out the back way, into the courtyard and then Kirov Street. Move, move—! Like a cripple who will not accept the uselessness of his legs. The doorway hanging open, white scars on the wood, inside everything dark, nothing moving.

He drew the Makarov from his shoulder holster.

"Oleg—Oleg!" It was almost a scream, from Puchkov now following him. "The bombs—the bloody bombs!" He turned at once, looking at the wounded, dying minibus, wheels still spinning slowly, two bodies near its open rear door. The FAE devices had to be in there, otherwise they would never have tried to escape as they had. He began to run, yelling as he did so.

"Keep away from there!" He had no idea what kind of ignition device they might have. The shock might have, the heat—? "Keep away from there!"

As Shubin had ducked back inside the warehouse, the group of white overalls and aprons had shuffled animatedly, like a flag waving to him, as if they thought he had come back to kill them. Then the window that overlooked the courtyard shattered and heavy bullets ripped through the woodwork. Then the door, each shot penetrating the old wood, the door knocked half off its hinges by the velocity and power of the shots. Shubin could almost hear the sniper's instructions in his head, and he knew he had the time it took to fit a new magazine to the rifle to get through the door, across the courtyard—

A belated, gagged moan—a stray bullet. It did not distract him as he ran, breath and footsteps very loud in the dark, flung aside the door, hesitated only for an instant, then heaved himself across the courtyard, turning sideways to ram his shoulder against the door he had previously selected—the butcher's shop—and the wood sagged, but did not give.

Bullets kicking up dust, concrete chips—Shubin leaned away from the door, then back into it and it still did not give and the sniper was shifting position because the firing stopped before the new magazine could be empty. Lean, thrust—no! Lean, heave against it—*come on, come on*—! Heave—back two paces, jump at the door—

A bullet at his feet, another whining away off the wall, and he was inside, staggering, stumbling, and cursing with relief over the door that had fallen in, both hinges and the lock giving way to his frantic efforts.

More bullets, one whining like a meat fly somewhere up in the ceiling, plaster settling like pattering mouse steps. Complete darkness. He moved forward, knowing he must not waste time—should have brought one of the butchers—and fumbled into a hanging meat ax, hanging saws. Clatter, fearfully loud, and he jumped, then sucked his thumb which was suddenly bleeding from its slight collision with the ax.

The doors of the cold room, and light from Kirov Street came through the distant windows at the front of the shop.

He walked painfully into the edge of the counter, which hurt his hip, then he could see the pale reflection of the checkered tiles all the way to the door.

He ran lightly, silently, then leaned against the glass door, feeling for the bolts, the catch. Open—

The door chimed as he pulled it open, like an old village shop. Maybe an affectation but now a signal. He went through the door, submachine gun now clasped in both hands, head swiveling from side to side. Kirov Street was deserted, except for the barriers and the police car—and that was empty. Flame, and its light, from the side street where the garage must be burning, noise and firing he had been unaware of in the deafness of the silent dark shop. Nothing in Kirov Street, no sirens as yet. He began to run.

Karen Gunston had heard the little quaint bell as the door opened. Using the infrared lens as a night sight, she scanned the shop doorways until she could make out the pale, red-rimmed figure in the doorway of the butcher's shop. She had wanted to run at the first explosion, the first shots, especially when the flames burst above the rooftops; but she could not, her legs weak, her feet anchored to the floor. She stood there, openmouthed, camera in front of her chest, then at her eye, archetypal spectator, unwilling and unable to move.

The single man, especially when he began to run toward her, did not make her afraid. He was something reduced to her scale, the compass of physical and mental activity sufficient to enclose him, even though he was carrying the submachine gun.

She began to take photographs of him, automatic wind-on purring, shutter clicking, everything normal even when he saw her, deliberately changed direction to head at her, the gun moving slightly aside. She still kept taking photographs, until he hit her sideways with the barrel of the gun, tugged at the camera strap and she felt the pain in her arm, then her leg as he kicked her, her ribs next, and the hurting arm being almost wrenched off as he struggled with the camera strap which she would not release.

She began to scream—he was almost weeping with rage and effort, she could tell—and scream. And he kicked her again in the ribs but she knew she must not stop screaming or hanging on, and then she felt her body slump, he released the strap, and she dimly heard footsteps running away.

Whistles, other footsteps—? She slid gratefully into unconsciousness.

Once they had removed one of the floor panels, having seen the slight pregnant bulge of the compartment that had been welded to the underside of the minibus, Kazantsev knew that the FAE devices were not in the vehicle. He had the bodies removed and laid out before he began to search the warehouse. But he had perceived Shubin's plan; and when the policeman who had lost the man who had run away and the sniper who had missed him reported, even before they began to search the warehouse, he knew that they would not find the bombs and that Shubin was alive and free.

He was left with the image of the fire engine spraying the forecourt, quelling the flames with thick white foam, and the face of the girl, Zenaida Federenka, staring sightlessly at the sky. Someone who had not intended mockery had folded their hands on their chests, all of them. Kazantsev, in frustrated rage, wanted to kick the girl's body, again and again.

PART FOUR

FINAL

CHAPTER 15

Greenberg seemed almost pleased that Gutierrez had brought the cassette player to their hotel immediately, to consult him and Allardyce; Allardyce thought it might have a paternal basis, but he made no comment, even a light one, forewarned by the strained appearance of Gutierrez's features. Immediately, the tape player, a slim Japanese package with brushed aluminum buttons and black plastic case, was handed him like a challenge.

"Listen to that, Davie," Greenberg commanded, a fierce light, combative and protective, in his eye. Allardyce watched Gutierrez. The young man was disturbed—but Allardyce, so often the victim of irritation when a deeper emotion seemed required of him, sensed that feeling in Gutierrez. Something was interfering with the smooth acceleration of Gutierrez's mind and body toward the 5000 Final, now less than fifty-two hours away, and he didn't like what it was doing to him.

"Is it ready to play back?"

Gutierrez pressed a button and stepped back again to Greenberg's side, as if requiring that slight distance so that he might measure his reaction.

A girl, speaking very bad English, with a thick, central European accent. He assumed, eyebrows raised, that it was Irena. Greenberg nodded confirmation. The message lasted only a minute or so. She explained her illness—which she claimed was real— explained that she was being looked after, and promised that they would be together again very soon, and he was not to worry. A skein of clichés unraveling.

The only thing not knitted tightly, securely, was the breathing they could hear. Emotion interfered with it, but not the kind of emotions that ought to accompany the message. False notes being struck, the wrong ground swell beneath the words. Allardyce wondered how many times they had made her record it until they'd had to be satisfied with this version

The girl ended with the sententious comment, "Your race, my medal, they don't mean anything, Martin—as long as we can be together. Nothing matters except that we will be together—and we can be. I love you—"

Gutierrez switched it off, mumbled that there was no more of it, and Allardyce was sensing the tears that had threatened in that last phrase, and a similar action somewhere by another hand which had cut off those tears. She did love him—that, at least, was genuine.

"When did you find this?"

"An hour ago I switched on the player. My tape had been switched for this."

"You believe it?"

"The hell he does—!" Greenberg began. Allardyce's hand made a chopping motion for silence.

"Then why did she send it? Who delivered it? And why? Have you answered all those questions, the two of you?" Allardyce motioned them to sit down. Greenberg perched on the edge of one of the beds, Gutierrez slouched in the second easy chair. A clean, functional room—the guilty cassette player lay next to Allardyce's own similar machine, both of them now innocent, harmonious with the decor, the furniture.

Allardyce dismissed the habitual irritation he felt at being used in other people's affairs, and attempted to feel that he *wanted* to become involved. After all, he had failed in Anna's case. He dismissed that thought, too.

"She's alive," he said, "and well. But the message was not to tell you that—mm?" He watched Gutierrez carefully. Yes, he did know, although he had tried to avoid the knowledge. "I'm afraid you won't get her back if you—win a medal."

He let the statement settle like a heavy meal on each stomach. He heard Greenberg shift on the bed, making the springs creak, but he kept his eyes on Gutierrez, who resented his inquisition but made no attempt to avoid it.

"Yes, everything for you and the girl hinges on the race. Oh, I shouldn't think she will come to much harm, but *you* won't see her again if you should win. And I think that's becoming clear to you, too. Am I right?"

Valentina was fussing again, but seemed for once utterly inappropriate—even insensitive, bovine—as she straightened his tie, brushed his jacket as if unaware of his mood. She seemed to avoid looking into the bleak eyes with the dark stains beneath them. Eventually, Kazantsev lost his temper.

"Give it up, Valentina—I'm tired of the ritual!" She looked at him as if stung, one hand to her cheek, but the other resting lightly still on his chest—over the breast pocket in which he had a buff envelope containing prints of the American woman's film of Shubin escaping through the butcher's shop and down Kirov Street. The foolish woman was in the hospital; *Do pobachenya* were all dead; and Shubin and the FAE devices were unaccounted for.

"Oleg—you're too tired to keep going like this." She had starched her voice—perhaps the ex-nurse in her reemerging—so that it was crisp, objective.

He put his arms round her, his head moving as he was distracted by the noises from the children's bedroom, some little argument about possessions. When he turned back to her, his mood was broken, and he could only toss his head in mock disapproval. "Take them to Gorki Park today, mm?"

She nodded.

"Sure, Lieutenant." He hugged her, the small dark woman, and she leaned her head against him. All she was aware of was the thinness of clothes, the fragility of his huge chest and rib cage. "It's a vendetta, isn't it?"

He shook his head, then confessed.

"Yes, it is. I have to go to Donetsk because of the bombs he has. If he didn't have them, I'd be pulling Moscow apart piece by piece to find him." He laughed, but the sound had no humor in it.

"Why?"

"Why? You disapprove—" He pulled her off her feet like one of the children, holding her to him, her face level with his. She sensed she was going to be patronized, fobbed off. "Usually, I treat it as a job, you were going to say? Well—this one I can't. Shubin—that's his name—is a lunatic." He shook his head suddenly. "No, he isn't. He's a fanatic, and that's much more dangerous."

"What does he want?"

"I don't think he wants anything. Except—oh, I don't know, Tina." He lowered her to the ground, as if recognizing her maturity. "Maybe he just wants to be famous—famous and secret. Some of them do, I'm told."

"Why Donetsk?"

She handed him his overnight bag, and began to usher him to the door of the apartment.

"Why? Because he got his bombs from there—and his bombs are his balls. And I want his balls!" He laughed. "What a gift for words. I want the bombs—I want to know about them, and where they'll be used, because they could kill a hundred thousand—like that!"

He clicked his fingers, kissed her quickly, and trotted down the first flight of stairs. She watched him go, and shivered—and this time it was less for him than, in some strange and unexpected way, for herself and the children.

Lydall and Ochengwe were training. It was a rest day in the athletics and all the events save the decathlon, the relays, and the 5000 completed. They jogged swiftly through the park complex surrounding the village, some accommodation to acquaintanceship having been made by their shared room, their shared loneliness, their unspoken mutual respect. Whatever it was, neither man regarded the other as a rival in the days before the Final. There was no commonalty of tactics or approach. Lydall felt always with Ochengwe that the man was in a different race—perhaps a different class. And Ochengwe had only the delight in running, in self-proving; he had no rivals who had to be outpsyched or tactically outplayed. Only other men in his event who had to be behind him when he came off the last bend.

"You miss her?" Lydall asked, aware of his intrusion.

Ochengwe looked at him, and nodded.

"Yes."

"What will you do—after this lot?"

Ochengwe studied the ground ahead of his feet for fifty or sixty yards.

"I don't know. Maybe the professional circus, uh?"

"Not your thing, is it?"

"How would I know that? Perhaps I will try it."

"You won't go back, then? You get a medal and all will be forgiven, won't it?"

Dappled shade, sun splashed on the short turf, down the trunks of the young silver birches.

"No, I will not go back. It was not my country in the first place."

Ochengwe spurted forward then, and Lydall, counseled to silence by the move, stretched out to catch up. They jogged on then in an imitation of intimacy that was the nearest to a relationship either of them could hope to create.

Tretsov, the robot in training, was going over and over the routines, watched by the coaches, the doctors, the psychologists. Round and round an empty stadium, the silence punctuated by the calling of lap times, the more distant calls at each quarter lap. The coaches consulted their clipboards like railway timetables, making charts of his times, lists of the figures they collected. Tretsov, under mild hypnosis, his mind empty of all extraneous matter, concentrated on every pace of the 5000 meters.

Then, after two thousand, they threw in, at unpredictable intervals, other runners, who hung on his shoulder or moved, erratic paced, ahead of him, tried to bunch him. Students mostly, used just for a couple of laps, breaking up his concentration, attacking his rhythm.

It would not work. The coaches orchestrated it as cleverly, as disruptively, as they could, even turning against their creation and urging him on, telling him to change his tactics. The runners hurried him, nudged him on the bends, talked to him, even yelled. He was being trained like a police horse—to take no notice.

He moved into a different gear on the last lap, having accelerated slowly at six hundred meters out, past the bell, then into a longer stride, but with a smooth acceleration curve, nothing dramatic even as he came into the last straight, passed the finish, jogged on.

He was handed over to the doctors and the psychologists immediately. The coaches from the High Performance Unit came together slowly, as if reluctant. Two of them had watches on the whole race, as opposed to laps or quarter laps. When these were checked, there was an unobtrusive but evident satisfaction, which became grins, and touches, then open backslapping and mutual congratulation. Hardly any of them, the authors of what they had seen, looked down at Tretsov, taped and wired like a dummy in a safety test, or someone dying.

The chief coach, with due protocol, voiced their thoughts.

"A second outside the world record—the second fastest time this year. Gentlemen—let us tell our Gold Medalist of his success."

Laughter, smiles, comradeship. The bubbling riders to the central idea.

"Irvine is finished—"

"Federenko will do as he's told—"

"The American and the African haven't gotten near these times—"

"What a *time!*"

Karen Gunston was sitting up against soft white pillows, her arm in heavy plaster and suspended from a pulley so that it stuck out as if she was attached to it rather than it to her. The arm was the first thing Allardyce noticed as he walked into the small, private room carrying the hideously expensive but no doubt expected red roses and his own private joke of a paper bag containing grapes.

Then he saw how bruised her face was, the eye puffy, the cheek and jaw discolored, the head bandaged. And they'd told him outside about the two broken ribs.

"You bastard," she breathed venomously. Her one good eye was fierce, her one good hand flicked to her hair, which was straggling and unkempt where the bandage did not hide it. Allardyce smiled at the confusion of philosophy and instinct.

"It doesn't matter, does it?" he said, bending over the bed and kissing the unbruised cheek. He presented the roses, which she indifferently allowed to be placed near her good hand on the bed, then pulled up a chair, opened the bag of grapes, and ate one. Then he smiled again, seeming well-satisfied and indifferent to further conversation.

The silence lasted while a nurse came in, took her temperature, removed the flowers, then brought them back, stiffly arranged in a vase, and left again with a puzzled look on her face.

Allardyce continued to eat the grapes, putting the seeds into the kidney bowl on the bedside cart.

"All right, thank you for the roses and, for Christ's sake, talk to me!" Allardyce shook his head. "Then why the hell are you here, Allardyce?"

Allardyce wanted to laugh at the mock-tough dialogue. The only time it sounded funnier than coming from an American woman was when he heard an Englishwoman attempt it.

"I came for a good look, and a laugh," he observed quietly, inspecting the last grape before popping it into his mouth. As he squashed it against his palate, he added, "And I must say, you do look an absolute sight." He winked, screwed up the paper bag, put it into the kidney bowl, stood up, brushed his clothes, leaned over and kissed her cheek, and walked out of the room, his "See you tomorrow, same time, same place" coming through the door as it sighed closed behind him.

She could not believe it. She disbelieved it so much that she screamed with rage and the nurse came bustling in, expecting her to have fallen out of bed. When Karen saw the nurse, she screamed again, moved and made her ribs burn, flopped back on the pillows, eyes tight shut in fury at Allardyce's superiority, at her helplessness and ugliness. She did not see the needle or suspect the sedative until it was in her arm and pricking her awake. Her face twisted at its suggestion of helpless idiocy, then she relaxed into the patient mentality that all hospitals try to induce, usually succeeding.

She slept, her ribs reminding her of their attachment to herself only irregularly, and the foreign position of arm to shoulder only slightly uncomfortable. She thought she woke, once, to see a dark-haired girl—frizzy, wiry mop of hair—staring at her. She thought—perhaps at the same time, perhaps later—she heard noises, but her eyelids were too heavy to open at that point. When she did open them again—hours later?—the girl had obviously gone. Student nurse, probably—

In a hospital gown?

Had she seen that? Allardyce, the bastard—she smiled at the treatment she had been given. Not that she admitted she deserved it. Simply that he had outoperated her, and had to be admired. She shifted her head slightly. She could just see the screwed-up paper bag in the kidney bowl; and she could see the roses on the cart.

She opened her eyes wide, in a moment of recollection, as she identified the dark-haired girl. The Polish high jumper who disappeared before the medal ceremony. She was here, in the hospital, as a patient.

Idling again, her mind drifted into a luxuriousness of half-memories. Allardyce's body, Allardyce's mood that had fouled up their first time. Her ribs, her face— So the girl was ill after all, just like they'd said.

Leonov knew he was poised on the fine wire of a critical moment, perhaps his most critical moment. His two sergeants, Georgi and Dmitri, were there, otherwise the low room was empty, the remainder of his team dispersed through the city on more routine inquiries and surveillance duty.

More routine—

This was the dacha outside Moscow belonging to Anna Akhmerovna, and they had just planted bugs in the main living room and in the kitchen and the bathroom. Even Leonov could not bring himself to place a bug in the bedroom where he had slept with, made love to, a double agent.

He had to say it—dark furniture, rich cushions and rugs intruding on his awareness. Shit and hell. They had drunk to each other in front of that fireplace, the previous winter, naked after making love, then made love again in the cold big bed in the next room—

Shit and hell, there was no way he could stop the images, coming like the questions of an interrogation, the photographic evidence to support accusations. Hell, it was *her*, not him—

And yet—

Say it, then.

"You understand, then?"

The two men, perhaps fifty years' experience between them—no, nearer forty. He'd had them with him for fifteen years or more. But were they with him now?

"No tape recorder, you mean—*Gennadi?*" Dmitri, thank you. Was that emphasis meant to reassure? Georgi seemed less at ease with the deliberate familiarity, his face contracting at the conspiracy that had hardly been voiced.

"No tape. Just the receiver in the car. Look—" The word like bloodletting, a bright arterial stream. Leonov walked to the window—he'd stood here before, looking at snow falling in the clearing in front of the dacha, an image heavy with sexual pleasure; for a moment, he saw himself with an eye that ridiculed. A man of forty who couldn't get a woman out of his bed, out of his mind. But he proceeded. "This agent could be valuable to us, now that she has been identified. I want her frightened off, *isolated*—but not arrested." Turn now. Look at their faces. "The case officer, he can be dealt with—an accident. The agent"—*don't even admit her sex, certainly not her propinquity, the way her body rolled onto his, taking him into her*—"must be frightened out of further contact. Then we can deal with the agent in our own time—"

Had he said it all, made it sufficiently clear? Dmitri was already nodding, then Georgi seemed to abandon reluctance. For him, they would agree to do it.

Do what?

Nothing more, or less, than keeping his mistress alive.

"Right. Let's check Reception, and get out of sight." He was businesslike, unemotional, while inside he was trembling with success and anxiety.

Outside, the day was warm, noisy with insects. He did not look back at the dacha. Georgi they left inside, and he was talking to himself—normal conversation level as he moved around the room—when they switched on the receiver in the car. Fade down to inaudibility as he moved into the kitchen, then loud again as he recited nursery rhymes, then his oath of office, then a poem by Pushkin, then hummed a Western pop song as he moved into the bathroom, and turned on the taps. By turning the volume all the way and straining, they could just make out what he was saying. An imitation of Andropov that almost everyone could do, Georgi better than most. Dmitri smiled. Leonov heard an insect loudly at his ear. Taps off, the voice clearer, fading, clearer, fading—and they could see him coming out of the door, relocking it. Dmitri gave him the thumbs-up.

"You and Georgi—" Leonov began as the detective walked toward them.

"It's all right," Dmitri reassured. "Georgi and me, we'll get our kicks from screwing the case officer. *You* take care of the other side of it."

Leonov nodded. Georgi climbed back in the car.

"O.K.?"

"Fine. Let's get out of sight."

Shubin stood at a shaving mirror in a white-tiled bathroom, studying his beard, then trimmed it until it was a poor and ragged attempt at facial hair. Then the foam, rubbed well in, stinging in the little nick on his thumb where he had touched the hanging meat ax, swilling the razor in the steaming water; shaving carefully, method-ically.

Pictures of him on a dark night. No pictures of him for years without a beard which he was now losing. The younger, sharper face with the weak chin he disliked began to emerge, watching him steadily from the mirror.

Suddenly, Zabotin was watching him from the doorway of the bathroom. He could see the man's worried face in the mirror, hovering over his shoulder like an omen.

"What do you want?" Shubin asked.

Zabotin coughed nervously. A tall, thin man, just like a doctor, which he was. But the face all nerves and incompetence now, no reassuring calm, no professional smile or concentration

"You look different," Zabotin offered

"Great. Thanks for noticing."

Scraping carefully round the chin that pudged a little, which was—weak.

"No, I only meant—"

"Yes."

"Tomorrow, then."

"Tomorrow."

Zabotin appeared satisfied, and about to return to the lounge of his bachelor apartment. Then he returned to the doorway.

"You have to kill him, do you?"

"Why?"

"Nothing—I just meant—"

"I have the papers, and they're good ones, Zabotin. I am the replacement security man at the stadium medical center. You have the rest of today and tonight to teach me enough about the medical problems of athletes for me to pass scrutiny, should there be any." Last flecks of foam, going over them with the razor as if he did not wish to mark the purple towel with them, then swill the razor out, rub the chin for its unaccustomed smoothness. He felt exposed, and unrecognizable. A sharp face with a chin that did not match. He turned to Zabotin, emphasizing with the razor.

"When you leave tomorrow night, you leave me behind. You'll have nothing to do after you've driven me and the cylinders through the gates in your car."

Zabotin nodded. He looked worried, probably by the thought of the four cylinders hidden underneath his workbench in his lock-up garage where he made little items of furniture and wooden dolls for his brother's children. Shubin dismissed him from his mind, and began washing his face in the shaving water.

The American had come, letting himself in—so Dmitri had reported, watching the dacha through binoculars from the shelter of a slight rise half a mile away—with the usual gimmicky master key, an hour or more after they had left the place. Anna did not arrive until almost five. She must have been shopping, or at the Ministry, Leonov concluded, for most of the day.

The car was hot, even with the windows open. The receiver

hummed like insects, and a gnat wandered round the windshield. Leonov squashed it with his thumb, and Georgi fiddled with the volume control on the receiver, perhaps to distract himself, shake off Leonov's tension. The silence that followed a door closing, and the light footsteps, went on so long that Leonov began to suspect the American had found the bug, and had cautioned her to silence. But he hadn't.

"Well? No, no introductions, please." It was Anna, taking command of the situation as he might have expected her to do. He wanted to smile, but it was a pressure not of amusement but of attempting to make innocent what he was about to hear.

"You're here to tell me the marvelous plan you have for getting me out. Be so kind as to do that, and leave."

Edgy, worn nerves just beneath her surface composure. She would be smoking already, taking short, rapid puffs, blowing the smoke out audibly. When they quarreled—infrequently—she did that, legs crossed, perched on the edge of the chair—which chair? He wanted to visualize her in the room; but alone, talking to the air. He did not know the American.

"Very well, Miss Akhmerovna." Georgi, at his side, smiled cynically at the Mormon-like politeness of the CIA man. "I'll get straight to it. You go out the day after tomorrow. A car will be waiting for you at the Lenin Stadium—just outside the complex, on the Komsomolski Prospekt, near the bridge." A pause. Silence from Anna. "O.K. The driver will be leaning on the car—blue shirt, checkered slacks. He knows you. The car will take you direct to the airport. A wig and change of clothes in the car. And luggage, tickets, passport, visas. Regular civilian flight, Pan Am, polar route to New York. Your seat will be next to one of our men, and there will be others on the flight."

Silence.

"Very well. What time, exactly?"

"Our man will be listening to the radio. The moment the 5000 meters ends, you leave your seat. It should take you ten minutes to get to the car, maybe forty minutes to get to the airport—the airplane leaves at seven."

"Thank you." Relief in the voice? "Now, please leave."

Leonov sat back in the seat, his shirt sticking to the hot plastic. Rivulets of sweat ran from beneath his arms, and his forehead was slick with it. Georgi watched him like a mother hen.

Click, audible and sharp, of the cigarette lighter—it might have been in the car—an exhalation of breath. Distantly, a door shutting.

"Switch it off," he said sharply. As if to continue listening would have been unforgivable, like a hidden camera in her bedroom or toilet. Dmitri's voice, then.

"He's getting in his car."

Leonov looked at Georgi, who was here instead of Dmitri because he was a better driver, and nodded. Below them where they were parked in a picnic spot, the road from Archangelskoe—a holiday resort—to Moscow snaked through trees that sloped away down to the Moskva. Leonov got out of the car.

"I'll watch from here. Don't make any mistakes—kill him!" The fury of his final words surprised even him, as if he had overheard some sexual assignation, some copulation and their climactic breathing close to the bug—*on the rug, in front of the fire, with drinks afterward*— "Kill him—but let her see it when she passes!"

The car had driven straight into a fir tree, its hood crunched into a hideous concertina of itself. The driver had come through the windshield, tearing open his face and head, and then broken his neck against the unyielding trunk. The body lay spread-eagled on the wreck of the hood, a white hand hanging down, its manicure hardly spoiled, the face averted from her as if in deference to her sensibilities. The flies feasting on the blood in the warm evening showed no such consideration.

After she had vomited, her body shaken by spasms until there was a sore, dry retching in her throat, she hurried back to the car, catching her stockings on undergrowth that had snapped and broken with the car's passage, tearing her skirt—

Get away, get away, she told herself, as the engine failed to catch until the fourth attempt. The rich headiness of the gasoline beginning to flood the engine made her want to vomit again. The engine roared as she pressed her foot down, the wheels spun as she pulled onto the road again. *Get away, get away—*

Already she knew what it meant. A warning from Gennadi. A dead body, with love.

Leonov watched her through the glasses until the car was out of sight round a bend in the road, hurrying back to Moscow. She looked very frightened. His satisfaction at her fear was masked by a desire to comfort her, show her that the horrors were cardboard, certainly not real—show her that she had to be slapped when she put her hand to the fire, otherwise she would burn herself.

Gennadi Leonov was at the mercy of his conflicting emotions, clinging to the spar of her survival in that angry sea.

Belousov was obviously the man to talk to, but he was away from the ordnance factory, suffering from a stomach bug. The director of the FAE project was an old man, formerly eminent but accepting this post as his last scientific sinecure, so the assistant director responsible for experimentation would be able to answer his questions.

Kazantsev had calmed down, understanding the need to know more about the possible FAE devices Shubin might have than about how he had obtained them and where they were now. If they ever came to light—and they would—then he would need to be able to deal with them, quickly and successfully.

Belousov lived alone—he was divorced from his wife, his file explained—in a dacha-style modern bungalow on a new development for managerial and scientific personnel from the Donetsk area, masked by new trees and hedges from the urban sprawl and in a dip of the land a few miles northeast of Makeyevka, near the river. A place Kazantsev could envy with its almost rural aura and its detached and semidetached houses. He smiled, pleased Tina had not seen it. Transfer to dirty Donetsk might have followed—and endless nagging before that.

He got out of the car, opposite Belousov's small bungalow which nevertheless asserted with its slightly larger garden and garage the status of its owner. It was growing dark, the sky a dirty orange over Donetsk, a pall of smoke through which a red sun was falling.

He rang the doorbell. Waited. Rang it again. Heard slow footsteps inside the door. Perhaps Belousov was disturbed by the huge shadow he must be able to see through the frosted glass of the door.

"Who is it?"

Something went on alert in Kazantsev's head. He could smell some night-scented flowers in the front garden, assess the bulk of Belousov through the glass, hear a car moving two streets away, and a lawn mower somewhere. Belousov was on edge.

"KGB," he said almost without thinking, added no mollification of the blunt fact.

"What do you want?"

Frightened? See how much he relaxes—

"Just a word, Comrade Assistant Director Belousov." The right ooze of deference. "We've met before—Oleg Kazantsev. I want to ask your advice about FAE devices—in general terms. May I come in?"

"I'm not well—" No relaxation. Instinctual impressions, professional sensors picking up something—

"I'm sorry for that. I won't keep you long."

Chain rattling back—chain? Bolt, catch. Rituals of security—why?

The door opened a crack. Belousov's weak white face.

"You'd better come in, I suppose—"

A frightened man. And one who hadn't been through the mincer—not yet. As Kasantsev went inside, he felt a tremor of excitement. There was an answer here, and he knew he would obtain it. Belousov had only begun to be frightened.

CHAPTER 16

"David—I know I look like meat the slaughterhouse rejected, but my brains don't rattle." Karen Gunston, her good hand resting on his as he sat perched on the edge of the bed—an imitation of domestic intimacy he had begun to enjoy—was staring at him with a pleading look in her eyes, a look he might have imagined her incapable of rendering. He nodded his head, jumping the little moment of doubt, the flinch from oncoming reality that had become habitual since his last contact with Anna Akhmerovna.

"All right, you weren't dreaming. You were sedated, but not hallucinating. Irena Witlocka is here, in this hospital. Now—what do you want me to do with the information?"

"God, David—why are you so damn *reluctant* all the time?" He noticed the proprietorial anger; she sensed she had acquired goods that were somehow faulty, fallen from the back of some cosmic truck. Allardyce subtly squared his shoulders, shaping up to events. He had decided that the Witlocka business was more within his scope—so be it. Do something.

"You don't know where she is?" Karen shook her head. The bruising was more yellow, her lips less puffed, and she shuffled her body in the bed without wincing too often. Allardyce was prepared to be in love with her at that moment. "O.K. I'll have a scout around—"

Karen shook her head again.

"Why is she here, David? Is she ill?"

"I don't think so. She's here so she can't defect—she's had a lot of time and effort invested in her over the years. Why should they let her go when they can prevent it? And—"

"And what?"

"It's a lever on Gutierrez—like the black market charges might have been on Irvine."

"You're joking, aren't you?"

"I wish I was. Perhaps I am—but these boys are fighting a war, not enjoying friendly competition. All's fair in—"

"Yes, I know that one. I majored in clichés, that's why I went into TV." She grinned. He squeezed her hand. "Bring me in one of those dinky cameras, like the ones spies used to have in the movies of yesteryear, mm?"

"You can't—"

"Oh, yes, I can. I'm one of the few who can move about this place without causing too much suspicion. If I can get a shot of the girl, then you and Greenberg and the kid—and CKR-TV, remember—can make an unholy noise." She touched the side of her nose. "Karen Gunston, fearless cub reporter."

"Don't forget what happened last time you took up photography."

"Screw you."

"My mother will be delighted with you."

"Go get the camera."

"I'll scout around a bit first. "

"No! If they see you, then they'll be waiting for me. Go and get the camera, then we can work things out."

Anna had sensed Leonov's strategy, and done everything to maintain the atmosphere of cordial superficiality he had used to cocoon the previous evening. She had washed her face in cold water as soon as she had returned to her flat, then decided that she needed a shower. She had stood beneath the hot water, then the cold, for twenty minutes, until the constant noise of the water calmed her, made the more oppressive of her thoughts recede.

She was able to think rationally, if only for a short time before she left for his flat. Gennadi Leonov had warned her. Somehow he thought he could save her, just so long as she made no attempt to get out. The dead American was a warning—*No entry*, or rather *No exit*. And perhaps it was a grotesque image of love, because he was either concealing everything from his men or had inveigled at least some of them into helping him.

The evening had been strained. He had sat—unusually for him—in the lounge all the time she was cooking their meal, attending with fierce concentration to the construction of a model aircraft. Even his sons, for whom the task was performed, seemed to have no part of his attention to the model. Dinner had been silent, smiles from him which she would have queried normally—*Is anything wrong?*—but which now she dare not.

He had drunk more than usual, too. Tried to talk about the Olympics, about anything—distracting himself more than her. She found herself undisturbed by his knowledge of her, more worried by his opinion of her secret life, the moral judgment he might have made. Was his silence, his aloofness, because he could not accept what she had done? Or was he merely confused as to her motives? Which had been—?

She put that part of herself aside like a handbag or gloves. A war machine which frightened her, a secret life that filled a void left by unsatisfactory lovers, ennui?

The soft glow of a table lamp illuminated the solid furniture that he had retained from his marriage, though he retained nothing else—she was sure of it—except the children.

They did not make love, but held each other for a long time until he fell asleep. She, too, eventually, narrowed her mental perspective to the illusion of comfort, of proximity, and slept.

And the morning was somehow soiled, and edgy, and unsatisfactory, his inquiries as to her day carefully indifferent, his departure for the office quick and that of a man caught in a dull and disappointing marriage.

And when he had gone, she knew that she had to talk to David Allardyce, at the stadium. It was risky, even foolhardy, but she knew he could not protect her. Gennadi might want to, but he would fail—he might even cease to want to. The KGB wanted her. Unless she got out—the thought caught at her throat like tears—she was finished.

Good-bye, Gennadi—

She handled his greasy breakfast plate as she might have done some talisman, before submerging it in the hot, soapy water in the kitchen sink.

"You make a noise, man—or screw this final—" Even as he said it, Gutierrez, looking into their eyes, knew that he had overplayed a weak hand, that they were angry, dismissive. Ballard, senior member of the U.S. AAU, Rickard, Assistant Track and Field Manager, Herter, Chief Coach, and Vandenburg, representing the U.S. Olympic Committee. All four of them were seated behind a table in the largest of the rooms in the village set aside for the use of the American administrators during the Games.

Gutierrez was standing in front of them, as if summoned for a reprimand rather than having requested the meeting to plead with them. He watched their faces now, knowing it was hopeless, that he had said too much.

Vandenburg resented him most deeply—resented the fact he was a Mex, that he wore denims and a vest whose lettering proclaimed that he had choked Linda Lovelace, and resented most deeply being offered an ultimatum.

"You're in no position to make demands, Gutierrez. You either get on with the race, or you go home—we want to hear nothing further from you except that you won a medal, sonny." Clipped, precise tone, the blunt vulgarity of power hardly masked by the Harvard voice. Ballard evidently agreed—Rickard and Herter seemed to bridle slightly at the counterthreat, as if they remembered old conflicts.

"Gutierrez—" Herter began. "We're not unsympathetic, boy. You believe that—?" He did not pause for a reply. "Now, we can make inquiries, but we can't do any more than that."

"We won't do any more than that." Ballard, who had to have everything simple, himself in the driving seat, athletes firmly in their subordinate role.

Gutierrez had known this would be the outcome. He had had to force it to this, but had expected no other reaction from these men. Now he would wait to be dismissed, backtrack by his silence from the point of challenge.

Rickard coughed, interjected, "This committee is now aware of the situation—" He indicated the cassette player on the table, from which they had heard Irena's words. "You'd better take this. We will make inquiries—"

Vandenburg must have considered he was being let off too lightly. "And don't ever consider threatening us again, boy. And—for you, newspapers are taboo. Understand?"

Gutierrez nodded, after a long silence. He stepped forward, as if in threat, and picked up the cassette player, then went out, slamming the door after him.

Looking for a joint, because Irena was getting to him and he was suddenly appalled that he was prepared to throw the race—not even *try*—for her sake.

Federenko and Tretsov, on the day before the Olympic Final of the 5000 meters, sat waiting to be interviewed on Soviet television in a special two-hour program of replays from the Games and a laudatory survey of the medal count. The two athletes sat in the hot, cramped studio watching a monitor which showed excerpts of the basketball, weight lifting, boxing, gymnastics, volleyball, and the other sports where the Soviet Union—and certain of its satellites—had achieved medals.

Then there was a rerun of the 5000 heats before the live interview. Federenko and Tretsov sat in separate silences, refusing to be jollied along by the link man between his sequences. Federenko—on one of the few occasions when he emerged from his blank misery—wondered whether Tretsov had been awakened by the hypnotist for the interview. The bitter humor of the idea of Tretsov pretending to be a dog, or taking his clothes off like someone hypnotized in a stage show soured even as he admitted it, and the dead face of Zenaida stared up at him from the hospital morgue table when they lifted the white sheet and he saw that she was at peace, and the sense of peace was the worst thing, the most terrible mockery of her life and what her death ought to have been. He wanted to have seen a toothless, wrinkled old face under that sheet, for she would have come to look like their mother when she got old, not that young, almost unmarked face with a tidied, cleaned scratch along one temple.

He had wanted to defile the body in some way, drag it off the table in his rage of misery, shake it back to life, to good sense. He knew she had *wanted* to die that way, as much as if she had told him so. Violent, glamorous death—they said you couldn't stop shitting in your trousers when someone shot you, but perhaps terrorists and fanatics didn't mind that, or it didn't happen to them.

She had belied everything, their whole mutual past, by what had happened. By gunfire, by explosion, by terror and exultation. To remember her as a child was to recall only an illusion.

The Australian press had been disappointed in him—not only in his performance in the heats, but in his performance for them. No jingoism—the Australian press was getting more and more insular all the time, he thought—no confidence, no bullshit. They wanted him with a fist round a tube of Foster's lager, white teeth set in a grin, sunshine and Bondi in the background. They wanted an ad for Qantas and the opportunities Australia offered. Supercobber.

He'd forgotten the necessary tricks needed to project such an image—or he couldn't believe in it any longer. He'd lost the script. He was a tired man with a buzzing, weary head, with a Gold Medal that had ceased to have any meaning for him. As he sat in one of the village's press lounges—a location which the team management had deserted along with the press, leaving him alone—the 5000 meters was beyond his mental grasp. He could not feel he was going to win it, or come anywhere near.

He felt he had hold of nothing. His mental grip closed only on air, and he moved within himself with a sense of dislocation, of being a stranger in that muscled physique, not quite knowing what to do with the fitness, the excess energy. A hyperactive child turning toward a destructive temper, having little or no control over his physical self. The will, the determination, had been lost—worn away so that everything was too much of an effort. He would be trying, if he went out there to win a second Gold Medal, to inject life into an affair that was long over, where the participants went through rituals of the familiar to disguise their strangeness from one another.

The KGB had him. He was tired, and small, and worried. He needed nothing less than a miracle, a resurrection. He was knackered, buggered, fucked, shagged out. He wanted to cry tears of pure self-pity.

It was a bucolic interrogation which obeyed a different time scale, into which urgency, perspiration, and threat could not intrude. Kazantsev, who used the powers of his office to remain in Belousov's bungalow through the night and the following morning, and the unspoken power of the KGB to make that presence implacable, nevertheless considered himself a policeman. No violence, no electrodes, no bright lights, which was why he had not taken Belousov to the Donetsk office, or called in anyone else. The Resident had called Belousov's number during the night, and Kazantsev had warned him off.

Of course, neither of them had slept, and the flow of conversation—question and answer, anecdote and memory—never stopped, running over the stone that was Belousov's secret—for Kazantsev knew he had one—smoothing and polishing it to something that could be exhibited. Kazantsev knew that a skilled interrogator—one of the men who had worked on the post office clerk, perhaps—would have broken Belousov by now. But he didn't have the technique. And he had to know that what he was told was the truth, the whole truth, and nothing but—

So, cooking a lunch of mushrooms in sour cream—*gribi v smetane*—while Belousov cut thick slices of black bread at the kitchen table, Kazantsev reviewed what he had learned with a weary brain that sought its own refuge from the ceaseless talk.

Belousov was a graduate of the same university as Shubin—not a thing the man had admitted—but with no apparent connection with the failed engineer and progenitor of *Do pobachenya*. He was a Ukrainian nationalist of mild sympathies. For a long time during the night and morning Kazantsev, seeing the essential timidity of Belousov, could not convince himself that he could be connected with bombers. He had drawn Belousov into a discussion of Soviet history, to the old bugbears of the famines of the thirties, the executions under Stalin, the war years, the postwar aspirations. Kazantsev, Ukrainian himself, knew the script, dredged his memory for other material.

A career in military hardware, scientific assistant on various projects, in different parts of the Soviet Union. Shells, tank guns, fragmentation bombs, FAE. Marriage to a fellow worker which hadn't worked out. Belousov had liked sex a lot, Kazantsev deduced, and in some of its more timidly exotic manifestations, judging by the clothes and the mock leather in the dusty, unused wardrobe. After the separation, dedication to work as an anodyne.

Once more, over the ground of his career in more detail. Kazantsev had jumped his hurdle. The man was not dangerous, but the technology of violent death was for him a piece of research or construction or design. Yes, he could make bombs. To him, they would be things that might never be used, only a set task, to be completed.

Did he know what Shubin would do with bombs?

Kazantsev finished cooking and shunted the mushrooms and cream onto two white plates with a wooden spoon. Belousov put the knife back in the bread bin, and sat down, setting two forks and the condiments on the table. Kazantsev, hungry, tore at the black bread, pushed a chunk into his mouth, forked up a mouthful of mushrooms, and beamed.

"Good, eh? My wife never lets me cook at home."

Belousov nodded.

"Good. My wife didn't let me do lots of things at home. Is your wife intelligent—I mean academic?"

Kazantsev, pushing another mouthful in. "No. Reads a lot— student of the human heart, maybe—but she didn't go to college or anything like that."

"But she's still with you, mm?"

"She is."

They finished the meal in silence.

"I've got some tinned fruit, if you like—?" Belousov offered. Neither of them remarked on the speed with which his supposed stomach trouble had cleared up. Kazantsev shook his head.

"We'll wash up, eh? Can't stand mess in the kitchen."

They did so. Then Belousov made coffee, lit a cigarette.

"Took them up again when she left," he commented. "Have one?"

"Thanks." They took their coffee into the small, neat lounge a fastidious bachelor with a decent salary might have created for himself. Kazantsev assumed that Madame Belousov's memorials were in the wardrobe, not in the lounge. Stereo—German import, by the look of it, and plenty of records. Taste catholic, but with the obligatory one-upmanship of foreign pop recordings. No ornaments, plenty of books—cheap paperback novels and scientific manuals. "Tell me a bit more about FAE weapons, Rudolf Ivanovich."

Slight cough, cup at his lips. Hesitation.

"Most of it's classified, you know."

"I know that. I've got the clearance. I wouldn't be in the antiterrorist mob without it, would I? What sort do you make down at the factory?"

Cough. "You're aware of general principles?"

"To a point. Bloody nasty things, wouldn't you say?"

"I don't think of it like that. They won't be used."

"Then why make them, for God's sake?"

"The Americans have them, therefore we must have them."

"Sounds a bit like a formula for not thinking—"

"Do you want to know about them, or not?"

Belousov, prissily challenged on the quality of his mind, showed a face thinned and pursed by ego. Both men, Kazantsev observed, had forgotten the purpose of the inquiry, forgotten their previous roles. Kazantsev's was a necessary surrender of his office; in Belousov's case it was also deliberate. He was prepared to talk and talk and talk because it postponed more unpleasant realities. Or he could just be lonely.

"Tell me, then. What are the most efficient types?"

"Those dropped by aircraft or helicopter—undoubtedly." And Kazantsev carefully sipped at his coffee, hiding most of his face behind the big mug. Something he hadn't considered. But it couldn't be, surely—? *Do pobachenya* were amateurish kids, apart from Shubin.

"Detonate at ground level—?"

"No." Belousov shook his head, disappointment in his pupil. "At a predetermined height, an outer casing comes apart—air pressure might even do it—and the FAE canisters are spread over a wide area. We're experimenting with glass ones, to give a better shatter-to-scatter ratio." He smiled at his professional witticism.

"What's the spread?"

"Depends how much you want—size of bomb, number of FAE liquid containers, whether you want the dish effect, or the lava type—"

"Pardon?"

"Do you want a spread at a set height, a wide saucer of the vaporized liquid which will ignite as if it's oil floating on water? It floats in the air at a certain height, then the ignition causes the whole dish of gas to burn at tree height, at man height."

"Charming." Pursed lips at the irrelevant reaction.

"Or, you can have it descend from that height slowly, say in a densely forested area, sliding like lava over every surface, and clinging to it. Then ignition burns everything that has been touched by it." Belousov's eyes were gleaming. He was sitting upright in his chair, attentive, pedagogic, determined that he should understand. Only understand—approval or disapproval were of no account in the aseptic atmosphere of the lounge.

"What if they're on the ground?" Kazantsev asked casually.

Hardly any hesitation, just an adjustment of the head as the brain considered. "Not so good. The scatter is small-scale—you need some means of propulsion for the containers after the outer casing breaks open. Oh, the gas will rise and spread, but more slowly. You'd still need a delayed ignition, you see."

"I see. So that wouldn't be an effective weapon, then?"

"No. Not effective in coverage by the standards of the other types."

Kazantsev said, "Fancy a stroll in your back garden, Rudolf Ivanovich? You much of a gardener?" Belousov shook his head. "Pity. Miss a garden, living in a flat in Moscow. Come on, let's have a look at it."

As they went out into the small, fenced garden with its untrimmed lawn and straggly flower beds and halfhearted attempt at vegetables, Kazantsev reflected that he knew that Belousov had not simply supplied the bombs, but rather had made them. But would the man have supplied something he evidently thought inferior, like a ground-dispersal Free Air Explosion device? Slow, small-scatter, delayed operation?

Unless Belousov had the egotism to have considered improving the design, and the talent to fulfill that ego?

Kazantsev realized he had to limit the conversation now, under the guise of scientific interest.

Standing beneath a stunted apple tree. Gnats in the heavy, almost stormy air. Belousov belched, more from the lunch than from nerves, Kazantsev suspected.

"Are they especially antipersonnel, FAE devices?"

Belousov shook his head, a mild look of outrage on his face.

"Of course not. Developed from the defoliant weapons the Americans used in Vietnam, and like some of our defoliant gases." Kazantsev nodded, since it seemed best simply to let the man talk. "The FAE weapon, which uses a napalm-type liquid which vaporizes but has adjustable chemical properties—such as the ability to reach the ground from a predetermined height in a set time or to spread in a thin film at a certain height depending on the wind—is designed for military use, against the terrain or military targets."

"O.K., don't get all prissy, Rudolf Ivanovich. I only wondered, since it seemed to make such a good and *effective* antipersonnel weapon—like the neutron bomb."

"Don't be emotive—it confuses the issue. You, as a bomb disposal expert, ought to be sufficiently objective—"

"Oh, I don't know. I get to pick up the bits when one's gone off, you know. Not nice. And I was wondering what Shubin might want with a weapon only for military use—since he's got one?" Kazantsev, smiling.

"Shubin—who is he?" Genuine shock at the change of tack, the jump in the conversation, as if Kazantsev had yawned with boredom.

"He's a terrorist. He would want an antipersonnel weapon. Now, tell me how good an antipersonnel weapon FAE would be."

Shubin minutely inspected the four cylinders hidden at the back of Zabotin's garage, traced the wax seals on the blow-out panels to make sure there was no shrinkage—there was none. Good, then he had finished. Now, he just had to load the four cylinders into the back of Zabotin's car with its official medical stickers on the window and windshield, and drive to the stadium.

The cylinders had changed their appearance since they left the ordnance factory—Shubin had stenciled in Cyrillic on each one XXII Olympiad—Medical Center—Pure Oxygen. He studied the readings on the fake dials—FULL, in each case. To all intents and purposes, even a close scrutiny would lead the observer to consider that he was looking at just the sort of oxygen cylinder that was wheeled onto an athletics track in case any competitor required reviving in such a manner. From each of the cylinders now dangled a transparent mask at the end of a length of tubing. Just like the real thing, just like—

Shubin felt himself giggling; the pleasure was wholly his, there was no sense of the culmination of two years' preparation, or of the other people, many of whom he had never met, who had placed him in that garage half an hour's drive from the Lenin Stadium with four Free Air Explosion weapons in his possession. Shubin with his oxygen cylinders was alone in his tight, complete cocoon of egotism. The organization in Munich, its members in Kiev, no longer existed—except the stupid, unrealizable demand contained in one of the letters he still had to post.

Do pobachenya, too, had ceased to exist with the deaths of the children. Except that he *was* the organization. The *Narodny-Trudovoy Soyuz* in Munich, the various Ukrainian émigré groups that were attached to it, or separate from it, the little mushrooms that sprung up and died, the little splinters or seeds that split away, had all in one way or another been used by Shubin. He had not kept any secrets, but he had used different contacts for different parts of his plan.

Belousov he knew. The doctor, Zabotin, was handed him by an émigré group more radical than most. Zabotin wasn't a radical, but his son who had fled to the West through Afghanistan and Pakistan was. And he was in Munich, and Daddy worshiped and missed him because he was a lonely widower. The letters were sent by another group, the papers manufactured by another.

And at the center of it all—and he saw himself only at the center—was Shubin. A couple of nice, tidy outrages during the fortnight of the Olympic Games. That was the general consensus. The older heads had reveled in the prospect of the bomb in the Lenin Mausoleum, with a suitable delay so that visitors could be evacuated to a safe distance, and the younger ones had clutched the second scheme to them like a child's comforter on an especially dark night.

The FAE device was *his* idea. And its location. And the letter that made the impossible demands but also contained the threat. And the detonation—oh, yes, the detonation of the FAE device was certainly his idea. There wasn't enough hatred of the Russians in the Ukrainian émigrés to permit an outrage which killed 100,000 people, a sizable proportion of whom would be Western visitors. But there was sufficient in him.

A great saucer of flame, burning.

He shrugged off the speculations, and swiftly loaded the four oxygen cylinders into the back of the medical estate car, covering them with a blanket before folding down the luggage cover. They were innocent, officially stenciled, innocuous.

As he went back into the foyer of the block of flats, he patted his breast pocket. One letter to *Pravda*, which would provide an express route to the Kremlin the following day, and another letter—he could post that now—addressed to Valentina Kazant-seva.

The address of the policeman who had killed the children was easy—the telephone directory. And the tickets, for the penultimate day of athletic competition at the Lenin Stadium, culminating in the 5000-meter Final, were those Federenko had sent to Zenaida. Three tickets, for the wife and kids of the KGB bastard. *Do pobachenya.*

And good-bye Arkady Federenko, arse-licker, time-server. And everyone.

He had no trouble passing through the security checkpoint at the stadium, parking the car in the place reserved for officials at the Games, near the door which led to the passageway to the medical center, or unloading the four cylinders, carrying them inside, storing them in a steel locker at one end of the long, clinical room with its red blankets, high beds, stretchers, oxygen cylinders, medical instruments, medicine cabinets, ECG machine.

When they were locked in, Zabotin, sweating profusely, dabbing at his forehead, gave Shubin his obligatory white coat which matched his new papers—supplied from samples sent by Zabotin to his son in Munich in the gas tank of a tourist's car, returned in the same manner—papers which declared that Shubin was a medical orderly to the general public and the competitors but also a KGB man on security attachment to the stadium, an identification he might need when he remained overnight in the medical center.

Once he was attired, there was nothing to do for the moment but to go up and watch the Finals of the high hurdles, the women's long jump, and the 400 meters.

And study the layout, for the first time at firsthand, of the track and field of the Lenin Stadium.

Anna Akhmerovna, in an agony of suspense, watched for the arrival of David Allardyce. The semifinal of the 1500 meters held no interest for her—African versus Russian and East German and American and Englishman, merely an array of different vests on slim, wiry bodies with ropy muscles and often narrow chests. Nothing had any significance since the endless evening and night with Leonov, after the dead CIA man on the hood of his car. The sleeplessness followed by dreams had become more horrible during the bright morning. She had come to the stadium for the morning events, triple jump qualifying and decathlon items in case he was there, and in case Gennadi decided to join her during the afternoon.

But Allardyce had not come, and she was left to ponder the weak and broken reed he was and the fact that he was her only chance. She would not deal with anyone else.

It was stupid, blind, and perhaps fatal. But strangers seemed to die more easily, and care less, and she had to feel there was some chance she would get out.

Gennadi had warned her—what else would he do? Stay here, he had told her. He knew all about her, but he had tried in his own way to divert her, as he would try, she knew, to divert suspicion from her if she stayed.

But he couldn't *do* it—! He would never get away with it, and he would be finished and so would she. And she wanted no compact in death, with Gennadi or anyone.

It was three o'clock before Allardyce arrived, coming up the steps with a casual thoughtfulness that appeared to her to be nothing short of jauntiness. She almost caught at his sleeve as he paused, smiling at her.

Sit down, she mouthed. *Please.*

Instantly, his face was wary, his eyes studying her, his mouth reluctantly pouted. But he sat down.

"David—have you heard from them?"

"No." He looked at her sharply, surprised at her breathless-ness. "I'm out of the game now."

"The American is dead."

"What?"

"Yesterday. His car was run off the road."

"An accident, you mean—?"

Second lap of the 1500. Neither of them remarked it, though the growing crowd noise deadened the volume of their conversation.

"It was no accident—Gennadi *knows* about me!" Anger rather than panic. Allardyce could not help admiring her control.

"What will he do about it?"

"He's trying to cut me off—he wants me to stay."

"Why not simply arrest you?"

"Don't be stupid—he's in love with me. He's trying to keep me, and save me."

"How did he find out?"

"I don't know. I'm sure he doesn't know about you." A propitiation. Allardyce resented being the child who needed to be bribed.

"The plan will have to be changed."

"*No!* The same plan—tell them I'll be there, *before* the race, and they must keep to their bargain."

"I'm not—"

"I won't trust anyone else, David. They're *children*, playing a game with my life. *You* tell them—you take me to the airport. No one else—you."

They were the only still and silent people in the stadium, as the 1500 finished, the Final to be run immediately preceding the Final of the 5000 meters, the next day. Or, so it seemed to Leonov, watching them through glasses so that her mouth was so magnified and so close he might have put his mouth on it or be able to read the pleas she was making. He saw Allardyce nod, pat her hand—spurt of jealousy there as if nothing else was real in the situation—and leave her. He studied her set face, staring sightlessly down at the track.

And the tears trickled, unnoticed, down his cheeks from under the eyepieces of the glasses. She was going ahead—she was leaving him, getting out, not trusting him to save her skin for her.

There was nothing more he could do.

Kazantsev and Belousov were moving deeper, like two frogmen slowly submerging into darker waters, diving reluctantly downward. Kazantsev had made a start on digging over a patch of garden that had become overgrown and weed-filled where Belousov had once made an unsuccessful attempt to introduce raspberry canes. They'd gone wild and unkempt and scratchy. But all the time he dug, or rested, or drank beer from the fridge, he continued talking, wearing at Belousov who weeded between rosebushes that needed pruning very badly. Earlier, they had cut back a hedge that had overreached itself.

Always about FAE devices, and increasingly now the breakdown of scientific detachment and mechanical enthusiasm—fuses, igniters, detonators, weight, size, shape, force, propulsion, damage, deployment. And the assertion of *casualties, effects, moral viewpoint, arms races, burns, fragility of the human body*—

And the reminiscences—the bodies, the bits of bodies, the bits that might have been bodies, the bits that could never have belonged to bodies, when bombs went off near people. Hearty talk, from the café or bar after a successful defusing, or an unsuccessful one and they all wanted to forget, talk it out of themselves.

"What effect would it have, though? Really. If you let one of these things off in Red Square, say—?" Mumble mumble—impossible, not for that purpose, ineffective— "But really—HE I've seen, a lot of it, but this? What would it do, if the spread occurred quickly enough? Char everything out of recognition over the radius the gas covered, eh?" No, no—mumble mumble, impossible. "But it would, wouldn't it. Thousands of people wouldn't stand any chance at all, would they. Burned to death— Hey! I know. Like the Dresden firestorm, something like that, eh?" Dig, weed, just for a minute, then— "It would, though, wouldn't it? Be like that, I mean? What would be the best conditions—wind or no wind? No wind, I suppose—?" Shut up, mumble mumble, it couldn't happen— "Burn like fucking matches, wouldn't they? Just piles of ash on the pavement, eh?" No, no, shut up, shut up, mumble mumble, I've told you already it wouldn't be like that, mumble mumble— "Go on, don't tell me they're not developing something that would burn the shit out of a city center—say Times Square or Trafalgar Square? Too good an opportunity, I'd say. I'll bet you're working on one!" No, no, shut up, shut up, shut up— "Spread like a dish, or drip down over everyone like molasses, vaporizing—"

Kazantsev was staring up into the sky, as if expecting a detonation, leaning on his spade.

"You feel a little tickle on your skin, like a shower, or hairspray misfiring—eh? Then, a little spark, over there near Nelson's Column, where that hippie is burning—burning? The silly cunt's set himself alight—your arm's burning by this time, look at it, your own St. Elmo's Fire and your skin's coming off in great gobbets and doesn't the fat burn with a blue flame. And every other bugger is burning, too—what a display! Cars, shops, the National Gallery, people . . . GUM, the Lenin Mausoleum, trolleybuses, shops, St. Basil's, the Kremlin, the Historical Museum—*people!*" His voice reached a climax he had only half-calculated, the inertia of his images overtaking him.

"Everywhere, the people are burning!"

And he stopped, then, as suddenly as the climax of a piece of music, leaving the audience drained and silent for that moment before the conductor turns to them—

Mumble mumble, shut up, shut up, shut up—feel sick, feel sick—

Belousov scampered toward the back door of the bungalow, his hand over his mouth, the other hand feebly pushing open the door and balancing his wild flight at the same time. Kazantsev let him go, his own stomach queasy as the rhetoric died and the images lingered. Let the clever little sod puke and puke until there was nothing more to come up, until the mess of mushrooms and sour cream and breakfast in the lavatory bowl revolted him all over again.

Then nail him to the wall.

He waited for ten minutes, then went inside.

There was a lot of blood, naturally. The wild, frenzied slashes at the wrists and forearms had become the more rational insanity of pressing against the kitchen knife as it was wedged in the jamb of the bathroom door. A lot of blood on the slippery tiles, over the white-and-pink bathroom walls, splashed on the pink lavatory and bath, and sliding in a slow red sheet down the bathroom door, onto Belousov's shoes. He was leaning against the door as if still sick or tired, his head resting there, the long knife still jammed in the door keeping the body half-upright.

Kazantsev smashed the bathroom mirror with his clenched fists, driving out the self-recrimination, the accusations, the revulsion at cleverness. The stupid bastard *had* made bombs, and they *were* to kill people, a lot of people.

And now he was sorry, and guilty, and horrified out of his scientific enthusiasm.

And he'd killed himself, when he should have put things right by confessing, explaining.

Kazantsev hurled the body aside, so that it fell into the bath, face-up, the knife protruding from the rib cage. Scientific to the last, the bastard knew exactly where his heart was. He slammed the bathroom door.

It was five in the afternoon—of the day before, the day before the day before, or *the day itself*—?

And *where*?

He wanted to cry tears of rage and self-loathing.

CHAPTER 17

A senior member of the Secretariat was reading Shubin's final letter to *Pravda*. The head of the Kremlin administrative staff, aware of protocol, was evidently disturbed by the emptiness of the huge office and by the presence of only the First Secretary of the CPSU and the Chairman of the KGB. Disturbed, too, by being made to read the thing aloud, as if by that means the words would gather threat from the dry, enclosed air, or its incipient threat be diminished by the high ceiling, the ornate furnishings, the huge dead fireplace beside which the two men sat.

"Go on, go on—" urged the Chairman, as if embracing the promised disaster. The First Secretary watched the letter's single sheet as it quivered slightly in the civil servant's hand.

". . . unless full national sovereignty is restored to the Ukraine and the Ukrainian people . . ."

Contempt pursed the Chairman's face like acid; the First Secretary remained impassive.

"Is that all they want?" The acid dribbled on his chin like spittle. "What else?"

". . . enshrined in a new constitution . . ."

"Go back to the threats!"

The civil servant, nonplussed, stuttered to a halt. A hand waved him to continue.

"Unless—unless the following rights of the Ukrainian people are recognized, a device will be detonated at the Lenin Stadium which will completely annihilate all competitors and spectators. The Mausoleum was simply a gesture of good faith. The First Secretary must broadcast, to the peoples of the Soviet Union and to the rest of the world . . ."

"That's enough," the First Secretary rumbled, shifting in his chair as if some sudden spotlight had fallen upon him. "Leave the letter—and be on call."

The civil servant coughed, grateful at dismissal, yet unsure of how to dispose of the sheet of paper in his hand, the coarse texture of which had become damp and gray under the impression of his thumb. His fingerprint was on it, and as if that implied complicity in its threat, he hurriedly put it down on the large desk. The two most powerful men in the Soviet Union, each in a separate and profound silence, watched the tall, stooping figure hurry down the length of the great room, open and close the door.

The silence went on for a long time.

"Impossible—" Chairman.

"What, the threats or the capitulation?"

It was as if the Soviet leader had made a joke concerning some deeply private matter. The Chairman of the KGB appeared affronted.

"The whole matter," he said carefully.

"You don't believe the threat?"

"I'm not prepared to dismiss it—"

The First Secretary rubbed his chin, then put both hands to his face, massaging his cheeks as if dissatisfied with their loose, old texture.

"What is to be done? A hundred thousand people, including you and me, will be in the stadium tomorrow and the following day. Perhaps two thousand million people will be watching television— someone is being very clever, wouldn't you say?"

"Is admiration called for?" The Chairman appeared ready to applaud ironically. Then he added, "What do you wish me to do? Round up all the Ukrainians, search the stadium from top to bottom—what else?"

"Those things, of course—perhaps as a matter of course. At present, there is no outburst from the Western press—what do you make of that? Is this an—*extremist* group without support in Munich or elsewhere?"

"I hope not. We might know nothing about them."

"They call themselves *Do pobachenya*—we know that much."

"Now we know *why!*"

"Yes—black humor. Yes, make your arrests, search the stadium. Meanwhile—I shall sit and perform the difficult task."

"Which is?"

"Doing nothing." A thin smile appeared like a knife cut in the broad, loose face. "We are—we have set our foot in the mantrap. We can do nothing. We dare not cancel the Games—if we do, we are shown as powerless, frightened, open to blackmail—think of the internal and external repercussions of that." The Chairman nodded gloomily. "We cannot give the Ukraine self-government—think of the internal repercussions of *that*—" The Soviet leader rubbed his cheeks again. "Yes, I know. What if there is a bomb, what if it goes off with the whole world watching—?" He turned his gaze from the empty fireplace, where he might have been reading the shadows of past fire pictures, and studied the Chairman, tried to catch the eyes behind their glinting spectacles. "You know your job, then—" He raised his hands, palms outward. "Don't maneuver for survival with me, Yuri. If it happens, then none of us will survive it. Get the Antiterrorist Squad all the extra help they need. Find that bomb, and find the bomber. *Then* we can maneuver for praise. Meanwhile, it's my job to sit on my backside, and do the worrying for all of us." The Chairman appeared about to speak. "No. The time for discussion is over. Find the bomb. And you and I will both be attending the Lenin Stadium, tomorrow and the next day. And we both want very much to live."

The Chairman, in his third-floor office in KGB Center, Dzerzhinsky Street, sat behind his ornate, massive desk, hands at each side of the green blotter in its leather folder, as if squaring paper. Puchkov, disturbed by the sudden elevation of the interview, and its implications, perched on the other side of the desk on a century-old upright chair.

"What of this man Kazantsev? Why does he persist in remaining over in Donetsk?" The Chairman's habitual suspicion—or ability to suggest suspicion, mistrust.

"Lieutenant Kazantsev is our most experienced officer—"

"Lame. Why is he there—don't you need him here? And the man he was interrogating—why did he not use an expert? He has allowed our *one* lead to kill himself."

"Yes, that was—"

"Listen, Puchkov. The First Secretary has just finished telling me not just to make the right noises and bury my head in paperwork. I'm telling you the same. Something has to be done. What do we know about the bomb and the bomber?"

"Very little, Comrade Chairman—" The Chairman's face puckered at the punctilious phrase. "Kazantsev is convinced that an FAE device or devices were made by the man Belousov, and have been handed over to Shubin the terrorist—"

"But what do they *look like*, these devices?"

"We don't know."

"So why is Kazantsev staying in Donetsk? Is he trying, perhaps, to contact the spirit world for his answers?" A brushing motion of his hand, ash or people swept aside, or just the hedge of intractibles the Chairman could almost see growing from the blotter. "I do not see the *necessity*."

"He believes Belousov must have left some clue there, at his place. The devices would have to have been manufactured outside the ordnance factory."

"And all evidence burned or otherwise destroyed?" The superiority that cynicism gave him seemed hollow and unsatisfying. "Very well. For our part, we must find the devices here. A complete search—the program begins at ten in the morning. We have twelve hours. Deputy Chairman Filipov is drafting in the extra men required and setting up the revised security arrangements. I suggest you make your way to the Lenin Stadium—at once."

When Puchkov had gone, the Chairman studied the growths of intertwining, suppurating anxieties in his mind—staring at the blotter as if he could see them as plant life emerging there. Occasionally, his hand continued to make a sweeping motion over the surface of the blotter—but without volition or anger. Almost nerveless.

Nine in the evening. The smoky Donetsk horizon was red and threatening through the window of the bungalow's lounge. Kazantsev had heaped the furniture, piece by piece in a methodical, cold anger, in the middle of the carpet, having operated upon each piece with a kitchen knife—not the one Belousov had used on himself, but the second sharpest—spilling the intestines of each chair, sofa, cushion. Then he had begun rolling back the carpets, tugging each of them away from the jagged rows of metal teeth that held them in place. The physical exertion quieted something else in him that clamored for attention—a sense of failure, a sense of growing desperation. Method, method. If he worked slowly, completely, then there was nothing he would miss, and he would be doing his job properly for a change and be able to tell himself he was.

Nothing under the carpets. Floorboards? He blanched at the task of ripping them up, one by one—then almost welcomed it. More work, more of reducing everything to the strength of his hands and forearms and back and thighs—pull, heave, strain, and the images from the bathroom didn't come back quite so clearly or insistently.

Belousov had been taken away by the Donetsk meat wagon. A team was being assembled to help in the search, but he still held them off. Some process of recovering self-esteem, or self-justification. It was *his* job, and only he knew what to look for.

The bastard had even swept the garage floor, probably washed it down. The little Volga sedan in there—which Kazantsev had started, backed out onto the drive—was neat and clean and hid nothing. Nothing on the shelves, no equipment that might have been used, no traces of material left behind, not even down behind the work surface that Belousov had built for himself at the far end of the garage, next to the vise and the small lathe. Nothing behind the neatly stacked tins of paint—the colors of every room in the house, even the paintwork outside; nothing in the toolboxes, in the jars of nails or under the pile of sandpaper.

Nothing in the bedroom, the kitchen, the spare room—and nothing but the blood in the bathroom.

Kazantsev was not seized by any mounting urgency, kneeling on the floorboards in Belousov's darkening lounge-dining room, bits of cheap kapok from the cushions of the sofa scattered around him. He was breathing laboredly but steadily, hands were pressed flat against the floorboards, as if absorbing the rough texture.

The Donetsk office was rounding up known associates and gathering information from the scientific staff at the ordnance factory. Trying to discover what the bombs looked like, how big, how many, how powerful. What was it the dead KGB man had seen when he was killed by Shubin? What had he instantly recognized, or suspected? Something obvious, clearly wrong.

Had he had one of the devices in his hands, and known what it was?

Kazantsev stared at his own big hands. How would one of the bombs fit into them, if at all? What would one feel like under his touch?

They could look like anything at all, he told himself. Just anything.

He would know it when he saw it—trace, fragment, drawing, note. He knew enough to know what he needed to see to solve his puzzle.

But the searchers in Moscow, at the stadium, just in case they came up empty, needed to know size, shape, number.

O.K.—forensic, and a lot of help. And up with floorboards, and the garden, even the concrete of the drive and the drains if necessary. And they could share his anxiety among themselves like passing round sweets he had given them. He continued looking at his hands, studied the nail of the finger with which he would dial the

Donetsk office. The answer could be in the dirt under the nail, picked up in every room in the house.

Forensic, then.

He dialed each number quickly, the urgency coming now with the sunset like a cold wind against his sweat-stained shirt.

The evening before the Olympic Final of the 5000 meters. Winston Ochengwe is jogging, lazily circling the main practice track of the village, with its football pitch within the running track. It is easy to perceive something of the delight, the satisfaction, that he feels, his body hardly sweating as he jogs for relaxation; his mind narrowed like the point of a knife, aware of the following day at the point of the blade, aware too of the haft behind him, the years and months and days that have led to this.

Winston Ochengwe is ready, and is aware that he is ready. His adopted country no longer exists, and his wife and child and mother are long buried under the routines of training.

A final lap, slightly faster than before, then he walks away. He is ready.

Peter Lydall is listening to music in one of the small lounges in the cultural center built by the Roskontsert Association and containing a theater, two cinemas, a dance hall, television rooms, a library, game rooms, and dozens of smaller rooms. The music is Sibelius, the fourth, glacial symphony. Lydall has always been able to identify with, immerse himself in, its chilly, understated intensity. This evening he sits, slouched alone in an easy chair, his feet up on a low coffee table, a paperback novel on the floor by his side, and the music speaks more mutedly, but nevertheless disguises from him the main thrust of his anxieties; masks for the moment a growing sense of tension, an excitement that enervates rather than energizes. He is not prepared to see the next day in any kind of perspective greater than that of the last two weeks. And if he does that, he knows that he, too, is ready—as ready as he has ever been.

The music seeps into him, almost having muscular power so that his hands close into fists and his arms seem tight with muscle. He is ready.

Kenneth Irvine cannot sleep. The room is empty except for his form stretched on the bed. The posture, if viewed from the door of the apartment's bedroom, is tense yet somehow suggests weakness, the bend of the knees suggesting a fetal curl rather than relaxed power. He does not move much on the bed—the counterpane is almost unwrinkled—but there is no relaxation. Only the eyes staring at the ceiling as if at some screen on which is being played back his time in Moscow. The interrogations—for that is how he now sees them—the press of people, the choking sense of never being alone, never hearing his own head, are in garish color, while the 10,000 is a grainy, half-recollected monochrome.

It has not come back to him as he wished, prayed. There has been no conversion of his experience with the KGB into a necessary *distraction*. It might, with luck, have worked that way, saving him from the boredom, the routine, of village life while he waited and trained. But it hasn't. Instead, it is a weight on his limbs, a weariness in his mind where he will have to come to rely on that sudden flash of insight and will that had happened near the end of the 10,000.

He thinks of getting the medal out of the bedside cabinet, but doesn't.

Tretsov, with sensors taped to his chest and arms, is sitting before a screen on which is projected nothing. There are no clocks in the room. He is being watched by his coaches, his doctors, his psychologists. He is dressed in a blue Soviet track suit, CCCP emblazoned on the back and pocket, the sleeves rolled up, the chest open almost to his waist. In his left hand he holds a button.

A minute passes without words, a humming noise in the background, the blank screen white, the lighting dimmed as if for a film show. Perhaps two or three seconds after the silent minute, Tretsov squeezes the button on the stalk of wire in his hand. Immediately, the screen shows a film of a running track, the finish line in the lower foreground. The camera, with the point of view of a runner, moves past toward the bend, then the screen goes blank again. There is some whispering behind Tretsov, among the medical experts, then more silence, until Tretsov presses the button again, and the white finish line is right at the bottom of the screen for a moment, then the camera has rolled over it.

Silence again, then repeat. White line at the bottom of the screen. Twelve times, and the white line is no more than two or three meters from the camera which shot the training film, a camera on a motorized dolly covering the circuit of the track in exactly the time Tretsov's coaches have decided he needs to run to win the race.

Except that on the twelfth time, the camera dolly speeded up to put in a last lap of fifty-five, and on the eleventh time, one of fifty-seven. Each time, Tretsov is ahead of the camera.

When it is done, he goes through the routine again—and then again, and again.

His coaches, his doctors, know he is ready.

Gutierrez, moving nervously, in sudden releases of nervous energy, strolls through the village like a child told to walk who really wants to run. Small stutters, uneven strides, breaking into a jogging motion more and more often.

He is ready. If he wins, which he knows he can do, then he will never see Irena Witlocka again. It is a simple dilemma, and if he were sure of his feelings for the girl, he could opt for the alternative that wasn't morally reprehensible, and that might romanticize the whole experience. But he is not sure of his feelings, not now that the girl is away from him, and he cannot envisage her circumstances. He is not worried that the girl might be hurt, or in danger. That is something he cannot conceive, or will not allow himself to conceive. She will simply be sent home to Poland, and all contact with her will cease if he should win the race.

If the girl were there, he knows it would not matter. He would choose her because he would be afraid to look into her face if he denied her. But she isn't there—and he wants a medal. So bad he can taste it, and he has the acute sense of betrayal of a child denied something it wants. If only the girl were there.

Greenberg and Allardyce have a stupid scheme like a caper from a bad film. Karen Gunston will take pictures, so that the girl will be safe, the authorities will have to release her or put up with the international news stories.

Gutierrez doesn't believe it will work, but he has to believe in it. Otherwise, he is left with an image of himself in a mirror that catches a hard light, and shows him what he is. Nothing, dirt, cheapskate, shit—

It isn't even real gold.

But he wants it. He can win. He is ready.

Arkady Federenko is sitting in the dark in his apartment as if there is someone to see his tears for Zenushka. There is a light from the street below, the light under which Vladimir stood when he shouted his defiance which then was empty—

But no longer.

Because Federenko has made his decision; he wants revenge, and he must assert his own identity, be something that the sacrosanct memory of his sister would not reject with a sneer.

He is ready. Sitting on in the dark, almost unaware of thought, conscious of the small sounds of the apartment block and the night street outside the window, he is ready. He will win the race tomorrow.

"Miss Gunston—you should not be out of bed." The night sister's English was good, and her presence sudden and surprising and damnable.

Karen, caught as if in a spotlight halfway down the empty corridor, shuffled the tiny camera into her pocket, then held her robe—the thick, lumpy one they had given her to replace her negligee—close around her. Then she turned slowly and tried to look dazed and overtired, a sudden inspiration which might prevent discovery of the camera, questions, prevention of a further attempt.

It was her damn arm, plastered so that she couldn't move quickly enough, and it had taken her too long to get out of bed and into her robe before the night sister made another patrol of the corridors.

The sister came toward her, smelling faintly of starch, her face framed by the crisp headdress, her eyes concerned rather than suspicious. No, she did look over her shoulder, toward the turn in the cream-painted corridor that led to the room where they were keeping Irena Witlocka. But only for a moment.

"Why are you out of bed?" she asked with professional, bullying sharpness.

Karen decided only her own character and reputation could extricate her.

"Because I'm fed up with staying in bed, Sister!" she said, still trying to look dopey and tired. The sister clicked her fingers against her side in impatience, and her tongue made a clucking noise.

"Your doctors will decide when you are to get up, Miss Gunston," she pronounced frostily. "Is there something wrong with your stomach?" She was looking at the bunched robe.

"No—how the hell do you think I could tie the belt?" Karen tossed her head, looked at her plastered arm in disgust. "I'm sick up to *here* with this fucking thing!" she announced with an excellent simulation of rage.

"Back to your room!" the sister ordered, offended and forgetful of their proximity to the unregistered girl patient down the corridor.

"Christ, can't you get it through your thick Russian skull—!" Karen began, louder than before. The sister took her by her plastered arm, and pulled her off balance and back along the corridor. Karen gritted her teeth against the sudden pain, and against the almost fierce delight she felt in having recovered from potential disaster. She moaned and complained, but went.

"You will wait here—I will send a nurse to watch you until I have prepared an injection." Arms folded, dignity outraged, patient effectively humiliated, the sister was pleased, even though it was an effort to breathe loudly through her nose rather than gulp down air. The American woman seemed suitably defeated, and she left the room, her footsteps clicking rapidly away.

Before she returned with a guardian, Karen stowed the camera at the back of her locker. And cursed her misfortune, and the sedative they would now administer, and her broken arm.

She had to get Allardyce to the hospital tomorrow—had to.

Shubin, in the medical center of the Lenin Stadium, the cleaners in the office with him, was hiding in the tall metal cabinet, his face pressed up against something that smelled of Zabotin—a white coat he could see if he opened his eyes, the light coming in through the three slits they always seemed to put in the doors of metal cabinets—and his body hunched as if desperately cramped. He had been still and silent for so long that he had begun to listen to what the cleaners were saying, and wanted to laugh at their stupid snatches of dialogue.

He was fifty yards from the cylinders, and he had a ten-minute space of time, a window, in which to arm the bombs. The time fuse that Belousov had installed in each cylinder had an eighteen-hour run, to the minute.

He held his watch up to the slatted bars of light from the cabinet door. Two minutes past nine. The window—the ten minutes during which he must arm the bombs if they were to explode exactly when he wished—began at 9:15. Four bombs; perhaps two minutes needed on each one.

The fat woman, gross and sexless, he had spied through the slats was still grumbling on about her husband's sexual appetite to the other cleaner, a thin, sticklike woman with a big nose and curlers under her headscarf, a cigarette drooping from her mouth. She wiped ash from the desk she was dusting, Zabotin's desk.

After the ribaldry with the security guard on his last round of the stadium offices, the women had moved into Zabotin's office, forcing Shubin into the cabinet where at first he skulked, angry and jittery, then fought a rising sense of his own ridiculousness and a savage contempt for the two women between him and the bombs.

"Twice the other night—" And Shubin wanted to yell out, a muffled, disembodied voice, that he was a brave man to try it once. "I told him I was coming on night cleaning with you, and he just laughed, the pig—" Bet he wasn't laughing after the second time, just trying to get his breath back. Mountainous thighs, and the sweaty fanny hidden between them—

Three minutes past. An agony of wanting to jump up and down in his confined space, desperate to move.

The fat woman emptied the wastebasket into the plastic bag that would be checked by security men before being incinerated. The thin woman coughed, and stooped to brush ash from the carpet where it had fallen from her cigarette.

Four minutes past nine. The window was open a crack, and he was fifty yards from the bombs, all four of them— Where the hell would these women go next?

"Finished?" the thin woman asked. Shubin could see a fat behind rear up just beyond the desk.

"Just cleaning under the desk—you know how that doctor complains!"

"Fussy sod," the woman with the cigarette offered indifferently.

The fat woman straightened up.

"Just run the cleaner over the carpet—"

Five minutes past. The window, the window—

"Why bother?"

Don't bother, don't bother—

"I'm not getting into trouble because of that long drink of rainwater."

Click, and the billowing bag, the noise of the cleaner. Six minutes past nine. The sound nuzzling closer, farther, like a dog seeking his scent. The cleaner banged against the door of the metal cabinet—

Suddenly lighter. The door had opened a fraction, perhaps a couple of inches. Shubin was terrified, his eyes flicking repeatedly from his watch face to the crack of light, then to the strip of light as it slid over his white coat, across one arm and down the length of the coat, onto his shoes. The sight pained him as physically as if the line of light was a weal from a lash.

Hand reaching, but frozen. The cleaner's noise moving away, then back and forth as if rubbing at a persistent spot on the carpet, then farther off, and the noise of a cracked voice singing a folksong—from the mumble, it was the woman with the cigarette in her mouth.

Silence.

Nine minutes past nine. The door still open, and fragile as if the slightest breath of air—his slightest breath—would make it swing wide, revealing him ridiculously crouched against the back of the metal cabinet, the steel damp and slippery against his cheek where he was sweating freely. The collar of his shirt wet, the second hand of his watch sliding round the numbers on the face with mocking precision.

"They don't even lock the doors—lazy pigs," the fat woman exclaimed. Slither of her slippered feet toward the door.

What if she opened it, what if she locked it, what if she—?

The door clicked shut, and Shubin expelled a breath that left his ears pounding, his body empty and weak, and he was aware of the need to relieve himself.

Eye to the slat—eye—! He had to tell his body to move, his eye to change its concentration on the watch face. Eleven minutes past.

They were at the door. He was clinging to the inside of the door handle, as if one of them might come back suddenly and jerk at it.

"We'll be here all night if we go on at this rate," the thin woman observed.

"All right, who's doing the toilet?"

"Your turn."

"Evening, ladies. Still out for a quiet stroll, then?"

The security guard. Twelve and a half minutes past, twelve and thirty-five, and forty, and all the time the seconds were disappearing they were just laughing, not even getting on with their conversation—

He silently urged them on through the vulgarities, the insults, to the end of the dialogue, his mind almost constructing the exchanges like a prompter in a theater.

"You've got the best life—" Fat woman.

"Very responsible job." Guard.

"What? Guarding empty offices? Who's going to break in here, terrorists?"

"Could be. You'll be off home long before me tonight, that I know for a fact."

Fourteen minutes past—the window widening. Four bombs, two minutes each. He had, at most, three minutes before he had to begin. He wanted to yell at them to get on with it, fuck off and do their jobs.

"She's going home to her husband and his dick," the thin woman offered, the habitual vulgarity breaking the surface again. "Who are you going home to?"

"My cat—"

"Does it with a cat! Even your Boris is better than a cat, eh?" Raucous laughter, then the plaintive admission.

"My wife—died."

"Left you, more like—!" Laughter, and Shubin's promptbook in his head carrying on the inevitable libel. *Couldn't hack it, couldn't keep his woman—*

Go on, then, insult him some more, make him walk off sulking.

"No, she died many years ago."

"What did?" Laughter, the cruelty of two people becoming a gang and the third a victim.

"She did—" The man rallied. "I killed her off—not like you, eh, Mother, killing off your old man."

The thin woman's laughter; the gang broken.

"I wouldn't give much for your chances—"

"I wouldn't give much either!" The guard reasserted his habitual self, the impulse to confession, to breach privacy, gone. Shubin could see the three of them in the doorway of the office, still taking no step.

Sixteen minutes.

The guard walked off, pleased with his exit line. The fat woman pushed the cleaner ahead of her, the cord trailing; the thin woman, taking the brake off an electric polisher, followed.

Shubin emerged from the cabinet, stumbled on weak legs, supporting his shaking frame with one hand pressed down on the surface of Zabotin's desk. When he could move, glancing at his watch, the time stinging him like a shock, he saw the sweaty imprint of his palm and fingertips on the mock-wood surface. With an instinctive action, he rubbed it away with his sleeve. Nine-seventeen.

He could see the cabinet, through the glass wall of the office, at the far end of the long medical room. He fumbled in his pocket for the keys, got them out, dropped them on the desk with a clatter his tension magnified, then went out of the office after picking them up, wanting to run the length of the aseptic, still room, striding almost weirdly until he was in front of the cabinet containing the four green cylinders. He would have carried them into the storeroom off the main room if he had had the time—but he didn't. Nine-eighteen.

He dragged out the first cylinder, watched agonized for a moment while two of the remainder tottered, rolled, but did not fall outward, then began to unscrew the valve at the head of the dummy cylinder. Then he held it up, recollected the slides that Belousov had given him, magnified through Zabotin's projector and thrown on his living room wall, and removed the gasket. He remembered—fished in his pocket, pulled out a clean cloth, wiped the copper surface of the valve head and the niche in the top of the cylinder. Then he screwed back the valve until it was tight.

Nine-nineteen. He wanted to savor it. He twisted the ON valve to OPEN, then through the restraint a further half-turn, using a tight grip and all the strength in his weak, nervous wrist. A hiss from the demand valve but no movement of the gauges already on FULL. The first one was armed. He rolled it to one side. No, no—

He dragged it back into the cabinet, pulled out the second one. Removed the valve, then the gasket, wiped, then refitted, turned it through the restraint. Two done. Nine twenty-two. Three minutes left before the window closed. One complete bomb armed.

He hefted it back into the cabinet, let it settle against the back metal wall. Began to pull out the third. It slipped, because his palms were sweaty and he had been wiping them on his white lab coat, not on the clean rag which was for the copper contacts—it clattered on the linoleum, rolled away from him.

He scrabbled to his feet, watching the cylinder in a terror of fascination, as if the panels, waxed in, might burst open, to reveal the horrific spinal column on which—

No, no! He dropped beside it, as if wrestling with something alive, held it pressing down, then tried to calm his breathing. Unscrew, lift out, remove gasket, wipe, *wipe*—! He did it, told himself he was doing it; his hands were so far away and so robotic they meant nothing to his brain.

Dragged it back across the floor, left it.

The fourth one. Nine twenty-four. A minute left.

Unscrew, lift out—

Then the footsteps, coming along the corridor outside the medical center, clicking in a measured beat he dare not obey, too slow and too fast, mesmerizing him. The gasket was tighter, and wouldn't peel—

Jesus-God-in-Heaven, the lights—they were coming to switch off the lights.

Footstep. Tug at the gasket, *footstep*, ripping the gasket off, rag, rag—*footstep, footstep, footstep,* before he got the cloth out, began to wipe—

Footstep. Wipe the niche, the contacts must be good. *Footstep, footstep* in the time it took to look at his watch. Nine twenty-five, the window closing. Leave it, leave it, *footstep, footstep,* he began to screw it in, *screw it in!* Turn, *footstep,* turn, turn, *footstep,* turn, turn, turn, *footstep, footstep,* hand slipping, turn, *foot*—turn—*step*—turn tight.

Valve open, turn, turn, turn, *footstep, footstep,* turn through—ugh! Noise of the air in his lungs as it expelled with the effort, turn, lock.

Four. Nine twenty-six. *Footsteps.*

He shut the door, and lay on the floor, no get up. He hid behind the cabinet, the two cylinders lay betrayingly on the floor, but maybe out of the line of sight of the guard.

He heard the main door open, then that in Zabotin's office. Less light. He waited. A faint whistle, of surprise—? No, a pop tune, tuneless and through the teeth, then darkness, and the closing of the door. Footsteps, already being submerged in the louder whistling. As if the man had felt something of the numbing effect of a hospital or a church in the medical room.

Shubin slumped against the wall, pressing his quivering cheek against the cool steel of the cabinet.

It was a long time before he moved to restore the two cylinders and relock the cabinet. It was a long time before he was able to tell himself, with a quiet chuckle in his throat, that the bombs were armed. They would explode at 5:25 the next afternoon.

He felt so tired, so tired—there was almost no room for congratulation. Relief kept pressing into his throat like bile. Almost no room.

Harsh floodlights bathed the little garden behind the bungalow. Cold whiteness, tinged with blue, fuzzy at the edges where the garden dropped into shadows. Men digging, methodically removing turf, then topsoil, or turning over the flower beds that no longer had color, the bushes and plants, tilted, collapsed, buried. They had started at the house just after full dark, working for an hour by flashlight until the floodlighting had been erected on long stalks and switched on, and had peeled away long strips of turf without really expecting to find anything. More promisingly, they had created a huge, untidy mound of earth alongside the trench that had once been the borders.

After five hours, they had found nothing. The night was warm, the diggers hot with effort. Kazantsev was alternately hot with impatience, cold with foreboding as his mind raced ahead or moved away, reacting to other possibilities, or no possibilities at all.

A small warehouse, an attic room, a cellar—anywhere. Or perhaps the remains had been taken away by the refuse collection, ground to pulp, buried on the outskirts of the Donetsk conurbation.

No, no—he had to contain those thoughts, believe in this scene of sweating, digging policemen and white floodlights. If he didn't, then Belousov supported by the knife against the bathroom door came back to him vividly and stayed like a persistent fear. He could almost hear him laughing in the shadows outside the ring of light—or perhaps he was trying to apologize.

No, laughing, Kazantsev decided, as a policewoman handed him a cup of coffee, and he wrinkled his face at the sugarless bitter taste. They had discovered the receipt—at last the piece of paper that betrayed the crook who fiddled a bureaucracy—in the ordnance factory records which had written off a consignment of FAE liquid canisters—the cluster-scatter type—as defective, and it was signed by Belousov. Two dozen canisters, self-propelling model.

Belousov had used them himself—nobody, least of all Kazantsev, believed they had been returned to the factory or destroyed. Then he'd siphoned off enough of the FAE napalm liquid to fill the canisters—but what the hell were *they* in? Something, something—

Traces—all they needed was a trace, a sign.

"Dig, you buggers, dig," he muttered half under his breath, the patch of overgrown raspberry canes behind him as he watched the scene. "There's something here, and we'd better find it."

He looked at his watch. Four-fifteen, and it was beginning to get light outside the ring of hard lights, though no one else had noticed.

Anna Akhmerovna stood at the window of her apartment, smoking a cigarette and half-aware of the conventionality of the posture that accompanied her restless thoughts. The light behind her made the spacious bedroom shadowy, soft lit but empty. Leonov had not come during the previous evening. He had telephoned to apologize with grave courtesy and with an explanation that pressure of work kept him from her. Those were almost the words he had used, old-fashioned, high sentiment of a kind almost amusing, but now pretended and artificial.

Gennadi went on being kind and considerate and polite, but it was the mockery of manners a jailer might display toward an aristocratic prisoner.

She did not think there was anyone watching her apartment—but surveillance did not matter now. The meeting would be as arranged, at 5:15 that day, when she walked out of the stadium with David Allardyce to the car that would drive her to Cheremetievo and a plane out of the Soviet Union.

Nothing else mattered and nothing could hurt her now. She puffed at the cigarette, pressing the filter with her lips as if it had offended her. She exaggeratedly blew the smoke at the ceiling, an imitation of a bad actress in a bad mood dismissing her lover.

She had to think of nothing, she told herself yet again. Not the past, or the future. She was just here, and now, and it would soon be light, and she would soon be done.

Someone would collect a suitcase from the apartment later in the morning. That was something she could do—pack. She pressed her cigarette into a jar of cold cream that she had left unlidded, smiled at the continuing melodrama of her actions, and opened the larger of the wardrobes.

A lot of clothes, most of which she fiercely liked, and displayed, in her own country—

Stop it.

Suitcase, suitcase— And she went out of the bedroom to get it.

Leonov saw her move away from the window, saw her shadow flicking larger and smaller on the ceiling, then disappear. She had left the bedroom. The silent empty apartment they were using for surveillance was a few floors below hers and across the street. He put down the night glasses.

Georgi was with him, a respectfully silent dumbwaiter, complete with cups of coffee from a flask, and German brandy.

"She's going today," Leonov said in a thick whisper which seemed to curl in the dark corners of the room like smoke.

"Chief?"

"She's going today. It's the pattern—she's uptight, more than ever, and we've made no move. She really believes she's going to make it."

"Yes, Chief."

Leonov thought—what could the poor sod say, to his superior officer whose mistress was a double agent? *Yes, Chief,* about summed it up.

He had made his resolve, she would not be allowed to leave. If he had to break her arm, she wasn't going away from him. Whatever the consequences, he would stop her and keep her. He would never consent to losing her either to the West or to the apparatus of the state. He had an idea about that, too. Even Georgi had no idea of what he intended—but he already had some of the necessary papers, and the dacha would do as the scene of the accident—

A small flicker of hope, like a tightness in his chest. No, no, he told himself. Don't think, not at the moment.

He could smell the brandy as Georgi unscrewed the top, poured out two large glasses. Warm, heady.

Puchkov, sipping vodka to keep himself awake, was sitting at the back of the main stand of the Lenin Stadium as his men began to check every seat, every piece of equipment, every exit. He was aware of the silence of the huge stadium, the day coming up behind the white floodlights, the insectlike figures, the regular punctuation of seats being tipped up, the hum of radio checks—

They were waiting for the men to check the electrical equipment, the huge scoreboard, the timers, the field-event scoreboard, the television cameras, the microphones, everything.

Four-thirty. They wouldn't let the crowds, or the bloody competitors, in until they'd finished. The only people inside the Lenin Stadium, apart from the KGB, would be Olympic officials who would assist the checking of their equipment and areas of responsibility.

"And don't forget the starter's gun," he muttered to himself. Then, after swallowing the last of the vodka from his flask, and disappointingly upending it, watching one drop escape onto the concrete between his feet, he added, "Come on, Oleg Kazantsev. Tell us what we're looking for."

Otherwise, they might have to begin dismantling the stadium itself.

Valentina had always liked the postman calling, ever since she was a child. A tiny, irrational excitement that something unexpected, surprising, birthdaylike might come through the letter box, be lying on the doormat or the hall carpet.

And this morning the thick, typed envelope, addressed to her, looked distinctly promising. Valentina Kazantseva. It might be from Oleg, though he usually didn't write and certainly didn't type his letters or envelopes if he did. From his office?

She might be, she admitted, a little disappointed if it was from her husband. She carried it into the kitchen-diner and opened it sitting sidesaddle on her chair, legs crossed at the knee, in a pink dressing gown that Oleg would have preferred to be something diaphanous, suggestive. As she flicked open the single sheet, she was about to reach for her coffee with her other hand when the tickets fell on her lap, then on the floor.

She bent, scuffled them together, then inspected them, hardly believing. Obviously, they had come from Oleg's office. He had managed it, even though he was in Donetsk, and obtained for the three of them tickets for the day.

And the events began that morning, didn't they? Where was *Pravda*, and the order of events? She laid the tickets down almost reverently on the table, got up, the excitement of a birthday plucking at her heartbeat and breath, and called out.

"Children, children—get up. We're going out for the day!"

CHAPTER 18

The Lenin Stadium, July 31, 1980, 10:30 in the morning.

Puchkov watched the last decathlon elements and the heats of the relays with a desultory attention, occasionally brushing at his head as if insects kept worrying his sweating hairline or his brow and ears. No fuss, no breath of the sinister—they hadn't found anything by 9:30, when the stadium, having been closed for the fiction of electrical repairs, was opened for the day's events. And every one of the thousands of early spectators, and every one of the hundreds of officials, had been subjected to a scan search as he or she passed through the gates into the stadium. Official cars had also been thoroughly searched.

All for nothing. Discretion had been used, naturally, and the spectators had become used during the past fortnight to being subject to scrutiny for their own safety.

Puchkov tossed his head at the thought, and swallowed more of the chilled Coke that was already beginning to become tepid in the hot morning. A hot bright day, little high white clouds, hardly a breeze in the great windless bowl of the stadium. Conditions good for running, perfect for an FAE bomb. And Oleg believed there was one.

Official opinion was, however, against him, or at least confident of the infallibility of the security machine. There was no bomb inside the stadium when they searched, and none had been brought in since then. Ergo, no bomb. And they'd all be there later in the day, in the *laager*, the bunker, the VIPs' concrete-topped, bulletproof-glassed booth in the main stadium, below which, carpeted from wall to wall in red, was the lounge and bar that served American cigarettes, whiskey, vodka, caviar, cognac. They'd have to come, of course, to show the faith—no bomb, gentlemen. Naturally, the First Secretary, the Chairman, and the rest of the Politburo would probably be the only ones safe in the whole Lenin Stadium. Down below ground, or behind the bulletproof glass—or would that melt?

Puchkov, who believed Oleg Kazantsev, hoped it would, because the Politburo had taken the most terrible decision—to risk the holocaust rather than the loss of face involved in owning up and canceling the events until Shubin and the bomb were found.

Puchkov finished the rest of the Coke, crunched the can in his hand, looked at it. That big? Bigger? How big?

Then the admitted thought, and its attendant fear: How big does an FAE bomb have to be to kill a hundred thousand people? And what does it look like?

The last of the experts was reassembling the scoreboard. Soon it would be functioning again. Together with everything else, they'd taken apart every one of the electronic devices used in the stadium, and found nothing.

He watched a man descending a ladder, saw lights begin to wink on the face of the board at the far end of the stadium. The other sixty-by-forty-foot scoreboard was already working again. Thirty tons of it, two and a half miles of wiring and cables—

He stopped there. It was impossible to have checked the whole board thoroughly. There could be a bomb in there.

Come on, Oleg—

Shubin looked up at the last man descending the ladder as he wheeled out, in his white coat and an official trilby, the second of the two pairs of FAE cylinders, now their final metamorphosis, strapped to a hand cart, oxygen mask dangling, white Cyrillic lettering clearly visible, and the addition of the label RESERVE the only other improvement.

He kept his head down, but he was smiling as he parked the cart with its two green cylinders near the finish line, back from the trackside. A genuine pair of oxygen cylinders were placed closer to the track, for immediate use. There were four points, in all, where carts were placed, with their appropriate reserves. The other FAE device was on the far bend, beneath the scoreboard just now beginning to work again. Together, they could effectively blanket the stadium with FAE liquid which vaporized on emission, spread in a saucer ten feet thick, fifteen feet aboveground, in a matter of minutes.

Do pobachenya. It had reached its linguistic apotheosis. Good-bye everyone.

Allardyce sensed that the article he was preparing on "The Electronics of an Olympics" for a sports magazine was another of the distractions he had entertained willingly since he became reinvolved with Anna Akhmerovna and the KGB. Nevertheless, he persisted with it, and waited now beneath the giant scoreboard as it began to flicker on its information concerning the heats of the women's 100-meter relay. He wanted to ask the electrician descending the ladder what had malfunctioned—a touch of immediacy between the facts and figures—

Twenty-four thousand 25-watt Osram Bellalux bulbs, controlled by a computer. Letters and numbers were formed by five-by-seven lamps, room for ten lines of thirty-four signs each on the board. Moving writing, vertical or horizontal, for longer signs. Enlargement of each sign up to four times, underlining, framing, tabular form. Drawings of the marathon route and the Olympic emblem, even animated films.

All a little bit dry, without the human touch of a bird's-eye view. Two men were looking at him, two men who were not part of the crowd, even though they were in summer shirts and light slacks. They seemed to be waiting for the last of the electricians to descend the ladder, just as he was.

Gun. First heat of the relays, the crowd noise disciplined to a gradual ascent of scale and volume, sharpest increase between the second and third takeovers. He turned to watch. He'd been a useful member of the British relay squad, never dropped a baton— He grinned, then the electrician was almost beside him.

"Press," he said amiably in Russian. "What was wrong with the scoreboard—?"

And suddenly the other two, staring at him, ushered the electrician away, who suddenly didn't have electrician's eyes when he heard the single word "press." Allardyce did not pursue it, because he knew the eyes.

All three were KGB.

Why were the KGB checking the scoreboard, for God's sake?

Tape broken. Stopwatches clamped. Placings and times decided by the photo-finish film cameras in the timing cabin set eighty meters above the track on the upper edge of the stadium. Twenty seconds, in a short race like the 100-meter relay, to produce a 3½-by-4¾-inch picture. For a longer race, a film of the finish up to 130 feet long. Time scale on photo or film made it possible to obtain results to within 3/1000 of a second.

Allardyce shook his head as if to clear it of the statistics that bubbled up like a fizzy, comforting anodyne, obscuring the other images, settling the nagging little headache of his growing sense of increased, sharper security.

All around the stadium the searches were more thorough, the lines longer, the hand scanners more in evidence. Cameras were opened, bags rummaged, step through the scanner here, please. And there were more people just standing around, the lounge of authority common to most of them. And they had inspected the scoreboards. Why?

He began to realize that it might be more difficult, even impossible—no, he would not admit that. It *would* be more difficult to get Anna out and away.

Winston Ochengwe, allowing no break in his normal routine, as if he were still running between his home and his job, was out in the park surrounding the village, the sun hot and taking the last freshness from the morning air, though he was oblivious to that, running as he ran every morning of his life. After a light breakfast, the only luxury the orange juice he had not had—chilled, too—back home. Except that he did not use that familiar, domestic term any longer, by a conscious effort of thought. Back—*there*. With the implication that it was all behind him.

Now, the past had faded, or was reduced to routines like his running or like breakfast, or which running shoe he put on first, or the slow, luxurious shower after he finished running. The future was uncertain, and blanked out. Everything narrowed down to today.

Orange track suit, moving beneath the young trees, catching the shifting pattern of light and shadow from the leaves. A black man, certain only of the physical on a day when the physical was everything that was required.

Peter Lydall, after twenty minutes' jogging—all he ever did on race day—and a light breakfast, was reading a newspaper he had taken back to his room. He avoided the sports pages, except for the cricket scoreboard, concentrating on the home news. A murder, another little girl who had disappeared in broad daylight and the police search of canal and waste ground and the neighbors beginning to whisper about the parents; exchange rate against the dollar worsening, unemployment up again—mainly school leavers—a local council scandal in the Midlands.

He was conserving the energy of body and mind as the minutes passed, the hours moving through the middle of the day toward 3:30 when the coach would take the finalists to the stadium.

His mind was breathing shallowly, like his body, scanning the news, turning eventually to the crossword.

Martin Gutierrez read the sports page of the *Daily News*,

psyching himself, or trying to, by going over and over the names between himself and the Gold, ticking them off on some mental balance sheet that always proved he was the best. Federenko, Tretsov, Lydall, Ochengwe, Holmrath, Jorgensen, Irvine. Something wrong with each of them, some minor fault or weakness, some flaw his mind turned up, transformed into a reason why that man would not win. Eventually, no one other than himself could win the race.

Except—

Don't even think about it—

Irena.

The room seemed small and stuffy even with the windows open, the net curtains hardly moving in the windless air. His roommates had left him alone—one of them had brought him his breakfast, and he had broken the rolls, applied butter with the knife with a surprising intensity. The orange juice remained untasted, the coffee was lukewarm by the time he remembered it.

He was alone, and the girl's image came in as if through the door, now and again during the morning, however much he resisted entertaining it. If he won, then he would never see her again. A simple equation—

A fourth-grade dropout could manage it. A simple son-of-a-wetback knew what it added up to, how it came down. Good-bye, Irena.

It wasn't easy to say. He hadn't said it, all the morning. At midday, even at two in the afternoon, when he began to pack his kit in the college-blazoned bag he always used, he hadn't been able to say it, right out.

Dependence.

What it was about. How the equation came out. Never mind *who* depended, it was there. For thirteen minutes and some seconds—maybe only a few at that—he would be able to forget the girl, not think of her at all.

Maybe he only had another fifty years' living after that. Remembering her. They'd make her watch the race on TV. She'd know, and so would he. All the rest of the time.

So, what the hell were Greenberg and the Englishman going to do about it?

He put it off like that, making it someone else's problem as well as his, and went back to the paper. GUTIERREZ COULD MAKE IT, the headline said.

Oh, yeah?

Tretsov jogged for thirty minutes at the almost deserted Army Sports Club track, keeping loose, getting the blood circulating, bringing up the heart rate. Mechanical functions from a machine to be examined later and for the last time. The machine was in perfect working order—according to plan.

Federenko, with the last of the tactical explanations over, was waiting to jog himself and warming up with a few exercises—running on the spot, easing out stiffness, losing the stale sense of a bad night's sleep, reinvigorating a body that had seemed slumbrous and overweight. Flapping his hands loosely at his side, lifting his knees high, rolling his head to ease the last stiffness from his neck. Watching Tretsov the robot.

And ready for him. On the brink of the fastest race of his life—faster, perhaps, than anyone had ever run 5000 meters before. To make *certain* he was the winner.

For himself, for the Ukraine, for Zenushka. It didn't matter now. It was a task to be performed.

Holmrath was lying in, skipping breakfast as he always did the day of a race, waiting instead for lunch. Staring at the ceiling and knowing he would not win a medal unless at least two people fell down or dropped out. He encouraged a smaller ambition—to race himself, and achieve his personal best for 5000. An acceptable compromise.

Jorgensen had announced his retirement from international athletics after the Olympic Final, in the main Oslo newspaper the previous day. And he was settled in his mind for the first time that year. One last, good performance. That seemed enough for him as he sat in the small refectory, taking an early lunch as he always did. Somewhere near his old European record, even inside it. Then he would accept the lucrative coaching job in the Middle East, making up to his wife and children for the lean times. Getting fat and bald. The image amused him. He would be ready for it, almost without regrets, when he had run one more good race.

Kenneth Irvine knew a thin crust of ice had formed during the night, when he had slept much better than of late. Now, lying on his bed, he could feel almost relaxed, put out mental feet and let them take weight as he tested the thin resolution, the slow return of confidence, and mental certainties and self-belief, and the absence of that stale smell in the mind every time he thought about running, about races, about the 5000.

He wasn't ready, not by a long way. But he was closer than yesterday.

Don't push it. Just let the ice that's now there take your weight, a step at a time. Another couple of hours before he had to get the bus, and his kit was already packed. He watched the slight reflected movements of the curtains on the ceiling of his room, letting his thoughts slacken, mind go blank, relaxing before the race.

François Diderot in his Paris apartment was going through the routines of bed making, washing up, making a shopping list that would blank out the hours before the race, provide some kind of alternative, knowing all the time that he would be drawn, ineluctably, to the television set in the lounge; inescapably, he would run that race mentally with all the *legitimate* competitors.

Diderot gritted his teeth, inhaled as if drawing back tears, and decided he needed onions, tomatoes, potatoes, leeks, and a bottle of cognac in a hurry.

If he went out, then he wouldn't keep thinking about the TV set.

Yes, he would go out.

Almost pathetically, he decided that he certainly wouldn't turn on the set until the 5000 was about to start, at five o'clock Moscow time. He looked at his watch.

Time to get the shopping, and get back. Have lunch out, he counseled himself, yes, have lunch in the corner of a bar somewhere.

And be back for the race. Just the race.

The TV set was at its loudest, so that Kazantsev could hear it while he searched the loft of the bungalow, his hands irritated and sore from the roof insulation as he pulled it away to expose the plaster beneath—and nothing more sinister than plaster, and dust, and part of the wrapping the fiberglass insulation had come in. He needed the TV, but whether for its conveyed urgency or its confirmation of normality he could not decide.

Triple jump final, decathlon pole vault, semis of the relays, heats of the 400 relays—the afternoon program had begun, leading to the 1500 semi and final, and the 5000. Good viewing, he thought with anger as his knees ached kneeling on two beams, his hands hurting with his fierce grip on the next strip of fiberglass. Damn it, the stage was set. He knew that, believed it utterly; but perhaps a human strand—Federenko, Shubin, Zenaida Federenka—had assumed too much importance for him. He could not tell, and wanted to reject the poetic inference that was too easy because of three people who knew each other and whom he knew, but it kept nagging at him. The mad logic, the lunatic justice Shubin might see in it.

He tore up the insulation, threw it aside, heard the commentator's voice rising up the scale as the last lap of a 400-relay heat began with the Soviet quartet having built up a lead. The voice floated up to him, enmeshing him in his fantasy of *rightness* concerning the Lenin Stadium, on that day, that afternoon.

Puchkov had told him over the telephone of the results of the search, of the bravado with other people's lives of the authorities— and pleaded with him to tell them how many, how big, what to look for, where.

Dust, newspapers, wooden boxes, and torn and heaped insulation.

Nothing else.

Normal search routines were being carried out that might lead to other dissidents or subversives being identified and arrested, or the whole network of *Do pobachenya* exposed and its links with émigré groups, even with Western intelligence services, revealed. The impetus was slipping from the investigation, it was becoming routine. The last part of the garden was being dug over, the raspberry canes gone wild.

Jesus, they even had two men going through the boxes of slides from Belousov's photographic hobby—trying to find faces they could identify, use later. Ridiculous, when there was—

Down below him, on the TV in the lounge, the Russian fourth-leg runner came home first, to noises of delight from commentator and crowd. The Soviet Union had won.

Some joke.

Anna Akhmerovna, arriving at the Lenin Stadium on the arm of Captain Gennadi Leonov, was nervous that her tension was communicating itself through the contact between his sleeve and her arm. They had lunched in a spirit of valediction neither of them could admit.

The flags were hardly stirring along the facade of the stadium, the noise from inside spilling over like some thick, treacly substance, slow and heavy. She carefully avoided any glance in the direction where the CIA car would be in two hours' time—it wouldn't be there yet. She tried to recapture her enthusiasm for that first day of athletic competition—but it was like trying to crawl back into a skin she had already shed.

Gennadi had been jovial over lunch, even amorous. But she had seen the strain behind it, assumed it was the strain of pretense and facade, nothing more. If she saw it like that then she was distanced from him just a little, and that helped, because she could not bear to think of her departure as yet another betrayal.

Leonov flourished their tickets at the main entrance, and as they passed into the stadium the noise increased, but to her in the sudden shadow it was a cold noise, like animals baying after her, picking up her scent. She shivered. Leonov patted her arm in a gesture of unexpected intimacy that puzzled her.

He smiled down at her. Nothing, he thought—nothing will harm her. I won't let any harm come to her if—

Valentina Kazantseva watched, while the children were buying ice cream and Coca-Cola and franchised potato chips, the tall blonde woman on the arm of the rather distinguished man. Cool, Western—somehow she knew the couple were Russian, but they preserved for her an illusion of magazine cultures only glimpsed when Oleg brought home confiscated material from the office. She felt herself untidy, hot, small, and dowdy in a cotton dress that was homemade and, though she was a good needlewoman, it was suddenly very drab against that woman's linen jacket and pleated skirt and striped shirt. Even Oleg, inches taller than the man, would have looked bearlike and bursting out of such a suit and sports shirt.

Then the children were round her again, and ready to move to the next of the obstacle course vendors. Their mouths and hands seemed full of bottles and cones and sticky things. Suddenly, she laughed. It was her *style*, and that was that. Tiny, dark, knowing, a little crumpled, always rushed, bouncing like a ball off her experiences. Oleg said so, and apparently that was the way he wanted her.

She had intended getting to the stadium for the morning events, but it had never seemed about to happen that way. Neighbors delayed her with gossip, the sandwiches had to be made, the children dressed—perpetually throwing her arms in the air in mock despair seemed to have characterized her morning.

Still, now they were here. She fished in her bag for the tickets, showed them with not a little pleasure at the main entrance, and allowed the security guard to search her handbag and the plastic bag that contained the sandwiches and woolens for the children in case it turned cloudy or cold and the plastic raincoats at the bottom.

Then they were in, and the noise was all around them, infecting the children, who might suddenly have been on their way to a party. She trailed up the first flight of concrete steps behind them.

David Allardyce saw Anna and Leonov take their seats below him. He had been watching the Final of the triple jump and the long glass panels of the VIP box, with the familiar faces behind the glass, emerging from reflected sunlight and reflected bobbing heads and bodies, but always there in some almost phantasmagorical way. The surface of Soviet life passed across the glass, and was caught and reflected—but always the strong faces were there, just behind the shallow, transitory reflections, and the faces were always the same strong, unsmiling faces. Lips moved, split, cracked, but none of it looked remotely like laughter. There was a class of face, he decided. If you had it, you were Politburo material. If you didn't—

He looked at his watch. Three, almost. At five, she would leave her seat. And Leonov should not go with her. Allardyce felt the tension in his body, but it was controlled. The last lap, just an escort job. He was to deliver the package. He had achieved that objectivity, that indifference, that had once characterized his intelligence work.

His telephone extension rang. Idly, he picked it up.

"If it's from Brezhnev, tell him we haven't got tickets to spare," Greenberg muttered at his side, his ball-point clamped between his teeth like a cheroot. Greenberg was high, Allardyce decided—high on expectation. The anticipation of Gutierrez's medal allowed him to forget the inconvenient little human problem of the Polish girl.

"Allardyce."

"David—"

Karen Gunston.

"How did you get through here?"

"Press, am I not?"

"Is everything O.K.?"

"The hell it is. I've been trying to make this call for hours. I can't get anywhere with our problem. You'll have to do it. Come visit me."

"Hell—"

"Thanks. But I can't do it, haven't done it. When you come see me, you'll have to do it yourself." The girl sounded angry at making the admission, resentful at Allardyce for giving her a task she had failed.

"O.K., I'll talk to Ben—see you."

He put down the telephone.

"She hasn't got it, right?" Allardyce nodded. "We promised the kid—" His face was darkened to something like threat. Allardyce resented his unreasonableness, but studied his reply.

"You and I are going to have to do it, then."

"How?" The journalist, the noncombatant, coming to the surface.

"We'll both go and visit Karen—and while we're there, we'll do the photographic session ourselves." He smiled brightly. "It will be terribly melodramatic, of course—you should enjoy it, Ben."

Greenberg was puzzled.

"Is there any other way?"

"Not unless you can think of one. Look, the girl's supposed to be back in Warsaw, but we know she's still in Moscow. If we have photographic evidence of that, then we may be able to get her released. Our people will make a fuss on her behalf, ask that Gutierrez be given visiting permission, all that sort of thing. When she's out—then they can go about sorting out their own lives. Meanwhile, the kid, as you call him, won't run a good race—his best race—with this on his mind. Now, do we go, or not?"

Greenberg nodded. "Let's go."

"We have two hours. I think we might try to borrow a white coat from the medical people here, don't you?"

The bus was waiting at the main entrance to the village complex. A fifteen-minute bus journey down the Michurinsky Prospekt and the Vernadsky Prospekt to the Lenin Stadium. Three-thirty in the afternoon. High, small clouds that seemed stationary, heat coming back up from the pavements of the village, no wind.

Lydall climbed on board the bus. Most of them were already there, ten maybe eleven of them. He did not study each face, did not count heads. Gutierrez in the corner of an eye, Ochengwe's black face, Holmrath, Irvine—

The bus was silent, the air hot and dusty, smelling of the seats and of plastic. The bus was large enough to give the fourteen runners a double seat apart from each other. It had to be that way.

He put his kit in the rack, then he sat down slowly, easily. One or two officials were on the bus, too, with lists of competitors—a normal precaution since the two American sprinters had sat in their room in Munich when their event was being called, mistaking the time. Lydall had been shooed out of his room by one of the British team officials like a boy late for school, his bag checked for its various items as if he were passing through customs. The Soviet Olympic Committee had guaranteed that all buses collecting competitors from the village would have on board at least one official whose sole responsibility would be to ensure that all competitors for any event were actually present on the bus before it departed.

Then Tretsov and Federenko, coming aboard together, a little piece of conciliation or showmanship, to travel with the others from the village to the stadium. They did not, however, sit together. It seemed Federenko's decision, and Lydall wondered about a race plan involving the two of them. Tretsov was too much a dark horse to be discounted as a passenger, and Federenko too obviously a favorite—Gutierrez had given him a very dusty look when he boarded the bus. Interesting, Lydall thought, but only in the abstract, as if it were a tactic in another race. Nothing interested him other than the race he himself would run, was ready to run.

The noise of the engine starting up cut across the heavy silence inside the vehicle. Fourteen men in track suits—names called out one by one so that Lydall was again irresistibly reminded of taking school kids on an outing or to the swimming pool—who were determined not to speak to one another.

The man who chatted to you over breakfast last week is little less than your mortal enemy now. Not true, Lydall corrected himself. He is an *object*, a challenge, a—whatever he is, he isn't a person anymore.

The bus pulled away from the village and Lydall began to stare at the passing scenery of the dual roadway, then up at Sadovaya as it passed over the Vernadsky Prospekt—but he was aware every moment of his body in that seat, at the light perspiration, the heart rate, the adrenaline poised. He was properly tense, sharp and warm, his mind pressing ahead of him with the right degree of impatience to begin the race.

He was eager to get onto the warm-up track, to keep loose. He concentrated on letting his body relax, find the shape of the seat, as he knew the others would be doing. But he didn't want to think about them.

Twelve and a half laps of the track, and each moment the forebrain—nothing of the misty back areas of the brain—ticking off his own lap times, analyzing the progress of rivals, weighing the effort, the condition of the organism in its progress.

He could feel his brain like a cold solid piece of machinery, sitting in his head, beginning—

Behind him, Gutierrez was trying to clear the persistent Irena from his thoughts, Ochengwe farther up the bus sat still as a rock, letting the townscape pass his closed eyes, hearing his body almost like running footsteps, the breeze through high grass, the road dusty and rutted in places beneath those footsteps. Every part of him was ready. Irvine, fragilely afloat on confidence, was half-afraid to begin and eager at the same moment. Tretsov closed and opened his eyes like a camera shutter, knowing to the meter the distance from village to stadium, measuring the times of his laps against the passing landscape, analyzing the speed of the bus, reducing everything to clockwork. Federenko wanted the race to have begun, as if they might discover his secret at the last moment and withdraw him.

Three forty-five. They descended from the bus, ushered by the official with a list of their names, as the red light above the warm-up track went on for the 1500 men to go to the reporting room. A gaggle of track suits trotted away to the far side of the track and the back of the stadium, one or two continuing to keep supple on the track until ushered politely, firmly toward the stadium.

The tension, then. The crowd of ticketless spectators, eating hot dogs or ice cream or drinking beer and Coke, the smell of onions in the still air striking Lydall immediately, almost wrenching at his stomach, making perilous and unreal for a moment the sense of absolute fitness, fine-tuned competence to run 5000 meters in that temperature, in that breezeless air. He jogged over to Harry, his coach, who waited for him, prepared almost as if he had a written script for the ritual of discussion. Lydall always *wanted* to talk, while others wanted nothing to do with their coaches or with officials who didn't understand that the only thing that mattered an hour before a race was the athlete's own feeling about himself. Lydall needed a mirror of himself; Harry's words, an admixture of tactics, flattery, reminiscence, concentration.

Gutierrez, looking like a lost sheep, jogged mechanically to get his temperature up, move the sluggish blood round the body. The American wasn't acting the part of a bystander, he was beginning to look and behave like one. Tretsov and Federenko were surrounded by Russian coaches, the East German also. Little groups and splinters of people who had only an hour together, an hour apart from one another. Irvine avoided the press, Holmrath signed a few autographs, something Lydall had never been able to do as a distraction—or an act of concentration—but which Holmrath seemed to treat as an assertion of identity.

Ochengwe was isolated, confident. Marked off by what had happened to him and his teammates, ignoring the flash of cameras, the whispers of the crowd.

And all the time, boiling over the walls of the stadium like an audible eruption, they could hear the noise from the crowd of a hundred thousand.

"Eat well?" Harry asked, drawing him back into himself, limiting the impressions he was to receive, note.

"As usual. You?"

"Got a couple of sandwiches."

"You should take better care, Harry." Lydall grinned. All part of the make-believe, all part of his preparation.

Greenberg and Allardyce, outside the main portico of the Pirogov First Municipal Hospital and Clinic, stared up at the classical majesty of the building's facade as it fronted onto the Lenin Prospekt, overlooking the Gorki Park and beyond it, to the southwest and across the river, the Lenin Stadium. The view from Karen Gunston's room, now that she was allowed out of her harness and able to sit at the window—that one, Allardyce decided, up on the fourth floor of the hospital.

"O.K., so what now?"

"We go and see Miss Gunston, like normal visitors," Allardyce replied. "Don't be put off by the lack of a white coat. This place should be full of them." He smiled.

"Why do I have to pretend to be the doc? You're the one with the command of the language." It sounded like an accusation.

"I have to be back at the stadium before the race starts—and that's all you have to know, Ben."

"Jesus—you're putting me on. You are, aren't you?"

Allardyce shook his head. "Forget it—everything I said or you suspect. Just take my word."

"And this is just the opener to the main event?" Greenberg narrowed his eyes against some internal sunburst. "That woman, uh?"

"Forget it, Ben—"

Greenberg looked at his watch. "Let's move it."

They showed their visitors' passes to the receptionist, and took the elevator to the fourth floor. Karen Gunston expected them, must have been watching them in the parking lot from her seat at the window. Her arm was still strapped, but slung beneath her breasts now rather than suspended from the ceiling in a sling. Her bruises had yellowed, giving her an appropriately jaundiced complexion.

"What in hell did you bring Greenberg for?"

"Hi, beautiful." Greenberg, in enjoying her discomfiture released his own tension which had accompanied him in the elevator like a hangover or a sharp, rank odor.

Allardyce proprietorially bent over Karen and kissed the top of her head.

"The camera?" he said. She pointed to the cabinet beside the bed. Allardyce pulled it out, examined it swiftly. Then he passed it to Greenberg. "You know where the room is. You go in, insisting on seeing the patient. Open the window as officiously as you can. Her room overlooks a lawn. Take as many shots as you can, and throw the camera out of the window."

Karen Gunston burst out laughing.

"Disguise yourself as a horse—they might take you in!"

"What's the matter?" Allardyce, peeved.

"It's so cruddy it's laughable." Her eyes sparkled. "Him, playing doctor—he doesn't even speak Russian." As if to belie the statement, Greenberg began speaking in Russian—and for a few moments Karen did not realize he was repeating the same two phrases again and again. "What did he say?"

"I am the senior physician at this hospital, and I wish to examine this patient." Allardyce translated. "And he's also saying that he insists and they have no authority in *his* hospital."

"And that's the plan?"

"Never mind. It will work—" And Allardyce was suddenly angry, fury making his throat tight, his words thick. "You think this Romeo-Juliet affair is *serious*, or *important*? In the country of Sakharov, Orlov, Scharansky, Ginzburg, *this* is important?" The name of Anna Akhmerovna was on his tongue, but he pressed it back. "It's a joke—!"

Karen and Ben Greenberg were appalled, as if they had looked at a scene of utter desolation for a moment, before a curtain of affability descended again. It diminished Allardyce; but, more certainly, it removed him from them and increased their sense of him as a complete stranger.

"O.K., O.K.," Greenberg said gruffly, the voice of ordinary

experience insistent. "Let's get on with the comedy. Go get me a white coat, for instance—?"

"Nothing simpler—staff rest room down the corridor. Or didn't you notice?" Allardyce was his unruffled, amused self—but neither of his audience was sure whether that image was his self or something adopted for the sake of rather pointless but time-consuming social intercourse. He was back less than a minute later, a white coat over his arm.

"Clever."

"Easy, old boy. When you speak Russian, and know the word for 'ulcer' or 'kidney.' Walk in, take your coat, walk out." He helped Greenberg into the coat, took the stethoscope from the pocket and hung it round his neck. "Camera in the pocket, and you're ready." Mocking or self-mocking—? Greenberg could not be sure anymore.

"O.K. You get moving—" Then a thought struck him. "What about the lady, afterward?"

Allardyce looked at Karen.

"She just isn't the sort of lady who vanishes." Greenberg laughed, an abrupt sound.

"Maybe you're right—and I don't intend to do too much vanishing myself—"

"They'll want orders. If they arrest you, there are a thousand pressmen slavering for the story. Remember that. *And* the exclusive when they let you out."

"O.K., I'm convinced. Lead on. So long, beautiful lady—"

Karen waved her good hand. "Take care, Ratman and Bobbin."

Allardyce went out quickly, and when Greenberg joined him, he pointed out the turn in the corridor, described the route once more. Then he patted Greenberg's shoulder, and walked away.

It's a *story*, Greenberg told himself as he turned the last corner and saw the man on duty outside the room look up, bored and undisturbed by the sight of the white coat. You're hustling for your by-line. Remember some of the old stunts, just to create news—?

He recited his sentence concerning his identity. The man's eyes narrowed, then he ducked into the room. Greenberg peeped through the door, saw the girl sitting up in bed, moodily eating fruit, watching the television. She appeared passive, even sedated. Remembering his assumed position of authority, he pushed open the door.

Just two men, one outside, one inside. Security gone slack around a docile prisoner with all the fight gone. Put in a couple of deadbeats to look after her. Ivan the Terrible, Boris the Even

Worse, two men of fifty or thereabouts looking after a girl of twenty, wanting to get home, wondering where the beer was, and would it be cold enough.

Hospital smells in the room; then the second man advancing, hand out to touch his chest.

He told them, again, who he was. Strong denial, lots of negatives thrown in as if he was asking for whiskey in GUM. He began to act angry then, told them his proprietorial interest in the hospital, moved to the bed. The two guards were bemused, the girl was taking just a small interest.

He pursed his lips, shook his head slightly as she recognized him. She understood, very slowly, and became tense, more upright; she stopped eating. One of the men was using the telephone, waiting for a connection. Greenberg opened the window. Allardyce was on the lawn below, pointing at his watch. Greenberg ignored him. The guard who had been outside, a short tub of a man with no neck and a face that was flattened and dumb-looking, hovered close to Greenberg as he fingered his stethoscope in what he hoped was a convincing manner. His other hand accepted the contours of the camera. He moved closer to the bed, studied the girl, brushed the guard aside, then had an idea. He pointed to the chair by the bed, made the guard sit in it, and stepped back. He wouldn't get the second man in, who was still waiting for his connection, but the guy in the chair was so beautifully KGB it didn't matter. He just couldn't be anything else—

Three shots. One for surprise, two for delay and shock, three while they came for him. He fussed with the venetian blind, as if trying to raise it, wanted to laugh, and felt his hand wet on the camera in his pocket—turned, raised, *click*. Enough light, had to be—*click*, and the man coming up in the chair, his hand restraining Irena whose reactions were quicker, more honed and who was beginning to struggle—slap, *snap*, and the second man dropping the telephone, getting up—

Click. The second man just in shot, the first guard struggling with Irena as if an accomplice in the charade. And *click*.

Five, five, and a hand reaching for the camera. Greenberg hadn't noticed his own knee lift, prod for the groin of the oncoming guard, who immediately fell away, his expression so comically pained that he wanted to catch it on film—

Blinds up, out of the way, tangling, rattling—Allardyce a long way down—out. Greenberg, as he was hauled back, watched the Englishman take the camera like a cricket ball, moving slightly to one side, hands together. Greenberg wanted to applaud, then he was punched in the back and his vision went foggy and his breath expelled—he wondered whether they would get angry enough to throw him out, then he was pulled away from the window, thrown on the bed beside the girl.

"Go on, Davie—run, boy, run," he grunted between clenched teeth.

Below the window, Allardyce was running for the parking lot.

The green light above the warm-up track signifying there was an hour before reporting changed to orange, like a traffic signal commenting on the directionless, darting activity of the fourteen finalists as they jogged and moved and fidgeted to stay warm and loose; movements of rats in a maze, or a pinball machine. To them, rituals of the familiar.

Gutierrez's coach knew better than to go near him thirty minutes before reporting. He'd been and gone while the green light was on, watching, nodding; a perfunctory analysis as if Gutierrez had applied for an insurance medical. But now that he watched Lydall fidgeting like a totem dancer round Harry, his coach, he began to regret the lack of distraction a voice might provide. He was losing hold of his concentration, the scene in front of him becoming less and less significant, more and more a blur of faces and track suits; he merely a spectator.

Someone had once said of him that he couldn't have been outpsyched if he received a telegram saying his mother was dying five minutes before a big race. It was an insult that he had always regarded as an affirmation, a compliment. But where the hell was Greenberg, and the Englishman? They'd promised—bring him the word, down on the warm-up track, so where the fuck were they?

He couldn't get Irena out of his head—couldn't. It was at once an admission of weakness and an unnerving subtle terror at losing her. Even now, he wanted to despise that feeling as weakness, but he could not achieve the necessary indifference. He could see the face with the dark, bruiselike stains under the eyes, the mouth tight with nerves, admonishing him. Even when Irvine crossed his path, it was only to signify to him the meaninglessness of a medal. He'd never seen the Australian wearing the damned thing round his neck all the time since the 10,000. So what was it worth when you had it?

He wanted it.

The black, the Australian, Lydall, the two Russians—why the

hell did the girl stand between him and the medal, along with them?

"Oh, Jesus," he muttered between clenched teeth at the cold recognition that all he amounted to was a running animal; he still wanted to exchange the girl for a medal, as if nothing else had the power to impress itself upon him. What the hell was the matter with him? He was sounding like his old man—that day in the orange grove, the white-costumed figure under the trees, admonishing him.

And he knew he was beaten because he was thinking like that. He didn't want, suddenly, to be a winner. At least, a part of him didn't, and that would be enough to finish him.

He screwed his hands into fists as he jogged mindlessly up and down, and clenched his teeth as if forcing tears or fighting to keep them back.

Where were those bastards—where were they?

David Allardyce was caught up in heavy traffic, most of it buses and trolleybuses and taxis, on the Volovaia section of the Sadovaya, leading into Dobrininskaia Square. Stuck solid, the little camera like a warning or a signal beside him on the passenger seat. His body was hot and damp with anger and frustration as he looked at his watch yet again.

The red light would be on. They'd be in the reporting room by now, then out on the track. He'd be too late for Gutierrez, and too late for Anna.

Guilt drove him, prompted the solutions no part of his assumed mask of confident world-weariness would have invented. That part of him would have lit a cigarette, sat in the car and waited, a small thankful shame growing in the pit of his stomach as he had nothing more to do with Anna and her escape.

How far was he from the Lenin Stadium?

He fished the map out of the glove compartment and found the scale. Smiling, he lit a cigarette for the pleasure of throwing it decisively away when he had finished with the map. He measured off the scale between finger and thumb, then applied it to the map. Oktyabrsk Square, across the river by the Krimky Bridge, down Komsomolski Prospekt to the stadium. A half mile, or three quarters.

He picked up the camera, left the map unfolded, draped over the passenger seat, and climbed out of the car. If he ran, he might just make it—just.

He slammed the car door shut with a gesture of decision, finality. A surprised taxi driver behind him called out some obscenity as he began weaving through the traffic. He took no notice, dropping into a swift lope along the crowded pavement.

The reporting room was under the main stand, directly adjacent to the entrance onto the track. A customs post for competitors. The orange light had changed to red, MUST REPORT, FIFTEEN MINUTES, as clear and familiar as if the words had been written in bulbs for them to read. Gradually, the warm-up track had emptied. Ochengwe was among the first to arrive in the clinical room with its benches and tables and blazered officials who checked their spikes, their numbers, colors, and their bags and track suits for advertising.

And then the wait for the stewards to summon them to the track. The clock on the wall showed 4:45. In five more minutes the wall of noise, the atmosphere, the tension gripping each stomach, the sense of impending failure that each of them would feel, if only momentarily.

A heavy silence, like that on the bus that had brought them from the village. Even the clock was silent, its red hand sweeping round, the minute hand moving with a strange, sudden jerk from one minute to the next.

Lydall scratched his ear, watched the Russians, each looking down at his feet, yogis having a quick session or perhaps already beaten men. Ochengwe, carved out of mahogany, his face showing nothing. Irvine, letting hope crawl like a slow infection over his face. Gutierrez, looking awful—concentration shot, eyes moving too rapidly for comfort, hands stifled in movements he could hardly contain. Gutierrez had already blown it.

Lydall bent his head, let his lips expose his teeth in a wolfish little smile. He was one closer now. The clock jerked off another minute—like the clock in the dentist's waiting room when he was a kid.

And you recollect that image every time you run, and meet one of these old clocks, he observed to himself. And it's all part of the ritual, like taking most of the next minute finding out how long you can take to pull up both the socks you wear contrary to the great tradition of British middle distance running. He looked over at Ross, the British number one, who was staring at the floor in front of him, knowing that Lydall was out to beat him, wherever they both came in the field.

Good-bye, sonny. Every man for himself—come back next time. He formed the words precisely in his mind, savoring the way they cut him off. The others were rivals anyway—getting rid of Ross was the way he established his sole and single identity; nothing to do with Britain, or Barnsley—only me.

Then the stewards were at the door of the reporting room, and they were summoned to the track. Gutierrez was first out of the door, like someone running for an urgent telephone call.

"Jesus, his fucking holiday in Tallinn!" Kazantsev's voice surprised the two men checking through Belousov's entire collection of prints, louder than the drone of the commentator as he heaped on the soupy prerace atmosphere required by television. Kazantsev let one little part of his mind be distracted by the television voice, just as another part of his attention recognized the Estonian capital, and the beach shots, from one of his own holidays. While in the middle of himself there was a growing urgency as the afternoon lengthened and he was aware—just because of one name, Federenko—that the 5000 event was coming up and he could not rid himself of the sense of approaching, intended climax. He looked at the screen, then at the projected slides. A girl, mousy as Belousov, obviously not his wife.

"After you with that," one of the two local KGB men commented. The girl was squinting not because of the sun but because she was myopic and vain about being photographed with her glasses on. Kazantsev, with unused emotions slopping in him like reserve fuel, felt suddenly sorry for her, angry at the KGB man's contempt.

"Nothing?" he said.

"No, sir. A few faces for us, but nothing for you."

"Hell."

"I always thought Tallinn was rather nice," one of them said in a whisper. Kazantsev wanted to be angry with him, but the TV commentary impinged as the athletes for the 5000 came out onto the track, to loud cheers for the two Russians, and prevented an outburst.

The cartridge of slides clicked, clicked again. Still Tallinn, with rows of beach umbrellas and fat women sunbathing, the mousy girl in the foreground, then the citadel and the cathedral, the sunlit square where he could envisage himself and Tina, she carrying Tanya and pregnant again while he snapped the sights before becoming father–baggage animal again. Click again, and the beach—

His own snapshots were just as boring, just as deadeningly encapsulating of something that might once have been enjoyable.

"Sir, they've found something—" A voice at the door, a sweaty, shirt-sleeved policeman. Federenko in close-up from a handheld camera at the trackside, the Russian runner taking off his track suit trousers; babble of commentary; his watch nearing five.

"What?" he snapped, believing for that moment in chance, fate.

"They're just getting it out now, sir—something wrapped in tarpaulin—"

"O.K., lead me to it."

Click.

"Funny, that—in his holiday snaps—"

On the screen, the projector humming more loudly, it seemed, as if exhaling its own tension, a white-line sketch on a black ground. Lines, little more than doodles, the lettering a little fuzzy. What was it, what did it remind him of—?

The policeman at the door, eager to get back, knowing where the body was buried. Click, and another, similar sketch, but the angles altered, an arrow showing a direction—

"Lead on," he said, moving to the door because he didn't understand the drawings. The policeman led him out into the sunshine of the garden, toward the wild raspberry canes at the far end where the diggers were now grouped, some of them bending, heaving at something.

CHAPTER 19

The runners on the track were trotting or jogging back and forth, keeping their muscles warm. The air was beaten upon by the last notes of the Kenyan anthem as the 1500 meters medal ceremony was concluded. The three runners waved, then trotted away past the 5000 men toward the dressing rooms and the press interviews and TV recordings.

Leonov shifted in his seat as if Anna's tension had communicated itself to him through some electrical contact. Should he tell her now, or wait? Explain that nothing would happen, that she would escape not by leaving Moscow and Russia but by remaining with him? Already, he was in the process of providing a scapegoat, planning the *accident*—the idea borrowed from the death of the CIA man he had engineered to warn her—that would remove the suspect from questioning forever.

And he was looking for a body, one that would burn in a car crash—Anna's car—as an alternative to framing someone else. It would be all right, it would be. He could do anything, now that he had leaped the hurdle of professional betrayal. As soon as the race was over, when she attempted to leave, he would—simple as taking her hand—stop her, and tell her. Allardyce was nowhere to be seen, and he hadn't even begun to use his office to save her. It would be all right. All she had to do was to believe in him—

The whistle, and the runners moved as if reluctant to the starting line on the other side of the stadium, a gaggle of cameramen with them.

Anna, fighting her panic at the absence of Allardyce, knew that she would go anyway. *Before* the race. Perhaps there was no car waiting, but she would still go, had to go—

Fourteen runners, bunched at the start, their names having spilled down the scoreboard ten minutes ago. Numbers, names, countries—Gutierrez, USA: Lydall, GB: Federenko, USSR: Tretsov, USSR: Ochengwe, UG: Vatainen, FIN: Ross, GB: Irvine, AUS: Holmrath, WG: Tolzer, DDR: van Riij, BEL: Jorgensen, NOR: Mostyn, NZ: and Tombi, TANZ.

None of them meant anything to Anna. Nothing took precedence over her growing nausea.

The gun, the surge from the line into the first bend. The Olympic Final at 5000 meters had begun.

Allardyce clattered up the final steps toward the entrance to the stand, his running footsteps along the concrete tunnels still echoing in his mind as he covered the half-circle from the main entrance to one opposite the start of the 5000 on the other side of the stadium.

He heard the gun as he reached the top step and came out into the hard sunlight and the noise, the atmosphere of accumulated tension and release now that the race had started was solid as a blanket against his face. The runners passed just beneath him, Gutierrez near the back of the fourteen, Federenko in front. He watched them stream away from him, round toward the main stand and the home straight for the first time, moving quickly and the crowd already sensing it would be a fast time unless the Russian changed the tactics of the heats. A roar from across the stadium as Federenko led them up the straight, the Tanzanian tucked in behind him, then Ochengwe and Lydall and the Finn—the field drawn like a comet's tail behind him, accommodating to his tactic because they dared not do otherwise.

He descended the aisle, passing a security guard with obtrusive machine gun—hadn't seen one for the last fortnight—down toward the trackside. A guard waited at the bottom, but his press ID was clipped to his jacket pocket, sufficient to excuse the unruly hair, red face, body panting with effort. The guard simply looked at him.

He waited, the camera poised as if he intended photographing the runners, his presence explained. As they came past, he did indeed photograph the field. Then, as Gutierrez, his face a grim but defeated mask, drew level, he yelled.

"Gutierrez—it's all right. The girl's safe!" Just once, as loudly, penetratingly as he could. Gutierrez was almost startled out of his stride, nearly stumbled as if suddenly awakened.

He raised his hand, acknowledging the camera Allardyce now held aloft. Then Allardyce turned, concern evaporated, before the puzzled guard could question or detain him, and went back up the concrete steps three at a time.

Now there was Anna. He felt resolve weakening like his body, but pushed it as he pushed his legs. Soon be over, he promised himself. Get it done, get it done—

An excuse to go to the toilet was insufficient. So, she dropped the ice cream she had made him buy on the lap of her skirt and smeared it in while she pretended to wipe it. The runners in the 5000 were passing beneath them for the first time, twelve laps to go.

"Damn—oh, damn, damn, damn!" A release of tension at the moment of pretense, making the act real. Leonov appeared startled and amused. "Do you know how much this cost, Gennadi?" He laughed, and she echoed it, knowing it was the last moment of intimacy they would share. "I'm going to sponge it out now. No, don't get up, I'll be back in a minute, soaking wet and very embarrassed." She smiled, moved past him into the aisle. There would be a clean skirt at the airport, in the case that had been collected.

She went down the steps quickly, dabbing, brushing at the stained skirt with her handkerchief, then turned down the steps to the gallery at the back of the stand. It was still hot down there, but cooler, and the noise not so oppressive, like the mere preliminaries of a migraine. Her head pounded with the tension, the accumulated fear.

Allardyce was there. He was there! Looking at his watch, and expecting her.

"David—!" She clung to his arm for a moment, steadying her body, her feelings. It was an illusion of clinging to Gennadi, which she could never do again, never even say farewell or thank you.

"You all right?" He'd been running, his face was red with exertion. She nodded. "Let's go, then—" Then he was looking over his shoulder, in shock, and growing fear.

All Leonov saw as he came down the last steps was Anna clinging to Allardyce's arm. The expected unexpected, changing the scene and the situation to some sordid assignation of sexual betrayal. He shook his head. It wasn't like that, why did he persist in thinking it?

"Anna—!" The voice not his, its anger quite terrible.

She was looking into the Englishman's face before she turned to him. He could see her extend her hand as if to protect herself, see her mouth open slowly. She had seen the gun in his hand, though he was hardly aware of it. It was meant for Allardyce—wasn't it?

"Go back, Gennadi—go back, please—!"

Allardyce was out of it now, still as stone, part of the hollow concrete gallery that made their voices bounce and ricochet. He moved toward her, three steps.

"Anna, don't go—! I have a plan, it's worked out. You'll be safe—"

"Gennadi—no!" *So final.* "I'm going, I have to go, I'm sorry, my darling, I have to—"

"No!"

She, turning to hurry the Englishman, not looking back anymore, had decided on her course of action. The gun was leveling almost of its own volition. She was holding Allardyce's arm—

"No! No!" A steel voice booming among the concrete stanchions, dehumanized.

She didn't look back, rather accelerated, dragging the Englishman—

He'd been in her, he knew. He'd been in her, sometime, whenever he'd recruited her. She let him, oh, yes, she'd let him all right—

Arms out stiff, gun level. She was hurrying away now, round the slow curve of the gallery, and he was calling out, over and over the single word "No!" in that terrible voice and she didn't take any notice, no notice at all until he squeezed the trigger three times, and she sprawled over against Allardyce, then slid to her knees, then on her face and lay still and he'd stopped her running away.

The pace was fast. Gutierrez, as soon as he heard Allardyce, emerged from the tiny, cramped cell in which his mind had functioned since they came out on the track and realized how strung out the field had already become, coming into the home straight for only the second time. There was a moment of elation concerning the girl, then she passed out of mind. He became all immediacy, a photographic plate on which emerged the impressions he absorbed. The crowd noise, surges of sound like great waves as the Russians applauded the boldness of Federenko's front-running. The leading group was tucked in just behind him, but making no effort other than to stay in touch. The second group, the possibles, then the stringers, then himself—

He kicked, moving past the East German and the New Zealander before they reached the bend. Eleven laps to go. He began to measure the number of laps required, the timing of each lap, to take him up with the group behind Federenko. Immediate choice—*when* did he want to arrive? Six laps out, four, three—? Four laps out, with Ochengwe and Irvine both fast finishers. Suddenly, he was in the race. They were lapping at around sixty-two and -three, and the tactics were going to be dictated by the front-runner for the moment. He would have to throw in at least three laps of sixty-one, maybe even a sixty, this early in the race, unless he wanted it all still to do in the second half.

Sixty-one, then. Irena was safe, he told himself. You almost blew it. And then there was only the race.

Lydall was in the leading group of five behind Federenko, with Ochengwe, Irvine, Tretsov, and Jorgensen, with Holmrath just detached behind them; then a second group of three—Ross, the Finn, and the Tanzanian—then the stragglers who were going to make no impression on the race. Gutierrez was somewhere back there, and it was all the thought Lydall spared for him. No one was going to come back in this race, unless the whole leading group blew up six or four hundred meters from home.

Federenko was doing what he had done in the heat, trying to lead from start to finish, and perhaps relying on the crowd to lift him during the last stages of the race. Lydall thought the Russian capable of breaking Irvine's world record, and knew he himself was not. But he clamped down on the thought, as if stamping it into the track. He felt good, even though the regular sixty-twos and -threes worried him. There had to be at least two slower laps in the middle of the race. Even if he had to take the lead himself, to make that happen. And if Federenko would be dictated to like that—

He knew, somehow but with certainty, that Irvine was going to fade. Just as he knew Ochengwe was a medalist. And Federenko—if Federenko faded, then he was in for the Silver. That decided him. When they'd buried the second group and the stragglers he would slow the race for at least a couple of laps, if he could.

Ochengwe, watching the red-and-white figure of the Russian in front of him, ticking off each lap's time, aware of the other runners, knew only that the pace was fast, but not too fast.

Into the home straight, four and a half laps completed, eight to go. Ochengwe considered beginning his midrace burst of four laps, just notching up the speed slightly, pushing Federenko perhaps far enough to make him blow up, or fade less dramatically back into the leading group—but decided to wait another lap, letting Federenko draw them in his wake away from the rest of the field.

Irvine, knowing he had to break his own world record to win the race, had already surrendered the Gold Medal, unable to recapture the feelings of that evening in Sydney, the sense of condition, of *rightness*, he felt then. The season hung over him like an admonishment rather than an encouragement. He was past his best, couldn't recapture it. And the medal for the 10,000—and the effort it had cost him to win it—worked insidiously on him, a whisper that suggested that he was ahead in the game, that the middle distance double was an impossibility.

He would have to slow the race soon—either himself or Lydall. It wasn't his day for front-running. He would hang on, wait—

Tretsov, assuming the strategy of the race was being fulfilled, fifteen meters down on Federenko at the back of the leading group, waited for the sense that Federenko was slowing, blowing up, and surrendering—knowing each lap he had so far run had been exactly to the time required. Everything was going according to the prerace plan, and he was satisfied.

Crane shot.

The two KGB men had left the television set on because there seemed little point in depriving the girl and the American journalist of the pictures of the race while they waited for someone from Moscow Center to come and sort out the mess. They were truculent, naturally, and fearful of the discipline they would incur.

Greenberg studied the crane shot down the home straight of the leader, the two little bunches of runners, Gutierrez, and then the stragglers. He had timed the laps, knew the world record was in danger and that Gutierrez had to run his best ever if he wanted the Gold. And he knew that Allardyce had made it, because the kid had moved up, was working out for himself a slowish route to the front, with maybe a couple or three laps left. The set was turned up loud, and the Russian commentator was evidently exclusively interested in Federenko's progress. Behind his voice, however, was the continuing noise of the crowd, as if they were cheering a 400, not a 5000—swells and shallows, sure, but almost continuous and deafening.

A trackside camera's view as Federenko swept past it into the bend, the tight group of five perhaps six meters adrift of him but showing every sign of hanging on.

Greenberg held the girl's hand, feeling rather foolish and sensing the excitement in her. Their situation had no significance whatsoever. It would become a diplomatic incident, and there was nothing to worry about except who won the race.

Zoom on Federenko from a camera on the stadium roof.

Sixty-three for the sixth lap, Federenko told himself, and no one wanted to take up the front-running. He was going to have to lead from start to finish if he wanted to win the race. And he *was* going to win it. If he beat Tretsov, he would beat part of the system. If he won the race, he beat the system altogether. The noise of the crowd was like a gale at his back or light at the end of a tunnel that pulled him down each straight, round each bend. Only *he* was in the race, as far as they were concerned. Maybe ninety thousand people wanted him to win. Good enough odds. He felt good, knew he had run this race before—front-runner from start to finish. If someone wanted to take it up for two or three laps, he would let them, now that the second group had become too detached to matter anymore—but only when he had burned off at least two more of the group behind him. Tretsov, running his race entirely in his head, had dropped a little as might have been expected, but the black man from Uganda, the British runner Lydall, and the Australian were still in a close group seven or eight meters down on him. The Norwegian had fallen back to the West German, behind Tretsov. The American was nowhere.

The runners passed underneath their seats. Valentina was absorbed in watching Federenko, the children were a little edgy, too excited—not by the race but by the electricity and tension of the huge crowd, the noise and heat of the late afternoon, and too much gassy drink and potato chips and sweets and ice cream. She felt herself ignoring them, except occasionally to pull them back into their seats, and becoming more and more fascinated by what was happening on the track. How could he do it—what kind of man was he? His sister had been killed just days ago, a terrorist or a silly child, Oleg couldn't make up his mind, but there he was, seemingly unaffected, running a race for a Gold Medal as if he hadn't a care in the world. Even Oleg had been more upset by what had happened than Federenko seemed to be. He was enjoying every moment of it, she considered, passing judgment. Callous, selfish. Perhaps he had to be like that, as an athlete. Even so, she did not care for it, and would pass no opinion that excused or favored him. Perhaps the black man was the same, hadn't she read about his wife and children—child?—being shot before he came—

Yes, she had.

She turned her attention to Misha and Tanya then, tidying and scolding them, as if making amends for ignoring them. She saw one of the young men in Oleg's department, standing at the end of the row of seats. She waved—he seemed surprised and worried, by his frown, to see them there. Then he walked away, quite swiftly. She returned her attention to the race, making a mental apology to the runners for her earlier judgments. She had no idea, after all. It might be, running down there, just like her own obsessive housework and washing up—single cups and spoons, sometimes—whenever she knew that Oleg was in a dangerous situation and while she waited for him to call, or come home—

Waited for someone else to call—

Suddenly, she wanted Federenko to win not because he was a Russian, or from the Ukraine, but because his sister had been killed and he was obviously trying to hide in this race from something that threatened to overwhelm him.

Lap seven, going past the finish line, into the bend, with the leading group six meters down on Federenko; Ochengwe second, Lydall third, and Irvine fourth but tiring. Holmrath and Jorgensen were still in touch with the group, but the second group, now augmented to six, were in a tight bunch perhaps forty meters down, and slipping away again. Gutierrez was in the second group, bunched in but ready to move outside, pass them during this lap and have the German and the Norwegian in his sights. He felt full of running, confident, but with just an edge beneath that which suggested he put in maybe two laps at around sixty and no slower than sixty-one—

Just in case no one blew it.

He elbowed through, someone gasped an expletive behind him, and he almost toppled as he became momentarily unbalanced by the New Zealander—then he was outside, lengthening his stride to move to the head of the second group as they reached the top of the back straight. Maybe thirty-five meters down on Federenko, with four and a half to go.

Irvine was going. Lydall could sense him slipping away behind him like a man sliding over a cliff or beneath deep water, not waving but drowning, losing his grip on the ledge of the race. Once he lost touch, he was finished. Lydall knew that because he knew it would happen to him if he couldn't keep up with Ochengwe and Federenko and Tretsov, who had moved up again in front of Irvine by the time the seventh was completed. He was running as if in a pressure suit, cut off from the rest of them, the race unfolding to some plan in his head. He looked half-hypnotized. Lydall wasn't afraid of him— strangely—as if the unchanging, robotic expression, the even regularity of his running, marked him as a loser rather than a winner. Perhaps it was based on Federenko blowing up, in which case, Tretsov was going to be disappointed. Lydall knew, as clearly as if he was in Federenko's body and mind, that the Russian wasn't going to break, he could only be broken.

And he knew he couldn't break him. Ochengwe might, the American might have if he was in any mental shape to win the race. But himself—?

He'd beaten Ross, Holmrath and Jorgensen were out of it, so were Gutierrez and the Russian. Better than he could have hoped, better than a dream.

And that was it. The barrier he couldn't get beyond. He would win a medal if he didn't tie up. He felt good enough, even at this sharp edge of it, not to tie up or fade badly over the last six hundred—but he couldn't get beyond that. His own expectation and that of the world had been too late and low for the Gold. He *couldn't* make it—

Lap eight, back straight. Federenko with Ochengwe closing up, the Ugandan having run three laps of sixty or sixty-one in succession, changing his classic tactics to answer the front-runner's domination of the race; Lydall third, six meters down on Ochengwe, Tretsov fourth, tucked in, going mechanically, then fifteen meters back from the leader Irvine fading back to laps of sixty-four, sixty-five with which he would finish the race. Holmrath, Jorgensen, Gutierrez, a newly formed group of three, seven or eight meters behind Irvine, moving to swallow him.

On the home straight, with a lap of sixty seconds, Ochengwe took the lead. Lydall, with a lap of sixty-two, closed marginally on Federenko. Tretsov slipped back slightly. Gutierrez was on Irvine's shoulder as they went into the bend with four laps left.

The tarpaulin had been unwrapped, and its contents spread out, cleaned of earth and laid as if to dry in the hot sunlight of the garden. Curved strips of metal, neatly cut out of something with a keen saw, and a dial, a gauge of some kind that had broken, since it registered full while unattached to anything except fresh air.

Kazantsev crouched by it like a scout who had come across some clear, but uninterpretable, signs. The strips of metal were clean-cut, obviously part of some container, and the broken dial was made to be set above a valve, since it was intended to measure pressure in something.

The afternoon was suddenly silent, the little garden close against their backs and faces like a suffocating curtain. The noises of insects, a match being struck, someone coughing to clear his throat and cutting off the noise as if it disturbed or offended. Flies settled on the strips of metal—one wandered over the face of the dial—a white butterfly drifted in and out of Kazantsev's intent gaze, a gauzy patch that suggested some astigmatism rather than a living creature.

As if he had willed the metal strips to give up their meaning, or arranged them physically so that they suggested the shape of the original container, he knew suddenly what they were. And on a screen behind his eyes flickered the slides the two policemen had discovered in the holiday snaps. A valve opening, and he could almost hear the hiss of air—his hands stroked the air, describing a rounded shape, then elongating as if he were a potter molding something invisible.

Lenin Stadium, cylinders with panels replaced—Belousov had called them shatter-scatter, shatter-scatter—the container blowing, the gas canisters scattered over a wider area, the gas spreading—

He got to his feet, looked round him wildly at the red-faced men, the sweat-stained police shirts, the garden implements, and the desolation they had made beyond the raspberry canes, and began running toward the house without explanation.

Lap nine, back straight. Ochengwe, putting in another fast lap, tried to burn off Federenko with the surprise of being passed and the cold shock of superior pace, but the Russian was hanging on. The crowd's noise was more thunderous and heavy than ever. Lydall, dropped by three or four meters on the bend, narrowed the gap to Federenko with the effort showing on his face and in the tight, stretched cords in his throat and across his arms and shoulders.

Gutierrez dropped Holmrath and Jorgensen, with Irvine

behind them now and making no further impression, then he began moving up on Tretsov. And there was a palpable sense that plans were being revised or torn up, that the heavy atmosphere and the inertia of the race and the noise had panicked them like cattle, and the challenge was down and only the fastest and the fittest would survive the remaining three and a half laps.

Into the home straight, Ochengwe was two meters up on Federenko who had begun to need the crowd and was beginning to dig into his reserves, Lydall was four meters down on the Russian as he came into the straight and he looked the wildest, the least composed of the three of them. Tretsov had been dropped by eight or nine meters, and Gutierrez was halfway through the bend, stretching out, building a flowing pace that most of the crowd had still failed to perceive but that the more expert commentators were trying to explain to their audiences, a pace that would put him in touch six hundred or so from home. For most, however, Ochengwe was the threat to Federenko in a more obvious way—or Federenko a similar threat to the black man.

Federenko and Kazantsev were linked for a moment in the mind of one of the two men running through Belousov's slide collection as the KGB man came through the door of the lounge and stared at the television set as if he expected it to have been damaged.

"We were just saying—" the young man began, nodding in the direction of the projector and the screen.

"Tenth lap, our boy's—" the other one added at a tangent.

The slides had moved on, to more holiday snaps, a wooded scene, a small dacha somewhere, maybe up near the Finland border, a hut that he had rented for a holiday.

"Where are those slides?" Kazantsev bellowed like a disappointed, desperate child.

One of the young men held them up, but Kazantsev had already turned his back on him and was picking up the telephone, dialing and looking up at the screen between each number.

"What shall we—?"

"For Christ's sake, put them on the screen!" He went on dialing, drumming on the table with his suddenly freed hand while he waited for the connection. "Kazantsev—give me the number of the main security office at the stadium—*now*, dammit!" Kazantsev's eyes were riveted to the TV screen. Back straight, Ochengwe and

Federenko shoulder to shoulder, the British runner trailing them by six or seven meters. The second Russian dropped by another eight meters and the American closing the gap behind Tretsov to four or five meters.

"Fast," one of the young men said, watching the TV screen. "This'll be a record."

"Is he trying to get a late bet on?" the other one whispered, nudging his companion.

Kazantsev held down the rest, then began dialing again, then drumming.

The bend, with Federenko nudging ahead of the Ugandan, and the British runner closing the gap slightly; Tretsov falling away, the American almost at his shoulder. Twenty meters covering the distance between the five of them, and perhaps another twenty back to Jorgensen, then Holmrath, then Irvine.

"Puchkov." Pause. "Get him. She's *what*—?"

Kazantsev stared at the screen as if at something alien and poisonous. Valentina was there, with the kids. Valentina was *there*—!

"Get Puchkov, *now!*"

Two laps to go. As they passed the finish line, Federenko challenged Ochengwe, who had held him off all the way down the straight, and nudged back into the lead. As he did so, he made his decision—to kick for home eight hundred meters out, and not wait for the back straight. Tretsov was long out of it, caught because the pace throughout the race was faster than the one he had been programmed to do—the time was inside the world record, at least a couple of seconds faster.

Lydall watched Federenko, almost saw the moment of resolution throw back the head, square the shoulders, lengthen the stride. The Russian was kicking for home with two laps to go and expecting only the African to stay with him.

Lydall looked over his shoulder. Gutierrez was away from Tretsov, and five or six down on him. Lydall had begun to strain at the pace of the race, grab at it, and his legs were beginning to feel heavy, demanding a rest. He kicked, still on the bend, and knew that Gutierrez was doing the same. Ochengwe looked capable of staying with Federenko.

Gutierrez knew he had to run two of the fastest finishing laps he had ever done. His gradual movement through the field had worked as he had planned, but the Russian and the African were kicking for home with two laps left and he had maybe fifteen meters to pick up. Neither of the leaders looked as if they would blow this close to the finish, but Lydall did look tired and his head was beginning to flop.

He surged forward off the bend into the back straight, moving perceptibly up on Lydall, who glanced over his shoulder. Gutierrez knew he had him then. The Briton had let the two leaders go, admitting he had nothing left to match them. He was interested only in protecting the Bronze position.

Up the back straight, and by the time he reached the bend, Gutierrez was three meters behind and closing. Federenko and Ochengwe, close together with the Russian just leading, were another seven or eight up. Lydall had nothing left—his stride almost faltered as he admitted it, then he tried to summon another gear or a last reserve only to discover systems shut down, burned out. The machine had done all it could, and now it was running down. The crowd's noise hid everything, and the silence of the tartan track prevented him from hearing the beat of the American's footsteps at his heels.. Nothing but the tunnel of noise. He was faltering, dying out there because his best wasn't good enough to beat a fucking Yank and a black bugger and a bloody Russian.

He kicked, expecting nothing, gritting his teeth together, lips stretched back as if with the force of gravity, nostrils and mouth trying to draw in the heavy, still, stifling air. And he caught the flicker of Gutierrez in the corner of his eye, trying to take him on the bend into the home straight.

"Fuck you!" he snarled, and Gutierrez dropped back. He saw it more as that than as his own moving ahead. His whole concentration was directed behind him, over his shoulder at the American who wanted his third place.

He had forgotten Ochengwe and Federenko, so much so that the bell became a shock to him, coming from somewhere dim and unexpected up ahead.

Federenko was holding off Ochengwe with 350 meters left. The African looked better than he did and he knew it; he was poised, but he still wasn't gaining. Three meters now. He struggled, gripping at something, and kicked again, his gesture having to be made, inconceivable that the black man could deny him the moment, the two fingers to the system, to everything and everybody—the Gold. *Stealing* it from Tretsov.

Ochengwe sensed something in the Russian, something that would not allow him to lose. Sensed, too, the pace of the eleventh and twelfth laps, and knew that he had never run that fast before. Ochengwe knew the Russian was going to win as they moved into the back straight for the last time. He stepped up his pace again, expecting to make only a temporary indentation on the distance between himself and Federenko.

Lydall held Gutierrez all the way down the back straight, all the time knowing he was still there, that he could not shake him.

Gutierrez, disbelieving the Briton could stay in front of him but trapped into concentrating on him, was letting the first two runners have the race; he sensed, too, that he might blow up unless he husbanded what was left, kept it for a final surge off the bend into the finishing straight. The tactics of recovery, the concentration and the effort to climb back slowly through the field and set himself for the kill, had taken more than he expected or knew until Lydall had come back at him, and kept himself three or four meters up. Then he had known he did not have enough to take the Russian or the Ugandan, unless they both blew it—

Federenko came onto the final bend with the crowd on its feet, the officials and competitors closest to him yelling, his concentration stuttering like a man falling asleep in a car, waking each time to find the truck ahead dangerously nearer. There was a collision of air, and Federenko felt restrained by the element, the finish ever more distant, the sense of the Ugandan and the rest of the field gone, everything gone now except the sense of the race never being over, of his mind going blank for longer and longer periods, the noise flashing in and out of it like a radio turned on and off. His legs almost going, his blood pounding in his ears, heart rate hideously fast and loud.

Ochengwe had run faster than ever before in his life. Coming off the last bend, he hit the noise of the crowd as a solid, impermeable obstacle, and felt his legs drain, as if some opened tap had drawn off his remaining body fluids. He could not beat Federenko now; the Russian, head rolling, arms pumping, legs heavy, was still too many meters up on him with too little left of the race. The very process of recognition, of admitting the red vest in front of him, was a decision to settle for the Silver Medal. He looked over his shoulder, hearing the crowd express their sense that he was beaten. Gutierrez and Lydall were into the straight together, locked into a race of their own for third place. They would not catch him. He pushed on into the palpable, treacly air around him, into the sea of noise, the seeming undergrowth of the tartan track, six meters down on Federenko.

Lydall's head rocked from side to side as if he were trying to throw it from its delicate perch on his thin shoulders. He pumped his arms like flails, hunched his shoulders, his eyes taking in only the track immediately in front of him, forgetting Federenko and Ochengwe as they claimed Gold and Silver. Gutierrez was up on his shoulder, taking the outside and not floating now, but driving almost as frantically as Lydall was himself. He had nothing left in his legs now, he had to be in as bad a state as Lydall felt—had to—

Into the straight, the American was half his skinny body in front, and Lydall pushed desperately, faltered, picked up like a cold or worn machine, and came level.

He held it for thirty meters, blind and almost stumbling in the bowl of noise, aware of Gutierrez roaring each breath in an ear deafened by his blood and his own breathing. Held, cutting out everything else but the sense of the American almost touching him—held, held—Gutierrez pulled half a meter ahead with less than twenty to run. Lydall had nothing left in his legs, tried to drive them, then accepted fourth place, easing with each remaining stride.

For Federenko, the crowd was the roaring of the sea which became the high screaming of a storm, then a wail that began to die away. He stumbled as if into deep water, felt arms catch him, turn him, lay him down like a corpse. He wanted to protest at their help, tell them he must finish the race alone, they were disqualifying him.

Blank, color, blank, then a black face looking down, teeth bared like something savage, nightmarish, breath roaring nearer than the blood or the crowd—blank, rolling his head until he saw the skinny American cross the line just ahead of the British runner—blank again, and he began to realize he needed oxygen.

Perhaps he had won—?

Someone kneeling over him, pressing a mask to his face as he moved his head to suck greedily at the proffered oxygen.

Sharp cracks, like the starter's gun over and over again in quick succession—cries of surprise, puzzlement as he sucked at the mask, swallowed the oxygen—then the mask slipped aside, and he had to fumble by his side for it while a metal ball landed only feet away, on the trackside, then rolled shinily away from him.

Where was his oxygen? Where was it—? Blank. Black face—another face, olive, then the thin, strained face that was the British runner, leaning over him—where was the oxygen? Blank.

Kazantsev saw the canisters bounce over the track and the field. The FAE device had been triggered, the panels that had been inserted in the oxygen cylinder had blown out, scattering the canisters that must have been attached to some central spine over an area big enough to—

He bit off the thought. Valentina, and the gas was beginning to spread. The kids.

"Puchkov?" he said, and the sweat broke out, as if the words had raised his temperature. "My wife and kids—" he could not help adding.

And he heard, distinctly, Puchkov's voice, saying, "Who the hell told you that?"

"Never mind, show them to me."

"We're wasting time, Oleg. The FAE devices have exploded."

"I can see it. The liquid has vaporized?"

"Yes—" There was the crackle of static over the line from Moscow. "For God's sake, have you got something for us?"

"I think so. Are your men ready?"

"Yes—what do we do?"

Kazantsev looked at the first slide projected on the screen. Puzzling, cryptic. He needed time, and there wasn't any available. How long would it take to form its saucer, when the moment of ignition would occur—and a great flat disk of flame would engulf the stadium, killing everyone. He felt sick, his eyes flickering back and forth from TV to slide projection.

"I have to work it out as we go along—"

"Oleg! How long have we got, man?"

"I don't *know*—" The two young men sitting behind the projector were riveted now. "Look, I'll have to talk it over. You'll have to put it on the screen for me—the bombs, in close-up, and I can talk them through." It was stupid, ridiculous, and all he could think of.

"A thousand million people—" Puchkov murmured.

"You must order them to keep transmitting!" Belousov's small lounge was hot now, dust in the air catching at his dry throat. "I can't instruct them otherwise. Now, do it."

Already, he could hear the first words of the public announcement, explaining away the devices that had cascaded at either side of the stadium, and explaining the necessity for an orderly evacuation.

"How long, Oleg?" Puchkov was pleading for some consolation, a fact that would make speculation more bearable.

"I don't know. Two minutes, ten minutes? Ours are airburst proximity or pressure fuses. This is homemade—who knows?"

"We can't clear—"

"I know it. Order them to show me Tina and the kids. Now."

"Where are they?"

Kazantsev remembered the numbers of the tickets he had given to Federenko to give to his sister. They were the tickets. Shubin's final twist. For what had happened at the warehouse, for the deaths of those silly kids. Tina and the kids, burned beyond recognition—

That's what would happen. It might take twenty minutes to clear the Lenin Stadium, and that was too long. If only he had some clue to indicate the type of fuel, ignition time—! Come on, come on—he had to be patched into throat mikes and headphones, and they had to get the cameras fixed on both bombs. He needed a split screen.

On the screen, the camera buzzed along rows of startled, worried faces, as if they couldn't find his wife and kids.

Lydall, bending over double, almost leaning in weariness against Gutierrez, the American himself retching with effort, felt the liquid splash his bare arm, cool like butane gas spilling on his fingers from filling a cigarette lighter, then vaporize instantly. A metal ball rolled near his feet at the edge of the track. It hardly impinged. His mind was revolving the last twenty-five meters of the race when Gutierrez had taken him and the Bronze. Fourth in the 5000 meters Final at the XXII Olympiad, hardly a footnote except in the more compendious of record books. His own best time, ever.

He felt light-headed but not in need of oxygen. The Russian looked as if he had almost killed himself for the Gold, and Ochengwe seemed unperturbed by second place. The rest of the field was still finishing.

He straightened, looked at the scoreboard as the lights flickered, spilled down its face, and the names appeared. Federenko, CCCP, and the world record light flashing next to the time, still to be confirmed. Ochengwe, a second down on that; Gutierrez a personal best; Lydall—all of them well, well inside Viren's old Olympic record, all of them inside everything except Federenko's time for the heat. Ochengwe inside Irvine's record, and Gutierrez and himself nudging it.

He had never run better, and the knowledge of that was an

anesthetic against disappointment. Then Gutierrez was suddenly beside him again, hand held out. He took it, felt still the last tremors of effort in the American's fingers. Ochengwe was grinning, the first time Lydall had ever seen a broad smile from the Ugandan. He nodded, hands on hips, breathing more regularly now. A recognition between them that included Gutierrez, and even the Russian receiving oxygen.

What were the noises he had dimly heard, the several close-set reports like the starter's gun over and over?

The scoreboard winked out, winked back with a message in Russian and English. Then the voice from the public address system in the sudden silence of the message that 200,000 eyes were absorbing, the words dropping heavy as boulders down a well, their sense unmistakable, even in Russian. Then the English.

"The security authorities have received a bomb warning. The devices have failed to explode—it is stressed that the devices failed to explode. Experts are preparing to inspect them. All competitors and officials will leave the area of the track and field immediately, so as not to hamper this inspection. As an additional security precaution, spectators will leave the stadium and assemble on the warm-up track and its surrounding area. Please do not hurry or panic—there is no danger. The devices have failed to detonate. Evacuation is a routine safety precaution." Then repetition in other languages.

Lydall looked around the stadium, seeing people stirring, hearing the hum and buzz of fear, curiosity, humor, but felt no kind of participation even when he saw the oxygen cylinders on their cart gaping strangely, and the scattered metal spheres. He simply could not consider those images as elements of a bomb.

Then armed guards were coming toward them, a more immediately chilling impression. Guards were in position in each aisle of the stands, and at each exit. People were lining up or waiting. Everything was unhurried, normal, like the time at Lords when everyone descended onto the pitch while the police searched the seats after a bomb scare. Unreal, just a practice—

They loaded Federenko onto a stretcher, and he and Ochengwe and Gutierrez trooped toward the tunnel. The heavy mutter of noise, the people lining up for the exits without panic or haste, suggested finality to Lydall. For him, the Olympics were over.

He did not want to think ahead. He closed his mind down like switching off a pocket calculator, and savored the last moments of being special, almost unique, walking with Ochengwe and Gutierrez and Irvine and the others, Federenko lolling on the stretcher just ahead of them.

Into the shadow of the tunnel.

Briefly, on the TV screen, he saw his wife and the two children, standing up, waiting to file to the end of their row, then to the nearest exit. His agony was to see her face, know that she knew it was an FAE device they were talking about, and what such a term meant. Valentina knew she wouldn't get out alive—but no one could have told that from her face as she talked to the kids.

The devices have failed to explode.

Brilliant. A harmless little exercise, putting into operation, with public cooperation, the evacuation procedures worked out a year before. *The devices have failed to explode.* But they will.

Valentina knew they would, knew there were minutes at most. He willed her to panic, drag herself and the kids screaming and yelling through the crowd to the nearest exit. But she didn't—she wouldn't.

He was almost grateful when the image cut to one of the dummy oxygen cylinders, then to a couple of the canisters like metal grapefruit on the track, more on the field like giant hailstones. The gas had propelled them as it escaped through maybe just a pinhole in each one—greatest possible spread. But—ignition? He looked across at the slide projected on the screen, wiping his eyes as he did so. Unable to understand its meaning.

The two young men were eager to change the slides, do anything to appease him, to assist. And helpless. The temperature in the small lounge was still going up. Kazantsev loosened his tie. He glanced at the screen. The commentator had gone silent. The cylinders near the finish line were in close-up, the dummy valve and gauge filling the TV screen. They'd decided, had to decide, in the Politburo glass house at the back of the stand. Safe in there, they'd agreed to broadcast an attempt to defuse two FAE devices to the rest of the world.

Then Puchkov was on the line, shouting tinnily in his ear, while the other ear heard the silence of the room in which a fly audibly buzzed.

"It's done—have you got it in close-up?"

"Yes—where's the split screen?"

"Broken down—"

"For Christ's sake! I have to have a view of both at once!" He was almost ranting, sensing every mile of the hundreds to Moscow and helplessly separated from everything that concerned him by each of those miles.

"NBC is going to rig one for them—it will take time. Look, talk to a TV man about it. He suggests cutting rapidly, at your order, from device to device—"

"That's no fucking good!"

"Oleg, calm down!" The older man's voice snapped at him, demanding obedience. The two young men in the room with him—why hadn't the others even come in from the garden, were they indifferent to it all?—were white-faced at his panic, his rage.

"All right."

"It is two minutes and fourteen seconds since the devices spread, and vaporization of the liquid. We have time."

"I hope so."

"You're patched into the demolition men and the TV director can hear you, and can cut in if he needs to. It's up to you."

Kazantsev nodded, as if Puchkov could see him. The cameras cut to each cylinder in close-up, only the angles slightly different. Handhelds, jogging slightly. They'd done their best in less than three minutes. Someone, probably the Chairman himself, had accepted, decided almost without pause. Perhaps the first hundreds were already passing through the exits, down the steps to the gallery. They might get five or six thousand of them out, including the competitors and the officials.

What was it he had said to Belousov, to frighten him? *Look at the hippie over there, burning?* Look at my wife, in the best seats in the grandstand, burning—

God, he thought, I don't understand the slides.

"Next one!" he snapped.

He didn't understand.

Leonov and Allardyce had carried Anna's body down to the medical center, laid it on one of the carts, and arranged it with care, covering the blood and the bullet holes with a blanket; then, after a long while, as if by mute, tacit agreement, they had covered the face.

Allardyce felt nausea catch him in waves, disbelief trying to keep out revulsion and a presentiment of madness. He could not look at Leonov, yet felt himself closely identified—much too closely—with the man, sensing that he shared some of his feelings, was a murderer manqué, or an accomplice. Leonov was docile like a spent animal.

The silence seemed to make the long, empty room cold. The public address system and its message of evacuation hardly impinged upon them. Allardyce registered more vividly the weight of her body as she was driven against him by the force of the bullets, then had become deadweight as she slumped into him. He could register that as a numb place down his arm and side, like a stroke.

His sleeve was smeared, badged with her blood, already seeming to go brown and old and meaningless. There was nothing more he could do but look at it, look away from it as he felt the nausea coming.

The young man who entered in a white coat, and who seemed surprised and suddenly guilty when he saw them, took only a small part of his attention. But Leonov seemed to seize on the intrusion into his own nightmare, snapping awake, questioning.

"What's happening?"

"A bomb threat, I think. They're evacuating—"

"What kind of bomb?"

"They think it's a dud."

Allardyce tried to attend, but felt his attention drawn back to his sleeve, to the shape under the blanket that seemed less insistently to suggest a human frame, a corpse. Old clothes, hidden. All the way down from the gallery, as he held her legs, Leonov her arms, he'd been aware of the pathetic, ridiculous ice cream stain on the front of her skirt, the dummy that Leonov had not bought.

"Are you—why are you not preparing this place for casualties?"

Allardyce focused. The young, dark man with the sallow complexion and the bright, narrow eyes was hanging up his white coat, making to leave.

"I—"

"There will be dead, injured. What are your orders?" The voice of a man desperate to climb back inside routines, forms of procedure without thought or decision. "What are your orders in the event of an evacuation?"

The young man was turning, about to hurry through the door, running away like he and Anna—

Allardyce realized it was happening again, and began to shout even as Leonov raised the gun, fired twice. The young man bucked forward as he was hit in the back and head, tumbled toward, *through* the plate glass which made a hideous, unexpected ripping sound as the body doubled over and disappeared from sight.

A rag of shirt, bloody, was left on the ledge below the shattered window, there was blood smearing the wall. Nothing else.

Shubin lay in the corridor outside the medical center, eyes flickering almost at the speed of the public address announcement, now in French. There was a vague, numb pain in his back and chest, and a stickiness he was noticing less and less at the back of his head. And a torn, open sensation near his guts.

When the announcement began again in German, his eyes stopped flickering and he lay still.

A helicopter hovered over the stadium, aerial surveillance. In the densely packed stands, people filed in an orderly, snail-like progression toward the exits. Only the first ineffectual hundreds had come out from the stadium's amphitheater toward the warm-up area. The track and field were deserted of competitors and ringed by armed security guards, the last of the press photographers and network handheld TV cameras being firmly and insistently forced to retire from two small areas, each with its own ring of armed men, facing outward—one near the finish line, the other on the opposite side of the stadium near the start of the 5000 meters.

A scene of little motion, almost stillness from that height. Two men in heavy padding—white, with red shoulder flashes clearly visible—moving out of the competitors' tunnel, carrying what might have been medical bags, each making for one of the small, tight-ringed areas. As the helicopter passed slowly over the stadium, the sunlight glinted on the metal canisters scattered over the green of the field and the red-brown of the track.

Puchkov looked up, envying the helicopter above the vaporized explosive, then looked across at the Politburo bunker. Heavy shapes behind the reinforced glass were slowly filing out, with dignity but as a precaution, down to the bar beneath, he assumed, to the whiskey and brandy and the protective concrete roof and walls. He knew where Tina Kazantseva was, but he didn't raise his glasses to find her. Somehow, he couldn't look at the crowd at all, the mugs who thought it was all just an exercise, with nothing much to worry about except getting back their original seats when the all clear sounded. There was still the decathlon 1500 to be run.

Puchkov fiddled with his earpiece and the volume knob of the handset clipped to his breast pocket, and felt old and tired in the hot sunlight as his two men, geared up, reached the carts on which the FAE cylinders had been mounted. He was patched into the communications circuit between Kazantsev and the two men out there on the defusing and the TV director.

The Politburo section was almost empty now, as if everyone was walking away from the scene of the accident, leaving him to deal with it. He wiped his forehead. Except that they weren't really walking away, just shuffling along their endless rows to the concrete steps toward the exits. Out of a hundred thousand, the bombs would certainly kill eighty-two or -three thousand. And the security team.

He looked at the stopwatch he had snatched from an official. It was three minutes fourteen seconds since scatter. How long did that bloody gas take to spread over this area?

He was saying it aloud, into his throat mike.

"Oleg—how long have we got?"

Kazantsev watched the screen. One of his team was approaching the cylinders near the finish line, the camera focusing down on the cart as soon as the man knelt by it and opened his tool bag. The image was close, steady. He looked at the slides, at the two helpless KGB men in the room with him—the door was now closed, jammed shut with a chair to prevent interruption—still sitting behind the projector, heard the fly buzz, felt the heat of the room striking against his body as if he had a temperature. Then he heard Puchkov, and responded.

"I don't know, there's nothing here, no writing, nothing but these slides which seem to be about arming the damn things—!"

"Do you want the other shot?" The TV director, a mask of professional calm, detachment. He'd probably been told he would be safe behind glass. Some safety.

"Yes, yes—where's the split screen?"

"Coming—"

"So is doomsday."

"Lieutenant?"

"Yes, Anatoli?"

"Testing—awaiting instructions."

"Who else is there?" Camera cut, joggle to a face he did not know.

"Ognev, Engineer Regiment, Moscow Garrison." The clipped, military tones of an ex-Suvarov cadet. Young face, intelligent and somehow brash.

"FAE experience?"

"Some. I understand the theory and practice, and the familiar types being stockpiled. But not this, I'm afraid." A small, almost winsome smile of self-deprecation.

"O.K., O.K. It's three minutes twenty-eight. I don't know about spread rate. It isn't going to have to matter. Cylinder, close as you can."

A shot of Ognev's cylinder, filling the screen. Kazantsev was seated on a chair in front of the screen, fiddling with the contrast button, brightening the screen. He could see where the panels had blown away, the central spine—like the remains of a corncob that teeth had stripped—where the canisters had clung like sea creatures until the time fuse had scattered them. And Ognev's hands hovering, waiting to be ordered remotely.

"Get one cylinder off the cart—both of you." He watched Ognev begin, then ordered them to cut to Anatoli, already feeling that he would never remember *his* directorial responsibilities often and quickly enough. He wiped his hot, damp forehead, tugged at his already open tie, pulled two buttons from his shirt as he opened it. "Careful, Anatoli. Now push the cart away, just as a precaution."

The director let him watch that, then cut to Ognev before Kazantsev could give the instruction. Ognev was listening to the remains of the cylinder with what looked like a medical stethoscope, not one of the amplified ones he might ordinarily have used.

"What now?" Ognev asked. "Nothing ticking."

Kazantsev glanced at the projected slide, waved his hand. Slide one, two, three, then the cartridge worked backward, three, two, one. The gauge and valve had been used in the arming process.

"Get the valve off—turn it first, all the way." Ognev's hand, then Anatoli's delicate touch. The hand was trembling, and the boy was thinking of the Lenin Mausoleum where two of his mates had died and Kazantsev knew he was going to have to keep an eye on him all the time. "Where the fuck is the split screen?" he yelled, startling the two hands he could see on the screen. "Sorry."

Three minutes forty-four. Five minutes had to be the absolute maximum. Time for Shubin to get clear, but not everyone else. Five minutes *had* to be the optimum time.

"Nothing. This has been turned through a detent." Anatoli.

"Confirmed." Ognev.

Kazantsev looked at the projected slide. Arming was done like that, yes. "Get the valves out."

He watched Anatoli take out grips, open and fit them to the valve head. Then a cut to Ognev, the director sensing the drama of the thing, perhaps even aware that he had an audience of one or two thousand million, every one of them watching what Kazantsev could see on the screen, the soundless pictures of a potential catastrophe. The director was aware of the tension, the possible scenario, and was beginning to respond to the actors and the action.

Slowly, slowly, the valve heads turned, the dummy gauges mocking, their faces turning like clocks or toys. Cutting, with more acceleration now—Kazantsev had to feel he saw everything, could countermand, instruct, cry out at the significant moment. This was the point of maximum danger, the removing of the arming section of a device, and the two men knew it, Puchkov knew it—the crowd did not know it—and perhaps a couple of million viewers *really* knew or guessed what they might be seeing.

Ognev's hands—pause, gingerly wiggling the loosened valve head, looking for some other, booby-trapped connection. Then breath sighed down the wire to Kazantsev, and he saw the hands lift the valve head clear.

"O.K., Anatoli—now you." Cut, and he watched again. Then to Ognev. "What have you got?"

"Nothing—"

"The cylinder head?"

"Mm." Close-up.

"Copper-faced plunger and seat, isn't it?"

"Confirmed," Ognev said with a certain amount of relief, as if Kazantsev had the blueprints and was consulting them with confidence.

"Right—get that seat out. Anatoli?"

"Yes?"

"You get to this stage with the other two cylinders—hurry."

"Sir."

"Do you want the split screen now?" the director drawled, confident, relaxed, professional. Quite unreasonably, Kazantsev loathed him.

"Please. Get the camera to go with Anatoli—to each of the cylinders."

Split screen. Anatoli taking his other cylinder from the cart, fitting the grips. The camera moving in, bobbing, and some shots of the crowd intruding—making Kazantsev gasp with widened perspective, just as it had reminded two thousand million people that the Lenin Stadium was still full to capacity with people like them.

"Get the seat out, Ognev."

"Understood." Right side of the picture, Ognev's hands, the camera peering over them into the little well where the valve had fitted. Pale gleam of copper. The seat unscrewed slowly while Anatoli strolled toward Ognev's second cylinder, began to fit the grips, casually—

"Careful—*both* of you."

Like a ghastly joke, a set of figures began ticking away in tenths of a second, seconds, and minutes in the corner of the screen—top right, as if timing a race.

"That's your time from detonation of the cylinders," Puchkov said in his ear.

Four minutes twenty.

"Sekonda Quartz." Ognev's voice, chiming crazily with the flickering figures on the screen. "I can see the face of an electronic watch—must be the timing device. *Really* homemade."

"What is it *doing*?"

"Who knows. Can't see a trigger, solenoids, power cells—no, no relays—"

"Anatoli—same procedure with the other three now. Copper seat out, until you can see the watch face—" Four minutes twenty-seven. "Get on with it!"

"Mm. That's interesting—"

"What?" His temperature jumped as he shouted, as if entirely governed by his emotional state.

"Down here, on the spine, so to speak—"

"Camera!"

"One of the canisters is still here—no, it's different."

Kazantsev could see it. Little stubby fins, like a nestling, sinister little bat with a round body. What did—?

"World War—butterfly bombs." Ognev, and then Puchkov.

"That's what it looks like here—"

"Oh, God—"

Four minutes thirty-four. Ognev scared out of his wits.

"What is it?"

"The gas—it's beginning to descend slightly. I can feel it around my head and shoulders, cold as hell—"

"Stay calm!" Kazantsev was shuddering as if he were there himself. "Calm down."

"We're very close," Ognev said quietly. "It's one of those with what we call a high collapse factor. It's sliding back closer to the ground the longer it's unignited."

"Then we're close?"

"Too close. It has to be almost—"

"Yes."

Four minutes forty-four. Anatoli was standing by the last of the cylinders, examining the butterfly bomb that Kazantsev could see in close-up on the other half of the screen. Something was catching the sun, and settling on Ognev's hands, darkly like liquid soot. The gas—?

He waited, almost half a second, to see Ognev ignite like the hippie he had created for Belousov. Then he breathed out.

"What's that on your hand?"

Hand rubbing hand—out of shot, sniffing noise.

"Oil—" Puzzlement.

"Close-up of the spine—quickly!"

Four fifty-one. Five minutes—it had to be no more than that.

The camera traced along the spine in the middle of the dummy cylinder. Catching the sun—?

"There! Like a pinprick in a water pipe—the oil's being forced out— See it?"

Ognev. "Yes—"

"A plunger inside the spine, pushing out the oil—that's the timer, the size of the hole. The butterfly bomb is the *ignition* system, and it's being operated—" Four fifty-six. "By the oil plunger. Plug the hole!"

A half second, stretching out. Then a thumb, slapping something on the pinprick.

"Anatoli—find the holes on your two—plug them. The Dutch boy. Use your finger, someone else's—!"

Four fifty-eight. Ognev stumbled against the camera, which joggled up to the sky, descending with a sweep across the crowded stands, then focusing on Ognev kneeling, pressing his thumb against the spine of his second cylinder.

And Anatoli, stumbling through a glutinous element or like a baby just learning to walk. Four fifty-nine, and yards to go before the last cylinder—a policeman was kneeling with his hand over the first spine.

Four fifty-nine point six, seven—

Anatoli dived, flinging himself upon the second cylinder like a man catching a greased pig, a wild creature that threatened him. His hands gripped round the spine, preventing the last of the oil being forced out and flinging off the butterfly bomb which was evidently some kind of thermite device that would ignite the gas—

Five-one, five-two, five-three—

Kazantsev luxuriated in the time that was now available. As if to further satisfy him, the director panned round the stands—perhaps now eighty percent full—to bring back his sense of proportion, or create self-congratulation.

"Ognev?"

"Yes."

"What was that you used—?"

"On the first cylinder? Chewing gum."

"Order some more. And now, show me my wife and kids, for God's sake."

When he saw them, huddling into the crowd that was filing up the steps, he began shaking with relief and he could not prevent the inappropriate and rather embarrassing tears that began to run down his bright-red, sweating face.

Acknowledgments and Author's Note

I wish to express my indebtedness to Lynn Davies, Olympic Gold Medalist in the long jump in Tokyo, 1964, for his invaluable assistance in providing—from his own wide experience—many insights into the techniques and training of Western athletes, and the atmosphere and detail of a great athletics occasion.

For the exercise of his technical imagination in projecting upon a basis of solid fact the nature of the FAE weapon that features in the book, I am indebted to T. R. Jones.

For the details of the electronics of a modern Olympiad that appear in Chapter 18, I am indebted to my brother, Gareth.

I would also like to acknowledge the principal sporting and reference books that I found helpful, especially *Track and Field Athletics* by Wilf Paish; *Athletics for the 70s* by Dennis Watts and Ian Ward; *Munich '72* by Christopher Brasher; *Mary, Mary* by Mary Rand; *Another Hurdle* by David Hemery; *The Big Red Machine* by Yuri Brokhin. Also the *Nagel Travel Guide to U.S.S.R.*, and *KGB* by John Barron.

The image of Soviet life and sport that appears in the book is my own, and any error, distortion, or license in the book is my own responsibility, not that of any of the above.

I would like to have been able to claim at this point that the FAE device that features in the book is a product of my imagination, or that of my technical adviser. Unfortunately, this is not the case. The Free Air Explosion device (or, as it is sometimes called, the Fuel Air Explosion weapon) is an uncomfortable, unpalatable reality, falling as it does—by design—between the maximum explosive power of conventional weapons and the minimal yield nuclear devices.

It is a matter of record that these weapons were first experimented with during World War II, that there was a revival of interest by both the USA and the USSR in the 1950s and 1960s, culminating in the use of what was termed the BLU-73 weapon in Vietnam, which contained ethylene oxide and was used to detonate mines or defoliate large areas of forest and jungle—what we have come to know as the napalm bomb.

Further development of these weapons has taken place, as in the CBU-55, which is a cluster bomb of 3x33Kg of ethylene oxide, a single kilogram of which is equal to five kilograms of TNT in its explosive effect.

Unfortunately, therefore, the FAE device concocted in my book by Belousov may not be simply a projection but, protected from the public domain by a TOP SECRET label, already a matter of accomplishment by both of the superpowers.